GETAWAY MONEY

BY

KIP JOULE

Argus Enterprises International
North Carolina****New Jersey

Getaway Money © 2009
All rights reserved by:
James Joule

A-Argus Better Book Publishers, LLC

For information:
A-Argus Better Book Publishers, LLC
Post Office Box 914
Kernersville, North Carolina 27285
www.a-argusbooks.com

ISBN: 978-0-9841342-3-6
ISBN: 0-9841342-3-9

Book Cover designed by Dubya

Printed in the United States of America

DEDICATION

To my mother, Madeline E., who gave me life more than once. To my father, James, who unknowingly provided challenges that confirmed whatever does not turn you into a spiritless puppet tends to make you stronger. To Aunt Sid Raynor, who cared deeply about me and for me, and who filled in plenty of blanks. To my wife, Vicki, and my children — JJ, Bart and Camy — who make every day worth living. And to Amy Wisniewski, coordinator for Western Nebraska Community College's Writing Center, who plowed through the earliest draft of GETAWAY MONEY. I am forever indebted to her for her comments, criticisms and encouragement.

"We can say nothing but what has already been said, the composition and method is ours only." — Robert Burton (circa 1621).

"There is always time to add a word, but none in which to take one back." — Baltasar Gracian (circa 1650).

Three authors seem to have used the title, *Getaway Money*, before I also chose to: Gail Brewer in Guilty Detective Story Magazine (November 1955), Elmer Davis in Liberty Magazine (Jan. 26, 1935), and Patterson McNutt in Colliers (Apr. 26, 1941) — all of whom used the title for short stories, none of which had anything to do with horseracing.

PROLOGUE

"Reservoir . . . reservoir . . . reservoir . . ."

Dazed and retching, the shaken jogger, a second-year Science major from nearby Mercury Community College, barely had been able to hit the speed-dial 9-1-1 button on her cell phone. The nearest patrolman, first to respond, discovered the tiny co-ed pitched forward on forearms and knees, in a tight, upright fetal position. Her surging, quick breaths — emanating as wheezing shrieks — were audible the instant he opened his car door.

Arriving a short time later, Lt. Bob Huber knew from her uncontrollable sobbing and choked-up voice that this young woman hadn't seen anything of consequence beyond her initial discovery. She had paused mid-stride while not truly identifying what the floating object was at first. As the mini-beats of water lapped upon the upturned corpse while it gently bobbed and bumped against the shoreline, her world had rapidly imploded. Sitting upright on the bank now, she shivered uncontrollably under a tightly draped Navy-blue blanket, even as the morning sun was baking everything it touched. For sure, this co-ed wasn't going to make it to her Sociology quiz later in the day.

At first glimpse, Lt. Huber, the local police force's lone detective, noted that the corpse, although fully mature, was the body of a small, but not dwarfish, thin but muscular, adult male.

"Good thing she had that cell phone, Artie," the lieutenant mentioned to the off-duty campus policeman he had called right after arriving. "Hell, even with that phone, if our dispatcher hadn't been on the ball, we probably still wouldn't be here yet. All the poor girl kept reporting was 'Reservoir . . . reservoir . . . reservoir . . .' Luckily, the dispatcher contacted our nearest morning patrolman without delay. He knew what to do. Quickly found her slumped over up the bank from where the body was. He's the best we've got. Been here a lot longer than me. Just wants to stay a patrolman."

"Yeah, some people are like that, I guess," the grateful campus cop nervously nodded, offhandedly telegraphing his own upwardly mobile intentions, while fighting the instinct to vomit. "We're forever reminding all our co-eds and female faculty to always have a cell phone handy, Lieutenant. 'Til now, we hadn't had a bit of trouble around here. But, with what you see on the six o'clock news and in the newspapers, you can't be too cautious."

"You know it," Lt. Huber grumbled, still scanning the scene. "We've got a countywide program going along the same line. Especially for our female after-dark joggers and walkers."

"What the hell goes on here, Lieutenant?" the fully nauseous security cop's hacking voice blurted out, unable to avoid succumbing to the scene any longer. "Jesus, this is way out of my league."

"Don't feel so alone, Artie," Lt. Huber quickly nodded. "I have no idea, either. I'll keep you in the loop best I can."

Perhaps the hands had been cut off to make fingerprinting impossible, thereby slowing down the identification process, the detective thought. Sure, it would take extra time for the DNA analysis or dental records to yield anything. But why the legs just below the knees? And, good lord, could this little fellow possibly still have been alive when he was dumped?

The only nearby set of fresh footprints along the bank was the jogger's. No sign of a blood trail. No tire tracks. Immediately, Lt. Huber knew this was the work of a dispassionately efficient killer. A calculating professional.

1

AMONG HIS PEOPLE

"Riders up!"

The gravel-voiced paddock judge's authoritative growl had cut through the observing murmur of the walking ring crowd moments ago, with his usual emphasis on "Up!"

Now, eleven immaculately-groomed Thoroughbreds glistening with coats of brown to gray-roan to jet black, and carrying their determinedly diminutive riders silhouetted on high against the slate-hued overcast of the afternoon sky, were filing toward the track. Destined from birth to look upward to most, the eleven jockeys now looked down upon everyone from the loftiness of their hot-blooded thrones.

Assured by his last-minute inspection of close-up details, Carson Bagwell turned with a slight nod of approval and began strolling leisurely toward the clubhouse.

"Great daily-double combo, Bagwell!" a voice shouted from behind. Bagwell long ago had schooled himself to keep walking in silence under such mortar fire. "Anyone can pick favorites, for Christ sake. Aren't pros like you supposed to know about thirty-seven-dollar horses beforehand? What the hell do they pay you for anyway?"

Meanwhile, the trackside trumpeter, attired in the traditional red long coat and black top hat of a Royal Guardsman, finished his "Call to the Post" with an inviting fermata. Sensing the anxious fervor of the buzzing crowd as they neared the track, the horses inquisitively pricked and pointed their ears, bobbed their heads and mouthed their bits, some rising into nervous prances while snorting their readiness. One bellowed an equine challenge.

Stepping onto the track, each entrant was reined in by a dutifully calming outrider pony. They know their single mission. Sometimes several times a day, these ponies courageously accompany their race-ready charges through the post-parade, pre-race warm-up and walk toward the claustrophobic confines of the metal starting stalls. As the post-parade unfolded, the announcer, from his booth high above, introduced the name of each horse, along their owner, trainer and jockey for the fifth race at Mercury Downs.

Bagwell, in the midst of his fourteenth year as a Mercury Times sports writer, had always been the paper's resident horse-racing pundit. Without fail, he had been a trackside fixture since opening day of the oval's first season.

"Nice 'Best Bet' yesterday, Bagwell!" a high-pitched, yet masculine, voice shrilled from his right. "How come you didn't tell us it was the best bet to finish fifth!"

As part of his survival, he long ago became socially impervious, but not aloofly detached. He had heard it all, and often. Prognosticating about a full card of races for everyone to see every day in the local newspaper is an open invitation to sordid ridicule. Only a special sort of person would want to constantly risk dangling by a thread over a swirling, gnashing pond of caustic piranhas.

No matter. Through every fickle flip-flop of thick and thin, these were his people. He understood horseplayers completely, and he loved them. Especially the superstitious, system-believing, rumor-feasting enthusiasts who frequented the general-admission side of the grandstands. Never pausing, his expressions acknowledged their wits and woes as he moved from one destination to the next amid any afternoon's sea of everstirring patrons. After every race there is blame to be meted out, self-important boasting to be broadcast. And, such things must be done quickly. Without fail, the results of the next race were certain to bring not only newer but also different circumstances of illogical chaos.

He hadn't gone another thirty paces when "Hey, Mister Carson Bagwell" was growled from the other side. "Yesterday, I boxed your three picks in the first two races for the Daily Double, and hit. Still lost four bucks. Hell, anybody can pick damn favorites, one odds-on. Thanks a lot!"

"Aw, shut up, will ya," a close-by voice retaliated. "He gave ya winners, for God's sakes. It's your own dumb-ass fault how ya bet 'em."

Bagwell long ago had learned that none of this acidic recrimination was worth a moment's worry. Horseplayers are born kibitzers. Chronic gripers. Their way of sheltering their eternal optimism. All part of the sacramental backdrop . . . the swirl and swill of a sweet afternoon of homestretch roars, intoxicating exhilaration and grounding disappointment. All forgotten in seconds under the ever-spinning wheels of renewed expectations. Always another race. Always a better tomorrow.

Ω

When the gates first opened for The Downs's inaugural season, Bagwell instantly became a man doing exactly what he wanted to be doing, when he wanted and how he wanted. Ever since, his life had bathed in the full warmth of that enjoyment. At a shade above six feet, his sinewy frame gave the appearance of slight gauntness. A black vest with a black and white mini-checkered front was single-buttoned over his white, long-sleeved shirt, with the cuffs rolled up twice. A polyester tie of diagonal half-inch-wide gray and red stripes hung loosely Windsored from his unbuttoned collar. Beige slacks, held by suspenders, partially covered his scuffed brown suede loafers. He was topped off by his usual camel-colored, wool Trilby that concealed most of his silky blonde hair and shaded his warm light-brown eyes.

Head-to-toe, Bagwell moved straight ahead at an unwavering gait, his friendly eyes habitually sweeping side-to-side, taking in everything. His left hand lightly tugged at the front brim of his hat as he nodded with a slight smile when passing the owner of a nationally respected racing stable. He genuinely liked her.

"Great race, Laura," he said quietly, referring to her mare's rousing wire-to-wire victory in last Saturday's feature race.

The well-maintained widow smiled widely in return.

As always, Bagwell was fastidiously clean-shaven. With obvious disdain, he avoided those media people who, consciously or otherwise, dressed and behaved like bums.

The tops of two pens protruded from his left shirt pocket, along with a pocket-sized spiral notepad. Intermittently, he tapped a loosely rolled local edition of today's Daily Racing Form against his upper right leg as he continually processed the information around him.

"Da favorite looks unbeatable," a voice, directed at Bagwell, rang from the crowd along the walkway fence.

"Perhaps you should give the race a second look," Bagwell spoke to the voice without looking. His stride remained unchanged, his head unturned.

"Whaddaya mean second look, dammit!" came the urgent response. "Ya pointed dat one out in yur column."

"Yeah, I mentioned him . . . as something to consider," Bagwell countered with even-handed friendliness while he kept walking. "But, I'm sure as heck not going to tell you how to bet your hard-earned money. I'm just saying, always be careful. No such thing as unbeatable."

"Jesus, that's a fine cop-out."

"Hey, I hope you win. Good luck."

"Yeah-yeah."

Wait a minute. He chose to answer this voice, but systematically ignored all of the others? Simple. This one was about an upcoming race. Still hope, still a chance. Those others were nothing more than crabbings over spilt milk. As far as Bagwell was concerned, a race that's been run is a race that's done. *Move on!*

Through it all, while choosing to respond or not, Bagwell's march toward the clubhouse maintained its methodical cadence.

As he entered, he immediately spotted Security Officer Frank Ogle at his usual post to the left, squatted on a beige collapsible metal chair just inside the door. The bulldogish, uniformed officer watched unblinkingly while Bagwell raised his left hand up in a loose fist as if he were going to rub his forehead. Suddenly, his hand opened wide, with all five digits spread; then, just as quickly, he closed his hand. After giving his forehead a slight rub, his hand dropped back along his side.

With a flick of his thick eyebrows, Officer Ogle acknowledged Bagwell's gesture and then returned to scanning the crowd. These two went back a ways.

Nowadays, one of the true denizens of the track scene also watched for Bagwell's finger-flashing mimes. Coiled at an advantageous distance to Officer Ogle's left with riveted nonchalance, Gordon Hammerstan, known to everyone who knew him as "Hammy," was familiar with everybody, but, with one exception, never became personally involved with anyone,

If you needed something that wasn't legally available, Hammy could connect you. He was a universal conduit, but never, ever the ultimate source. Every cabbie, bartender and motel desk clerk within the working vicinity of Mercury Downs knew how and under what circumstances to get through to Hammy in short order, or they knew someone who quickly could do that for them.

The way he dressed, you'd swear to God that Hammy was terminally colorblind. Hell, flat-out blind! And, with subtle quirks, he helped people to believe this was true. Added in, the severe prescription of his oversized, black-rimmed glasses gave the impression that his eyes were twice their actual size. Yet, when watching a cluster of horses racing down the backstretch through his binoculars, Hammy always knew precisely where each one was and what they were doing each step along the way, having memorized the colors of the jockeys' silks and the saddlecloth numbers during the post parade.

Slovenly and portly, Hammy constantly slouched, with a shaggy crop of brown hair and a bushy, unkempt mustache. And he did nothing to improve this seedy image. Blending in perfectly, he cultivated his facade of a typical racetrack degenerate. He smoked and chewed on the cheapest cigars he could find, and reeked of them.

With simmering voracity, Hammy's patron demon incessantly pulled him toward the instant action and euphoric atmosphere of horse racing, but failed to anoint him with any need for the more grounded gratification of winning money. Hammy simply evaluated his net situation of the moment by whatever handfuls of crumpled bills happened to have found temporary residence in the pockets of his baggy khakis.

Talking excessively only when genuinely irritated, Hammy watched everything. You could be talking with him while standing directly up in front of him and, even though he would be just as intensely involved in the conversation, his eyes might be roaming the tote board behind you.

Hammy regularly achieved nirvana. All that he required was some tickets on the next race and then to be standing trackside while waiting for the starting gate to open, puffing on one of his rank cigars in anxious anticipation of something that rarely happened.

Routinely, by the time a race went off, Hammy had a cyclone of hearsay information swirling around in his head from his myriad of can-do sources. Invariably, he gathered convincing evidence that every horse in the race was an absolute shoo-in. Consequently, his final choices almost always ended up being emotional and arbitrary . . . no better than the people around him who had absolutely no information and were relying on birthday numbers or pretty jockey silks as their rock-hard method for losing.

Regardless, on his annual tax returns Hammy declared himself to be a professional gambler with a prodigious profit. Carefully providing this information on Schedule C, he masked every cent that he had underhandedly collected from fees for providing connections throughout the year. Early on, as accountability for his illicit sources of income began to loom, Hammy had entertained the idea of declaring himself to be an independent financial consultant. But the justifying paperwork for this masquerade seemed tedious and fraught with two-party trappings. Professional gambler was much easier to handle on a single-person scale.

At the track every day and continually in line at the betting windows, how could the IRS ever doubt his participation in this rarely profitable practice? Mostly though, and by design, Hammy bet minimally small. The exception was when he had a line on a personalized suggestion of Bagwell's. Then he bet, as they say, "with both hands," and, after the race was over, made a point of bragging profusely as he headed off to collect.

Written as a seemingly indecipherable code in very small notebooks entitled "Gambling Winnings" and dated by year, Hammy recorded every fee that he clandestinely collected. If he were ever nabbed on some misdemeanor or minor felony charge, he did not want the episode to unravel into a humongous tax-evasion rap.

Only he knew, for instance, that a winning daily-double entry in his tiny book was actually an illicit referral fee linked to a specific call girl; a specially numbered exacta winner was a cocaine-connection fee, etc., etc. The decoder for this maze of encrypted deceit wasn't written anywhere. It existed only in Hammy's head and was never spoken about.

He maintained accounts in all three of Mercury's banks. From these, he automatically paid the semi-annual rent on his remote local apartment, along with payments to the insurance policies on his apartment and late-model Dodge Duster, as well as a substantial term-life policy written to a coded anonymous benefactor. From time to time, he also wrote checks to a local broker for purchases of shares of blue chips and other low-risk, solid-yield common stocks. He systematically accumulated, and never sold, blocks of these stocks, declaring the dividends as part of his annual income. On the surface, Hammy appeared to be a cleverless buffoon and honest taxpayer.

As part of his daily meanderings through the grandstands and clubhouse, Hammy quietly collected losing tickets that had been tossed aside by disgruntled bettors. Careful to avoid the obviousness of stooping for tickets on the floor, he found adequate supplies at the main restaurant, concession stands, beer bars, and various other bettor-friendly roosts with tables and chairs.

Each night, he sorted through that day's collection, selecting out high-dollar straight bets and multi-combinational exotics that added up to sizable single-ticket bets. He religiously stored these keepable "losers" in shoe boxes. Periodically, by balancing the potential year-end total of these losers against his gross income from collected fees for the year, he tallied his declared "professional gambler's" net income. Based upon this total at year's end, he calculated his federal and state taxes, and faithfully wrote checks to both offices prior to the Ides of April. He had never been questioned, let alone audited.

Hammy slouched wherever he sat, and wherever he stood, deliberately skirting any pretense of ostentation without backing into terminal absurdity. Beneath this motley, rumpled, easily disregarded morass of sloth lurked a steely deliberateness of meticulous record-keeping and instantly serious accountability.

Occasionally, in cahoots with a trustworthy ally and under very sound circumstances, Hammy would agree to become the cashier of record for a windfall winner who wanted to remain anonymous. These fleeting partnerships usually involved signing for Daily Double or Trifecta payoffs having odds exceeding 300-to-1 or becoming the taxpayer of record for winning Pick-6 tickets amounting to thousands of dollars and requiring immediate state and federal tax deductions from the total payoff.

Impostors ready to step in and represent others who do not want their identities revealed after scoring an instantly taxable pari-mutuel windfall are a regular part of the trackside human paraphernalia. Known as "ten-percenters," this is the going rate for providing their handy sort of conspiratorial misrepresentation. Without a doubt, Hammy would have performed this service for free, though he never let on as such. He wanted the notoriety of this paper trail that "proved" he rather frequently cashed big-time pari-mutuel payoffs. These "factors" helped to launder — taxably justify — his more-than-comfortable income from the seamy sources he could not possibly declare.

Bagwell unknowingly caught Hammy's attention several years ago. After stealthily watching for a few days, the cigar-smoking stalker had concluded that "this newspaper guy might know something." He began trailing Bagwell wherever possible, going to the paddock, following him as he went toward the off-limits-for-Hammy press-box elevator, and edging into line behind him during those uncommon occasions when the writer used the betting windows on the clubhouse's main floor. But trying to overhear what Bagwell was saying to a mutuel clerk proved frustratingly barren. The writer always leaned forward and mumbled too softly for anyone but the ticket puncher to discern.

Somewhat unexpectedly, a dangling brass ring rewarded Hammy's tenacity . . . he stumbled onto Bagwell's daily signals to Officer Ogle. Most days brought a silent walk-by signal that nothing of special worth was on tap. But the wait was worthwhile. On those semi-rare days when Bagwell's fingers lit up, Hammy sauntered to the nearest mutuel window and emptied his pockets.

With the unwavering scrutiny of an ambushing predator, Bagwell patiently watched every race, had the latest Daily Racing Form with him at all times, went to the paddock for the saddlings of significant races, and watched most post parades. He locked onto every race from the start to well after the horses passed the finish line. He also watched all angles of every replay on one of the TV monitors after each race, and was at the track the next day in time to study the replays of the previous day's races that were always shown prior to the start of that day's card. With a wrinkled brow, he worried endless details into submission.

Ω

Today, as he headed for the elevator that would take him up to the press box, Bagwell brooded about the silent, windless drizzle that had shrouded the scene for the past two hours. Ten different ways he nagged at himself: Could unaccounted-for moisture on the racing surface possibly have a costly affect?

The cloud bank had recently lifted from the western horizon as if a gray curtain, water-colored toward the bottom in masterfully tinged transitions of lavender to pink and finally hemmed with brilliant orange, was rising to give the day a second act.

"That damn drizzle hasn't left any puddles," Bagwell self-argued in silence, constantly wrestling with the demon-born apprehensiveness of a tormented perfectionist. "Can't possibly bother things?"

Just then, the mid-afternoon sun forcibly peeked from under the lifting orange hem and began screaming back onto the area with a shimmering golden blare. Stunningly sunny and drizzly at the same time, the penetrating rays now outlined every moisture-coated object with a sharper sheen. Some of the watery prisms glistening along the railings and painted benches ricocheted the sun's beams with the impression of emitting a white-gold incandescence of their own making. As the curtain continued to rise, the sun became nested in robin's-egg blue. While the afternoon shadows reached out, the drizzle subsided and a muggy stillness of evaporating warmth began to saturate the air. Soon, any tenebrous inklings should be forgotten. But, not by Bagwell . . . not until the next race was safely over.

Ω

Earlier, about twenty miles to the west in the city that gave the track its namesake, another Mercury Times reporter had put his byline on a very different unfolding story. The leeches had left their telltale circular incisions on the naked, pallid body that had been pulled from the shallow edge of the city's reservoir early that morning. The corpse had been spotted from the bank-side gravel path by a sunrise jogger.

Leech marks meant the body still had been warm, perhaps still breathing, when tossed into the water. But, the hands were missing, and the legs had been cut off just below the knees. A white-cord tourniquet had been carefully tightened to each arm and leg about an inch above where each extremity had been cut away.

What wasn't reported was Lt. Huber's instant recognition that this desecration had been meant to be found quickly . . . meant as an unrepentant and unambiguous message.

2

KNOWING'S NOT ENOUGH

Without fail, each time he silently tipped Officer Ogle about some horse's immediate chances, a triggered microsecond inside Bagwell relived the origin of their friendship. During his first year with the Mercury Times, Bagwell had interviewed a boisterous young trainer about a mare in his care that was returning to racing after a long layoff due to a nagging tendon problem. The trainer had assured Bagwell that the mare was entered way over her head, and would be out there simply to put a race under her belt before getting back into a plan for winning. Bagwell mentioned this information in his column the day before the race. Instead, the mare, off at 27-to-1, broke on the lead from the starting gate and, never challenged, won by three easy lengths.

A week later, the same trainer mentioned another of his horses to Bagwell, emphasizing that this one was ready to win comfortably. This time though, Bagwell warned his readers that, although this particular trainer was exuding confidence, bettors should note that his horses have been known to run opposite of how he tells people they will. The next day, the colt, off as the 7-to-5 favorite, finished seventh, never in the hunt.

Entering the clubhouse after one of his regular paddock visits two days later, Bagwell suddenly was struck hard from behind, just below the left ear. Reeling against the wall, he heard, "I'll teach you to call me a liar, you sonofabitch," as the furious trainer closed in for a haymaker directly into the writer's face. Seemingly from another dimension, the sharp crack of a nightstick across his forearm instantly stopped the trainer in mid-assault. Officer Ogle's unquestioning quickness had surely saved Bagwell from permanent injury, and the writer remained steadfastly grateful. They had seldom spoken to each other since, their knowing bond preferring to thrive in reverential silence.

During his daily watch as the clubhouse's chief security officer, Frank Ogle never seemed to respond to any sort of spoken language. "Talk means nothing — everybody does it," he had once confided to Bagwell.

All afternoon, the banal crowd noise reverberates between a droning buzz and a semi-emphatic murmur. Then, ten times each day, an all-inclusive sacred rite is faithfully performed. Ten times, between gate opening and finish crossing, a clanging magma of mega-decibel humanity frantically erupts. As the runners surge through the far turn and begin entering the home-stretch, the feverish yelling, screaming, cursing and praying reaches out in an ever-whitening wave of broiling anxiety, spilling over as the front-runners reach for the finish wire, then ebbing to its usual spectator buzz before the last of the trailing also-rans cross the line.

Body language was Officer Frank's motivating dialect. Any perceived irregularity drew an immediate evaluation or instinctive reaction. Before retiring to Mercury, his special mix of lawful authority and innate survival had served him through thirty years of patrolling the nights of Brooklyn and The Bronx.

Racetracks everywhere have forever been bastions for heated debate, abusive language and the invocation of deities for all manner of intervention, as well as for raucous bragging, loosely veiled threats and a generally combative atmosphere amply thickened with testosterone. None of this usual turmoil jarred the routine calm of Officer Frank's constant surveillance in the least. But a questionable human movement, no matter how subtle or silent, instantly zeroed his full focus. The quiet awareness of Officer Frank's presence, along with perhaps others like him, made Mercury Downs one of Bagwell's two perfectly-styled comfort zones.

Bagwell hated being labeled a gambler. Few things upset him more than being unmeritoriously dismissed in such offhandedly abrasive terms. During rare moments when the situation was private enough among trusted associates, he would elaborate at length about why he described himself as an information developer, not a gambler. Enough information was always available to make an astutely profitable decision, he constantly emphasized to his listeners. All one has to do is know where to look and what to do with the discovery.

Ω

Today's trackside drizzle wasn't nearly enough to change the officially listed racing condition from "Fast," yet even the slightest departure from an otherwise completely dry surface irritated Bagwell's educated vision of how this race was expected to unfold. Realistically, the dank afternoon shroud, though dismally moist, was not likely to threaten his immediate aspirations. Slight dampness notwithstanding, everything seemed in order. Bagwell was thoroughly familiar with the trainer's genuine capability for preparing his horses for a winning effort. He also knew about the jockey's skillful reliability to "put a horse across" when it was ready.

Number 5's last race, nineteen days ago, had been a solid prep for today's all-out effort. After an easy first six furlongs, the colt had accelerated through the home stretch and continued on after the finish line for another furlong, methodically passing all of the galloping-out horses in front of him in the process. The young horse's two published workouts since then, which Bagwell had verified with his own stopwatch, telegraphed that the colt was razor sharp. Now, back in with the same level of competition over the same distance, the jockey had only to make sure that he didn't get boxed in and then start his mount's closing surge a bit earlier.

Tony, the clubhouse's uniformed elevator operator, knew where Bagwell was headed and, with a welcoming nod of recognition and a smile, automatically pushed the press-box button. A shorter-than-average, heavier-than-average cordial sort of fellow, Tony revealed his bald pate whenever he readjusted his black-billed, white operator's cap. The thick, wavy, coal-black hair along the sides and back, accompanied by sideburns cut at the base of his ears, masked any hint of a hairless crown with his cap on.

"Bet the Number-5 horse, Tony," Bagwell said flatly, with only the two of them in the elevator as it ascended. This brief utterance marked the first time that Bagwell had chosen to mention anything about racing to Tony in the three months since he had been hired to operate the elevator.

"Yeah . . . sure . . . OK," Tony nodded blankly, thumping out his I've-heard-it-all-before tone like a dull drum.

Bagwell remained silent.

"Good luck," Tony said, with robotic cheeriness as the door opened to the press-box floor.

After stopping by the self-serve betting machine that accommodated the members of the press corps, Bagwell walked toward Bill Leegrum, the Eclipse Award-winning turf writer who more recently had become a freelance stalwart for several dailies and weeklies. Leegrum, a hopeless chain smoker of unfiltered Camels, still maintained the rush of a fire that reignited each time he heard the sound of a starting gate opening. When Mercury Downs's season ended, he headed to whichever location would be hosting the Breeders' Cup championship series that fall, after which he always overwintered in Miami, covering the major East Coast handicap and Triple-Crown prep races at Gulfstream Park. Then, during the rejuvenation of Spring, he chased the Triple Crown circuit all the way to Belmont Park before migrating to Mercury for the summer.

Bagwell and Leegrum were trackside chums-in-common. Through the integrity reflected by their writings, they had developed a respect and fondness for each other before ever meeting. Later, they discovered that they also could trust each other, a rarity to depend on anywhere. Occasionally, they hoisted a beer or two together at Rocco's Finish Line Lounge after the races.

Right now though, one of the track management's office flunkies, Blake Zimmerhoff, had Leegrum cornered with some tedious nonsense that, out of courtesy, the scribe was having trouble freeing himself from. Leegrum waved distractedly as Bagwell rolled his eyes and walked on by. In cadence with his overly-loud small talk, Zimmerhoff's head bounced side-to-side and his openhanded right arm artfully chopped up-and-down at Leegrum as if taking the measure of a block of unbreakable wood. In every other respect, however, a martial arts demeanor did not fairly describe Zimmerhoff's exasperating facade. Forever the gentleman, Leegrum continued to stare back patiently.

Ω

The track announcer's observation abruptly blared above the general buzz, informing everyone that the horses were entering the starting gate. Quietly, Bagwell moved to the nearest front window of the press box to watch the start of the mile-and-one-eighth route for Allowance 3-year-olds. That the race was being contested on the inner turf course was what rubbed him most about the nagging drizzle. True, the turf course continued to be listed officially as "Firm". Even so, a wet grassy surface can become spongy and slippery, impeding an otherwise skillful horse that might be trying to make up ground during the latter stages of a race.

"They're all in line," the announcer said with trained urgency. "An-n-n-nd . . . they're off!"

Bagwell watched through his binoculars with calm, but sharpened, interest as the eleven-horse field charged from the chute to his left, passed by the grandstands for the first time and then headed into the clubhouse turn. As the field began to string out and enter the backstretch, he moved away from the window and over to one of the nearby surveillance TVs for a closer look.

"Like something in this race?" Leegrum, having finally pried himself away from Zimmerhoff, asked while sharing a look at the TV screen.

"He's running third, but he won't be there for long now," Bagwell said with dry certainty.

The Number-5 horse, Heed Johnny, moved up three-wide with the co-leaders on the far turn. Then, into the homestretch, the announcer began his anticlimatic description of how Heed Johnny, in workhorse fashion, was uneventfully moving away from the other two under a rhythmic hand ride. The jockey gave Heed Johnny one gentle backward right-hand tap with his whip in mid-stretch to make sure his steed switched leads and kept his mind on business, and together they passed by the finish line four widening lengths ahead of the place horse.

"I'm sorry, Bill," Bagwell said sincerely. "I tried to get to you before the race, but that damn Zimmerhoff wasn't letting go. Geez, Bill, this was one of those where you just take everything you've got in your pockets and put it on the nose. I've been waiting for this one to run back ever since his last race three weeks ago. I didn't want to say anything until I got a good long last look at him in the paddock today . . . what the hell was Zimmerhoff talking to you about, anyway?"

"Oh God, something about turf writers being viewed as superstars by the general public, and that we should become more visible to the common man . . . especially here at the track," Leegrum said with a sneer, trying to avoid griping about his missed opportunity. "How the hell can you walk around down there like that? They won't give me a moment's peace. Everybody always wants the low-down."

"I know. I just try to be nice to everyone," Bagwell shrugged with a short, low laugh. "The secret is to keep moving at a steady pace while you're among them. Don't stop for anything. Don't pick up the pace either. That can be construed as offensive. You don't want that. Just nice and easy."

"Yeah, easy for you to say," Leegrum snapped back. "Why tempt fate unnecessarily?"

"As usual, you have a point, my friend," Bagwell patronized, but Leegrum, unaffected, knew there was a punch line still in the bag. "Look, you're a hermetically sealed syndicated writer. I'm a local yokel. It's good for business for me to be seen."

Leegrum let it go with a final word and a smile, "Humbug."

At final odds of 7-to-2 and the third choice among the betting public, Heed Johnny paid $9.60 for each $2-win ticket. Bagwell's $1,000 wager netted a $3,800 profit. He avoided betting horses with post-time odds of less than 3-to-1, and usually passed up any race where the favorite's odds dropped to even money or lower.

"You should have pushed that goddam Zimmerhoff the hell out of the way," Leegrum, after a long moment's lull, quipped with disappointed understanding. In the past, he had profited plenty from Bagwell's solid suggestions, and knew there always would be others up ahead.

"What's he really supposed to be doing around here anyway," Bagwell whispered with disgust about Zimmerhoff.

"Damned if I know . . . he's an assistant to the assistant manager of something or other," Leegrum shook his head, still grinding over having missed out on Bagwell's horse. "He doesn't even know enough to leave us the hell alone when the races are running. He's a pain in the ass . . . a goddam nuisance. Somebody's friggin' nephew or something."

Bagwell remained in the press box for the next two races, then headed back down to the paddock. He wasn't planning on betting again today, but wanted an up-close look at the fillies and mares in the feature race, a Grade-III six-furlong sprint for 3-year-olds-and-up.

"You bet the 5-horse?" he asked in a friendly manner, stepping into the elevator alone with Tony again.

"Ah . . . no," the operator answered with uneasy honesty. As the elevator quietly descended, Tony adjusted his black bow tie with newfound interest in his passenger, cleared his throat with three quick muffled coughs and shyly asked, "Who do you like in the next one?"

"Forget it, Tony," Bagwell answered dryly. "Those don't happen that often. It might be another month or so before another something like that comes along."

3

LEECHES AND LEGS

By mid-afternoon, the Mercury Times had the story on the local streets, complete with pictures of the discovery site and the body bag being loaded into the ambulance. "Mutilated, Unidentified Body Found" blared across the top of the Front Page. The accompanying story was squeamishly graphic with its descriptions.

Mercury, a town of nearly 9,000 industrious citizens, is typical in its design for a Midwestern rural community. Relying heavily upon the year-to-year whims of Mother Nature for the success of its wheat, corn and soybean crops, Mercury's steadier commerce is generated by its massive Caterpillar and Allis Chalmers heavy-equipment manufacturing and assembly plants. In concert, while the weather and blue-collar sweat routinely lubricate the backbone of the town's economy, Mercury's God-fearing families adequately provide for their children without tending to spoil them with material opulence.

One of the town's two main thoroughfares, Belgrade Avenue, runs east-west through its the center, while the other, Main Street, bisects north-south. Where these two major avenues intersect, Mercury's main business sector fights to flourish. If you travel east from this intersection, Belgrade Avenue quickly feeds into Interstate Highway-75. After twenty miles, you'll pass by the barn area and grandstands of the Mercury Downs horseracing community, and after twenty miles more you'd reach the outskirts of Goldspar, the second largest city in the state.

Along Main Street, two blocks north of Belgrade Avenue, Mercury's city hall and fire station complex consumes one entire block. The police station is across the street. On the same west side of Main, the county courthouse, fronted by six imperial white pillars, is another block to the north. The police station also houses the city-county jail.

Strewn observably at random throughout the city limits and just beyond, Mercury's well-attended churches offer a baker's dozen variety of the Christian persuasion during Sunday services and Wednesday evening Bible studies.

The town has two elementary schools, located on the east and west sides, that struggle with kindergartners through fifth-graders. Next, all advancing students converge into centrally located John Brown Middle School, and then, after three years, become part of the buzzing hallways and classrooms at Mercury High School, home of the Wing-footed Mustangs.

Mercury's twelve-person police department, including two part-timers, serves the town and its rural outskirts. A four-person sheriff's office oversees the rest of the county. Stretching out along Belgrade Avenue in both directions from the main intersection, the town's self-sufficiency is showcased by its post office, public library, five-screen cinema, and handful of self-serve gas stations and convenience stores that intermittently close and then reopen, usually changing hands in the process. Along the east end of Belgrade Avenue, within ready reach of the Interstate off-ramp, a cluster of nationally recognizable chain restaurants strive to satisfy everybody's sit-down and takeout fast-food urges. And, Mercury is a Pepsi town. The scoreboards at the football stadium and basketball courts are ablaze with Pepsi symbols. All of the pop machines in town are Pepsi machines, filled only with Pepsi products. If you want a Coke, Dr. Pepper, 7-Up or A&W Root Beer, you have to go to one of the three supermarkets that appear at strategically opposing intervals along the town's two main thoroughfares.

The independently-owned shops that spread from the four corners of the main intersection are the same as you find in most Heartland towns of Mercury's size. Donut shop. Jewelry store. Flower shops. Gift-pharmacy shop. Shoe store. Two video-rental outlets. Laundry and dry cleaning. Several small unisex hairstyling salons. Three clothing stores offer differing price ranges. Mixed in are the law firms, insurance agencies and realtor offices, some of which are housed within rental spaces provided inside the town's three banks.

Rimming along the outskirts, several liquor-driven dance halls and lounges provide a hodgepodge of rock 'n' roll and country-western ambiance. Some offer weekday amateur karaoke nights. Two showcase live-band performances on the weekends.

Pistol-Packin' Annie's downtown restaurant serves the nearby employees and local shoppers, mostly for breakfast and over the lunch hour Monday through Saturday, and closes by 3 o'clock in the afternoon. But it is the donut shop and the hairstyling salons where the local gossip is cared for, nurtured and embellished.

In every way, self-sufficient Mercury, with its small-townish demeanor, satisfactorily fits the classic blueprint that the metro citizens of Goldspar and erstwhile Interstate passers-by from both coasts, with their unsolvable crime rates and welfare burdens, summarily dismiss as Podunk, the sticks or the boonies.

Ω

By the following day, a preliminary autopsy confirmed what Lt. Huber already knew.

"Except for one thing, Bob," Dr. Shannon L. Sugihara, Barksdale County's medical examiner and forensic pathologist, pointed out. "Some of those round marks on the torso aren't from leeches. They're probably cigar burns . . . too big to be from a cigarette. For some reason, this little fellow stumbled into hell on Earth. That same cigar probably is what burned his eyelids to a crisp. And, his mouth was sewn shut with monofilament fishing line. This was a monstrous ritual."

"I know, Doc, I know," Lt. Huber impatiently scowled back with nauseating dismay. "Christ, we don't even know where to start looking for his lower legs and hands. Obviously, this was all done somewhere else and then just dumped in our reservoir"

Dr. Sugihara, a stocky, strong young man of Japanese heritage, consciously tried to keep his white lab coat clean as he maneuvered around the body on the examination table, peering through octagonal, wire-rimmed bifocals while he vividly described the ghoulishness of the details for Lt. Huber. That he secretly enjoyed tormenting his friend a little was deftly hidden inside his austere, cheerless monotone.

"The leeches had made their marks early and then abandoned the scene before we ever got there," Dr. Sugihara moved on, undeterred by the lieutenant's visible disgust. "Take a look under the stereoscope over there, Bob. Excuse me for saying, Bob, but you do look a little squeamish, Bob."

"I know, Doc, I know," The detective winced as petty irritation began creeping into his uneasy anguish. "Sometimes I think if I ever start taking something like this completely in stride I better get the hell out. It'd be telling me I've become just as inhuman and lowdown as the damned devil that did this."

Still ghastly disturbed by Dr. Sugihara's clinically thorough explanations, Lt. Huber hovered like a pale, apprehensive robot and peered unsteadily through the binocular eyepiece of the scope into the Petri dish underneath, half-filled with water.

"See those little gliding critters that maybe look, at first glance, like baby leeches?" Dr. Sugihara aptly described. "Well, they're not. They're flatworms. Planaria. Primitive little aquatic beasts that grow naturally around here. High-school kids play with them in Biology class. They feed on dead meat, among other things. Behaviorally, they're as different from leeches as mosquitoes are from flies. You know, you have to be alive in order for a mosquito to like you well enough to want to suck out your blood. Around a cooling corpse though, it's only flies that are buzzing."

"So, the leech marks mean that this body really was still alive?" the lieutenant offered.

"Yes, or so warm and near-alive that it fooled them for a while," Sugihara elaborated. "If it's any comfort though, if this little fellow were still alive when he was put in the water, I think he was beyond any semblance of consciousness at that point. Probably didn't feel a thing by then."

"Sure, doc, that's a great comfort," the lieutenant growled, trying unsuccessfully to hide the tremor in his voice. "How the hell do we know what he felt?"

"We'll know more in a few days," the examiner said, disregarding the officer's bleakish inquiry without so much as a pause. "Psychology of the criminal mind aside, I can't tell you whether what we're looking at here is the driven work of a methodical sadist or, as you described him, a baseless monster completely detached from any semblance of humanity as he goes about his work. The most bloodcurdling screams might not faze him one way or another, but he'll want those who discover his work to be haunted by imagining those shrieks."

Dr. Sugihara estimated that the body, if the legs had been intact, would probably have measured out at about five-foot-three and weighed in the neighborhood of 100-110 pounds.

Ω

During his career, Lt. Huber had seen numerous corpses resulting from murders, mostly before he had arrived in Mercury. Some, of course, he had discovered in horrifying condition. But twelve years had passed since anything close to this had happened within his jurisdiction. The last had been a murder-suicide, made particularly messy because a double-barrel shotgun was used. Even so, all the loose ends had been neatly tidied up within a few days, and the incident had been quickly and professionally tucked away in the "Case

Closed" files. Helpful also, from a gallows-soothing perspective, the expired couple had not been Mercury residents for very long. At least the townspeople had been spared having to suffer the gruesome loss of two beloved pillars and left dwelling under a sustained cloak of lingering grief.

"This one's different, Doc," Lt. Huber grimaced to the pathologist, continuing to broadcast his lack of recent practice with crimes of this caliber. "This little guy was worked over somewhere else and then dropped on us for a reason. And, I think it was to slow down any investigation while, at the same time, attracting lots of notoriety. The killer's probably betting we're a bunch of small-town yokels who don't normally handle stuff like this."

"He'd be right, too," Dr. Sugihara responded with an agreeing tone. "We don't. Notice I said he. I can't convince myself that a woman would be capable of doing such a thing."

"Don't bet on it, Doc. It's a new day, women's lib and all that."

"If a woman did this, I quit."

"Jesus, don't do that. We had a hellava time finding someone as good as you."

"The upper legs and wrist areas have tourniquets, but I'd still like to know where all the blood went."

"See ya, Doc," Lt. Huber said, nodding in agreement as he headed briskly for the only door, then mumbling, "All my years, I've never seen anything so methodically vicious."

"One more thing, Bob," the pathologist stopped him. "If I were a betting man — which I'm not — I'd wager that this little fellow was a jockey or an exercise boy over at Mercury Downs. His overall size, muscle and low amount of body fat tend to say that. Also, this was a strong little guy, both in the arms and from what I can tell by the upper legs. And, his midriff is tight as a drum. I wouldn't presume to tell you your business, Bob, but I'd start by asking questions over at the track."

Lt. Huber nodded good-bye again and departed without pause while Dr. Sugihara discoursed over some Tower-of-London details about not killing people too quickly, but keeping them torturously aware while making some insanely atrocious point.

Ω

The lieutenant had received his early training at the state police academy in Virginia and then, while working the night and weekend shifts as a full-time Lexington PD patrolman, had pursued extensive criminology training in investigative research and analysis with the FBI's nearby forensic field office. He had achieved the level of detective before moving to the Midwest.

Responding to the Mercury Police Department's nationwide advertisement of search for a detective-level officer, he had flown in for an interview and abruptly decided that Mercury was the place where he'd want his kids to grow up. He was right. His son and daughter had done well all the way through high school; then both had gone away and graduated from college. Now successfully independent financially, both were married and tending to families of their own. Their career commitments had taken them well beyond the reach of regular cup-of-coffee visits.

Not long after attending their daughter's wedding, the lieutenant and wife Judy looked at each other and passively agreed that, without the kids around, they really had little left in common. More than four years ago, Judy had moved back to Virginia to be closer to her roots.

These days, the lieutenant cohabited with Marcus, an ageless black-and-gray neutered tabby who came and went as he pleased through a small swing-door leading into the backyard. Marcus's particular job — self-imposed, of course — required that he crouch his oversized body at various points along the stone-and-mortar backyard patio wall, thereby denying the visiting fauna access to the copious peanuts and birdseed that the lieutenant faithfully supplied. When the weather suited him, Marcus remained silently poised for hours under his slowly waving tail. By keeping their smorgasbord teasingly unavailable, Marcus's spiteful dog-in-the-manger act orchestrated the yard's daylight hours into a raucously shrill clatter led by nasty squirrel chatterings and stark blue jay screechiness.

Marcus was one family possession that Judy happily had left behind. When the cat had first appeared, seemingly from nowhere, Judy tried her best to warm up to him. At first, she talked to him in offhanded kitty language, and then, after a few weeks of frustration, with harsh directness. Regardless, Marcus would only sit, unmoved, and stare blankly at her, or, more precisely, through her. Exasperated into dismal defeat, Judy finally declared the cat to be a sullen ceramic fixture that they must have purchased from some cheesy lawn ornament shop. Yet, whenever the lieutenant finally arrived home, an instantly perky Marcus would immediately leap onto his lap with purring delight and, while rubbing his chin and both cheeks against his chosen compatriot with softly shut eyes, beg to be stroked.

Under Chief-of-Police Richard Millington, Lt. Huber served as second-in-command and remained the local police force's lone detective. He preferred that combined status. Acting as the departmental leader during Chief Millington's vacation breaks always reconvinced him that it wasn't something he wanted to do on a permanent basis. Each time the chief returned, the lieutenant gladly re-embraced the freedom and latitude of his personal purpose for choosing law enforcement as his life's calling. Among the regular duties he enjoyed was being Commander of Operations. This made him the upfront go-between whenever the department had to make statements to the press about local crimes or was invited to speak at the local Rotarian, Kiwanian or Lions lunches, or high-school assemblies.

Lt. Huber moved slightly slower these days, but cunningly smarter. Bolstered by his years of experience, he now used far less random energy getting from Point-A to Point-B in most intuitive situations. And, he had developed a tenacious fever of eminent domain about his town of Mercury. The citizens of Mercury were his people.

"Goddam . . . local yokels, huh? . . . country bumpkins?" he silently growled, gritting his teeth while on his way back to the station after seeing Sugihara. Inexorably, the discovery at the reservoir had boiled his territorial mood into the red zone of reactive comprehension. "How could someone dump a horrifically mutilated body into my reservoir and even remotely expect to get away with it!"

4

QUIET ALLIANCE

"Agent Maxwell?" Lt. Huber asked, in a friendly tone, and Maxwell nodded. "How was your flight?"

"Like they say in the business, any landing you can walk away from is a good landing," Maxwell shrugged straight-faced, then asked directly, "There some place quiet we can talk?"

Retired FBI operative Jason "Jace" Maxwell was easily spotted by Lt. Huber at Goldspar International Airport as soon as he stepped from the jet-bridge walkway linking the parked Boeing 747 to the concourse. The wide-brimmed Stetson hat, brown leather jacket, Navy-blue turtleneck, faded jeans and Asics Duomax running shoes sorted him from the flow of exiting passengers. Or, maybe it was the searching look of his eyes.

"Sure. How's a beer sound?" Lt. Huber said as they headed for the baggage-claim area.

"Fine, but let's do it here," Maxwell suggested. "After we leave here, I don't want to be seen hanging around with you." The operative's blunt assertiveness instilled a paused silence in the detective as they continued walking.

"Your flight's damn near forty-five minutes late . . . how come?" the lieutenant finally asked with guarded interest, brushing off the agent's directness as a geographic gap in mannerisms. Certainly wasn't Midwestern.

"Aa-aa, late leaving Dulles International," Maxwell said, waving his right hand across his midsection toward Lt. Huber and shaking his head with offhand disgust. "Some bigwig senator or something had to get to the West Coast in a hurry. They held the damn plane for her. After we finally got going, we made good time."

The waitress was on them before they had finished settling into the farthest table at Ellen's Runway Lounge on the second level of the main terminal. For the moment, only a handful of other patrons ringed the smoky bar near the entrance. None of the booths or other tables were occupied.

"So, what do you have that you didn't tell me over the phone?" Maxwell said in a low tone as soon as the waitress had left.

"Nothing I can think of . . . not even a routine plan about what to do next," Lt. Huber whispered back. "I'll admit it's eating me up. Oh, we're doing some things. Nothing that's going anywhere. One guy, Frankie the Flea, a real lowlife, couldn't come up with an alibi right off the bat. Then, when he finally says he recalls where he was, his buddy, who verified his whereabouts, is an even bigger loser. Truth is, though, neither one of them really knows where the hell they were at the time. Probably stoned out of their skulls somewhere. No matter what, they don't have a brain cell between them. Not nearly capable of doing what we found at the reservoir."

"That's it?"

"The other guy we're always watching is a sleazy track urchin. Goes by the name of Hammy. Into everything. Women, drugs, lone sharks, fences, strong arms . . . you name it. If there's a need and no apparent supply, Hammy can fix you up. Never gets directly involved though. A goddamn walking referral service. He swears to God he knows nothing, but says he's keeping an ear open. If you try to sweat him, he won't lawyer up. Just smile and clam up."

"One of those, huh."

"Yeah, he's actually a reasonable person."

"A reasonable sleaze. One of a kind."

"Hell, he's even used our help on occasion. One time, for about a week or so, there were these two trollops parading around the grandstands, openly hitting on prospective Johns. Real cheap act. Together, they looked like a walking painted menagerie."

"I get the picture," Maxwell interjected impatiently.

"Anyway, Hammy put us onto them. We picked them up and ran 'em back over to Goldspar. He commented that they were giving the place a bad name. That's the thing with Hammy. No matter what he's into, on the surface everything's smooth, quiet and clean. So, we almost always leave him alone."

"Mercury's no different than any place else in that respect."

"Tell me, Agent Maxwell, why the hell does something like this happen right under my nose? How'd your office get interested anyway?"

"They didn't, at first — I did," Maxwell nodded, deciding to lay it out. "Actually, the bureau forces its agents to retire at 55. But, there's a special budget for guys like me."

"Once an op, always an op?" the lieutenant was feeling more comfortable.

"On the side, I'd been onto something for a while that looks like it could connect up with that body in your reservoir," Maxwell leaned back in his chair, toying with the condensation on the outside of his beer glass. "Little over a year ago . . . one of the leading jockeys on the Maryland-Delaware racing circuit was discovered by a tugboat crew. His body was tangled against one of the pilings under the Delaware Memorial Bridge. Crabs and fish had done enough that we had to wait for the dental and DNA cross checks before being certain whom we had."

"Cause of death?" the lieutenant asked.

"A few months later, another top jockey," Maxwell chose to keep going, "this one in Southern California, was found shot in the head at pointblank range in a parking area near Seal Beach. There was a .38-caliber pistol in the car with only the jockey's prints on it. No note. Quickly went into the books as a suicide. But heck, this guy was riding good at the time. A family man, too. Kids and all."

"Two isolated things, coast-to-coast?" Lt. Huber shook his head. "That's not going to catch your attention."

"More recently — excluding the one you've got here — a leading jockey at the Fair Grounds in New Orleans was found dead from a hotshot of heroine. Didn't make any sense. Never tested positive for any controlled substance during his entire racing career. Didn't even drink beer, for crying out loud. And, he was at the top of his game . . . brought in three winners the day before. On top of all that, the nurse at the track's infirmary swore to God that the guy was deathly afraid of needles. One day — she said — while he was in the hotbox to drop a quick pound or two, he became so dehydrated that she had to rush him to the hospital. When they went to give him an I-V to get some liquids and electrolytes back into his system, he saw the needle coming and passed out cold as a mackerel, mumbling 'Oh, no, no' on the way out."

Maxwell explained to Lt. Huber that his report about the mutilated murder of the Mercury Downs jockey, since identified as Enrique Mendoza, pushed any earlier thoughts of coincidental accidents onto the back burner.

"Someone's killing jockeys all over the place, and scaring hell out of the rest," Maxwell summed it up. "Man, there's two prominent ones missing up in Canada in the past year. Nobody's been able to find them. I just took all of this information, including what you gave me over the phone, to my old boss and laid it out for him. He agreed."

"So, here you are."

"It's not generally known for good reasons, but there's a special operative budget for stuff like this. They've just put me back on the payroll under that amorphous status and turned me loose. Obviously, I have to check in once in a while, but that's all . . . unless I need something. Otherwise, I'm on my own. By the way, just call me Jace. Everybody else does, except my parents . . . and one other person.

"Sounds like a peachy setup, Jace," Lt. Huber interjected.

"I like to think I earned it," Maxwell smiled. "But, I'll tell you another thing that really helped. When I spoke to you about coming out here, you didn't give me lot of that usual junk about 'We don't need no help from no outsiders. We take care of our own problems our own selves out here.' Quite the contrary. You more than just invited me to come ahead."

Looking across at Maxwell, Lt. Huber knew this was a man he could trust and depend on.

"I'm happy you're here, Jace," the detective said with firm sincerity. "But, I've got to admit I've got a great big Medieval-size ax to grind about this one. Nothing like this ever happened before on my watch or anybody else's in the history of our police force. When I came away from looking at that poor kid's body with our medical examiner, I still couldn't fully grasp what I'd seen. It's hard for me to get inside how somebody could do something like that to man or beast. Hell, I've seen plenty of stabbings and shootings, mostly before I came out here to Mercury. But, Jesus Christ, this one was such an evil ritual."

Maxwell looked down at the table for a long few seconds, weighing the relative worth of what he was about to say.

"You're right about a monster like this not being from around here," he said quietly. "Creatures like this crawl out of a deep hole somewhere else, do their heinous bidding and then crawl back in. The area around Mercury can't provide that kind of continual cover. Goldspar might. But, if he was holed up there, he wouldn't pull a job as close by as Mercury. Distance is a factor here. Yes sir. This is danger on a whole new level. If you want to get into this, you'd better convince yourself, straight off, that you're probably going to have to do some things that you've never thought about doing before, or ever wanted to."

"I don't see where I have any choice."

"Hell, you asked the right question when you saw that kid's body. What sort of deranged evil could do something like that and just call it business as usual in the same way that you and I go to work? Because, like or not, this kid was killed professionally and for calculated reasons. Wasn't a random slashing by some serial nut case trying to sort out some repressed anxieties, and it's not the usual mob hit by a run-of-the-mill torpedo. This one will look at you the same way that you look at an inconsequential piece of paper that comes across your desk. Just something to be dealt with routinely and placed in the out-box, without so much as a lingering thought. It's the way he handles things that makes him special. All in the details."

As Maxwell spoke, the detective had been nodding his head up and down with quiet reservation.

"Look, this guy's got to be like everyone else," Lt. Huber broke in. "You shoot him, he'll bleed. And, he's got to have flaws, same as you and me. Flaws that will betray him. Hell, Jace, everybody's got flaws."

Maxwell smiled thinly. He expected this.

"You didn't find a speck of trace at the crime scene, did you?" he said rhetorically. "I mean, not the slightest hint of how the body even got in the water. Right?"

"No forensics," Lt. Huber answered solemnly. "Locard's Law is dying of loneliness. No trace evidence. No tire tracks. No footprints. No nothing, dammit. Our night shift was just ending when Mendoza's body was called in by that co-ed jogger. The weather was real mild overnight. Nothing that would have destroyed evidence. My best patrolman was on it first, so I know the scene wasn't compromised or contaminated . . . or tampered with. Hell, other than the body itself, there wasn't any evidence to contaminate. We don't even know where to start looking for the hands or leg parts. And, where the hell is all the blood? Jesus, Jace, that reservoir site is a secondary or tertiary crime scene at best."

"Absolutely right," Maxwell nodded.

"We're fortunate that Goldspar's office has a great lab setup. I personally drove everything Sugihara gave me over there. Even so, we already knew everything we were going to know before the lab got back to us with their findings. I had some track people come over and ID Mendoza's remains."

"That's got to be driving you nuts," Maxwell said flatly. "Especially since the body was mutilated some-where else. You're right. Where you found Mendoza was just the dumpsite. Look, this guy doesn't do this just for the money . . . and, believe me, there's plenty of money behind this. He does this because that's what he does. Period. The money just comes along."

For a moment, both were silent.

"And, this guy blends in just as normal as can be," Maxwell looked down at the tabletop and grimaced with a low snort. "Huh, if the three of us were walking down the street together, to anyone else he'd look saner than you or me. Look, when you get off work, what do you do? Go home and relax, or go some place and have a beer with your buddies, right? Not him. He goes home and reads FBI handbooks, criminology and aberrant psychology textbooks, and law enforcement training manuals. And, everything he reads is something he can use. Right now, he's got a heckuva lot better profile on you than you've got on him."

Lt. Huber took a long, deep breath and, sitting straight up with puffed cheeks and hands clenched at the nape of his neck, slowly let loose a resigning exhale.

"OK, so what do we do?" he said earnestly.

"Try to trap him," Maxwell said in a tone that be-came lower than the rest of the conversation. "But, that's up to you. This guy's a modern-day phenom. He doesn't exist, at least not the way he does, without to-day's easy access to high-speed, global transportation and communications. We're going to have to make it interesting enough for him to want to slither back here. I'll bet he's got some sort of bedrock rule about never coming anywhere near one of his previous scenes."

"Trap him?"

"Let's call it a day for now . . . I'll get the check . . . I'm budgeted for this kind of stuff. From now on though, we don't talk directly. I've got other ways of getting hold of you. If you see me around, no matter in what capacity, don't even let on that you recognize me. Just remember the password . . . 'Mercury hasn't had an earthquake in a hundred years'."

"Password! Sounds like nine words," Lt. Huber muttered in a drab attempt at dry humor.

Not amused, Maxwell quietly shook his head.

5

MAXWELL'S HAMMER

With the current racing season still in its early weeks, Maxwell quickly found work as a groom for one of the more successful stables at Mercury Downs, under trainer Will Harrison. Although the city of Mercury's neighborhood is almost completely white, the colony of workers along the track's shed rows remains a noticeable exception. With its glorious mix of whites, blacks, Hispanics and Asians represented by young and old men and women alike, one of the more improbable ways to hold anyone's attention in the stable area is a person's ethnicity.

One aspect where there is plenty of common ground is the lack of much formal education. Dropouts and runaways, along with occasional waves of illegal immigrants, are not uncommon. As long as you do what is expected and keep your nose clean, everybody remains friendly. To anyone even remotely connected to the horses, the backstretch is a very democratic hodgepodge of humanity. All opinions are given a chance to be heard, as each horse's handlers constantly search for and stoke the embers that will produce more speed and over a longer distance. Throughout the entire racetrack community, nothing else is nearly so important.

When told by Harrison that his wages would "not be very high," but that he could sleep in the general quarters in the barn area that boasted of electricity and a hot-water shower, Maxwell replied optimistically, "Dat's awrat, suh. Ah knows ah kin make dew. Ah can't hep it. Ah jess luvs bein' aroun' da hawses."

While they were talking, Maxwell, outfitted in faded jeans and a flannel green-and-black checkered shirt, suddenly took a step back, then walked over to a near-by colt that was showing mild signs of discomfort. Running his hand down the colt's left front leg and cupping the ankle, he commented, "Dar's a slight inflummashun in the suspensories. Overextended a liddel, huh? Not much heat rat now, but it'll turn bad ifen it don't git luked afta."

"By God, you spotted that!" the trainer said with a frown. "That's exactly what we've been doing with that one . . . giving him plenty of rest and a chance for that to heal. Listen, you're going to be responsible for that one and a couple of others. This one's Bright Boy. The other two are in racing shape right now. I'll see you in the morning. Four-thirty, sharp."

"Yessuh, Mistah Willy-am," Maxwell answered slowly with his toothiest grin. "Ah-be heer."

Ω

Harrison's shed row was immaculate to a distraction. Other trainers never failed to kid him when they visited, pointing to rare instances where items were slightly out of place or a small piece of paper had fallen on the floor. Maxwell had purchased a body-worn dark blue Dodge Charger with a good motor, meeting his desire for as inconspicuous a vehicle as he could imagine. He also maintained a motel room adjacent to Goldspar International Airport where he kept most of his regular belongings. This was his information base if the bureau needed to contact him.

As part of growing up, Maxwell long ago had learned to be a chameleon. At first, from one day to the next, nothing about life seemed to make much sense. So, he simply and passively accepted the blur of each new day as another cleanly erased slate. While quietly biding his time, he began to recognize latent similarities as his surroundings continually reaffirmed themselves. Gradually, through analytical deduction, not blind faith, he realized that he could confidently connect with these redundant cues, and react and adapt in accordance. From then on, silent patience became the stoic pacemaker behind the rigidly accountable fairness of his fiery spirit.

As the fourth of five children, with all of his older siblings being brothers, Jason was low man in the pecking order. One constant within this hodgepodge of brotherly strife was Arliss, closest to him in age and his unmerciful tormentor. Almost a four-year difference existed between the two. Arliss was born five months after their father had shipped off to Seoul, Korea, as an infantry soldier with the U.S. Army's First Cavalry Division. During the time her husband was away, Jason's mother held the family together as the housekeeping supervisor for the town's lone hotel, overseeing the laundry and dishwashing as well as the day-to-day rejuvenation of all forty-four rooms.

Jason knew precisely when his father had been discharged from the service. He was born nine months later. Two years later, the only girl of the generation, Carmella Anne, arrived. As far back as he could remember, Jason had been Carmy's caretaker and protector. The more he was made miserable by Arliss, the kinder and more doting Jason became with his younger sister. Occasionally, one of the older brothers would catch Arliss being mean to him and step in forcefully. Even so, that sort of vigilance was not nearly common enough to be relied on.

Not that Arliss harmed Jason physically. In fact, although there was an unspoken threat that he could, he never did. One day, they dug into their mother's clothes. Arliss made Jason put on one of her dresses and then completed the sculpture by forcing stockings and high heels on him, along with generous swabs of rouge and swipes of lipstick, then topping him off with a strawberry-colored straw hat. Then, ordering a sniffling-in-silence Jason to simply stand there, Arliss sat on the bed and howled helplessly with laughter. That particular antic happened only once, however. When their mother discovered the disheveled heap of her belongings, she quickly got to the bottom of the caper. Arliss was grounded for a month.

Another time, Arliss decided Jason was a goat and tied him by an ankle to the base of one of the clothesline poles in the backyard. The restraining string was too strong for Jason to break. He whined and tugged, but couldn't figure out how to undo the knot. Mother Maxwell, watching from the kitchen window, allowed this escapade to play out for a while, knowing that her son would be goat-tied more than once during the years up ahead and might as well begin learning how to deal with life's little inconveniences right now.

The caveat in Arliss's sibling lordship over Jason was its unforeseen termination. While Jason grew taller and filled out with muscle, Arliss seemed to stay about the same. From the beginning, Arliss purposely threw baseballs and footballs too hard to Jason, and blocked basketball shots back into his face with painful regularity. Slowly though, through badger-like perseverance, Jason began handling everything Arliss threw his way, and found he could launch a clean jump shot over Arliss's outstretched defense without the slightest interference. The more successful Jason became, the more Arliss verbally taunted him . . . until that day toward the end of Jason's eighth-grade school year when Arliss, a high school junior by now, was being particularly nasty. Chiding Jason's manhood every time he drove toward the basket during a late afternoon one-on-one skirmish, Arliss also began using his hips and elbows. Suddenly, Jason shoved the ball aside and smacked Arliss squarely in the mouth with his right fist. Then, without wasting any motion, he covered up, awaiting his brother's compulsory retaliation.

After a long moment, Jason peeked from behind his crab-like crouch. Arliss wasn't on the attack. He was ten feet away, head down and both hands covering his mouth as he sobbed in utter resignation. They played no more that day. As they walked home together, both boys realized that their worlds had changed forever.

"Don't think you can just move down and start picking on Carmy, either," Jason said with newfound frankness. "So help me God, if I ever catch you doing that, I'll come at you with everything I've got." Never before had he noticed how soft and pudgy Arliss was.

Ω

Jason's parents, both of whom had been forced to go to work before finishing high school, had vowed that every one of their children would earn high-school diplomas.

"We shouldn't have them if we can't afford to give them a good start in life," Mother Maxwell said in agreement with her husband's only request when they began openly discussing their plans for marriage.

The two oldest Maxwell brothers had already graduated from Lincoln High School by the time Jason enrolled as a freshman. Arliss was now a senior, Carmella Anne a seventh-grader at nearby Benjamin Harrison Middle School. Already the starting strong-side safety on defense, Jason, rapidly developing as an exceptional athlete, earned his way onto the Tigers' offense as a starting halfback after the third game of the season. In accomplishing this uncommon feat, he had forced a senior and two-year starter onto the bench. Jason always credited Arliss's earlier barbarism with molding his toughness.

The Tigers' varsity games were played on Saturday afternoons, so Friday's practices were mandatory . . . no excuses. Missing Friday's practice meant forfeiting the honor of even suiting up on Saturday. Going into their seventh game of the season, the undefeated Tigers were tied with their archrival neighbors, the Franklin Pierce Rhinos, for the conference title. If the Tigers beat this Saturday's opponent, the lowly Strathorne Rams, then next week's matchup would be a championship battle of unbeaten teams.

On the Friday before the Rams game, Jason was not there when practice started. All session long, the Tiger coaching staff, while intermittently gazing toward the locker-room door, went over final preparations for tomorrow's game. The previously demoted senior was situationally reinstated at Jason's halfback position. Then, while the players were walking off the field after several practice-ending wind sprints, Jason came out of the locker room in full pads, carrying his helmet in a full run.

"Coach, I got here as soon as I could," he pleaded to Head Coach Harmon Kellogg in between short breaths. "The biggest Algebra test of the semester is Monday. Miss Davis offered us a special after-school review session today. I need all the help in there I can get. Let me do some wind sprints and hit the blocking dummies so I can say I've been here today."

"I'm sorry, Mr. Maxwell," Coach Kellogg lamented. "Can't do it. There's enough people here who know you missed practice. Besides, I'm the one who made the rule. Can't very well not enforce it, wouldn't you say?"

Deflated, Jason nodded and turned away. The next afternoon, the Tigers squeezed out a 34-32 victory over the inspired Rams while he watched helplessly from the stands. His replacement scored three touchdowns, including the winning points with less than two minutes to play.

As always, on the Monday following a game, the varsity Tigers never went near the practice field, let along put on pads. It was a day to physically recuperate from Saturday's wear-and-tear and do some post-game analysis of Saturday's game films. Also, the scouting films for the upcoming game were usually seen for the first time. This one, against the conference co-leading Rhinos, would be for all the marbles.

As the players were leaving after the review, Jason approached Coach Kellogg.

"Coach, I'm very sorry I missed the game," he said remorsefully. "I knew the rule, and had a decision to make. But, I missed it because of an academic conflict. I don't know of any other reason short of a deathbed sickness that would've kept me away."

"I believe you, Mister Maxwell," Coach Kellogg said, giving his best running back his due.

"Coach, it killed me that I let my teammates down," Jason felt there was a congenial opening for further expression. "If we'd lost that game, I don't know what I would have done. I don't know if I could have faced anybody today. Trouble is, if the same situation comes up again . . . I mean, if I had to take care of something concerning Algebra or English Literature or whatever . . . something important with my studies, I'm afraid I'd have to make the same choice the same way again. I'm here to learn and get good grades. Then comes football."

Eyebrows raised, Jason stared, seeking out any sign of understanding, while Coach Kellogg smiled back, marveling at the youngster's maturity.

"Son, you're a freshman," the coach finally responded with a quiet directness. "But you've got more savvy than most of my seniors. You had what I consider to be a very valid reason for missing practice. But, if I go around splitting hairs — you know, this excuse is a good one, but that one isn't, sort of thing — I'd be opening a whole can of worms that I don't need to be opening."

They nodded to each other in collective understanding, then the coach turned and walked away.

As Friday's final prep for the crucial Rhinos game was winding down with the traditional wind sprints and war whoops, Coach Kellogg announced that, beginning next season, there would be a slight change in the rules. Anyone who missed a mandatory Friday practice would not be able to start on that Saturday, implying that, once the game was underway, the coach's discretion would determine who should or shouldn't get into the game.

Ω

While football forced Jason to face up to his personal priorities, springtime on the Tigers' track team taught him the most about the uniquely American cultural mystique looming between black and white people. He was a skillfully competitive high jumper and long jumper. But, sharing in the camaraderie of the school's championship mile-relay foursome did the most to open his eyes. Although Jason also was an accomplished basketball player, he did not try out for that school team. After the distracting pressures of football season, the growing scholar used his basketball-season hiatus from organized sports to ensure that he was on top of all of his studies. He was a straight-A student and co-captain of the debate team.

Whenever there wasn't a weekend meet for the whole track team, Coach Arthur Becker found special competitions for his crack mile-relay team, which, on some occasions, required a couple of hours or more of travel each way. Coach Becker, along with his assistant, would load his four regular runners and one alternate into the school's Volkswagen Microbus. Hours of traveling in close quarters, and stopping to eat along the way, gave everyone plenty of opportunity for an interracial familiarity that was rare among Lincoln High students at the time.

Scholastic integration had long become a comfortable routine at Lincoln High. Yet, while the students mingled in more than a simply cordial fashion in the classrooms and hallways, there remained a lingering social barrier of former times. When the school day was over, white students went their way and black students theirs. The black section of town was predominately occupied by members of two rather expansive families, the Taylors and the Maxwells. It was common among the local white dropouts and other rigidly backward types to pompously refer to that section of town as "Taylorville."

As the third leg on the Tigers' all-senior relay and its lone black runner, Jason received the shiny metallic baton from a white hand and passed it to another white hand. The unbroken chain reaction from this inter-ethnic flow of energy led to a showcase of gold medals and trophies for each member of the foursome and a significant spirit of accomplishment for the entire school. In unison, the Tiger quartet tore through an ever-warming season of unharnessed exuberance that none of them would ever find again.

To earn a leg on the relay, Jason had to beat out one of Lincoln High's regular varsity sprinters in a best-of-three series of match races, overseen by Coach Becker. After the first two races, there was no need for a third. He had glided to the finish a convincing five yards ahead of the sprinter in both quarter-mile confrontations.

Relegated to the role of alternate on the relay, the sprinter, also a senior, didn't take it well. Unbeknownst to Jason, the demoted runner began spreading injuriously false gossip, concocting that Jason had told him the reason that he lost was because he was white. "Any black guy could beat the likes of you," the Caucasian sprinter hatefully misclaimed, grasping to soothe the pain from Jason's proven superiority.

Right away, though, the other relay members caught onto the ruse. John and Davey, the first and anchor legs of the relay, quickly warned Jason of the situation, assuring him that it was he they wanted as part of the squad. They also made Coach Becker aware of the sprinter's denigrating remarks and requested permission to take care of the matter internally. The coach acquiesced, provided that the situation didn't escalate.

At that afternoon's practice, after warming up for a few laps, Jason approached the sprinter during their stretching exercises. They hadn't spoken to each other since their match races. Nearby Tiger teammates paused with whatever they were doing, poised and ready to break up what they fully expected.

"The things you've been saying behind my back are getting back to me," Jason said directly, in a quiet monotone, while the sprinter, in the midst of a butterfly routine, slowed and stared at the grass in front of him. "I've run into your kind before. You're no surprise. If you aren't good enough, you'd rather see your teammates get beat without you. A real team player. I just want to encourage you to keep repeating those things you're saying. The people who I want to hang around with know exactly how to deal with your type. And that's all that you are. Just a predictable type. There's nothing special about you. I hope that someday you'll find a place where your sort of behavior is viewed with something other than disgust. Good luck."

The sedentary sprinter showed no signs of responding. Moments later, Jason quietly jogged away.

The following afternoon, before practice, without comment, the sprinter turned in his track uniform to Coach Becker. The coach nodded without a word.

Ω

On the road, the Tiger relay would exhaust their opinions on any subject of the moment. Preferences in clothes, music, dance styles and, of course, whenever the conversation turned to women, the one doing the talking instantly had everyone's undivided attention. Larry, the second leg on the relay, told about his mother making him take lessons in ballroom dancing and how all of those hours hadn't helped him one iota when it came to capturing the essence of the twist, Watusi or funky chicken.

"Ballroom dancing doesn't get girls," Larry chirped desperately. "It chases them away!"

"I guess it all depends on the kind of girl you're looking for," Jason spoke up. "I know some who would look rather kindly on that approach."

"Maybe so, but he sure has showed everyone how scary mixing the fox-trot with the twist can be," Davey, used to seeing Larry cavort unyieldingly at the school's Saturday night victory dances, piped up. "Talk about a stork with its head down, wading in ankle-high water, looking for unsuspecting tadpoles! How about waltzing a Watusi?"

After the laughter, pushing and shoving subsided, Jason shared how his grandmother had an uncanny secret formula for making dandelion wine. The intimate exchanging of these endless personal tidbits laid the groundwork for plenty of lifelong understandings.

6

AGELESS ARCHANGEL

Early in his senior year, Jason received a handful of scholarship offers for athletics and academics. Meetings with Lincoln High's guidance counselor had sharpened his interest in wanting to study the law. Accordingly, he was drawn to the partial academic scholarship offered by Northwestern University, preferring it over several opportunities afforded by full athletic scholarships from small colleges and other universities. The counselor agreed. But, where to make up the prohibitive remaining portion of the financial nut that had to be cracked in order to attend a school of Northwestern's caliber?

One of the town's most socially active dowagers presided over a trust fund that breathed life into a scholarship program created by her deceased husband solely for the purpose of giving a local graduating student a needed boost toward pursuing a college education. In addition to requiring a consistently outstanding record of academic excellence and personal character, a special stipulation of the trust was that the student must demonstrate full intentions to pursue a career in either agriculture or law.

Jason's counselor urged him to write a letter of application to the widow. Some years, the counselor noted, the funds from that source were not even given out because no one could be found who met its stringent standards.

Four weeks later, Jason received word through his counselor that he had been awarded the widow's annual stipend. Furthermore, the letter informed him that, if he showed continued success with his chosen pursuit of pre-law, the funds would be renewable each year until he graduated.

While celebrating openly with his counselor, Jason promised that, along with writing a formal letter of appreciation, he would visit the widow in person.

Ω

"Thank you for coming, young man," Mrs. Dahlia Cranford smiled. She was a tiny, seemingly physically frail lady in her early eighties, made smaller by the enormity of the overstuffed crimson felt armchair in which she sat rigidly upright.

"It's the least I could do, Ma'am, considering how happy and grateful I am," he said with emphasized sincerity. "Your foundation has made all the difference in my present choice of opportunities. I'll try to make the intentions of your scholarship proud that you have chosen to support me."

"I know you will, young man," Mrs. Cranford said, continuing to smile as they looked each other over. "Mr. Cranford would have been proud to know that you will represent the Cranford Foundation Scholarship this coming year. Northwestern should provide you with a proper challenge."

"One thing though, Ma'am," Jason just couldn't let the issue go. "I hope you didn't give me this honor just because I'm black."

Mrs. Cranford broke into an amused giggle.

"Truthfully, Mr. Maxwell, I didn't know you were a Negro until you walked in here just now," she shared. "We don't ask unimportant questions when we're seeking the best person."

Her response made him take a momentary mental step back. Not since he was very young had he been formally referred to as a Negro. Black, yes. Afro- or African-American, yes. But Negro? Oh well, that's one way to accurately measure the generation gap. What's next? Colored?

Ω

The discussion inside the Maxwell home was very different. There had never been any thoughts of college educations in the Maxwell family. Over dinner, with Arliss and Carmella Anne also at the table, Jason carefully laid out for his parents all of his academic plans and the financial support available for his intentions. As was his growing manner, Jason respectfully explained and re-explained every detail in its most basic terms. Adrift on uncharted waters, everyone remained quietly puzzled after he had finished. Desperate for a sign, Jason nodded in askance to each of them as he slowly looked around the table. Finally, his father broke in.

"You know, Mother," Mr. Maxwell spoke up, while leaning back in his chair and smiling to his wife. "With Carmella Anne still to go, each one of our children has fulfilled our dreams of an education the way we first planned . . ."

"Yes, but . . . " Mrs. Maxwell sensed his drift.

"Let me finish first, Mother," Mr. Maxwell said gently. "I've seen how a college education prepares a young man for the world. There was a whole bunch of them over there in Korea. Instead of drafting them right when they reached eighteen, the Army allowed them to go to college . . . something called a deferment. Then they were grabbed up right afterwards. Didn't seem to matter what they had studied in college. They just had more confidence, understood things quicker and were better prepared for anything that was thrown at them."

Mrs. Maxwell smiled back at her husband with quiet reassurance.

"I know I speak for myself and the other brothers," Arliss suddenly joined the discussion. "All we ever wanted to do was get that diploma, get a job and start making money. Simple as that. I don't know anything about this college stuff. But, if Jason is right in saying that everything's taken care of, why not? If that's what he wants."

"It was our duty to make sure the next generation in our family all earned their high-school diplomas," Mr. Maxwell said. "But then, in turn, it also would be up to them to make sure their children did better. Maybe go to college? Maybe Jason here has given us the chance to take that next jump a little early?"

Then Mrs. Maxwell spoke.

"Evanston, Illinois? That's an awful long way away from home, baby," she said, looking directly at Jason with a wrinkled brow. "You've never been away before."

"I know, Momma. I'll be OK," he said smoothly, putting his hand on her arm. "I'll be in the freshman dormitories with a whole bunch of homesick kids. We'll help each other through it. I'll miss you, too. I'll write as often as I can. Just keep taking care of everybody at this end."

Everyone laughed at the truth in that last comment. Mother Maxwell had steadfastly remained the glue and hub for the family's strength.

"And, we'll send you some money whenever we can, son," Mr. Maxwell interjected, reinforcing his encouragement. "All work and no play . . . " His sentence trailed off as Mother Maxwell gave him a stern look.

Ω

That summer, before heading off to college, Jason washed dishes at a local restaurant during the day, banking all of those paychecks, and pumped gas for three hours in the early evening for his regular spending money.

Regina Taylor, daughter of a local doctor, had been Jason's steady girl all through their junior and senior years at Lincoln High. Together, they had been chosen as part of the senior royal court for the Homecoming Queen. A tall, slender, athletic girl with sharp features and a serious outlook, Regina could shoot pool with the best players in the area. Around her family's pool table, Jason and she conspired against whatever other plans the adults may have had in store for them.

Jason and Regina knew what they wanted, with or without anyone else's blessing. He would go off to Northwestern and complete his pre-law studies with a Liberal Arts approach. Then, she would join him when he began pursuing his law degree. Meanwhile, Regina would enroll as a History and Language Arts double-major at the state university. As the only child of Dr. and Mrs. Thomas Taylor, both college graduates, it was a foregone conclusion — even before they knew whether they had conceived a daughter or son — that she would earn a college degree before doing anything else with her life. Her disenchantment with this apparent cradle-to-the-grave management of her life by others fanned the fires of many volatile discussions around the Taylor dinner table.

Ω

After delightfully looking forward to his first invitation to dinner at the Taylors, Jason ended up visibly disturbed. Having meticulously rehearsed his stock answers to the predictable barrage of questions about his plans for the future and his intentions with their daughter, he instead had to endure a meal-long onslaught of blistering salvos between Regina and the doctor. Shortly after the introductory niceties were performed, and the soup and salad appetizers were served, it started up.

"What if I don't want to go to college, Daddy?" Regina snapped at the doctor, with the tone of an ultimatum.

"Oh, you'll go, young lady," he answered evenly in a tone that sounded like soft-rolling thunder, but not unfriendly. "And, it won't be the local junior college, either, where you're coming home every day. No siree, it'll be a good college or university somewhere, with room and board and all the rest of it."

"Is that why you're a doctor, Daddy?" Because someone made you be that? You had nothing to say about it? And, don't young lady me, either! I'm not all that young . . . and the jury's still out on me wanting to be a lady."

"Look, back then I was flat-out grateful to have the opportunity. I wasn't some privileged brat who stuck my nose in the air at everything."

"Oh, my aching ass. Here it comes. The black Abe Lincoln and his humble log-cabin beginnings."

"Now, dammit, that's off-limits."

"Rule number one, Daddy, nothing's off-limits at the Taylor dinner table. That's the way you brought me up. Your rules."

"Well then, certain aspects are so ridiculous, they warrant no further discussion. Let's leave it at that."

Mrs. Taylor sat quietly by, satisfied that she had nothing to add to her daughter's expressions of her own feelings. "Please don't let this stuff bother you, Mr. Maxwell," she smiled at Jason, noticing his uneasiness. "These two characters have been going at it like this as far back as I can remember. Just relax . . . enjoy the dinner."

By dinner's end, the battling twosome had touched all the bases — politics, religion, sex and sports. They seemed to enjoy the special audience that Jason provided.

"Holy mackerel, Gina, maybe you should go off to Northwestern, and I'll just stay here and pump gas," he moaned across the pool table once they were alone after dinner.

"Oh my, Jason. Daddy and I have been going at it forever," she chuckled, echoing her mother's dinner table appraisal, while enjoying his discomfort to an unconcealed extent, with a smidgen of friendly cruelty in her tone. "I don't even pay any attention anymore. I'm truly sorry if it made you so uneasy. If I had known that, I'd have cut it short."

"Oh, really?"

"Trust me, it beats heck out sitting there hearing him drone on about Mrs. Storer's diabetes or Mo Jones's gout or any of that other medical-talk drivel. Your turn, stud. Shoot!"

Regina's aggressive directness had him. He knew she enjoyed needling her scholar-athlete beau occasionally, but would never, ever leave him out to dry. Her high cheekbones rounded downward to a tight, but not pointed, chin, giving her face a creamy Valentine radiance, especially when she broadened that comely heart-shapedness by smiling her widest smile. In the clutches of self-discipline though, her soft hazel eyes took on an instant steeliness whenever she drew down on a cue ball. Her wardrobe, tonight, a beige pantsuit composite, was chosen to eclectically announce, without accentuation, that she was joyously prepared to uphold her part in nature's bargain. Someone an escort would be confidently comfortable with anywhere. Together, Jason and she would clear their own special path through the thick underbrush of life's uncharted forest.

"What does he think about my background?" he asked with quizzical concern. "I mean, heck, you come from a doctor's family, and mine's a bunch of relatively uneducated laborers."

"He knows about your family, Jason," she now looked at him with calm sincerity. "Each of them do what they can to make our community a better place in which to live. That's all my father tries to do. No different."

"No different?" Jason exclaimed. "Then what's all this fuss about going to college? Law degrees, and all that?"

"Oh hell, they may not be able to keep up with Daddy's medical talk. So what? If they started talking about what they do, they'd darn sure lose him just as fast. Besides, don't let tonight's dinner confuse you. We don't have lobster tails all the time. Momma likes you. Wanted to impress."

"Well, tell her she did," Jason nodded assuredly.

"Tell her yourself," she said, only half-kiddingly, then sternly redirected. "Your mother's the one who has me in awe. How she held that household together, with all those boys, while your father was off fighting in that war?"

"Yeah, Mom's pretty cool. Given me a lot — a lot that I probably haven't even figured out yet," he answered quietly.

"Besides, why do you make the same mistake most people do?" Regina returned to her dinnertime tone. "Just because Daddy's a doctor, he must be super-well-rounded? Knows all about everything? A lot you know about pursuing a medical career. After their bachelor's degree, they have to focus through years of very narrow training. If they want to be educated beyond that, they've got to do that on their own. I know that's why Daddy likes — even instigates — our supper-time arguments."

Ω

Jason remained at the top of his class throughout his four years at Northwestern, and in early December of his senior year he received his letter of acceptance from Yale Law School in Connecticut. Over the Christmas break, Regina and he sharpened their plans to be married in mid-June and then travel to New Haven. She began seeking a teaching position there.

He chose to remain on campus during Spring Break. Taking an overload of elective courses, Jason was using the extra time to finish up some reading and complete some reports. From there, only the formality of final exams stood between him and his marriage to Regina.

He had become a solid young man during his growth on campus. While still a freshman, he had toyed with the idea of becoming a walk-on for the football team. Soon though, his observations of the obvious difference between the demands at the high school and college levels of the sport squashed such thoughts. He did, however, long jump and high jump for the freshman track team during his first spring on campus, scoring points in a couple of dual meets. That, too, soon became an unworkable imposition as he delved deeper and deeper into his studies.

Even so, Jason stayed in excellent physical condition by regimenting time to jog-run and lift weights a few times each week. This caring attention to both body and mind would be part of his character for the rest of his life, except for one relatively brief period.

7

SOFT-SHELL TO HARD-SHELL

"Oh, Jason, I'm so sorry, baby" his mother wailed when Jason took an unexpected phone call from her on the Sunday afternoon before final-exam week was to begin.

Regina was dead.

Instantly engulfed by a numbing fog, Jason helplessly fought to grasp what his mother was talking about as she described some of the details of this impossible turn. *"This can't be true,"* he silently ruminated over and over, fading in and out of a world of dull nothingness. Her words became broken nonsensical intrusions into his devastated consciousness. Only the lucky ones who have never met this terrible sort of ambush upon humanity face-to-face tend to explain away the effects as trivially as though being stunned by a sledgehammer. Suddenly and unexpectedly losing an everyday heart mate — an uncompromisingly affirmed partner in life — is to be gripped by a darkly heavy tentacle jutting from some anti-dimensional murky undercore of despair, and being pulled harder and harder downward, while knowing it will never, ever be undone. Unlike a hammer blow, there is no recovery from the clutches of finality that abruptly severs a shared personality.

According to the coroner's report, the cause of death was accidental asphyxiation. Dr. Taylor and Regina apparently had sneaked away very early Sunday morning to pick up a low-mileage, white Cadillac El Dorado convertible about sixty miles to the north, in

Olsenburg. The pair wanted to have the vehicle parked in the driveway by the time Mrs. Taylor arose. Regina had lovingly created the gigantic red "Happy Birthday" bow they took with them.

The predawn air had been irritatingly cool and damp as the mid-May vestiges of a frigid season fought a losing battle with Spring's rolling out of the carpet for Summer. After acquiring the vehicle and leaving Mrs. Taylor's Oldsmobile Cutlass behind as a modest trade-in, Dr. Taylor and Regina began the journey home with the heater on and the windows rolled up. The coroner suggested that Regina must have felt drowsy and climbed into the back seat to lie down. Approaching the outskirts of town, according to nearby motorists, the El Dorado suddenly had slowed, drifted onto the shoulder of the road, then come to a quiet stop in the adjacent drainage ditch.

First-arriving witnesses found Dr. Taylor slumped over the steering wheel and Regina lying motionless across the back seat. The motor was still running and all four doors were locked. While one witness phoned for emergency help, another had broken the passenger's side window with a nearby brick. Both unresponsive bodies were pulled from the vehicle, and CPR was being performed when the first emergency medical service ambulance arrived. Regina was pronounced dead at the scene, and attempts to revive Dr. Taylor failed as the ambulance screamed toward the local emergency room.

The vehicle's exhaust system somehow had an over-looked, yet sizable, puncture near the manifold leading from the engine, and, with the windows tightly sealed on that dreary morning, carbon monoxide fumes from the unchanneled exhaust had seeped up into the pass-engers' area. As if grinning with satanic irony, Regina's huge red bow reclined upright on the passenger's side front seat.

"How's Mrs. Taylor, Momma?" Jason whispered, dully aware that the full brunt of this emotional cata-clysm still waited in the shadows of the moment. "I ought to come home and see her."

"She collapsed at hearing the news," his mother answered after a moment of silence. "She's been taken to the hospital. The funerals will be this coming Wednesday. Son, I know this is going to sound callous to say, but maybe the best thing you can do is stay where you are and finish your studies."

"Momma, I loved that woman more than myself," Jason said with a returning, but dull, awareness. "I'll be there as soon as I can."

He went directly to campus and in zombie-like fashion found his major advisor. An academic workaholic, Dr. Alex Fleming habitually spent his Sunday afternoons in his office, tinkering with his latest manuscript in self-imposed isolation. Explaining what had happened, Jason asked the professor to contact his other instructors about the possibility of taking make-up exams quickly enough to still allow him to graduate on time.

"I'll only be gone a few days," Jason promised. "I'll be back before the end of the week."

And he was. The combined funeral service, attended by a seemingly endless stream of grievers and consolers, had gone off quietly for Jason, except when one out-of-town reporter stepped in front of him as he was leaving the grave site.

"How do you feel, sir?" the reporter asked with a recording microphone thrust forward.

"How do you think I feel, for God's sake!" he lashed back with verbal restraint, his puffy reddish eyelids holding back an upwelling of unshed tears.

Momma was right. Mrs. Taylor had become inconsolable since the tragedy. Jason returned to campus without visiting her; and, under the collective understanding of his somber professors, he mechanically waded through the ritual of his final exams. Fortunately, his classroom performances earlier in the semester had established a record that could robustly withstand the distracted disregard with which he now wrote out his answers.

Once home again, he called the dean of the law school's office at Yale to say that he would not be attending classes this coming Fall. After a brief explanation, he assured the dean that a formal letter confirming his decision would follow.

"I wanted you to know as soon as possible, sir," Jason said. "I know that this is terribly late. I hope that you can still find a suitable student to take my place."

"You are among the most highly qualified candidates in our incoming class, Mr. Maxwell," the voice at the other end confided. "Oh, we will fill the vacancy. However, I doubt we will do it quite so well. Should your situation change and you wish to reconsider in the future, by all means, please contact us right away."

He also made an appointment to see Mrs. Cranford. Her foundation had offered additional funding to defray much of his law school expenses, with the understanding that, upon passing the bar exam, Jason would agree to return to his hometown to practice law for at least three years.

"Time doesn't allow us to forget, but it allows us to go on after a while, Jason," Mrs. Cranford, now in her mid-eighties, shared in quiet reflection. "It never really heals us, just allows us to go forward. Be thankful for that . . . I suppose I ought to know. I've buried three of my five children . . . There's a special unnatural sort of sadness anytime a parent has to bury a child. It's never right . . . When you decide to pick up again, our money will be here for you. You've made our foundation quite proud . . . I appreciate you coming to tell me in person. God's speed, Mr. Maxwell."

He marveled at widow's directness. They had reached an understanding without having to dwell endlessly on the circumstances. *"Indeed,"* he self-mused, *"occasionally wisdom and age truly do go hand-in-hand."*

Quickly aware of the discontinuity in his educational pursuits, the local draft board requested that Jason come in for a physical exam and aptitude testing. He knew that his attributes would guarantee a 1-A induction status now. Only a matter of weeks remained before he inevitably would be asked to report for duty. So, when he reported for his preliminary physical, rather than simply succumbing as an aimless two-year draftee and being arbitrarily stationed wherever Uncle Sam decided and doing whatever job matched the location, he volunteered for a regular three-year commitment. This way, he would be given a much stronger measure of choice over how he wanted to serve his commitment.

Ω

In the years to come, Jason would always wonder why the government had ever discontinued the draft. All able young men could use at least a couple of years of contemplation and reflection, he felt, between doing mainly what others had told them to do and preparing for what they wanted to do for themselves. Also, serving in the military was a solid measure of gratitude to a country that had provided an early, safe, nourishing stage for life. His gut feeling on this issue never softened, but later expanded to include young women, though he couldn't envision them as combat soldiers.

Heck, he would always argue, in most other countries there is a short list of only a few things that are acceptable. And, if you're caught doing anything else, you'd better be convincing with your explanation to the proper authorities. In America, though, there are only a few things that you're not supposed to do — unreasonable infractions such as murder, theft and so forth. Otherwise, you can do just about anything you choose . . . as long as you're willing to live with the consequences.

Ω

During basic training at Fort Dix, New Jersey, he was introduced to the rudiments of killing people with a rifle, bayonet and his hands, Then, having volunteered for Officers Candidate School, he became familiar with the theory and practice of leadership. While at Fort Benning, Georgia, he also took three weeks of infantry airborne training, and then went way beyond simpler static-line jumps by joining the "Hi-Lo Club" — soldiers who jumped from planes in a silent free-fall and then, manually, didn't pull the rip chords of their parachutes until moments before it wouldn't do any good. By now, Jason was completely immersed in being a capable war-time machine. Even without a weapon in his hand, he was willfully dangerous. He topped off his first year of military service with Special Forces survival training in the swamplands of Louisiana's bayou region.

Walking out of the backwater ooze and slim where the alligators and water moccasins play, Jason immediately stepped into the leadership of a counterinsurgency squad designated as the Crab Claws. For the next eighteen months, extended from an original twelve, his covert unit roamed the jungles of Cambodia, putting dents in the Khmer Rouge's ongoing reign of atrocities.

His first kill would haunt him forever. As skilled as he had become in the use of all sorts of small-arms weapons, it was with a sawed-off 10-gauge shotgun full of double-O buckshot that he blasted his first enemy soldier into oblivion. Silently coming around a dense stand of bamboo, Jason had surprised the young fighter who was squatted, relieving himself. At pointblank range, as the startled soldier reached for his nearby pistol, Jason shot him squarely in the face. That instant-before terror on the youth's face became engraved in Jason's memory. Infinite times after, he wondered where the fellow might have called home. Did he have a loyal, loving sweetheart like Regina waiting? Perhaps he was a daddy?

The rest of his kills became a dehumanized blur of sub-anthropomorphic vertebrates whose life-rules merited an instant death sentence in any way possible. Remarkably, the Crab Claws lost only one member under Jason's watch, when one of his scouts apparently misjudged a booby trap while attempting to disarm a land mine. Conversely, the unit grew in size whenever, usually under cover of night, a courier parachuted into their ever-moving location with the latest top-secret information about their newest targets. Instantly, these couriers also were absorbed as permanent members of the Crab Claws.

Their only mission was to create organizational chaos by assassinating whomever they determined as having a stranglehold of cruelty and terror on a village's inhabitants. The Crab Claws never remained long enough to find out if their intrusions had any lasting effect. They only hoped that fairness and democracy would be given an opportunity. Having once experienced the horror of cruel occupation, the assumption was that the villagers would become more aggressively protective of their former order when given a chance. A village-by-village checkers game of death.

Without the expected attrition rate within his squad, and with regular additions of parachuting couriers, by the time Jason left his Crab Claws, the hit-and-run unit had ballooned into a mini-platoon. They were at the bursting point of no longer being capable of virtual invisibility and the element of surprise.

Whenever assured by reconnaissance that a general area was secure enough for an overnight bivouac, Jason would post sentries along an expanded perimeter and allow his otherwise stoically silent men to relax and carry on in relative quiet. He would intervene after a short while whenever the chatter became heated over religion, sex or politics. However, he always allowed arguments about race to run a fuller course. With a solid mixture of whites, blacks, Asians and Hispanics under his command, Jason crystallized his lifelong effort to break through color lines by means of natural familiarity. In the clutches of a steamy jungle, all Crab Claws were thoroughly convinced that the color or creed of a person didn't matter a hill of beans while they watched each other's backs.

After eighteen months in the corrosive heat of a Southeast Asian, disease-infested oven, Jason was assigned to Fort Lewis in the state of Washington for debriefing and to begin processing for his discharge back into civilian life. On July 15, he knocked on the door with a wide toothy smile and Captain's bars on his shoulders. When his mother opened it, he fell into her arms. They kept each other from falling.

"Thank God you're safe," Mrs. Maxwell sniffled uncontrollably. "Come see your father. But, I have to warn you, he's not been doing real good."

A year ago, Mr. Maxwell had retired from the rubber factory with a good pension and a lifelong guarantee of full medical benefits. Lately though, he had been bedridden off-and-on in a weakening and wasting condition. Jason tried to mask his astonishment when his frail father gingerly sat up and smiled. Jason sat on the edge of the bed, and they looked each other over with knowing smiles. As fellow war-zone soldiers, they communicated without uttering a word.

Ω

The world that Jason had come back to was the residual decade following the stormy upheaval carved from the patient nonviolence preached by assassinated Dr. Martin Luther King Jr. and the even earlier assassination of Malcolm X and his black nationalist solution to black people's endemic problems, cross-matched with the more volatile immediacy of H. Rapp Brown, the Black Power credo of Stokely Carmichael, and the proactiveness of Huey Newton and his Black Panther Party, along with the writings of James Baldwin. Adopting an Islamic name after winning the world heavyweight boxing championship, Cassius Clay, now Muhammad Ali, encouraged people, especially black people, to speak their minds in defiance of the encrusted social structure into which they had been born.

Seemingly providing the necessary tinder in the mid-50s, Rosa Parks' quiet resistance to the established southern rule of yielding her seat to a white Montgomery bus rider reached farther than all of Angela Davis's high-pitched radical rhetoric that followed. Somewhat earlier, the image of Nobel Peace Prize Laureate Dr. Ralph Bunche had been too lofty, too singular for the average American, and, more importantly, black Americans, to latch onto as an enlightened direction. This newer multifaceted movement had everyday substance and promised something for everybody. Now, riding the crest of President Johnson's civil rights package, millions raised their fists against the deadening status quo of America's caste system of racism.

As this broad brush of social correction was repainting the American landscape, it seemed to blindly stimulate new allowances of any sort. Draft evaders found as much, or perhaps more, solace as those who had dutifully answered their country's call. While amnesty for draft evaders was being debated, and would subsequently be granted, many of those who had served were encountering hopeless practicalities as they sought to reposition themselves and find peace within the society that they had fought to preserve.

As he became more confused and depressed, Jason began drinking heavily to escape into a pickling hermitage. Each time he reawakened, flashbacks of murder-torn Cambodia, and especially the image of that first young soldier whom he had vanquished with the simple flick of a trigger finger, were there to greet him. He began avoiding people, and staying away from places that afforded any sort of social contact. He was afraid of himself . . . fearful that something, very likely unintentional and remote, might suddenly bring the dormant ferocity of his combat training back to the surface; and that he would involuntarily hurt someone, or worse. He needed his unreachable Regina.

Within six months after his release from active duty, Jason had plummeted to the nadir of his personal despair, hospitalized in complete mental and physical disarray. Six weeks of proper sleep and reasonable meals without alcohol lifted his confusion and began giving his spirit a healthful chance. Visits by his mother and clinical psychiatrist Dr. Ivan Zapinski, followed by twice-weekly encounters with cognitive psychiatrist Dr. Jonathan Rhent, while he rested at the home of his parents, provided him with the time and support to regain a grip on the direction of his personal worth in contemporary Americana.

Ω

A short time later, his mother candidly reminded him that the GI Bill for Education had been re-established by Congress in the previous decade. Though the financial support provided by Congress was not nearly enough to cover the economic burden that someone would incur by taking up that course of action, the concept was enough to antagonize a self-anchored person into giving additional education a second thought.

Beckoning overtures of law school began revisiting Jason with increasing intensity and frequency when he was alone. Skeptical of how deeply his academic focus might have been eroded, perhaps even permanently destroyed, in that Cambodian jungle, he enrolled in two courses at the nearby junior college: American Literature of the 20th Century and History of Russia. Combat pay that he had stored up by default during the detached nature of his duty in Southeast Asia now bought him time to study and cogitate.

Midway through the semester, he contacted the dean's office at Yale's law school. Informed that his original application had remained on file, Jason was strongly urged to submit a newer form with any updated information. Three weeks later, he received a letter of acceptance for the coming fall semester. However, due to the relative lateness of his application, no scholarship money would be available until the following year.

Ω

Mrs. Cranford, now heading into her early nineties, acknowledged Jason instantly with an ear-to-ear smile.

"She hasn't aged a day," he thought as he stepped forward to take her welcoming hand. *"I'll bet she can't say that about me."*

"Oh my, Jason, you've become a man since we last saw each other," she said with gleefully warm pride. "Oh my, yes."

"Outwardly perhaps, Mrs. Cranford," He smiled back. "But, there's a lot left underneath that needs maturing, Ma'am."

In the midst of his explaining that Yale had accepted him again, that he felt he had his academic mind back, and that between the GI Bill and what he had left of his hazardous duty Army pay . . . she interrupted.

"Jason, ever since you told me that you had joined the Army, I have always felt this day would come," she looked at him squarely, with the hint of a tear, as if the confidence she had always borne was suddenly re-emerging with more meaning than even she had expected. "The foundation's funds are still here. They've been waiting for you. One thing, however. Our agreement that you return here and practice law for at least three years after passing the bar still holds."

Jason could not believe his ears.

"I understand perfectly, Mrs. Cranford."

Ω

He became part of Yale's law review in his second year, and graduated magna cum laude while feeding his special interest in criminal prosecution. During the intervening summers, Jason returned home and clerked for Bradley Sutherland, the county prosecutor. An understanding developed between the two men that he would join Sutherland's private firm after passing the bar. Unplanned, though, when the FBI offered a field position that would rescue him from being chained to a desk, Jason knew he had found his calling. Certain that Sutherland could fill the coveted position at his private firm in a New York minute, there was a much more serious complication . . . his promise to Mrs. Cranford.

Ω

"We've altered our agreement before, without breaking it, Mr. Maxwell," the majestically tiny widow, now in her mid-nineties, chortled to him. "I think we should do that once again. I detect happiness here. So, when the FBI ruthlessly cuts you loose — something they'll call retirement — please come back here and honor that three-year promise. This time, however, I'm afraid our agreement must be set in stone. I have a feeling I won't be here to haggle with you too much longer . . . By the way, Jason, there is no such thing as a good retirement."

Passing up routinely enticing promotions and pay raises, Maxwell remained a field agent during his entire career with The Bureau. He was offered, encouraged and finally almost ordered to take a permanent position in the home office, including a sectional directorship. Recently "retired" now, he was back in his hometown, fulfilling his promise to long-deceased Mrs. Cranford. While nestled in a routine manifested by probating wills, presiding over uncontested divorces, weekly dinners with Arliss and his family, and playing lots of golf, he read about the Mendoza mutilation.

8

THE TALON AND THE CHURCHMOUSE

More than twenty-three-hundred years ago, Aristotle proclaimed, "Poor is the student who does not surpass his teachers." Surely the wise Greek hadn't envisioned the likes of Richard Pierce as his benchmark example. Early on, Pierce outran his given name: Frances Xavier Spagnoli. He did this purely to reduce his personal discomfort with the presumptive ethnic bigotry that all Italians are somehow linked to organized crime. The change was easy. He owed nothing special to any family tradition. The rough, unforgiving night hours of Cicero's streets had been his weaning ground.

These days, he was a well recognized and respected resident of the Richwater community, located halfway up the Gulf-side coast of peninsular Florida. He made a point of being well recognized.

Pierce, with an always colorfully attractive tie swaying against his white shirt, systematically dined at the several restaurants in town, shopped at every store and used every convenience gas station within reach. Avoiding any hint of absurd flamboyance, he was known with nice-guy familiarity everywhere. A regular churchgoer, he was lauded for his generosity. And, he played golf as a country club patron. He spoke to everyone, if only to nod with a smile and a "Hi, how are you?" in passing. The citizens of Richwater "knew" that Pierce "was in real estate," although not one of them had ever purchased or sold a house, or even an undeveloped piece of property, through his office.

Pierce's true calling had festered downward via a lineage of message killers from Chicago's Capone days. He had originally learned from a guy who had learned from a guy, and now he took the utmost pride in being the very best at what he did. Genetically driven, his life was committed to improving upon whatever he learned.

Pierce began as a rubout thug, part of a trio known as the Arachnids who took people for rides or broke into houses, apartments and places of business to quickly finish off lucrative contracts. Mostly, these belligerencies were against other crime figures or down-and-out deadbeats. And, with the trail usually fairly cold to begin with, less-than-vigorous investigations were mounted by local law enforcement. Invariably, the authorities, even the run-ragged, incorruptible types, would chalk each of these atrocities up as one more internecine casualty in the eternal drug-prostitution-gambling wars.

During his days as an Arachnid, Pierce learned about forensics and, most importantly, how to leave a message without leaving any trail of implicating evidence. The leader of that early break-in, rubout trio, One-Shot Lenny Lewis, a true veteran of the profession without so much as a parking ticket against his name, had taken Pierce under his wing. The master found pleasure in sharing minute details from his experiences.

"Yur a good listener, kid," One-Shot Lenny complimented him after one complicated, tedious and particularly nasty caper of contractual revenge. "I'm proud-a-ya. Yur gonna go places."

A while later, when One-Shot Lenny decided that he had had enough and was preparing to retire to a warm climate, he was found dead in bed — a single small-caliber bullet having entered through his left eye at close range. Beyond doubt, a professional reply. When Pierce inquired why such a thing should happen to a longtime loyal craftsman such as Lenny, he was flatly told by Big Mike, the third member of their suddenly undermanned Arachnids, "Ya don't decide if and when ya can leave. They do. Everything we do is always a matter of permission . . . respect."

Soon after, Pierce became his own boss and planner. Now, if and when reaching an agreement for a "job," he carefully used a broken string of fictitious IDs on his way out of Richwater and back. Obsessive about keeping plenty of distance between his work and his hometown, he rarely took on a contract that involved completion south of the Mason-Dixon Line. He'd drive his personal car to Pensacola Regional Airport, about 130 miles northwest of Richwater, and, unassumingly, would park in the outlying economy lot. From there, he'd rent a car under an assumed name and drive to Atlanta's Hartsfield International Airport, New Orleans's Louis Armstrong International Airport or Montgomery Regional. Occasionally, he would drive the extra few hundred miles and use Houston's George Bush International Airport. After dropping the rental car off, he'd book a flight to his appointed destination under another assumed name. Afterwards, he would always backtrack using an entirely different route and set of assumed names. With his underworld connections, fake IDs were among the least of the items that he ever had to worry over.

From an initial cryptic message on his answering machine, Pierce never knew what any potential job really entailed. That's because the initial message would sound very similar to a prospective real estate client wanting him to consider a piece of property or one of his motel managers with a problem. In response, he'd go out for a drive and, on a throwaway cell phone, get back to the "client." He used a lot more cell phones than jobs he finally agreed to. Many times, he immediately turned the job down. Other times, if the job was simply too cheap, he'd recommend someone else. If, however, he agreed to do the job, he would make one more call before jettisoning the phone.

These throwaway-phone clients knew him only by the underworld moniker of "The Talon." His "jobs" were never simple hits; there were always special "needs."

Otherwise, there wasn't any real point to calling The Talon. He knew all about guns, knives, ice picks, ropes, knots, tape, tourniquets, garroting wire, cleavers, chain saws, acids and electricity. And, he always planned immaculately, in the same way as any master artist becomes completely immersed within the exuberance of his perceptions. He was completely devoid of empathy and suffered not one iota of transferential backlash from his horrible work.

For a long time now, having done away with sniper work altogether, he maintained a self-imposed policy of never having a gun. Completely without remorse, The Talon had hardened into the most dispassionate crystal of cunning inhumanity.

After hearing the details of the job, and before returning home, he'd contact his advance man, The Churchmouse, who, following his own set of rules and escape routines, would immediately head for the instructed location. While The Talon patiently passed away some days sightseeing in Atlanta or New Orleans, The Churchmouse would locate the mark, study the general routine, ferret out detailed information and derive the best places for completing "the job." Using pay phones exclusively and their own special vocabulary, the duo then rounded out the details.

Through quietly circuitous recommendations from The Talon, The Churchmouse also did surveillance work for several others in the "business." With The Talon's help, he skillfully avoided any crossover between clients. Soon, the income from his legitimate accounting firm became uninterestingly meager by comparison.

Ω

Christened Emil James Carth, The Churchmouse had been the apple of his parents' eyes — a demanding, but loving, father, who was a general surgeon, and a doting mother, who kept the Carth household warm and sparkly. Dr. Carth never wavered from intending that his only child should follow in his footsteps in the medical profession, preferably also as a surgeon. Instead, young Emil's path to success in medicine abruptly dead-ended long before running up against the proverbial "sight of blood" or "making that first cut" roadblocks that traditionally provide ample fodder for those special living graveyards strewn with would-be doctors. He couldn't stand to hurt insects. And, the chronic nausea brought on by the conventional dissections of frogs, crayfish and worms during his high school Biology classes firmly put an inarguable end to any thoughts of medical school.

While withstanding the castrating jeers of his father's vilifying disappointment, Emil developed into a bright, extremely sensitive post-adolescent who graduated fifth in his class from the state university's Hutton College of Finance.

Emil and The Talon had met on a long shot. A kited stock deal had gone badly, and the realized value of the "borrowed" retirement pension fund for a cardboard box workers' union had evaporated into a faint shadow of its recorded worth. During the ensuing days of the federal government's drawn-out hearings, while Emil was tediously wading through the misery of the debacle on his way to coming up with a bottom-line suggestion for the union, The Talon's assignment, from a completely unrelated source, was to find the person most responsible for the entire mishap and then deliver a nonfatal, but attention-getting, message. As the hearings crawled forward, the public's perception of who was most responsible continued to remain aggravatingly vague. Each day, The Talon silently grew more frustrated.

The day before the information-gathering segment of the inquiry was scheduled to end, when the hearings had broken off for lunch, Emil and The Talon, through sheer necessity, happened to be seated in the same booth at the nearby, jam-packed diner. Recognizing each other from the courtroom, they cordially introduced themselves. After a slow beginning, Emil began talking at length about the details of the financial collapse, noting that only the general information had been adequately summarized by the newspapers. The Talon was taken by the way this littlish, exquisitely dressed fellow first outlined with a broad brush, then painted with minutely accurate details, each phase of his one-way conversation. Along the way, Emil also unwarily exposed the identity of the union officer who had charted the mismanagement of the pension funds. Three days later, The Talon sought Emil out while lunching at the same diner.

"Thanks a lot," he smiled with a hush as he sat down, then quietly slid an envelope containing fifty crisp one-hundred-dollar bills. "You saved me a lot of time and trouble. Oh, I'd have ended up with the same conclusion, but you definitely helped."

"What are you talking about?" Emil frowned frantically, staring into the envelope. "What is this?" he whispered forcibly.

"Maybe it's better that you don't know," The Talon shrugged, then motioned him to come closer.

Emil squinted and leaned forward.

"You read about Faison, the vice-president on the union's pension board, right?" The Talon said, speaking in a very low tone with seeming delight while Emil turned pale, eyes widening without once blinking.

"You?" Emil whispered loudly.

Ω

Everybody had read about it. The local EMS crew had responded to an anonymous 9-1-1 call and found Mark Faison unconscious in an abandoned garage. His right leg had been cleaved away below the knee and a tourniquet applied. With his dismembered lower leg still oozing blood beside him, Faison moaned that he knew nothing about what had happened. The next day, he still denied having any additional information, confident, with The Talon's message still ringing in his ears, that remaining absolutely silent was his only ticket to avoiding further harm.

Handing Emil that envelope full of money had been a test, and The Talon liked where the conversation led. Emil, now dubbed "The Churchmouse", became a flawlessly efficient wellspring of detailed information and suggestions about where and when to finalize future contracts, while ardently insisting upon not knowing anything about how The Talon finished off these transactions. And this was precisely to The Talon's liking.

When their dark pact was first sealed, The Talon, without ever revealing his motives to The Churchmouse, concocted a mini-series of dry-run situations, verifying the soundness and precision of his partner's advance information with follow-up surveillances of his own. During this charade phase, The Talon's network of background checking also quelled doubts about loyalty. Soon, he had complete confidence in The Churchmouse's advance work, which in many ways was more pictorially graphic than his own. At that point, The Talon designed an airtight information relay system that fronted the bland Churchmouse and minimized his own time in the general area of a designated bloodletting.

Through the intervening years, the pair silently had agreed to avoid direct contact with each other, relying solely on their pay-phone system for communicating and a neutral courier relay for The Churchmouse's payoffs.

Ω

On one rare, unplanned occasion though, The Churchmouse had completed his surveillance call to The Talon and was waiting for a connecting flight at Memphis International Airport. Meanwhile, The Talon was en route from Atlanta, through Memphis, to the target site. They bumped into each other in the airport. Instead of feigning no knowledge of the other's existence, and with a couple of hours to kill between flights, they nodded and headed for the bar, taking a booth at the far end.

"It's on me," The Talon declared, laying a $20 bill on the table.

There were neither the gruff snickers nor the scowling sneers so often portrayed by Hollywood's mobsters. These were men who cared dearly about the precise meaning of words and a clear interpretation of the English language. Purposely, they lent themselves to the light browns and grays who trudge about their inconsequential work-a-day business unnoticed. Not a hint of rigid immediacy here. And yet, an understood direct- ness pervaded the calmness of their collective aura.

They shared a quiet zeal of satisfying comfort in what they each did. And, it showed in their accommo- dating faces. Relaxed and confident, these two not only thrived, they also flourished in a land where the laws, and consequences from not being heeded, were focused upon thwarting their interconnected mission. One was little shorter, rounder and balding, like millions of Americans. His companion on the opposite side of the table was slightly taller than average, sinewy and hair- headed, like millions of other Americans.

The Churchmouse, his removed fedora having re- vealed his balding pate, blandly noted they had come a long way since that bogus pension-fund disaster.

"OK, yeah, what the hell, let's talk shop," The Talon thought, and he began quietly describing, with a chatty, offhanded demeanor, how he had extracted some needed information, using only an ice pick, from a fel- low that The Churchmouse had located and set up. But before he could get into a thorough elaboration, The Churchmouse bolted for the men's room and began vomiting, barely reaching the nearest sink.

The Talon laughingly caught up with him. While commenting sarcastically that airport terminal food wasn't to be trusted, he promised, at The Chur- chmouse's weakened, but desperate insistence, to never again talk about what he did with the advance informa- tion.

"OK, sure, no more shoptalk," The Talon chuckled and patted him heartily three times on the back.

In the moments while waiting for the out-of-sorts Churchmouse to recompose himself, The Talon stood by in split reflection about why he had acquiesced to "talk shop" anyway. It certainly wasn't to idly reminisce about some ice-pick incident. That was intended as a small hors d'oeuvre to the main morsel that he wanted to make use of . . .

Ω

Prior to recruiting The Churchmouse, The Talon had always done his own advance work. One such situation had involved a local ambulance-chasing lawyer who had climbed into the upper-crust section of town through means that couldn't possibly be explained by his visible sources of income. Under a quiet cloak, the lawyer's house, with his wife and two daughters completely unaware, was being used as a go-between depot for the area's cocaine and heroin traffic. This conduit in the circuit continued to be routinely profitable for the lawyer until he became delusional about his personal power. He began boisterously voicing his intentions about becoming the kingpin of the distribution, and squeezing the current controllers out. He was taking on the veneer of a loose cannon. Soon, he was looked upon as a potentially dangerous whistle-blower. The Talon got a call.

Doing his own surveillance, Pierce tracked the lawyer family's weekday comings and goings for almost two weeks. Midway into the second week, while all members of the household were away for a predictable couple of hours, he masqueraded as a tree surgeon concerned with how any trees and shrubbery might be rubbing against the neighborhood telephone wires. Disguised with a reddish beard, sunglasses and a pulled-down baseball cap complete with false company logo, he parked in front of the home to the left of the lawyer's in a cream-colored van with a bogus logo blaring in red letters on both front doors. After spending a few minutes diligently inspecting the phone lines, poles and trees on both sides of the lawyer's home, The Talon quietly and routinely went into the lawyer's backyard which had been neighbor-proofed with a high, opaquely wooden fence along the entire perimeter, and made even more impenetrable to viewing by the numerous tall Blue Spruces rimming the inside of the fence. With a complete feeling of security, The Talon instantly jimmied the backdoor lock, and, moving briskly, in less than five minutes had absorbed a mental image of the intricacies of all three floors of the home, including the basement.

Monday night of the following week, The Talon parked his rental Datsun in the lot of the all-night Wal-Mart, within a mile from the lawyer's neighborhood. Dressed in a tight-fitting deep maroon sweat suit and a reflective headband, he began slowly jogging through the quiet streets toward the lawyer's home. Slowing to a walk and tending to the shadows, he discarded the headband atop a mailbox as he turned onto the single-block street that harbored his destination. Slipping into the lawyer's backyard, he lodged himself between two spruces and, donning a black ski mask, began his sur-veillance of confirmation. As expected, the two daugh-ters were already in their rooms upstairs. The parents were capping off their downstairs activities by taking in the late news in the front living room. Reacting with methodical approval, The Talon silently jimmied the back door open again, crept up the stairs from midway in the hallway and into the walk-in closet of the master bedroom. Once settled, he waited and watched.

Soon, the couple appeared. With a minimum of conversation, they shared the adjacent bathroom in preparation for bed. Neither had a reason to approach the walk-in closet. Following a very routine, somewhat brief intercourse, the pair reclaimed their opposing sides of the king-size bed and drifted into an afterglow of deep sleep. The Talon waited until the first snore. Walking quietly to the wife's side on his left, he sedated her into a securely motionless stupor with Demerol, then dropped the empty syringe to the floor.

"What's on the agenda for today, hon?" the lawyer asked upon arousal in the morning, his back still turned to his wife as they lay in bed. Not getting an immediate response, he quipped, "You alive?" Again, no answer.

He rolled over to nudge her. The crimson spew of drying blood obliterated any outline between the wife's upper body and the surrounding pillow and bed sheet. Her throat had been sliced to near-decapitation. Within a week, a realtor's available-for-occupancy sign appeared on the front lawn. Heeding The Talon's message, the lawyer disappeared into silence.

Whisking away from the lawyer's home that night, The Talon had reclaimed his headband at the end of the street and discarded his trademark weapon of choice under a ground-level curbside evergreen shrub while leisurely loping his way back to his parked rental vehicle. Using this example, The Talon had intended a show of appreciation. Had The Churchmouse been on board back then, The Talon's risk at the scene would have been reduced from a couple of subjective search-based weeks to very few hours of planned focus.

Before The Churchmouse became part of his well-oiled network, The Talon was already using an expert metal artist known as The St. Louie Beaver. Through trial-and-error, the two had designed and modeled a lightweight, four-inch, double-edge blade of cadmium steel. At rest, the razor-sharp blade resided inside an open handle of aluminum-nickel alloy. To arm the knife, The Talon had only to press a guarded bead on either side of the handle. The blade instantly sprang straight from the end and locked into position, rather than having to swing out in a 180-degree arc in the manner that street-use stilettos are fashioned. During endless hours of enjoyment, The Talon practiced producing the knife, with lightning speed, fully armed from anywhere on his body, and what to do with it once it was out.

The Beaver not only manufactured The Talon's knives in his suburban two-car garage turned makeshift metal shop, he made as much money from deliveries. Using truck routes and train schedules, from his centrally located position he could deliver an innocent-looking package of a dozen knives anywhere in the country within two days. He usually had more leeway, since The Talon would alert "The Beev" where the job would be at the same time that he was launching The Churchmouse into his advance work. Two days later he would make one more call to The Beaver to find out where to pick up the knives, usually from a silent courier or an ultra-safe drop site. This scheme circumvented any worries about having to get knives past airport security or carrying them long distances in his cars.

During their chance meeting in Memphis, The Talon, in his own spur-of-the-moment way, had decided to express to The Churchmouse how much he appreciated his work. By describing his own intricate advance work when dispensing with the misguided lawyer and his wife, he intended to show, by this example, how important The Churchmouse's work was to him. Nowadays, The Talon could turn what might be more than two weeks worth of risky stealth into a single instance of finality. Much less chance of becoming recognizable.

The Churchmouse's instinctive aversion to any hint of physical abuse cut The Talon short, before he could reach any mentioned of the lawyer.

Watching as his advance man pathetically retched into the sink, The Talon had approached as close to remorse as his creed would ever allow.

"Please don't do that," The Churchmouse pleaded three times, broken up by intervals of silence as he gasped for breath.

"Yeah . . . yeah, sure," The Talon thoughtlessly answered each time while his mind still toyed with reflections of the lawyer job. *"Ah, what if the lawyer's family had had a dog or two,"* he silently mused, practically oblivious of The Churchmouse's immediate circumstances. *"Still would have been business as usual, I'm sure. Any extra details would have depended on the dog's personality. That's all."*

Ω

By all outward appearances, The Talon and the Churchmouse were woefully bland creatures whenever they traveled, made plainer by how they dressed. They hazily blended in among the endless streams of nameless humanity that you look at, but do not see, while patiently waiting for them to pass by on the street or in the airport, with the hope that their bland commonness might reveal, but certainly never cause, something of interest in their wakes. If this inwardly sinister pair deviated at all from their dull outwardness, their attention to neatness was their shared flaw. Both were always clean-shaven, with their hair carefully combed and recently trimmed. With practiced care, they were always mildly polite while purchasing a drink or a newspaper.

The Churchmouse was helpless to do otherwise. His eternal fate was to remain painfully plain in the face of universal change. The Talon though was an unchallenged master player of cryptic narcissism. As aggressively as he worked at being noticeable throughout his adopted community of Richwater, the ambushing stalker put that same energy and discerning eye into modeling inconspicuousness on the road. Along with a well-groomed persona being a consistent thread of his home-and-away image, he also tried to find time and a place to work out every day, lifting weights or jogging or both. The Churchmouse did neither; and The Talon hadn't failed to mention how soft he appeared.

Privately, The Talon already had decided that the Mendoza killing was to be his last. He, of course, hadn't confided to The Churchmouse about his planned departure. This hardened decision had compelled him to take greater care with each monstrous detail during his brutally Gothic torture and dismemberment of that Earthforsaken jockey. Not just a mysterious drowning this time, or a gunshot to the head that could be misconstrued as a suicide, or a drug overdose that perhaps had been self-inflicted. No, every detail of the Mendoza mutilation was one more direct statement to the racing world, and to jockeys in particular. The Talon had come away from Mercury's reservoir having methodically positioned Mendoza's partial remains, convinced that, *"Now you little runts . . . When certain people ask you to do something, you had better damn well do it — no questions asked."*

Ω

At first blush, the upshot of the "Mendoza thing" seemed to be when the rider threw in a double-cross after dutifully carrying through on what had been "requested." But, what about those earlier jockey deaths? All they ever did was immediately turn down an offer, which likely had turned into a request and then to an outright demand. With each escalating urging, the independent pride and character of those fellows apparently had held, never wavering from their ethical allegiance to the profession that they revered and respected. Seemingly, too, not one of them had blown the whistle after being approached. Yet in the end, their simple refusals were enough to earn a visit from The Talon.

So, would Mendoza have been killed anyway, even if, after complying with the Twin-Tri scam, he had kept his mouth shut? Or, having once crossed the line of no-return, would he now be in their pocket, a caged pigeon waiting to carry out their next caper? How many jockeys out there had once succumbed as requested and, having kept quiet afterwards, were forever chained to the whimsical demands of the hoodlum backwaters? Perhaps none. In the underworld code of paranoiac silence, even the chance of a threat apparently is routinely eliminated. If so, Mendoza's fate was decided the moment he was approached, though certainly not with the horrific suffering he subsequently endured.

With his substantial nest egg already positioned to ensure that he could enjoy a life of leisure well beyond any unhurried visit from the reaper, The Talon, with bone-deep confidence, was sure that he could recede into an untroubled future. One-Shot Lenny's fatal flaw was the faith he misplaced in openly announcing his intended retirement, even making a point of visiting "trusted colleagues" to say good-bye. The Talon was in the very final stages of his preparations to silently vanish when the tongs of an unavoidable distraction gripped his attention.

9

FALLING IN LOVE

Carson Bagwell loved horses from the day his mother first lifted him up for a pony ride at the state fair. He was nine years old, and the slow-footed gelded Shetland under him instantly became his Pegasus above the clouds.

That same summer, Carson began taking lessons twice a week, first learning how to post with a western saddle while guided by the stable instructor's lead pony, then quickly graduating from solo trotting to a purposefully breezy canter, and later to the euphoria of a full-out gallop.

By the following summer, Bagwell's now thrice-weekly lessons at Reed Stables pretty much entailed paying to saddle his favorite horse, Harry, and taking the gelding out for a run, either along the county's dirt roads or around the huge sandy-loam track that ringed the acres of soybeans behind the stables. At first, enthralled by the speed and power that horses generated at his command, he soon fell under the spell of communication that developed with Harry. Sitting just behind the thick-necked bay's black mane, Bagwell became submerged within the deeper regions of horsemanship, coaxed along by Harry's patient guidance.

Abruptly though, before the next summer, Reed Stables fell into bankruptcy. The entire farm halted operations. Weeds began to get the upper hand, rust bled from the hinges and latches as paint peeled everywhere. Worst of all, Harry was quietly sold and unceremoniously vanned away. Bagwell was careful never to inquire where. It couldn't matter, and he didn't want to know. He had neither the funds nor the facilities to be with Harry for more than few rented hours a week. If he were told where Harry had been taken, this most certainly would have put pictures into his imagination that would scar his tender memories of their time together. Still, through the years he would haunt himself with recurring regrets of having let Harry down.

Through osmotic happenstance, his mother also had introduced him to Thoroughbred racing. When she wasn't at the track, Mrs. Bagwell listened to the daily race results on the radio, which usually included an invigorating live-call of the day's feature race. She religiously wrote down this information as fastidiously as a breakthrough scientist recording virginal experimental data. Mama was a systems player.

Mrs. Bagwell was convinced that the neighborhood track maintained a speed bias near the inside rail. And so, one of her favorite "systems" was to crisscross the horses from the three inside post positions in the first two races with $2 daily-double tickets for a total bet of $18. When she hit, which wasn't all that infrequently, she would proudly brag to Carson that she had "had a big day" and give him a dollar or two. This intrigued him.

"The horses leave me cold," his father, who invested heavily in the stock market, sternly told him. In silent turn, Carson chalked this up as just one more attribute that his parents didn't have in common. He often wondered how they ever came close enough together to have him, and, at times, was thoroughly convinced that he must have been adopted.

Ω

Bagwell was a child of the Great Depression, although born seventeen years after Black Tuesday's crash. His father, Dr. William Bagwell, a dentist, had weathered those lean years by keeping his office open and continuing to practice his profession while others abandoned theirs in hand-to-mouth frustration and despair. Dr. Bagwell, with jaw jutted, had gambled that sooner, rather than later, the nation inexorably would pull itself up by its bootstraps and once again be able to take pride in the care of its teeth. Meantime, he continued to peer into his patients' dental problems throughout the Depression, giving proper professional attention to those who couldn't pay by using the income from those who could to cover the burdening costs of maintaining his nurse-less office, and to keep a roof overhead and food on the table for wife Ruth.

By the mid-1940s, the New Deal had the country well out of the Depression and mighty enough to crush Hitler in Europe and Hirohito in the Pacific. Dr. Bagwell's steadfastness in the community during the strife of the 1930s had permanently etched him among the most solid of local pillars. In good health and with the family's income back in line with the expectations of a successfully practicing dentist, Carson became William and Ruth Bagwell's first child.

A chain-smoker of Chesterfields, Ruth had put out her last cigarette when William first announced that they were financially in position to start a family. She never was a drinker, except for a very rare after-dinner Creme de Cacao.

$$\Omega$$

Four-and-a-half years later, brother Richard arrived and Carson was no longer the baby of the household. Although his mother continued to dote on him after Richard was born, mealtime was always an occasion of anxious silence except when his authoritarian father chose to speak. Dr. Bagwell had not only decided when Ruth and he would start having children, he also decided what each of his kids would do with the rest of their lives.

"It's the way life has always been with the Bagwells," Dr. Bagwell stated dutifully, as if harkening back to an ancient tribal tradition etched on the walls of a European cave. Then he would go about describing how, without the slightest discussion, his father had guided him toward dental school and completely financed that training. Now, too, without any debate, Carson would trace his father's footsteps and become a next-generation's keeper of the tooth. Other than during dinner, Carson saw his father infrequently, and then usually only in passing.

Having survived the Depression with sheer rock-hard, jaw-clenched determination had convinced Dr. Bagwell more than ever that his way in all things was the right way, and this was his smothering mantra whenever he conversed with Carson. Once, when Carson courageously attempted to explain his desire to pursue a Liberal Arts path at college, with a special interest in Literature and History, his father sternly glared and asked, "How many college degrees do you have?"

"None, sir," Carson quietly and defeatedly replied, staring submissively at the ground between them.

"All right then, do as I say," his father flatly directed. "Where's the money in Liberal Arts? Literature and History? Good lord!"

Ω

During the summers of his high-school years, Carson began working in the valet parking lot at the local racetrack. Within a short time, through a connection made while parking cars, he moved over to the barn area of Teddy Darcy, one of the track's leading trainers. He learned by mucking out stables, rubbing and wrapping, hot-walking horses after early morning workouts and hitching those who didn't have a workout scheduled for the day to the walking wheels for up to an hour. Darcy knew right away that Bagwell could ride, but, except for rare occasions, the trainer wanted him nearer to the barn area to help with the overall management of the early morning operations.

Each afternoon, Bagwell watched every race, either from the backstretch on days when Darcy's stable had horses running and would require hot-walking, baths and rubs afterwards, or from the grandstands when he had a rare afternoon off. With the suction capacity of a black hole, he absorbed the past-performance lines and all of the other information in Daily Racing Form. When on the grandstand side, he was a fixture in the paddock area before each race. From within the ethos of his quiet demeanor, he watched the jockeys and the trainers and the owners, but mostly he watched the horses. Early on, he had discovered that figuring how the entrants for a particular race stacked up on paper was only one important aspect. That information only told a discerning eye what the horses had done before, not necessarily how they were going to perform today.

He had once overheard Hall-of-Fame trainer Woody Stephens say that he couldn't possibly be living at the level of comfort that he and Mrs. Stephens were enjoying if it weren't for the betting that supplemented his income. From that rather terse statement, Bagwell surmised that, if a person really knew what he was doing and maintained an even temperament, he really could glean an income from betting on horse racing. That sudden slant was diametrically opposed to what he had observed and heard trackside up until then.

In those days, Bagwell bet small and infrequently, and when he didn't cash a ticket there was usually an obvious, unforeseeable reason. He was an excellent high-school student and an average athlete who practiced diligently to get better each day. He usually had a rather steady girl, instead of dating around, even though his six-foot frame, with blond hair and warm brown eyes, would have ensured that he always had a date for the dance on Saturday night.

Under the guidance of Mr. Andersen, the school's English, Speech and Journalism teacher, Carson put together and wrote much of the school's biweekly newspaper during his senior year. He also designed the yearbook and directed its layout. Bagwell was far more of a listener than a talker, and he frightened people with his uncanny ability to remember details about everything without notes. He could spiel back the contents of any conversation, lecture or speech verbatim. He became locally famous for having a recorder-type mind. Although he usually socialized with a specific group of classmates, he got along with everyone and was completely at ease cross-cliquing with other groups or one-on-one.

Under his father's strict guidance, Carson began college by enrolling in the state university's pre-dent/pre-med curriculum. His grades were terrible. Right off, he despised attending classes without self-purpose. He was a spiritless prisoner in a situational destiny that he felt powerless to confront. So, midway through the first semester of his sophomore year, while his father offhandedly pondered how his son could possibly be accepted into a reputable dental school with such a poor early academic record, Carson walked into the nearby U.S. Army recruiting center and volunteered for a three-year hitch.

His father never forgave him.

10

GETTING IT TOGETHER

Carson remained truly dismayed that he had disappointed his father. Fortunately, he never forgot how infinitely more unhappy he had been when trying to be insincerely pleasing.

Stationed with the Adjutant General's Office at Fort Knox in Kentucky, Carson longed to be transferred overseas . . . anywhere, everywhere. Holding to the timeless adage, he wanted to see the world on Uncle Sam's dollar. What he saw were the bars and clubs of Louisville on Saturday nights. But also, twice a year, for about six weeks each time, Churchill Downs's Thoroughbred racing season was in full flight. During these stints, he spent his Saturdays, and whenever he could break away for an afternoon during the week, trackside.

He still bet small and infrequently, mostly to cover his costs of purchasing Daily Racing Form, and a hot dog and soda. Servicemen were given free admission to the grandstand. On the few occasions when his horses didn't pay off, what of it? The U.S. Army still provided clothing, a roof over his head and three square meals a day to tide him over until next month's payday.

Bagwell was honorably discharged in May, just as the rumblings from Watergate were becoming too loud to be ignored. The Presidency of the nation was under attack: Misuse of power and the abuse of the public's trust were being interrogated. Amid tapes of Oval Office conversations, smoking gun hypotheses and "I'm not a crook" theatrics, President Nixon would resign during the ensuing summer.

May also meant the local racing season was about to unfold, and Bagwell instantly picked up his old routine as Darcy's top assistant. First day back, something whispered that whenever he strayed from the barn area for very long, the distinctive smells of horses, leather and hay were sure to demand a thorough accounting and a promise of firmer loyalty. And, Darcy had had much to do with this, having cultivated his assistant's fervid admiration for the business.

"Some owners view their horses simply as pets, and could care less what they do on the track," Darcy explained one dawn, while the two hung over the fence along the backstretch watching an exercise girl put Stormy Joe through a special half-mile blowout over the turf course. "And, most bettors don't even bother to learn the horses' names. Give me a ticket on Number 6 is all they ever know, for whatever reason.

"Other owners treat them as mechanical pieces of property that should always win, or else. Hell, a two-buck bettor will curse a horse or a jockey after a loss as bitterly as if they were a millionaire investor. And, in neither case have they really looked at the horse or dared to question their own judgment.

"You and I know different. These animals are neither pets nor windup mechanical monsters. They have different feelings, potential capabilities and subtle mannerisms that need to be discovered, understood, nurtured and attended to in the same way you would any prize athlete. They're not all champions, but it's in their blood to run and compete. And, that's where we come in. It's up to us to find out how good each of them can really be.

"How would you like it if every second of your life was planned from the time you first hit the ground? Hell, some third-party agenda even decided when and how your parents got together to have you. That can add up to some pretty cold prospects to have to start out with, and then have to deal with day-to-day."

Bagwell looked over and nodded in agreement, without Darcy knowing the full measure of why.

Despite his father's narrow regimentation, Bagwell knew that he needed more formal education. Although the level of funding from the G.I. Bill didn't bridge the gap between his current circumstances and attending college, the money provided by Congress urged Bagwell to look harder into this possibility. To supplement his summer income from Darcy's stable, Bagwell worked as a counter clerk at the local 7-11 convenience store until midnight, five days a week. He lived at home and paid his mother a small weekly gratuity.

Usually arriving home late, and up and out very early, on rare occasions he still saw his father who now openly referred to him as "a bum and a total loss." With a Spartan's determination, Bagwell used his summer income from Darcy to pay for tuition and fees. The hourly money from the store bought his books and provided some spending money, and the monthly stipend from the G.I. Bill covered room and board. He did this for five years, with one alteration. Beginning with his third summer, Darcy formally promoted Bagwell to assistant manager of the entire stable. With the healthy raise involved, he was able to stop working at the store in the evenings.

During his final weeks before graduation from the University of Missouri's School of Journalism, with minors in History and Mathematics-Statistics, Bagwell interviewed with several prestigious newspaper chains that had set up career booths on campus. They mostly showed sincere degrees of interest, and he quickly received four firm offers through the mail, all with reasonably competitive starting salaries.

Notwithstanding, when he saw an ad announcing that an entry-level position for a general assignment reporter was available with a small independent daily newspaper less than 50 miles from his hometown . . . ability to report on sports a plus . . . he responded with a letter and a resume.

"Mr. Bagwell, if you're still interested in our reporter's position, we've looked your resume over and you seem very much like a person we'd be interested in hiring," the voice said over the telephone the following Tuesday, after introducing himself as Tom Leidring, the managing editor of Harmon County Courier. "If it's not terribly inconvenient, could you find time to drive over and visit us for a day? The publisher and I'd like to show you around our newspaper plant and buy you lunch."

Ω

Two days later, Bagwell was driving down Main Street in Rushburg, looking for the office of the Harmon County Courier.

Over lunch, the publisher, Paul McGabe, who also owned the paper, sat quietly while Leidring spoke at length about the Courier, about Rushburg, about his family . . . Bagwell never got a word in.

"It doesn't occur to these people to play poker," Bagwell mused silently. *"Their hole cards are all face-up and out in front. They know what their mission is and what kind of help they need. And they can't afford to make mistakes because of misunderstandings."*

Later, after he had toured the building and met the staff, including Ralph Gomez, who was in command of the paper's other reporter position, Bagwell finally was given an opening.

"How come a guy with your academic credentials is even looking at a place like ours?" Leidring asked frankly, while they stood together by Bagwell's car outside the building, getting ready to say their good-byes. "Damn, the big dailies should be falling all over each other to hire someone like you. Is there something I don't know about?"

Bagwell reacted with a shrugging smile.

"Tom, it may seem a little strange," finally, he was about to get a meaningful word in, "but, this is the type of position I'm looking for. Sure, I've got offers from bigger papers with much wider circulations. But, with every one of them, I'd be pigeonholed. They've got virtual armies of reporters and staff writers. Management tells you exactly what they want you for when they hire you. Nice tight little niche. And, if you've show any initiative about branching out or expanding, right away you're stepping on some other guy's toes. Here, you've got Gomez and whomever else you decide to hire to cover the whole show. That means there's plenty of range for everyone. On top of that, Gomez says he hates sports and can't wait to get away from it. Looks like we'd be a good fit."

Leidring nodded silently. For a change, he seemed to be enjoying just listening.

"Oh, I know, Tom. The money. You can't afford to pay nearly what the big guns can. But, for one thing, the difference in cost of living between here and where those big papers are is Grand Canyonish. Don't get me wrong. I'm not completely against getting paid for my work. But, damn, what would I do with a friggin' Mercedes-Benz? I'd have to spend all day polishing the damn thing instead of writing."

Leidring — still more than halfway convinced that they were just going through motions here, and that, when Bagwell came to his senses, he would go elsewhere — offered him the position at somewhat better than the paper's base starting salary.

"I've enjoyed my visit, Tom," Bagwell said graciously. "I'll call you tomorrow for sure. I'd like to sleep on it."

Leidring, as seasoned as they come at hiring entry-level reporters and then bringing the good ones along, commented cordially as Bagwell pulled away, "You're right. Your car could use a trip to the car wash."

Ω

Bagwell quickly caught onto the differences between the sterile, formulated journalism in the classroom and vitriolic vacillations of street journalism. Leidring was firm and demanding, but never threatening or demeaning. With Gomez as a teammate, the Courier's local stories began taking on a more aggressive luster for giving the readers what they wanted to know about and also what they should know about, whether they wanted to or not . . . even when it meant reporting the dull limbo of Rushburg's political scene or the unnervingly general details of a crime scene involving children. With sports in particular, Bagwell not only reported, he also taught with his beckoning explanations and vivid descriptions that strove for meanings beyond the aboriginal rah-rahs of the home crowd.

"I try to tell the people who weren't lucky enough to be there what they missed," he discussed with Leidring over lunch one day. "And, I also tell the people who were there what they saw. Look around the stands during any Friday night game. How many people are intently glued to what's going on out there every second? Hell, half the time they're yakking with whomever's close by, or buying something to eat or drink, or the play-of-the-game happens at the opposite end of the field or court and they can't hear the ref's explanation of what just occurred. And, even if they do see what's going on, our story the next day is a colorful reaffirmation for them.

"Tom, I'm always hoping that the information and descriptions in my stories will get our subscribers, the next time they go to a game, to look at the entire picture a little closer and a little differently than they ever have before. I want them to come away thinking things like, 'Now I understand why they do that,' and 'My goodness, I never noticed that before'. And that's all because of us."

"Look, you don't have to sell me on where you're coming from," Leidring quietly agreed. "I see that same attitude carrying over into any story of yours, regardless of whether it involves any sports."

Approaching two years after Bagwell had arrived, the publisher's wife died of a rapidly spreading, inoperable brain tumor. The ordeal consumed McGabe. Permanently grief-stricken, he lost all interest in owning the paper and soon put it up for sale. He too would die within a year.

Leidring, whose personal fortune wasn't nearly vast enough to allow him to make a reasonable solo bid for the paper, hurriedly scoured his contacts about becoming potential partners. In the end though, they could not meet the bid by the small Midwestern chain that took over and began moving in its own people.

Most insulting was the new ownership's overview of the relative worth of the Editorial Department and newspapering in general. All of the new personnel were positioned in the Advertising Department in an all-out attempt to increase local revenue and stretch the umbrella of the paper's circulation range. The Editorial Department suddenly was seen as a necessary evil that brought in zero revenue and loomed as potentially harmful to the general bliss of the readers. There were serious rumors that the main office was evaluating ways to cut the editorial payroll. Word was that Gomez would be let go, without any replacement, and that Leidring would be asked to take a severe pay cut. Bagwell would be retained. He was the cheapest item on the department's payroll; and, with his workaholic tenacity, he more than fit into the new owner's cost-effective scheme . . . if he could just be steered into covering what the Advertising Department felt was appropriate.

Bagwell always gave the local sports scene the fullest coverage possible all year long, regardless of which sports were in or out of season at the time. In addition, he did his readers' homework for them prior to any of the big annual national events such as the Super Bowl, World Series, March Madness, Indianapolis 500 and Kentucky Derby. Like clockwork, a few days before any of these premier events were to occur, he would write a thorough, yet skillfully concise, overview of what to expect and from whom.

With his special trackside acumen, he had written about the 1985 Kentucky Derby, providing his readers with plenty of details about the lineup and pointing out that most in the thirteen-horse field were pretenders, not contenders for the Roses. Chief's Crown, the Breeders' Cup Juvenile winner from the previous fall, was going into that Derby as the strong prerace favorite at just about even money. Bagwell wasn't buying it. Most of the turf forecasters on the Chief's Crown bandwagon were basing their faith on a very fast time that the horse supposedly had run in his final prep race. Trouble was, three other horses of rather pedestrian abilities had finished very close behind Chief's Crown, supposedly indicating that they too had all run a quantum-leap faster than ever before. To have all these horses suddenly improve that much at the same time was impossible, Bagwell surmised. So did Andy Beyer, by then the nationally respected turf writer for the Washington Post. Both came to the same conclusion. Those horses in Chief's Crown eye-catching race hadn't suddenly become that much faster. More likely instead, the clocking of the race must have been grossly inept.

Another horse, Spend a Buck, had caught Bagwell's eye. As the distances of his prep races increased, Spend a Buck had carried his front-running speed to wider and wider margins of victory. Plus, Triple Crown-savvy jockey Angel Cordero was in the saddle. Bagwell wrote his pre-Derby column from the angle that Spend a Buck would win, and closed it out with "They ain't gonna catch 'im." They never did.

With the strife at the Harmon County Courier becoming more obvious and unavoidable, Bagwell forwarded his resume and some racing articles to "Homestretch," a weekly news magazine published on New York's Long Island that specialized in coverage of the national Thoroughbred racing scene. They were looking for a combination staff writer and copy editor with a solid knowledge of horse racing.

"You're going to leave me here to fight with these clowns alone?" Leidring quipped with a touch of genuine sadness.

11

ROOM FOR MORE

Within a year, Bagwell took over as the senior editor of "Homestretch," coordinating an in-house staff of fourteen and a network of field correspondents blanketing every Thoroughbred racing venue in the U.S. and Canada, and also Tijuana's Agua Caliente Racetrack.

Each edition of the magazine also offered Bagwell's personal interview with a trainer or jockey from throughout the racing network. He alternated between the Hall-of-Fame celebrities of the premier racing circuits and those who were very successful, but less well-recognized nationally, at the smaller tracks.

The truisms he had first learned at his hometown track wore well as he now moved from interview to interview on the national scale. Once the word was out that he could be trusted to tell his stories with sincerity and caring accuracy, the racing community opened its nationwide heart to him. He discovered an endless stream of fascinating moments that hadn't been shared in print before.

Laffit Pincay Jr., the Hall of Famer who would later become the winningest American jockey of all time, told him that, while rating Swale along Churchill Downs's backstretch, he knew nothing from behind them had a chance and, with dead aim on front-running filly Althea, they already had the 1984 Kentucky Derby won.

Ron McAnally, the Hall of Fame trainer who turned a bottom-line gelded claimer into an international champion and multiple Horse of the Year, confided with Bagwell about becoming worried when he shipped John

Henry into New Jersey's Meadowlands for an important handicap race. McAnally reveled in his horse's other-world keenness for knowing exactly where he was every step of the way on a racetrack. If the jockey tried to start his finishing drive too early, John Henry would simply ignore the prodding and keep cruising along. Nor did he wait if the jockey was too late in asking. John Henry ran the way he wanted to and always knew precisely where the finish line was. But Jersey's Meadowlands involved night racing, something John Henry probably hadn't encountered before. During the post parade, the horse, always a curious sort, kept looking up at the lights. McAnally anguished that John Henry might have his mind on other things besides winning the race. Once the starting gate opened though, the noble gelding had his game-face on and won convincingly.

Ron Turcotte spoke similarly of Secretariat, saying that he never rode the horse, he just sat there. The horse knew what to do and when to do it, Turcotte confided, and, man, he had the gear to do it with. He spoke of Secretariat's early race-controlling surge in the Preakness and, of course, his supernatural performance in the Belmont. As Secretariat and Turcotte were moving through Belmont's homestretch toward a Triple Crown-sealing victory of 31 widening lengths, trainer Lucien Lauren had shouted from the stands, "Just don't fall off, Ronnie!"

And, journeyman jockey David Neusch, while describing a Thoroughbred's inherent tenacity for winning, spoke about a front-running mare that he had ridden early in his career. The mare not only dug in and ran harder when challenged by an oncoming closer, she suddenly craned her neck to the side and tried to bite the opponent.

"I'd never seen anything like that before!" Neusch exclaimed. "Colts, yes, but not from a filly or mare."

By contrast, Hall of Fame jockey Braulio Baeza winced when he spoke of Buckpasser's will to win in the face of excruciating pain. During the walk from the paddock to the track and during the post parade, Buckpasser would suffer with every step he took, Baeza recalled. But, when the gates opened, the horse's heart always took over.

Regardless of which trainer or jockey was being interviewed, Hall of Famer or not, it always boiled down to stories about the horses, not the humans. It was the horses that made everyone great. It was the horses that provided them with a living. And, without fail, each interviewee reaffirmed this deep respect.

Bagwell never sensationalized or embellished his stories, let alone introduced fabrications that might tend toward inaccuracies. The stories themselves did the talking. All that had to be done was to make sure that they were well-written enough to reach out to the readers with vivid accountability. And that was what he quickly became known for.

Riders and trainers began being obvious with their availability to share a story or two with Bagwell. Once, while introducing himself to great New England rider Carl Gambardella and attempting to explain what his professional intentions were, the jockey stopped him in mid-sentence, "It's OK. I already know who you are, and that you're a standup guy." Gambardella would amass way more than 6,000 trips to the winner's circle before an injury during a morning workout instantly ended his career.

Ω

While his income as senior editor of "Homestretch" didn't leave much after all the bills were paid and food was in his belly, by now Bagwell had honed his patience and confidence to the level where his pari-mutuel skills provided him with reasonable funds for recreation. Occasionally, he would go for two weeks or longer without making a bet.

Still convinced that no one could consistently collect on bets without being aware of the information in Daily Racing Form, it also remained obvious to Bagwell that such information, by itself, was inconclusive for determining how those same horses might perform today. The skills that he had developed during those summers with Darcy's stable remained at the forefront. Knowing what to look for, he studied the habits of the individual jockeys and trainers. He watched the reruns of races over and over, and he was at the track early every morning with stopwatch in hand, constantly seeking an edge as the horses worked out.

Ω

Returning to his news desk one morning, Bagwell found among his daily correspondence a letter from a Kathi VanBach. Her letter thanked him for commenting in his recent column that front-running horses have a decided edge when the track was muddy or sloppy, but are at a decided disadvantage whenever a strong headwind swirls down the backstretch.

Bagwell wrote back, warning Ms. VanBach that those two generalizations were only part of a quasi-infinite picture of handicapping angles, and that she should know a lot more about the horses in any particular race if and when she were to consider risking her hard-earned money. She wrote again, asking for more of his advice. He sent a quick Monday note, "Meet me at the clubhouse side of the paddock area before the third race this Saturday. I'll be wearing a bright yellow tie."

He picked her out before she spotted his tie. Kathi was alone, with no possible reason under the sun why she should be. No one, he mused, with that flowing blonde hair, stately posture, suntanned face and light-blue pantsuit grounded by black block-heeled boots should ever be left unattended.

Now she saw him approaching, and greeted him with the broad smile of her round face, small sharpish nose and half-closed, happy light-lavender eyes. "She should be with somebody," he kept silently agreeing. "It's a sin to see someone such as this alone."

They began meeting every Saturday and soon were having dinner after the last race. A short time later, they began stretching their evenings with a movie or an off-Broadway play. She talked rapidly and verbosely; he spoke slowly and succinctly. She had plenty of time; he had only Saturdays for them. She seemed to have a wealth of disposable income; he watched every penny. Though she didn't openly convey it, he began to sense the sort of idle comfort in her that he had long ago branded as the anathema of achievement.

While they observed the horses being saddled and paraded in Belmont's paddock, he would talk with her about which ones seemed "up on their toes," ready for an all-out battle, and shake his head at those that appeared to be indifferently heading out for "just another day of going through the motions."

"You talk as if they are humans," she looked at him with a tilted head and an inquisitive smile.

"Well, they're not machines or puppets," he said in a low voice, matter-of-factly. "They all have feelings, personalities and dispositions. It's up to us to figure them out."

She liked the action of betting lots of races. She saw him make two bets in the first three months that they were together.

"In the old days, other than race tracks, if you wanted to gamble legally you had to go to Nevada," he remarked later, while they quickly grabbed a bite at a Denny's restaurant before rushing off to a playhouse rendition of "Who's Afraid of Virginia Woolf?"

"Now, there's Atlantic City. Now, there's the river boats and the Indian casinos. And stupid things like lotteries, Keno and pickle cards on every corner. It seems that every week another state legislature is approving another absurd measure that will expand gambling. Because the tentacles from these quick-and-dirty forms of gambling are reaching deeper and farther almost daily, people's gambling dollars are being sucked dry practically before they ever leave home. The result is, some horseracing tracks are closing up and others are drastically cutting back their racing days. On the flip side, the simulcasting of the races from the tracks that are left is reaching out like crazy. Horseplayers are being urged to trade in their trackside savvy and become fast-and-loose spectators of multi-TV racing. My

God! The nation's racing format has been taken over by Ronald McDonald!"

"What's so bad about that?" she asked. "More racing, more options."

"In every conceivable form, swarms of gambling options are sweeping the country and are being eagerly promoted by state and local governments to cover up their addictions for squandering the taxpayers' money. Each new gambling enticement is simply one more way to tax the people. OK, they don't walk up to you and just take it out of your pocket in the usual IRS way. Instead, they give you a little scratch game to play along with some cooked-up vision of get-rich-quick returns. Trouble is, it's a regressive tax. It burns the lower-income people to a much greater extent. Anyway, with all these opportunities for gambling around, everybody has three choices. Either don't gamble, period, or try to control the amount that you let it drain you."

"That's two . . . you said three choices," she fired back as a measure of her attentiveness, waiting a second or two before filling the unexpected void.

"Yeah well, the other one's so remote that it's almost not worth mentioning," he snort-laughed. "Learn how to win. Use it in the way it wasn't intended. Show a profit. Right away, that cuts out the lotteries, slot machines, all the video games, the wheels, craps and the rest of the table games. Ask any casino executive which game he'd play and, to a person, they'll emphatically answer 'None!'"

"So? I've seen you bet," she half-stated, half-queried.

"How do you match wits with a slot machine that is calibrated like a monkey wrench to turn a profit at a certain steady rate?" he was not about to offer a short answer. "Your best chances are when you match wits with other players, not the house. Poker or horseracing. True, in these situations, the house rakes a part of every pot as a surcharge or handling fee. This also pretty much guarantees the game is on the level and that you're going to get paid off if you win. Not always the case with a backroom card game or playing the ponies with a bookie."

"You've said more than once that I'm foolish for betting every race," she explored.

"So, you not only have to beat the masses, you have to win at a little higher rate to cover the rake," he stayed on message. "Here's where knowledge, skill, patience and experience replace dumb luck. No windfall stroke is going to put you into a life-changing bracket like you see on TV with those mega-millions lottery winners. Playing the horses successfully is a lifelong grind that will only give you back what you put into it."

He paid the check and they hurried off to "Virginia Woolf."

Waiting for the curtain to rise, she replied, "Sounds like you're trying to take all the fun out of it."

"Not unless in some yet-explained way you find losing amusing," he whispered, nodding his head slightly as the curtain started to waver. "Remind me to tell you about this guy I used to hang around with when I was first learning the game."

After the show they grabbed a table at the nearby Encore Lounge for a beer.

"I love that play," he said. "As many ways as I've seen it done, it never gets old. Weren't Burton and Taylor a great fit in the movie?"

"Yes, but I also thought George Segel and Sandy Dennis were perfect as the straight couple to Burton's and Taylor's diabolical antics," she said as he held her chair for her.

"Oh, there's nothing diabolical about it," he smiled. "They're just having a little mischievous fun while masking their own shortcomings."

"Oh, sure!" she laughed. "If you call premeditated social torture, and a Niagara of anxiety and disgrace, fun. Hey, both of those women got Oscars . . . Anyway, what did you want to tell me about this guy you used to hang around with?"

After ordering two Budweisers from the waitress, he nodded to Kathi. They were completely immersed in each other.

"OK, here was this guy whose annual income was probably five or ten times mine back then," he smirked, with his head bobbing slightly. "We had gone to school together and, for a few years after, we used to meet at the track once in a while when he was in town . . . just for old time's sake, I guess. We really didn't have much else in common anymore."

"Nothing unusual there," she quipped.

"He'd always stoke the fire, betting handfuls of money on every race," Bagwell described, while agreeing with her generalization. "He never let a race go by without plenty on it. He'd say, 'Hey, I'm not here to watch.' And, he stayed true to that. I don't specifically recall him ever cashing a ticket, but, in my mind, I can see him running over to me on very rare occasions after a race and holding a ticket up in my face and laughing."

"Why does that type always do that?" she revealed an inner wisdom.

"One day while we were waiting for the first race to start — Christ, he already had a handful of daily double tickets, a bunch of quinellas and a big fat win bet on something — I began giving him one of my you-can-beat-a-race-but-you-can't-beat-the-races talks," he kept on, acknowledging her observation with a nod. "He just brushed me off. Jesus, it was like me talking to my image in the mirror. You know, you're right arm becomes your mirror image's left. Everything turned around, reversed. That's how his logic hit me . . . entirely the opposite of everything I held sacred."

"And, there's no stopping them," she agreed.

"Right, but here's the kicker. He told me that the amount of money he lost at the track heightened his social standing with the people back home. While gabbing around the barbecue pit in the backyard of whoever's turn it was that week, all he'd have to mention is that he'd dropped two or three grand at the track yesterday, and his standing in that crowd ballooned. The dark logic being that anyone who can afford to drop that much at the track without batting an eye must be worth one helluva lot more. To him, so it seemed, there was power in losing. Like I said, we didn't have much in common anymore. I'm sure I just stood there and stared back while he told me his story. What the hell could I say to dignify that?"

They were quiet for a long moment, and then Kathi broke in.

"I know lots of people who would fit your friend's description like a glove. Logical or not, I can't stand that whole facade. I come from stuff like that. And, I can't stand it."

Kathi explained that her father owned VanBach & Son, a company he had built from nothing that designed, constructed, installed and maintained the elevator systems inside skyscrapers. Her older brother had already been groomed to take over the company. Other than being well provided for, Kathi was not, nor would she ever be, involved in any of the family's business. With the social connections made available as part of her birthright, her parents presumed that she would marry well and enjoy life that way . . . more of a sterile two-family merger than two people finding romance. Meanwhile, her brother would gain access to most of the family fortune, since it was mostly tied into the business.

"Ah," Bagwell interjected. "As Daniel Webster might have said if he were defending you against a pact with The Devil, 'Tis the right of every woman to raise her hand against her fate, but when she does, she's at crossroads'."

Ω

Kathi had upset the family apple cart when she accepted a full scholarship to Cornell University to study pre-veterinary medicine. Graduating in the top five percent of her class, she was working as an operating room assistant for Caring Care Animal Hospital during the current summer, before starting her first semester in the university's veterinary program.

Her father had huffed openly that such pursuits only made her less attractive to the types of men he had in mind for her. Real men are uncomfortable around intelligent women, he advised. Especially women who telegraphed their abilities with advanced degrees. Up to now, Kathi had kept this mostly to herself, feeling that any such explanation to Bagwell was uninteresting or worse. Why detract from the moments that they enjoyed together? She liked him, and he was falling deeply in love with her.

Perceptively, Bagwell also knew that, if he remained with "Homestretch" much longer, he would likely be forever pigeonholed as strictly a Thoroughbred horse-racing specialist, rather than as the general news wordsmith that he envisioned for himself. With the presidential election little more than a year away, and Ronald Reagan unable to run for re-election after two terms, Bagwell suspected that the upcoming campaign trail was going to turn into a wide-open battlefield and an excellent opportunity to study the fiery practice of top-level politics up close. His go-for-broke gamble was his silent prediction that Massachusetts's Governor Michael Dukakis would eventually land the Democratic Party's presidential nomination. If that happened, the Massachusetts newspapers, especially the dailies with regular beats nearest to the Boston area, would be taking on additional staff at many levels.

12

CLOSER, BETTER

In Editor & Publisher magazine, he came across the Chelsea Daily Tribune's search for a general assignment reporter/staff writer. With resume in hand the following Tuesday, Bagwell drove up to Chelsea, about ten miles north of Boston, and quietly barged into publisher Edward Evans's office.

"I think you're going to need more help than you're currently advertising for," Bagwell asserted, as a way of direct introduction.

Evans leaned back in his chair and glared at Bagwell. He didn't ask him to leave.

"Governor Dukakis has the nomination all but sewn up, and Bush, Reagan's obvious successor, can be had," Bagwell took advantage of Evans's silence. "Hire me as your assistant editor in charge of the political beat for the coming election year, and I'll only need one other reporter to help me."

"I'm not saying you're wrong, whomever the hell you are," Evans finally spoke, after a squinted hesitation. "Even so, what you say I'll need is still a little ways away. Right now, what I need is another reporter."

"Can you hold off until early November?" Bagwell said, his hands out in front, palms up, while explaining that, loyally, he had to stay with Homestretch until the looming Breeders' Cup Day spectacular was over. "I'm committed in good faith until then. After that, there's a lull in the sport until the prep races for next year's Triple Crown heat up. It'll give whoever takes my place plenty of time to get situated. You have my word, I'll be here right after Breeders' Cup."

"You'll come in as a general assignment reporter," Evans said straightforwardly, eye-to-eye, "We'll see how things go from there."

Bagwell quickly informed his publishers at Homestretch of his intentions. During his final three weeks before leaving, he was leisurely able to show his replacement the ropes and introduce him to several of his reliable grandstand and backside connections on the New York Racing Association circuit.

Ω

"Boston's not that far away," he attempted to assure Kathi during their next after-track dinner. "My weekends'll still be free until the campaign trail heats up. Even so, that won't last forever either."

Kathi hadn't touched her salad or her beer, but seemed quietly reserved.

"When you know what you want and go after it, how can anyone fault that or be selfish enough to try to interfere?" she answered. "Shucks, everybody's situation is different . . . where they come from, where they are and what they want to do next. I know that as well as anyone. But, I also know that I love you, and I'll fight like heck to stay with you. Carson, out there going after what you want is very different than just being adrift. Go after it."

He, too, had stopped eating.

"The whole time we've been seeing each other, it's been weekends only, except rarely," Bagwell said, carefully maintaining the same low tone that the conversation had evolved into. Anyone watching without being able to listen would have surmised the couple was putting the finishing touches on a minor agreement, not looking uneasily across a magma-filled chasm of unmapped depth.

"During other times, we both have had plenty to do," he said emphatically. "I love you very much. I'm in uncharted waters here because I've never felt anything like this about someone, and I doubt that I ever will again. But, a young woman like you . . . the way you carry yourself and what you've made of yourself so far . . . I'm sure I'm not what your people have in mind for you."

Abruptly angry, Kathi took a sip of beer.

"That's not fair, and you know it," she whisper-barked back. "How the hell can you decide what's good for me and what isn't, based upon what the hell my parents might have had or not had in mind, for God's sake! All we do is talk about not having other people make up our minds for us, and then you start doing the same damned thing that you supposedly detest. There's only a couple of reasons why people interrupt another person's plans — ostensibly for that person's own good, of course." She tilted her head and drew it back to emphasize the disgust in her sarcasm, her lavender eyes afire. "Most of the time it's for fear that you'll succeed and make them look foolishly bad. Otherwise, it's because they're just flat-out control freaks. Why the hell don't we just try to figure out how we're going to deal with this Boston thing?"

God, she looks great, he smiled silently. *What the hell does she see in me? Wow, she never cusses!*

"Look, I don't even give a damn about money," he said with a monotone, determined not to fall in line with her sarcastic air. "How the hell can you expect to get anywhere near what you want by hanging around with me forever? All I care about is getting enough together to exist on so I can keep on writing."

At that moment, the waiter, who had been standing perplexedly out of sight, broke in with, "Is there something wrong with the salads?"

Bagwell abruptly awakened from the conversation, "Ah-no, they're fine. Just give us a little more time."

"But sir, your entrees are ready and, even if I keep them warm for a few moments, they will not be as inviting as when freshly prepared," the waiter pleaded.

"Fine, bring them right away," Bagwell consoled. "And leave the salads. We'll be OK."

Bagwell and Kathi quietly stared at each other while the waiter put the salads aside and carefully placed the main courses in front.

"I can't be worried about how much money I'm making or going to make and be true to my purpose at the same time. Every time I see something, first thing I try to do is put it into words that someone else will understand and have the same feeling for. No matter what consequences might develop. I can't be worrying about how much it's worth in dollars, or how much somebody else might be willing to pay. Now, do those sound like serious prospects for a woman who wants to spend her summers in the Hamptons or out on Montauk? One thing though, if I could ever truly put into words what I feel for you and what you mean to me, I think I could begin to do battle with it. The way it is, all I can do is helplessly try to reason with you. We've had a better time together than most people ever enjoy. Shouldn't we leave it at that?"

He reached across to hold her hands. She reacted by withdrawing them.

"Hamptons? . . . Montauk?" She muffled her shriek as her eyes welled up with tears. "I could have never written to you in the first place and had that! It frightens me to think of it."

What might have been the best T-bone and lamb chops they would ever encounter were abandoned with hardly any nibbles. Regardless, by the time they left the restaurant, they had a plan for dealing with this Boston thing.

Ω

Bagwell moved into his position with the Chelsea Daily Tribune the Wednesday after, in a rare battle between Kentucky Derby winners, Ferdinand edged Alysheba in the 1987 Breeders' Cup Classic at Hollywood Park. And, he was right. The next July, at the convention in Atlanta, Gov. Dukakis claimed the Democratic nomination for president. Right after the convention, Dukakis's rating in the polls gave him a decisive lead over the Republican's uncontested nominee, Vice President George H.W. Bush.

Bagwell and assistant political reporter Sandra Burns had begun tracking Dukakis's campaign more closely during the New Hampshire primary and Iowa caucuses. During the final month before the convention that's all they did, night and day. And, as much as the Massachusetts governor's rise in the nation's public eye was intoxicating, every savvy pundit knew that post-conventional polls were apt to yield false positives, especially whenever the opposing party's convention is still on the horizon. Still, Dukakis more than gave Bagwell what he sought while the two traveled along the campaign trail, especially when the over-spoken candidate used Boston as his oratory backdrop.

Notwithstanding, Vice President Bush's previous experience as director of the CIA trumpeted that he was ruthlessly skilled at exploiting political espionage. If it hadn't been the Willie Horton episode, it would have been something else. Outgoing President Reagan was beloved by a great majority of Americans, and, since he couldn't run again, Bush was the closest transference for their adoring passions. By Election Day, Dukakis's edge had evaporated and, after all the votes were counted, the electoral points slam-dunked the White House safely into Bush's corner, 426 to 111.

With the election over, Evans quickly began putting his Chelsea newspaper back on an everyday keel. Accordingly, the paper's national political reporting effort was going to be scaled way back and most of its duties refocused toward additional coverage of Chelsea's city council, county commissioners and school board activities, same as Bagwell had been doing before Dukakis's campaign heated up.

"Hell, Sandy, I would have been satisfied to leave right after Dukakis got the nomination," Bagwell told his assistant over lunch after both of them had been made aware that cutbacks were in the wind. "By then, I had what I wanted from why I came here. Watching the entire election process up close from then on was just icing on the cake."

"Well, I'm glad you're here, Carson," Sandy interjected. "I'd have hated to go through all that on my own, or with anybody else."

"You like it here?" Bagwell asked.

"I love it," she confided. "But, I'm low girl on the totem pole . . . and Evans'll be cutting quickly now."

"I'm looking at a spot in the Midwest that has great possibilities for what I'd like to do next," Bagwell confided with her. "And, even if that doesn't pan out, I still want to move on. Evans knows that. But, I'll reaffirm it with him and recommend you for my slot."

"Oh, come on. There's got to be better qualified people, with much more experience?" she shook her head with disbelief. "You don't need to say things just to be nice."

"Look, aggressiveness and the willingness to learn and be committed to whatever it takes, among other things, count for a lot with a guy like Evans," Bagwell urged with firm conviction, then suddenly gave out a reflective chuckle. "Heck, I once got a job I wanted by just asking, without an ounce of experience to back it up. When I told the fellow I didn't know anything, but was willing to learn, he answered with a noticeable degree of sarcasm, 'You're hired! I just fired a guy who knew everything.'"

"Why would you even want to do something like that for me?" Sandy asked with growing confidence. "Chrissakes, other than my internship with the Boston Globe the summer before, the only other thing I've ever done is work on school newspapers. Why don't you just move on, and not give a damn what happens behind you?"

"At least a couple of reasons come to mind," Bagwell answered with quiet reserve. "Hell, none of us makes it anywhere on our own, no matter how good we think we are. When I think my hat-size is getting too big, I try to catch myself and reflect back on the people who adopted me for a moment or two along the way and gave a part of themselves. Stuff I could take with me. They each made me a little better than I would have been if I'd never met up with them. And, in situations like that, when you move on, most of the time there isn't even a chance to say good-bye, let alone a satisfactory thank-you. And, maybe that's the way it's supposed to be. It's never really good-bye. If you truly do take part of them with you, then the only way you can truly thank them is by doing the best possible with what they gave you. God, they're great people, all of them.

"The other thing, when you see someone — such as you — with something on the ball, you want to get in there. Help them take the next step. Be part of it. Like they say, you can't take it with you in the end . . . so it has to be what you leave behind that counts.

"And, one other thing . . . this one's personal. Whenever I leave a place, I hope it's in better shape than when I arrived. And, I want to see it do even better after I'm gone. That's the only way I can be sure that I've really made a lasting contribution to the important picture, and wasn't just putting on some sort of one-man show. And Sandy, you're just the kind who will take what you learn and run hard with it."

Ω

Bagwell had gotten wind of a brand new Thoroughbred racetrack, Mercury Downs. Its construction had been completed ahead of schedule, and the initial racing season would begin the last weekend in March and carry through Labor Day Monday. His credentials put him at the top of the list for an interview as the new turf writer for Mercury Times, the local daily newspaper.

While at the Chelsea paper, he had been able, in 1988, to write his usual prognosticative column about the Kentucky Derby. Even with Suffolk Downs right there in Boston's backyard, and Rockingham Park just up the road in south New Hampshire, the Chelsea sportswriters didn't focus on horse racing at all. Any racing stories that appeared in the paper were invariably pulled from the Associated Press's wire service. So, when Bagwell asked them if he could do a pre-Derby column, the Sports Department applauded.

For his 1988 piece, Bagwell had given good mention to California filly Winning Colors, trained by future Hall-of-Famer D. Wayne Lukas, who back then was being maligned by Thoroughbred racing's blue bloods as a brashly abrasive interloper from the quarter-horse ranks. Bagwell liked Forty Niner even better. He liked the horse's connections — owned by Claiborne Farm, trained by Woody Stephens and ridden by Pat Day, both Hall of Famers.

He always felt that Forty Niner should have won that Derby. Winning Colors was a massive freak of a roan filly with lightning out-of-the-gate speed. Day had been right to take Forty Niner back, away from Winning Colors's early fractions. Nearing midway through Churchill Downs's endless homestretch, Forty Niner began closing the gap on Winning Colors like crazy, just missing at the wire by a neck. Bagwell felt Day could have kept Forty Niner closer before starting his charge, but he never commented about that in print then or in the years that followed. He always had great respect for Day. And, who can say that, if kept closer early, Forty Niner would have had as much punch left in his stretch run? With severity, however, he did comment about the absurd debacle that occurred when the two horses rematched two weeks later in the Preakness.

Intent upon landing this job, Bagwell flew into Goldspar International Airport and drove his rented Datsun over to Mercury, about forty miles to the west, passing by just-completed and currently quiet Mercury Downs about halfway there.

"Everybody says good things about you, Carson," Mike Marston, the Times's managing editor, said. "I'm sure you can handle the turf writing end of it, but what kind of a gambling habit comes along with you?"

"Oh, I've been known to place a bob-or-two if the situation looks right," Bagwell answered right away, not exactly sure what Marston was up to.

"Look, gambling, drinking, sex . . . I've got nothing against any of that, as long as it's done the right way," Marston said directly. "You know you're going to get a name for yourself as our local turf writer right of the bat. You know, somebody who's in the know. Or, at least somebody who knows more than The Average Joe. Just figure out a way to be discrete with your betting, so The Average Joe doesn't even know you're doing it. Damn, I don't want them following you up to the windows and then squawking that they lost a bundle because they bet the same thing that Mercury Times's expert did."

"I understand," Bagwell nodded in agreement. "I'll take care of it."

"The track closes for the season just when football's starting up and doesn't reopen until just when basketball season, except for the pros, is getting over," Marston methodically described. "So, you'll be part of my football-basketball staff when the ponies aren't running. OK?"

After meeting with the publisher, Jackson Grey, over lunch, Bagwell drove back to Goldspar International for a late afternoon return flight to Boston, knowing he had the Times job sewn up.

Ω

Kathi, knowing how badly he wanted the job, drove up to Chelsea on the Friday evening after Bagwell returned. The next morning, when they went over to Boston, he showed her Plymouth Rock, chuckling as they looked down at an uninspiringly small slab of worn-smooth igneous stone.

"The job looks good, Kath," Bagwell said, reiterating what he had told her over the telephone. "I'll have to be there about the first of March, just when the barn area starts to fill up and the horses begin their first workouts over the track. I'll hate being apart from you. I can't even remember what that was like."

"There's no stopping you, Dear," she reaffirmed as they walked over to the little Quiet Clam seafood stand across the street from the bay. "And, I wouldn't want to."

The largest collection of impressionist Claude Monet's art ever gathered under one roof was currently on display at the Boston Museum of Fine Arts. Bagwell had tickets. Their self-tour time would begin at 2 p.m. sharp. They had just enough time for a lobster sandwich.

"We'll get together when we can," she reassured him after their tour. "It won't be forever, and I'm not going anywhere without you."

"How'd you like Monet?" Bagwell asked, thankful for an expedient reason to change the subject.

"I loved the Freudian interpretation of his haystack series," Kathi answered genuinely. "And, that time-lapse, natural-lighting series of impressions of the "Church at Vatheuil" is one of the most remarkable creations I've even seen."

She still had two years of vet school remaining, and no intentions of stopping her studies at Cornell or transferring to be nearer Bagwell until after she had graduated. They had dress-rehearsed this separation scene before, when he made his move to Chelsea. Other than rechecking a few cues, there was little new to talk through this time, except how to suture the wider breach that would temporarily separate them this time.

13

TWIN-TRIFECTACIDE

"Good evening, Carson speaking," Bagwell cheerfully answered the phone in his den, masking his irritation at the intrusion.

"Mr. Bagwell, I presume," the voice at the other end stated in monotone.

"How quaint . . . who the heck is this?" Bagwell scowled, now openly irritated. Dinner over and a swirl of potential ideas in mind, he was just settling in for an evening of writing.

"Oh, I hope we'll meet soon," the voice seemed assuring. "Actually, we've worked together before without being properly introduced."

"Is this some sort of game?" Bagwell quickly quipped, not hiding his displeasure. "When am I supposed to start guessing?"

"No, no, wait. I'll try to level with you in a nutshell," the voice said with a quieting determination. "Remember the Dukakis campaign?"

"How could I forget?"

"Well, we crossed paths."

"I don't get it."

"You recall you were recruited by the Secret Service detail that was with Dukakis back then?"

"Yeah, but only while trafficking in the everyday information surrounding Dukakis. If I saw or heard anything that seemed to be a threat, I was supposed to call. Nothing came of it."

"I was in charge of that detail. The way things turned out, there was never any reason for us to meet"

"I remember. I made it very clear that I would come forth right away if I thought there was a clear and present danger. And only then. Otherwise, no. I wasn't going to sit around ratting on every little coming and going, especially about my fellow journalists."

"And we never expected anything different."

"So, we were on the same page . . . That's nice," Bagwell had had enough of idle chatter. His word processor was beckoning. "Why the call now?"

"A few reasons, all having to do with the same thing . . . the Mendoza killing."

"Hey, I don't know anything. Leave me out. The way the papers described his body is nothing compared to the way it really was. I know. I was there right after the body was found."

"Wait, wait. you won't be involved. Strictly back-burner stuff, just like before. You're such a fixture with the local racing crowd. You can move around at will and not even be noticed anymore. That's all I want. Just a messenger. If it will help, we've been a lot closer more than once recently. I mean, 'Brighty's comin' along jess fine. He be back on de track afore ya knows it.'."

"God, that's you!"

"Yezzah."

"Unbelievable."

"No, believable. So, you can see how easy it will be to pass information to you to give to some other trust-worthy soul."

"Are you kidding? How the hell am I supposed to know trustworthy when I don't even know who I'm going to be talking to?"

"Did you get burned during that Dukakis thing?"

"No, but this is different."

"Different how?"

"Somebody's already dead here. I don't like that!"

"Yeah, but I'm betting you'd like to help catch the sonovabitch that did it. I know you liked Mendoza. Wouldn't you like to help, if you could do it safely? You know you would."

"How the hell do you know you can trust me?"

"I'm betting that's a sure thing. I'm also assuming you're in. Relax. I've got your back. I won't let you get near the fire. Right now I need you to help with some general details. Strictly background stuff. Tell me about this Twin-Trifecta thing at Mercury Downs?"

"You want the 25-cent tour, or the one-dollar super-special?"

"I want anything you can tell me. Fill me in. All I know is it's one of those get-rich-quick deals."

"Yeah, right. Get-poor-quick. But, that never stops a lot of 'em. You're right though. The Twin-Tri is sort of rare these days."

Without further comment from Maxwell, Bagwell went on, starting with a little summary of history. He sounded like a textbook on the subject. And he should have. He had written enough about the subject over the years.

"The Twin-Trifecta, also known as the Triple-Double, is one of the more fanciful gambling heads of the voracious hydra that was spawned when horse racing's traditional pari-mutuel betting system met up with modern computer technology," he described in monotone.

"Remember the old pre-computer days? Punched-out tickets with codes? Back then, racetracks compiled their pari-mutuel betting pools using a rudimentary system of relatively slow electronic counters and calculators. Win, Place and Show, along with one Daily Double per day and perhaps some Quinellas, were the only types of bets available. Also, legal bets could only be made at the racetrack, and only on races that were actually being run at that particular track."

"I've never hung around tracks," Maxwell interjected. "My work is my vice. Yeah, I've seen those old tickets."

"Wait a minute," Bagwell retorted in disgust. "I hang around the track every day. It's not a vice . . . it's a whole world unto itself."

"OK . . .OK."

"Then, suddenly," Bagwell returned to the topic at hand with renewed vigor, "the advent of high-speed computer equipment, with sophisticatedly complex capabilities, and made small enough to be easily moved around and conveniently put into service at will, fostered a quantum leap in how betting money could be handled for horse racing. Overnight, an entirely new frontier of novelty bets sprouted. Exacta, Trifecta, Superfecta, Pick-3, Pick-6 — hell, pick-anything — and rolling Daily-Double pools could be handled automatically and the winning payoffs calculated in milliseconds. Nowadays, an enthusiastic bettor can wheel, part-wheel, crisscross, key or box almost limitless combinations of horses on one ticket."

"How the heck do the pots get so big on some of these bets?" Maxwell pleaded, needing a breather before moving forward.

But Bagwell was in high gear. He went right on explaining that not long after the Pari-mutuel Computer Age arrived, the nationwide simulcasting of races between betting sites, both trackside and at off-track betting parlors, mushroomed every bettor's opportunities. From there, it was a simple techno-step to be able to commingle all of the betting pools from all the different betting sites for a particular simulcast race, thus creating gigantic single money pools involving the entire nation. Through a mega-network of phone lines and satellite dishes, even races at the more remote tracks, fondly known as bullrings, could generate enormous pools with money now gushing in from a limitless ocean of bettors located at myriad distant tracks, OTBs and casino race books.

"With the advent of this pari-mutuel cornucopia, the lone roadblock to getting at the bettors' money was the lack of imagination in making a particular type of bet attractive," Bagwell said with inflection. "Hell, Pick-3s, Pick-4s, Pick-6s and Pick-9s are all daughters of the traditionally attractive Daily Double — a Pick-2, so to speak. But now, instead of picking the winners of just two races in a row, you could pick the winners of a broader array of consecutive races, with the payoffs to winning tickets inflating exponentially as more races are added to the sequence!

"With high-speed, economically concise and user-friendly computers, the payoffs for these ultra-complex bets now can be sorted and reported more quickly than rudimentary Win-Place-Show prices were during the pre-computer days."

Bagwell pointed out that, as a combative measure, commingled simulcasting became horse-betting's backlash to its waning popularity when hordes of action-seeking gamblers began gravitating toward more serving venues. Greyhound racing, with races every twelve minutes and upwards of fifteen-race cards, and with matinee and evening racing the same day, offered pari-mutuel bettors chances to put down their money faster and more often.

"Omaha's Ak-Sar-Ben race track was the celebrated jewel of Midwestern Thoroughbred racing for about seventy years . . . until nearby Council Bluffs, just across the Missouri River in Iowa, introduced dog racing and then casino gambling," he said, using his favorite example. "Then, too, lottery tickets beckoned at the checkout counters of most convenience stores, and Indian casinos, local Keno games and other dollar-eroding distractions, such as pickle cards, began beckoning within easier reach."

Ak-Sar-Ben, he noted, had folded under this pressure, fallen into disrepair and later went the way of the developers. The entertainment dollar that horse racing once monopolized — nowadays inanely referred to as "disposable income" by the Yuppies and Generations X and Y — became spread too thinly and was grabbed up more quickly than Ak-Sar-Ben could withstand. In a troubling trend, the Ak-Sar-Ben model for racetrack extinction was occurring in other parts of the country as well.

Ironically, from the ashes of Omaha's once-auspicious live-racing industry a transplanted simulcasting facility is managing to do a large-scale busi-

ness. To assuage a quirkiness of the Nebraska state legislature, Horsemen's Park, a full-scale live-racing facility is pontooned onto the side of the elaborate simulcasting building. Live-racing is held there three days
each year to meet a special minimum legislative stipulation for anyone wanting to operate an off-track betting
site in Nebraska.

"In states where legislatures are more accommodating – like Iowa, West Virginia, New Mexico, California
and, more recently, Florida," Bagwell recited, "racetracks have brought in slot machines, video poker and
other casino games, not only to save, but shoot new life
into their live-racing programs. Purse money has ballooned for these places."

"You seem to know your stuff," Maxwell said plainly.

"It's what I do."

"So they say. It's why I called."

"Even though most people gamble with fanciful
dreams of winning, they are more than just tolerant of
losing," Bagwell emphasized, sharing a deep-seated
opinion. "Hell, those magnificent edifices along Las Vegas's Strip are nothing more than stunning testimonies
to the human species' universal acceptance that casino
gambling is ultimately a one-way arrangement."

"They're really that stupid?" Maxwell asked, with an
uneasy hint in his tone.

"I wish it was that simple," Bagwell jumped right
back. "Sure, many realists defer to losing before ever
sitting down. They know that when hopes based upon
chance face off against foundations steeped in statistical control, the long-range outlook is complete ruin for
the fortune-seeking opportunist."

"So, why?"

"What can I tell you? Humans, down through history, have remained fascinated. Even a remote chance for
success is worth mounting a challenge. Forget the relatively few out-of-control gambling addicts. That's not
what built Vegas. It's not what keeps the racing industry going. It's the millions and millions of people losing

small amounts of money that add up to billions and billions in profits for the house."

"The house wins, and they lose . . . and they dumbly keep marching off to slaughter. How can you say that's human?"

"Call it willful resignation. One way of breaking the monotonous routine. Most levelheaded people who are bent upon doing a little gambling routinely set aside part or all of their 'disposable income' for that."

"So, right away, they plan on losing . . . even calling it disposable dollars. Maybe I'm too old, but I don't have disposable dollars. I earn my money. It's not disposable."

"OK, call it entertainment dollars. You do like to have fun once in a while, don't you? The way this conversation is going, I have to ask."

"All right . . . all right."

"OK, well, the traditional Win-Place-Show horse-racing approach, while ever-appealing to the plodding purist — like me, I might add — doesn't come close to satisfying the inner burn of the give-me-action "recreational gambler." You know, the spin-a-wheel, turn-a-card, roll-the-dice types. Anyway, modern technology gave racetracks a chance to counter the casino-instant tsunami that continues to sweep across the nation. With newer exotic ways to bet on horses, racetracks still can't promise quicker returns, but they are now capable of creating lottery-like potentials for windfall, life-changing-size payoffs on initial bets as small as one dollar."

"Yeah, I know that much. Instead of going a track, they just go to a room somewhere and look at a whole bunch of TV screens."

"Right, except the farther you get away from the real thing, the less information you have. And, the more it becomes a flat-out gamble instead of an informed wager . . . just like the rest of it. Action plus hope equals thrill."

"So, that's we're talking about? Win or lose, they're just looking for the biggest jolt?"

"Hey, you called me. I think I know why though."

"You do?"

"Look, I get paid to handicap things. I thrive on it, too."

"So, you're handicapping me?"

"Comes natural. But, this could go on all night. I've got a life to live. You'd like to know a little bit more about what's the big deal about the Twin-Trifecta, right?"

"Get on with it."

"Well, obviously, as the complexity of these exotic bets — like the Twin-Tri — increases, the chances that anyone might hold a winning ticket decreases. And, therein lies the bait for the modern pari-mutuel marketer's hooks. On occasions when no daily winners exist, the pools for some types of multi-race bets are carried over to the next day, greatly inflating that day's pool before the first bet is even taken. Carryover pools can add plenty of excitement to bets such as the Pick-6 and, in particular, to a revolving exotic bet such as the Twin-Trifecta."

"Revolving exotics? Inflated pools?"

"With the Twin-Tri, you have to correctly pick the first three finishers in one race in exact order, same as for any regular Trifecta bet. Then, between races, you must turn that winning ticket back into a mutuel clerk for the opportunity to correctly pick a second Trifecta in another race designated later in the day. Hence, a Twin-Trifecta."

"Sounds a little complicated for the Average Joe's taste."

"You'd be surprised. Especially when the pool starts to snowball."

"Yeah, what's that all about?"

"Every track does it a little differently. At Mercury Downs, any bettor who hits the first Trifecta of the twin bet collects a payoff from 50 percent of that day's Twin-Tri pool. Then, if no one successfully completes the Twin-Tri that day, the other 50 percent of that day's pool is automatically dumped into the next day's potential Twin-Tri payoff. On occasions when, day after day, the carryover pot remains untouched by short-falling bettors who hit only the first half, the cumulative Twin-Tri can grow into an enormous sum."

"How long's that take?"

"Sort of slow at first. This type of bet is so difficult to hit, so to speak, that initial interest can be relatively small. Early on, the chances of winning are so low compared to the size of the pot that even some not-so-smart money tends to avoid it as a sucker bet. But, when there have been no winners for several days, the inflating carryover pool becomes much more enticing, and a blood-fever of interest begins to really snowball in size and speed. After a while, an un-hit Twin-Trifecta pool can swell into a life-altering nest egg, much the same way that an un-hit lottery pool occasionally does."

"Hundreds of millions of dollars?"

True, Bagwell's claim as a handicapper par excellence was without argument, but Maxwell knew precisely how and when to interject brief, urging questions to keep testifier testifying.

"OK-OK, so we're talking in terms of a lousy million or so dollars as a Twin-Tri windfall, not that hundreds-of-millions interstate lottery stuff. But, wouldn't the way you are planning the rest of your life take on a whole new aura if you suddenly were handed an extra million?"

"I like my life the way it is."

"Yeah, me too."

"So, what do you do with an extra million dollars? Give it away as fast as you can, so it doesn't interfere?"

"Not a bad idea," Bagwell quipped, then returned to why Maxwell had called. "Those pools that can build from one day to the next don't grow as fast as you might think. That track always gets theirs first. Pari-mutuel betting is never a zero-sum game. Not all the money bet during any given race is ever distributed back to the holders of the winning tickets."

"Ah yes, the handling charge, or, in some circles, the vig."

"Right off the top, baby. The track doesn't care who wins. They get theirs the same way every time. Before the payoffs to the winners are calculated. Along with paying state taxes, this take-out revenue goes toward the prize money for the races at the track and the administrative costs of operating the facility. It can be as low as 10-15 percent for straight Win, Place and Show betting, depending upon which state the track is located in, or as high as 25 percent for exotic bets."

"Like the Twin-Tri?"

"You betcha. Bettors always gripe about a track's handling charge. But, whatever it is, it's far less debilitating than the monstrous chunks extracted from the pools of any state-run lottery or Keno game."

"So, what's the big deal about the Twin-Tri?"

"Probability-wise it's hard to hit. What makes it even harder to hit is the way the racing secretary makes sure that both races are full of the most inept, unpredictable horses on the grounds."

"That's what a racing secretary does? Make up the races?"

"Same way at every track. With upwards of 14 horses, each Twin-Tri race will be either very cheap claiming horses or the epitome of disadvantaged racing animals — rock-bottom maiden claimers."

"So, it's a dice roll?"

"Worse. Do the math."

"Meaning?"

"Look, all things being equal, the odds of any one Trifecta combination in a 14-horse field is a formidable 2,183-to-1. That's tough enough. Yet, it pales by comparison when you realize that the simple odds of being sure to hit a Twin-Tri from two fields of 14 horses is an astronomical 4,769,855-to-1. Anybody who doesn't know that going in, shouldn't be reaching into their pockets to bet."

"Even if they do know, they shouldn't."

"Seems that way to me. But, there's a big difference between horse races and simple probabilities. Sure you've got time for this?"

"I'm listening, aren't I? My dime, handicapper."

"Yeah, you called . . . Obviously, not all the horses in any race have an equal chance of winning or even finishing in the money. It's the racing secretary's job to know all about this. Based upon each horse's background and racing history, certain ones have better expectations than others. That's why, for any given race, horses are assigned differing morning-line odds in the track's published racing program. Simply the racing secretary's estimate of the probable outcome of the race."

"Any good?"

"Nothing more, nothing less than one knowledgeable person's educated guesses. Besides, those morning-line odds only hold until the betting starts. From then on, the racing secretary's opinion is out the window. From the first bet until the race goes off and the betting closes, the odds displayed on the tote boards are established strictly by how the bettors have been putting their money into the Win pool. Or, in the case of exotic bets, the relative amount of money on each combination. This is the true essence of pari-mutuel betting. Horseplayers don't bet against the house the same way as the players at a table only go up against the dealer in a blackjack game. Horseplayers bet against each other's financial opinions. The old 'My horse can beat your horse' stuff."

"I've always stayed away from this stuff," Maxwell sighed. "Guess I just took my chances in other ways."

"Had enough? I'll stop . . . or talk as long as you want."

"No, no, keep going. I can see how people get hooked . . . trying to beat the odds . . . or just liking the action. A bunch of horse running down the homestretch is exciting, and more so with a bet on it."

"Like I said, it's your dime, Look, the amount of knowledge and information that a horseplayer can accumulate means a lot toward being able to correctly predict the outcome of a race. This is what makes placing money on a horse race a wager, rather than a simple gamble. With a simple gamble, the odds of any event happening are ironclad. They're known beforehand and never change. The long-term odds always favor the house. The gambler just hoping he'll get lucky over the short hall — before the Law of Large Numbers eats him up. Craps is a great example. Regardless of who blows on the dice before rolling, or how the dice are shaken above the head or to the side, or any of that other hocus-pocus, it is a simple rigid fact that the odds of any particular outcome from an unbiased pair of dice remain forever the same."

"And yet, there's never any shortage of takers at the dice trough."

"The pinnacle of macho excitement. Almost as if winning or losing takes a backseat."

"Kinda shallow, isn't it?"

"Ah, who can say? One man's pleasure is another's . . . Anyway, the more you know about the horses in a particular race, the sharper your chances. The more you know about each horse's pedigree, lifetime racing record, trainer, jockey and owner, along with the horse's recent performances and workouts, the distance of the race and the conditions of the race, the keener are your chances. Some swear by a narrower slice. Specialists. Number crunchers. Sheet disciples and speed freaks. Blinkers and leg-wraps specialists. And, those who worry over the use of legal medications, such as Lasix and Bute."

"Does that work?"

"They all work at times. None of it works all the time. None enough. No system is a rubber stamp to easy street."

"So, most end up losing?"

"Lots more than just most. Try finding someone who makes living at the track. The probability of running into one is next to zero."

"So, for most it's strictly recreation, like going to the movies?"

"A little more. There are endless angles for any horseplayer to ponder. And, that's what keeps people

coming back . . . certain that this time they know a little more . . . this time they surely will finally outsmart
the game. People who wouldn't go near a lottery ticket,
Keno game or slot machine, can't resist the Sirens' call
to post."

"What about this Twin-Tri thing?"

"More recently, many tracks that originally offered
the Twin-Tri have become less enamored with its relative ability to generate revenue per effort. At many places, Pick-6 and Superfecta wagers have pushed the
Twin-Tri into retirement. For instance, before they
dropped the bet altogether in 2000, Ruidoso Downs's
record Twin-Tri payoff was $792,446.40. There were
4,345 'live ticket holders' after the first half that day,
but only one correctly nailed the second half. But, it
had taken a race sequence of 27 straight days of unhit
carryovers to build that pot.

"Isn't that too bad," Maxwell chided in a low tone.
"All of 27 days."

"You don't get it, man," Bagwell was emphatic.
"These go-for-big guys aren't plodders. They want bigger
and faster. They want that life-changing stuff. God
knows what they think they want to change to."

"OK, I get it. Greed'll never stop by itself. It just
wants to keep feeding and growing."

"Yeah well, the Twin-Tri just doesn't get it done
quick enough. Before Maryland's Laurel-Pimlico circuit
dropped the Twin-Tri, the record payoff at Laurel had
been $1.8 million, but that was split between 31 correct
tickets. Meanwhile, the best that Pimlico ever did before
abandoning the bet was a $414,043 payout on April 4,
1991."

"How the hell do you pull that crap off the top of
your head?"

"You doubt my capacity?" followed by a slight, but
contrived, pause. "Actually, I'm sitting here at my desk.
As soon as we started talking Twin-Tri, I pulled my file
on it."

"How very efficient."

"Here's an interesting exception," Bagwell noted, ignoring Maxwell's jab, "Tampa Bay Downs has kept their Twin-Tri alive, amid its Superfectas and Pick-6s, by promising to clear the carryover pot every Tuesday, whether it's hit or not. By week's end, if no one has a correct ticket for both halves, the pot is split among all bettors who correctly pick the first half that day."

"Tampa's rule ensures a timely payoff," Maxwell cut in, showing that he doing more than just listening. "But, with their mandatory weekly cutoff, it seems highly unlikely there will ever be a rainmaker-type return."

"Right-o. Since their every-Tuesday innovation, Tampa's Twin-Tri carryovers have topped out at the low- to mid-$30,000 range," Bagwell answered with enthusiasm, spurred on by Maxwell's remaining on top of the conversation. "But, like Tampa's mutuel manager told me, it does add excitement and bring people out on Tuesdays, which otherwise is not usually a big day."

"So, anyway you look at it, get more people to bet more money . . . and faster. Greed, greed, greed."

"Heck yes. Tracks know they serve as havens for bunches of these incurable moon-shooters. So, they strive for bigger, faster-growing carryover pots. And the Pick-6 outperforms the Twin-Tri, hands down."

"Is there really that much difference?"

"You decide," Bagwell needled, referring to his files again. "On August 4, 2004, for instance, Del Mar set a new record when it paid one bettor $2.1-million for a correct Pick-6 ticket — after only two days of carryovers! Heck, Pick-6 payoffs in the hundreds of thousands of dollars are so common nowadays that they really don't draw much comment anymore."

"I see," Maxwell acquiesced. "So, what's Mercury Downs doing?"

"You mean, why did they keep the Twin-Tri? . . . Go against the grain?"

"Yeah."

"In large part, precisely because the other tracks were forsaking it. It was the Mutuel Department's decision. Mercury Downs simulcasts their races everywhere they can. The Downs's decision-makers speculated that there were plenty of "Trifecta experts" out there who would still enjoy having the bet available. They were right. The Downs's Twin-Tri gained momentum because others chose to drop it."

Over the past winter and throughout the new year, Mercury Downs's racing fans had continued to buzz about the week when the Twin-Tri's carryover suddenly went nova near the end of the season.

"Sure, there had been some nice little pots in the low-to-mid hundreds of thousands before," Bagwell knew what Maxwell really wanted. "This time, though, when the money began frantically flowing in from hasty partnerships and syndicates, all it did was add to the momentum of the snowballing carryover. Nobody hit."

"Wait a minute . . . partnerships? Syndicates?"

"Yeah, very temporary things. Nothing clandestine or criminal. They always materialize to spread the burden of the stake money needed to cover the reasonable possibilities for hitting the right three horses in the right order on two different tickets. This time, though, nothing worked for days. The pool inflation from the unsuccessful carryovers soared."

"You're going to have to spell this out."

"Are you sure you want this?"

"Try me."

"Look, the economical killer for Twin-Tri bettors is this. You have to bet each combination of horses that you like on your first ticket enough times to ensure that you will have enough winning tickets to cover a bet on all the combinations you have figured for the second race. Believe me, this gets very costly in a big hurry."

"Dollarwise, what are we talking about? Geez, the pot was a million-seven."

"Maybe so, but check this. Say you have figured that half of the 14-horse field in the first race of the Twin-Tri has a reasonable shot of finishing in the top three positions. To cover all of the possibilities for those seven horses finishing in the top three places would cost 7 times 6 times 5, or $210 in one-dollar tickets."

"Doesn't seem like much of a wager when there's a pot approaching two-million dollars at stake."

"Wait a second. That $210 for the first race doesn't get you anywhere. Say that you also have seven horses figured in the second half, or another 210 combinations. Now, to ensure that you can cover all 210 second-half combinations, you must have 210 winning tickets from the first half. So, the initial Twin-Tri bet now becomes a formidable $210 x 210, or $44,100! To soften that blow, temporary partnerships and syndicates frantically begin to arise out of this maelstrom of financial need."

During the final Wednesday of the previous season, when Mercury Downs's Twin-Tri pot had hypnotically skyrocketed to an intoxicating local record of $1.72 million, there was one winning ticket.

14

BLACKJACK FOR DINNER

LaVona Scott was among the first of Mercury's citizens on Lt. Huber's must-meet itinerary when he visited during his job interview. She had shown him several apartments to consider temporarily while making up his mind about permanent housing. Judy hadn't come with him for the interview, but, ultimately, the choice of where the Hubers might settle in Mercury would be hers.

Quarter of a century later, long after Judy had left for good, he remained in the house that she had selected. At first, he was uneasy over how little the sudden void bothered him. Had life with Judy been that synthetic? Even in the quietness of late evening, no ghosts of a shared past came haunting. All remnants of her spirit seemed to have vanished with her.

"My God, had we really become that distantly sterile?" the lieutenant muttered to Marcus from his reading chair on more than one occasion when his wandering mind sought value in an adult life faithfully shared under the same roof, at the same table and in the same bed with one other person.

The lieutenant employed a daytime housekeeper, twice a week. Along with the general cleaning and laundry, Mrs. Alvarez cooked breakfast and supper on those days. Once a week, she also did the grocery shopping and, during the summers, helped to keep the grounds weeded and trimmed. He mowed the lawn in synchrony with the weather's nourishing whims: Every ten days or so during the dry spells, every week whenever the late afternoon showers were prevalent.

He was ever home for lunch. On those days without Mrs. Alvarez, which included the entire weekend, he was completely on his own for food. Though he made it a point to dine at various places, he preferred the steak-and-potatoes menu at Charlie's Wagon Wheel. Ambiance meant little to him. Cleanliness and reliable food counted for plenty.

When Judy left, he continued to bury himself in his work. Several months past before he began taking notice of the happenings around him during his off-hours. One of the first objects of his rekindled focus was LaVona Scott. She also was having a late supper alone at one of the Wagon Wheel's tables. The only other customers stood at the cash register near the doorway. Charlie's evening shift waitress was cheerily counting out the change from their check. Nodding as he passed by, he took his regular chair at his regular table.

Idly scanning the room, he smiled and, with genuinely shy evasiveness, gave a quick head bow to the woman at the other table. A little later, having given his order to the waitress, the lieutenant awkwardly stood and approached.

"I don't know if you remember me, but you helped me get settled here some years ago," he stammered.

"Don't remember you?" LaVona said rhetorically, but in a soothingly cordial manner. "Everybody in town knows you. I'd say you've settled in pretty well. How's the house holding up?"

"I'm still there, but I'm afraid I haven't improved the place much," he said abruptly, wondering instantly why he had said that. "My wife went back East a while ago to be nearer her parents, but I'm still there." *Gad, this is getting worse by the moment,* he thought. *Why don't I just go back to my own table, sit down and shut up.*

"I probably knew about that right after it happened," LaVona nodded straightforwardly, very much intending to avoid any pretense of coy naiveté. "I never inquired about any of the details, but you can't keep a thing like that a secret around here. Won't you join me?" She made sweeping motion to all three empty chairs at the table.

"Thank you, if you're sure I wouldn't be intruding?" he said, unable to hide his fidgetiness. *Oh God,* he thought, *she asked you, didn't she? Just pull a chair up, dummy.* Then, without waiting for an answer, he waved to the waitress who was in the midst of bringing his salad. "Miss, I've decided to sit over here."

During the ensuing weeks LaVona and Lt. Huber dined together several times and then one evening caught a movie afterwards. After insisting upon buying her own ticket, she allowed him to pay for the bucket of buttered popcorn and diet Pepsi they shared.

Ω

LaVona had been married for five years and divorced for quite a while now. The fiery prospects of togetherness had permanently cooled into the irreversibly nauseating rigors of confinement and accountability for her, and there was nothing that her now-former husband could do to quiet her all-consuming restlessness. Seeing other men had nothing to do with the wall that thickened between them. She simply found that she wanted to come and go as she pleased, and keep her own counsel. Fortunately, so it seemed to her, kids hadn't become part of their temporary union.

As a successful businesswoman, she also served on the boards of directors for the Mercury Museum and the local Carnegie Arts Center. And, she spearheaded the creation of "Keep Mercury Beautiful," a volunteer organization that had developed the local recycling program and periodically mobilized the county's scout troops for highway cleanups and helping senior citizens with spring cleanups. Her organizational skills were also sought whenever car washes, canned-goods donations and walk-run fundraisers were needed to support local citizens struck by unforeseen tragedy.

Ω

Each fanatical about privacy in their own personal lives, LaVona's and Lt. Huber's current lifestyles soon meshed comfortably into the pleasure of each other's company. Then suddenly, on a lark of conspiracy, they planned their getaway.

Just after noon on the second Friday in March, she had gone to Goldspar International Airport to board a 2:30 p.m. direct flight to Reno, Nevada. Three hours earlier, he had headed for Chicago in his car. From there, he made reservations to Reno on the earliest possible flight.

As planned, they ritualized surprise at running into each other at the Salamander Gift Shop in the mini-mall area of Circus Circus casino, as if the good people of Mercury didn't know by now that they were an item. Public sightings of any two people together were sure to keep the gossip mill churning in Mercury . . . marital status or sexual preference of either party notwith-standing.

After an initial spat over the relative merits of slot machines versus roulette wheels versus blackjack tables, they went into a moderate-stakes blackjack hot streak that lasted a full two-and-a-half days. Imme-diately, they had agreed that neither had any idea what was going on at a craps table. Using the house's money, their weekend hiatus added a Monday and then a Tuesday. They slept late and played blackjack during the day, then dined elegantly and took in a late stage show each evening.

On Saturday, they rented a car for the day and drove to South Lake Tahoe. The lieutenant spent most of the day at Harvey's sports book playing the March Madness college basketball games and simulcast horse races. LaVona shopped, then settled into the less-threatening oblivion of the quarter slot machines.

That night, while late-dining at an Italian restau-rant after taking in singer Tom Jones's show at Har-rah's, they finally talked about something besides gam-bling and the general glitz.

"Thanks for taking me," LaVona said with a bouncy sparkle. "I've always wanted to see Tom Jones in per-son. He's even better than I expected."

"As comedian Alan King said, 'He gets more out of Delilah than Sampson ever did'," he quipped, while silently relishing the glow of her happy cheeked face, wreathed by the gentle bushy flow of her auburn hair. *God, she's beautiful!*

She nodded an agreeable smile in seconding King's comment, and then they were quiet until she broke the silence.

"Before Roger and I finally ended it, we agreed to seek help from a marriage counselor," LaVona dryly reflected while leaning back pensively and slowly twirling the stem of her empty wineglass between her thumb and forefinger. "Actually, she was a rather expensive psychiatrist. About midway through the third session, she had had enough, saying, 'Usually, I try very hard to help couples work things out, but I can't see how you two ever got together in the first place.'"

The Lieutenant nodded in knowing silence. Nothing to say.

"Roger didn't argue much after that, and we rather smoothly backed away from each other's lives. He lives in western Kansas now. Teaches History and coaches basketball. Seems happily remarried to a stay-at-home wife and has three kids. What brought yours to an end?"

Lt. Huber looked down at her glass. Taking an accentuated breath through his nose and, while pressing the thumb joints of his intertwined fingers of his folded hands against his lips, he then, with a squinted frown, peered into her eyes.

"I'm not sure it is," he answered frankly while hesitatingly drawing his now tilted head back a little.

"Oh, really?" she said, leaning forward, no longer twirling her glass.

"We hadn't put much of anything down on paper by the time Judy left to go back East," he said directly. "Oh, we had informally decided that I would keep the house, and she could have both vehicles. I bought the Ford after she left. God, by the end we were the dullest, most withdrawn twosome you can imagine. Worse than shy first-daters. We'd see each other when I finally got home, and wait for the other one to start some sort of conversation that we could share. Emptiness and silence was all that remained."

"I know the drill," she shook her head.

"There wasn't even any sex left. But hell, there never really was much of that."

"Do I really need to know that?" LaVona had kept quiet long enough.

"She was a virgin on our wedding night," the lieutenant kept on, seemingly without the slightest acknowledgment of her subtle despair. He was in full stride and not about to be easily put off.

"Not that there's a thing wrong or right with that," LaVona interjected. "Virginity on the wedding night has a lot of history."

"Well, it just happened to be the way she was, and I respected her viewpoint while we were courting," he shrugged. "She was very adept orally, though. Christ, she knew her way around with that mouth and those hands of hers. Somebody must have gotten her aside before it was too late. A wily aunt, perhaps, or her sorority sisters . . . maybe even her mother."

"Isn't that quite enough?" LaVona interjected directly. "I think I get the picture."

But, he wouldn't be put off. "Somebody clued her in with, 'Look, honey, with your looks and style, there's going to be plenty after you, hot-and-heavy. There'll even be times when you'll get turned on yourself and want to give in. But, there's ways to calm things down without losing that all-important cherry'."

The waiter, having earlier introduced himself as George, suddenly glided toward them with a hearty burgundy. That seemed to stop Lt. Huber, or had he finally made all of the point he wanted to?

After uncorking the bottle, George leaned to pour a splash into his wine glass. Instead, the lieutenant smoothly waved the gesture off by covering his glass with his right hand and pointing to LaVona's. Dutifully, with an all-out smile, she sipped and then nodded to

George, who filled her glass halfway and then the lieutenant's before quickly departing.

"So, it's sort of, as long as you've got it in your mouth or in your hand, you know where it is," LaVona picked up lightly where the lieutenant had left off.

"Seems so. And, whoever told her such things also must have elaborated pretty well on the art," he responded without missing a beat as they touched glasses. "But, after we married, we never did develop really intimate intercourse or share much in the way of exploring each other's ideas about sexual ecstasies or fantasies. I guess I carry plenty of that blame. Most of the time I was so damn tired by the time I got home, I wasn't in the mood for a lot of zest and creativity."

"Why the hell are you telling me all this?" LaVona said crisply, dissatisfied that her previous comments hadn't put a lid on the subject.

"Don't really know," he nodded. "Never gone on like this before. Maybe it's because, underneath it all, I'm a stickler for details . . . and you seem like a detail kind of woman. I'm sorry. I just feel so damn comfortable talking to you about it."

"Yes, I wonder what that really says about me?" she retorted with comely sarcasm, no longer off balance in the slightest. "Anyway, you really haven't answered that end thing."

"Oh, about seven-eight months after she left, her attorney sent me some papers to sign, along with a request from her, asking me to pack up the rest of the stuff she wanted and send it on. I did. Just about everything, except for the living room and kitchen furniture and the bed."

"You didn't fight to keep anything?" LaVona asked with renewed interest. "Just settled for what she didn't want?"

"Hell, I didn't care," he shrugged. "We had often argued over the merits of material stuff and having nice things, and so on. My position's always been that material junk bogs a person down. People waste their lives away worrying about how to pursue and acquire material, and then, if they happen to attain any, they spend the rest of their lives worrying about how to protect it and take care of it. Outside of when the kids were growing up, I guess my work is the only thing that's ever really mattered. And, she couldn't take that from me."

He suddenly paused again while George served the shrimp-marinara-for-two main course. They gave the appropriately timed raised eyebrows of delight and approving smiles of anticipation while the seasoned waiter went through his presentation.

"So, you see, I couldn't really squawk too much when Judy up and left," the lieutenant picked up again as George stepped away and they began delving in. "Anyway, after the papers were signed and the stuff was sent off, I never received word that the divorce process had actually been completed. I've always assumed that it had."

"Seems you still love her and don't want to let go completely," LaVona said seriously, without malice or determination. "As long as it isn't finalized, or at least you haven't verified that it is, there's still a ray of hope."

"Oh-h-h, please don't read something like that into what I've been saying," he quietly pleaded, leaning forward softly. "It's a ghost of my past that I'd prefer faded well into the background. I'd rather leave it that way. Even if it means not knowing certain things for sure. What we're doing right now is what's important to me. By the way, you're looking even more ravishing than usual."

"Must be part of the upscale Tahoe package," she smirked in very friendly fashion. "I feel as good as you say I look." Indeed, his last comment had conjured up an even more comely sparkle in her eyes and broadened the welcome of her glisteningly scarlet lips.

"Something's got me," he murmured. "I've never said things to anyone, even to Judy, the way we've been talking since we sat down here."

Through their days in Reno they had rigidly maintained their unspoken pact of not talking shop. Nothing about law enforcement or real estate. Aside from filling each other in on bits and pieces of their personal pasts, Lt. Huber conducted an ongoing verbal treatise about the finer points of playing blackjack and its revealing ramifications for human nature.

His lecture mode had continued ever since they first moved into a moderate-stakes table where the fifth and sixth chairs were open. The people occupying those seats had just pulled away. The dealer reached for the dead-card file to her right, emptied the remainder in the shoe and prepared to shuffle the six-deck stack. Lt. Huber immediately motioned LaVona into the fifth chair while he settled into the sixth.

"The house doesn't have to beat everybody all the time to keep the profits rolling in their direction," he began slowly and quietly while the dealer shuffled parts of the formidable mass in front of him. "With blackjack, look at it this way. Of the six players at a full table, with everything else being equal, the house only has to beat four to show a solid profit. So, you always want to be one of the other two."

"How does one make sure of that?" LaVona wanted to know.

"Before the dealing starts, you place how much you want to bet on the chip spot in front of you," he said, implying that the answer to her question would be somewhere in his explanation. "There are two methods of play. If the game is being dealt from a multi-deck shoe, each player initially gets two cards dealt to them face-up." That happened to be the situation at the table where they were currently sitting and he pointed over to the shoe at the dealer's left to emphasize his point.

"If the game's being dealt this way, you never touch the cards. When it's your turn, you just point at your cards if you want another card — a 'hit,' so to speak — or wave your hand over your cards, palm down, if you want to stay, or 'stick' with what you already have."

"There are other ways," she noted.

"Yep. Look around at some of the other tables here. Where there is no shoe and the dealer is dealing from one or two decks right out of his or her hand, the first two cards are dealt face-down to each player. In that case, you pick both cards up to get a look. Now, if you want another card, scrape the table felt in front of you lightly with the bottoms of your cards. If you want to stick, just slide both cards, face down, under the chips you have out there as your bet."

"What difference do these differences make?

"Regardless of which way the game is being dealt — both up or both down — the dealer always deals one card up and one down to himself," he avoided the directness of her question. "So, you always get a look at half of the dealer's hand to start with. And, everybody's always still in the game after the first two cards have been dealt. It's impossible for any two cards in the deck to add up to more than twenty-one. The important part comes next. That's when you've got to decide whether you want the dealer to 'hit' you with another card in an attempt to improve your hand. Or, do you want to 'stick' with what you were originally dealt? It's the most dangerous part of the game. Subliminally, it also has a sort of sado-masochistical aura. I mean, where the hell else, if someone asked you if you want to be 'hit,' would you answer 'yes'?"

LaVona smirked quietly at his humor.

"Anyway, as long as your hand doesn't exceed 21, you are always still in the game. And many times, that's all it really takes to win. Just staying in there is huge because of the house rules which dictate that the dealer must take a hit if his hand totals 16 or under, and must stick if he has 17 or above. Oh, there are special house rules in Reno about the dealer hitting a 'soft seventeen.' But, that's a minor technicality we can talk about later. Right away, you know something about the dealer that he doesn't know about you, who, on the other hand, always has the option of taking a hit or sticking with anything.

"If your cards and the dealer's count up to the same number, it's a tie, called a 'push,' and you simply keep your bet. But, here's the dealer's big edge. If you take a hit, and your hand suddenly counts up to more than 21, you're 'busted,' and the dealer immediately rakes in whatever chips you've put out there. Later in that same hand, if the dealer also 'goes bust,' he still keeps your money anyway. If you go bust, and the dealer goes burst, that's not a push. And that, my dear, in simple terms, is the house's time-honored edge. That simple event gives the house a small, but reliably consistent statistical edge over the long haul, provided both sides are playing the game at the best level under the rules. More about that later, too. Let's play."

As he finished up, the dealer flipped the red cut-card in front of him and held the multi-deck stack on its side for him to cut, accompanied with "Good luck, sir."

Lt. Huber laid two crisp hundred-dollar bills on the felt in front of the dealer who made the appropriate chip-stacks for the couple.

Lt. Huber had explained that all picture cards — jacks, queens and kings — are worth 10 points and all other cards are worth their face value except aces, which situationally may be assigned a value of one or 11, depending entirely upon how the holder chooses to use the card.

"If, after your first two cards are dealt, using an ace as 11, your hand adds up to 21, you have "blackjack" and you automatically win, except if the dealer also has blackjack, then it's a push . . . unless you've insured your hand," he kept on with his monologue, thinking that, if she grasped any of what he was talking about, she should win some sort of medal.

At first, after they had both looked at their initial cards, he would then murmur to her whether she should take a hit or not. As the hands went on, he began urging, "Go ahead. What do you think?"

Nervously, as though a million dollars were riding on every turn of a card, she began pointing with her index finger or waving her down-turned palm without his help. He laughed nervously when she took a hit with a queen and an ace, momentarily counting it as 11 instead of an instant blackjack. But then the dealer turned over another queen for her and she became a winner anyway.

"See, no harm done, sir," the dealer said.

"Except for a couple of things," Lt. Huber conversed back. "Blackjack would have paid her one and a half times her bet, instead of just even money. Also, anytime you take a superfluous hit, it changes where the ensuing cards will come around. It could change the whole flow of the game."

The dealer shrugged, and smiled gently.

"Tell you what, sir," her pocket tag said her name was Linda-Lu, "if you're right that every wrong move changes the flow, then from where I'm standing, the flow changes an awful lot. Who cares if the flow changes, as long as your winning trend doesn't change into a losing one? And, you don't think that can ever happen, do you? You've got this game beat, right?"

Lt. Huber chuckled back and nodded, unsure of whether what Linda-Lu had just said was sincerely for the lady's benefit, or was just part of her usual shtick for egging suckers on. Either way, you had to think twice about trusting anybody who's being paid to take your money.

Their streak persisted and, again on house money, steaks were in order Sunday.

"All I've yakked about so far is the basic mechanics of the game," he began while they glanced over the menu.

"What else is there?" LaVona frowned. "I mean, it's not like poker, is it? You can't bluff anybody, or inflate your bet according to what you see in your hand, can you? I'll take the prime rib, medium, and the baked potato and broccoli, with the Caesar salad to start."

"That's not exactly true," he answered, pointing his right index finger at her. "You've seen you can double-down after getting a look at your first two cards and the dealer's up-card, if your cards add up to eleven or less. Or, you can double your bet by splitting two cards the same."

With that, the waiter was upon them. He ordered the prime rib for LaVona, then asked, "What do you recommend?"

"The lady's prime rib is a good choice, sir," the waiter diplomatically smiled, the maitre de having announced him as Michael a while ago when he had seated the pair and handed out menus individually with the deftness of a sophisticated dealer.

"Fine. Michael, I'll take that, too, along with the baked and broccoli, but I'll have the clam chowder instead of a salad." Lt. Huber said. "Medium's fine."

Then, after also ordering a chardonnay with the main course, he turned back to LaVona without a hitch.

"Still, you don't double-down just anytime the mood suits you or just because your first two cards happen to add up to ten or eleven . . . although you'll see plenty of crystal-ballers who do. There has be a solid reason why. You want a situation to be one that also doubles your chances of winning. You want your original two-card hand to add up to either 10 or 11. This way, with one additional card, you can potentially pull a 21. But more to the point, and just as important, you want the dealer's up-card to be a six or less. This way, if you don't catch a face card or something else that gives you a high-count hand, at least the dealer has to hit his hand and has a chance of busting out. So, see? Just because you happen to be dealt an 11 with your first two cards doesn't mean you automatically jump into a double-down mode. The dealer's up-card must signal something, too."

Ω

By Monday evening, Lt. Huber could see that their streak was turning. They had doubled their original bets and, with a show each night and good food, they were getting near to tapping into the money they had brought with them.

Comedian George Karlin was trying out some new material, along with some of his standard stuff, at the El Dorado. Since it was Monday, good seats were still available. Lt. Huber called in a message to his police station that he would be detained another day. Molly, the dispatch operator, assured him they would manage.

"Don't hurry back on our account," Molly laughed. "Things couldn't be quieter."

Then LaVona called and postponed the two client meetings on her books, and arranged for the vice-president of Keep Mercury Beautiful to preside over the organization's regular Tuesday meeting.

"Let's get something to eat, and maybe some more blackjack afterwards," Lt. Huber said as they marched out of the El Dorado's main showroom minutes after Karlin had said his last good-byes. "A couple of drinks and Karlin are enough to give anybody their second wind."

"Look, there's a China Wall, just like in Mercury," LaVona chortled.

"I'll bet it's not owned by the same people," he laughed, pointing at a neon lion that roaringly dispelled any of Mercury's homespun quietness. They headed for the restaurant's main door.

While looking over the three dinner-for-two specials, this time they couldn't agree on anything.

"OK, a la carte, what's your pleasure?" he surrendered.

He opted for the combination chop suey, an ambitious mix of beef, chicken and shrimp with white rice, and she, the spicy kung pao shrimp with fried rice. To settle any dissension about the appetizers, he ordered a wooden poo poo platter that promised everything.

"Blackjack is such a simple game . . . if you don't give a damn," he said, testing whether she had had enough of that conversation. She still appeared interested. "Everybody's trying to get 21. But, all you really have to do is beat what the dealer has. Taking a hit is the most dangerous thing you can do. Let's say you have 13 and the dealer's got a face card staring at you. So, you assume, with a 7 or more underneath, he could beat you, flat-out . . . and there's a reasonable chance that's true. So, you take a hit to try to improve your hand. If you don't catch a 9, a 10 or a face card, you're still in business, and, if you catch a 7 or an 8, you've got a heck of good chance of winning the hand. But, say the dealer hits you with a 2, 3 or 4. What do you do?

"I'd still assume the dealer has the better hand, and probably ask for another hit," she said, hesitantly.

"Ah, Huber's Rule is 'One Hit to a Customer,' regardless of its worth, if it keeps you in the game," he smiled and shrugged. "Besides, if you pull a small card with that hit, that means the proportion of high cards in the deck has automatically shifted upward. Which, in turn, means the next hit would have a higher chance of putting you out of the game. Huber's Rule is simple. One hit and then stay in the game."

"OK, Huber's Rule," she nodded. "Power to the people!"

"There's also a reason why you need to get into that sixth chair," Huber's Rule or not, now he had arrived at his point. "A blackjack table, with its six chairs plus the dealer, is a micro-community of disjointed personalities."

"Huh?" LaVona squinted, indicating the conversation might suddenly be bordering on the ridiculous.

"The person in the first chair to the dealer's left can't possibly know or care what he's doing. Essentially, the first chair is playing the dealer heads-up and sooner, rather than later, the house always wins that one. Usually, while his money is dribbling away, the first chair is just content with the free booze that flows from the comely bosomed cocktail waitresses who keep stopping by as long as he keeps playing. Hell, drinking and gambling at the same time is a guaranteed one-way ticket to the poor house. But, who cares as long as you're having fun, right? Hell, if you want to drink, drink, If you want to play, play. But, not both together. Anyway, the first chair is a no-no, with or without the booze."

"You're kidding me, aren't you?" LaVona said lightly. "If I didn't know you beforehand, I'd think this was just one more line I hadn't heard before."

"I'm deadly serious," he answered, thankful for a break in his discourse. LaVona and her kung pao shrimp were way ahead of him and his chop suey. Silently, he had been somewhat perplexed all along that someone with her all-around experience didn't know a little more about blackjack than she was letting on. Was she just leading him down a merry lane? _If so, she's doing a damn good job,_ he concluded. No matter, he was enjoying the ongoing tutorial.

"I didn't come all the way to Reno just to get you into bed," he said with sarcastic jest, then taking another quick bite. "I'm serious about anything I do. I came here because I'm very serious about enjoying being with you, period." _Did that come out right?_ he wondered.

After a pause, while he took in the full moment of LaVona as she sat quietly in the chair to his left, he raised his wine glass across in front of him and they toasted the moment with two touches.

Quietly, he made inroads into his chop suey until he was satisfied that they would end their main courses appropriately close together.

"Many times, the people in the second and third chairs are together," he started up the blackjack trail again. "A couple of honeymooners or a couple of buddies just enjoying sitting at the table, perhaps for the first time. No matter what, assume these players . . . and I'm using that term very loosely here . . . in these two chairs don't have a clue about what's really going on. They usually ask the dealer lots of questions and giggle at his dry humor . . . even when they happen not to get it. A lot of absolutely stupid moves come from those two chairs. Part of your ongoing mission is to not let their stuff get under your skin . . . throw your own game off."

"No problem," She quipped. "My game's not on yet."

"Now, the players in the fourth and fifth chairs can usually be relied upon to be pretty savvy," while nodding that he caught her drift. "They'll usually play some pretty good blackjack. You can even talk to them about the game while you're playing, and they'll actually know what you're saying. The sixth chair is what it's all about. It's the only chair with its own name of respect. Called 'third base.' The player in that seat gets the best read on all the recently played cards because he gets to see all the hits that have been taken in the first five chairs. And, honest to God, some of those people in those other chairs will hit anything and keep right on hitting, as long as they haven't reached 21 yet.

"Third base has two strategies to think about, instantly. Stick or hit? Me or the dealer? Third base has the maximum possible information at its disposal . . . all the earlier hits, as well as the dealer's up-card. If a huge run of low cards has shown up and it looks like the dealer is going to have to take a hit, a skilled sixth-player will forego any consideration of a hit to his own hand, regardless of whether it might help him or not. He'll simply force the dealer into a situation of having to take the next card. Very likely a high one that will bust him.

"On the other hand, if the trend for the preceding hits is mostly face cards, the sixth-player may take the chance that a low card is next and hit his hand. It gets imperfectly complicated. As such, third base carries a lot of extra pressure. An instantaneous decision by third base can mean the difference between a win or a loss for the entire table."

"Lots of responsibility," LaVona observed. "I'm not ready for that."

"Like I said, it's imperfect," he agreed. "But, make the right decision, and sometimes the entire table will applaud you. Make a decision that turns out badly for everyone and endure not only their jeers. But, worst of all, their half-assed suggestions about how the game should really be played. That's why plenty of pretty knowledgeable blackjack players will take either the fifth or fourth chairs, but avoid the heat of the sixth like the plague. Had enough?"

"Well, you're right. It's a completely different slant on what, at first blush, appears to be a rather sterile, simple game," LaVona confessed.

"These casinos weren't built because the owners relied on luck and superstition," he shrugged. "So, why should a player take that attitude? It's all about details, and when and how to make the right move at the right time. Over the long haul, with the odds slightly in their favor, and with way deeper pockets, they know they can get to you if you let them. Over the short haul though, you can have one hell of a good time in Reno or Vegas on their money."

"The way we are," she answered emphatically.

"As for sizing up the other people at the table . . . I didn't want to bring up anything close to shoptalk during our excursion here . . . but, I guess, once a profiler, always a profiler. I plead guilty to being a creature of habit."

While Lt. Huber finished up his chop suey, LaVona saw her chance.

"You're not the only one at this table who's a student of human nature," she said pointedly, leaning toward him and touching his left hand. "I'm not just a real estate agent, period. I'm a real estate agent in the town of Mercury. The people of Mercury are my people. If someone tells me they are interested in a certain house and nothing else will do, there's not much I can do about it . . . except maybe set them straight on some details. Like you said, sometimes you just have to play the hand you're dealt with in the first two cards. But, whenever someone is moving into Mercury and wants my help in getting settled . . . Ah, that's where you and I meet in the middle, buddy. Putting the right person in the right house is a winning hand all around. Most of the time I have to figure out what they really want, because they really don't know. So, don't feel like the Lone Ranger. You're not the only profiler here tonight."

Lt. Huber smiled, full of interest.

"Small world, isn't it?" he winked. "I knew there was a solid reason behind my gut feeling that you would enjoy blackjack."

"Yeah, but do you really believe that you can bottle and label a person's character and personality just by which chair they sit in at a blackjack table?" she winked back with a shrug. "I usually like to do a little talking and a lot of listening before I arrive at those sorts of decisions."

When the fortune cookies came with the check, they silently reaffirmed what they had agreed to earlier about the substance of luck and superstition. The cookies were pushed aside, unopened, without the manufactured forecasts and character summaries being read.

"There's one other thing . . . and it's real . . . you can see it, even though, up to now, nobody's satisfactorily explained it," he leaned forwarded with a determined sincerity that he hadn't shown before. "Some call it bad luck. Some call it a losing streak. Some just blame the deck for turning cold. Whatever hocus-pocus you want to put on it, it's there."

"Beware, beware of the green-eyed dragon with the thirteen tails, who feeds on puppy dogs, frogs and big, fat snails," she kidded.

"Bear with me here," he laughed back. "It has to do with cycles, and the good and bad parts of them. There are times when every hand that isn't a blackjack or a winning double-down is a dealt 20 or makes 21 whenever you take a hit. Man, you can't lose, and the chips are just piling up. It's euphoric. All-consuming. You start thinking, 'What an easy game!'"

"Sort of what we've been enjoying since we first got here?" LaVona interjected.

"Yeah, but then comes the downside," he answered in a warning tone. "You can't see it coming right off. Maybe it's suddenly taking a hit that puts you over when you weren't sure what you should have done. Maybe the dealer has an underneath blackjack after you've pulled a 21 with three cards. It's barely perceptible at first. Something subtle always signals that the downslide has started. Soon, you can feel it. It's over for now. Trouble is, most people try to ignore it or fight like a dog against the increasingly obvious consequences . . . continue to ride their wave of misplaced optimism or damaged ego all the way down."

"Another slant on human nature?"

"It gets more sickeningly obvious with time. If you have 18, the dealer has 19. If you have 20, the dealer will hit for a 21. Of the six players at the table, you may be the only consistent loser. It can become that precise. Soon, everything you've won is gone, and then they start working on your own hard-earned stuff."

"So, what do you do about it? Stop playing?" LaVona wanted to know.

"That's not a bad idea," he nodded. "Get the hell out of Dodge for a spell. Hopefully, while you still have some of their money. Go somewhere. Take a breather. But, here's the kicker. More times than not, next time you go back to the tables, no matter when or where, that same downward slide is still with you. It's like a baseball batter in the throes of a ruinous hitting slump. It follows him from city to city. That's why I'm more inclined to feel that these card cycles are internal, and we carry them around with us, no matter where we go. It's spooky. But, it seems to have more teeth than just blubbering about good-luck-bad-luck, or blaming someone else like the dealer or the other people at the table, or the lighting, or God knows what. "

"My question's still unanswered."

"I find the only way to shake the bad part of my cycle is to play through it, just like a baseball player does. Benching a slumping player doesn't usually help an otherwise good player. Same with playing blackjack. My personal remedy is to find the cheapest table around — a dollar table if you can find one — and then just sit there and play until things get back on an even keel. Sort of like a player being shipped back to the minors for a little while to get his stroke and his eye back. Then, you can think about going after them big-time again."

After dinner, they played losing blackjack for about an hour. Agreeing that they had squeezed all the juice from the orange, it was time to head back to their separate routines in Mercury. Returning to their hotel room, they booked separate next-afternoon fights — LaVona to Goldspar, the lieutenant to Chicago. Then, suddenly consumed by an accumulated exhaustion that had been masked by adrenaline over the past few days, they crumbled into a collective deep sleep

Ω

What seemed like minutes later had actually been the stillness of several passing hours. Quietly, he began coming out of the fog of an unrecountable dream. Something was calling him. His erection was at its bursting fullest. Her quivering lips slowly were moving down the fully blossoming head of his penis. She slowly ran her tongue around the ridge of his circumcision as she held his shaft firmly with her left hand and gently cupped his scrotum with her right. With her tongue, she feathered the orifice at his tip, then, slowly and attentively, began to take him. More intensely, she began all over again. His back stiffened and his buttocks tightened as he arched his neck to thrust his pelvis toward her. He held that position, clutching the headboard of the bed as she increased the ecstasy of his passion. Suddenly, he exploded, and, as he ebbed, her hands massaged the remains of his pleasure out of him and gently squeezed his scrotum.

Then, looking up at him, she asked softly, "Remind you of old times?"

Ω

By Wednesday evening, the realtor and the lieutenant were comfortably in their favorite booth at Charlie's Wagon Wheel. Charlie, a retired New York City chef, mostly stayed in the kitchen, out of sight. This was a moment he couldn't resist this.

"Hey you two, nice to see you back," Charlie said with a singsong needle in his voice. "Funny how you both disappeared for the same amount of time . . . at the same time. Whoever said there's no such thing as coincidences?"

Grinning sheepishly, the wayward couple silently blushed in unison. Yet, in his own way, Charlie had told them they might as well stop worrying about what other people might think about their always being together.

15

JOCKEY'S STRIFE

Thinking only of heading home for the day, Lt. Huber received a brief anonymous phone call. The muffled voice told him to meet at the trackside railing directly in front of the infield tote board at Mercury Downs at one o'clock the next afternoon. Nothing more.

He arrived by 12:45 p.m. and stayed in plain sight. Leaning forward with his arms cradled atop the railing, he idly scanned the racecourse and watched as the odds on the huge tote board flashed their telling changes every minute or so. Hatless, his right hand shaded his eyes from the overbearing glare of the midday sun. Post time for the first race was 1:15.

"Mercury hasn't had an earthquake for a hundred years," a voice murmured from behind him as soon as the infield clock flashed precisely one o'clock.

"Bagwell!" Lt. Huber snapped back in recognition as he whirled around. "What in hell does this have to do with you?"

Bagwell stepped up beside him and cradled his arms atop the rail. Lt. Huber resumed that same position, and the two men appeared to be leisurely dissecting some last-minute details about the day's opening race. The lieutenant continued to shade his eyes with his right hand, and Bagwell tilted his camel-colored Trilby forward to just above his eyes.

"Maxwell wants to meet with you tomorrow," Bagwell said, while continuing to look out into the infield. "About three o'clock, but he didn't tell me where. Said you'd know the place . . . same as when you two first met.

"How the hell do you know Maxwell?" Lt. Huber asked his same question another way. "I'm sure he didn't just pull you out of the hat after he got here."

Bagwell laughed, and chided, "Always the detective, huh. Apparently we go back a ways, but I'll let him explain that . . . if you need explaining. I'm supposed to fill you in up to a point on something else. Remember Cossie Jarvis?"

Lt. Huber squinted at Bagwell for a long few seconds, then shrugged, "Can't say I do."

"Christ, don't you guys read the papers?" Bagwell shot back pointedly. "I thought that bunch down at the station at least kept up with the Sports Pages."

Pausing, Bagwell saw that his line of talk still wasn't ringing any bells.

"Geez, it even made the Front Page the first day. It was plastered all over, complete with pictures, for about ten days. The horse Jorge Vicone was on happened to be leading the way down the backstretch in a distance race on the turf course. The feature race on a weekday card early last August. Just as they were approaching the far turn, the right front leg of Vicone's horse snapped."

"Oh, wait a minute," Lt. Huber barged in. "Now that you mention Vicone . . . yeah, I remember. That was a bad one."

"It was," Bagwell emphasized, and went on. "Vicone apparently felt the horse giving way under him and bailed out to the outside. Unfortunately, the horse Cossie was on was just beginning to make its run to the outside. As Vicone was going down, a hoof from Jarvis's horse nailed Vicone squarely in the head, cracking his helmet almost in half, killing him instantly. Real freak-accident stuff. The driver of the ambulance that was trailing the race became visibly sick when he reached Vicone's lifeless body. Not a pretty sight."

While Bagwell spoke, the horses for the first race had filed out onto the track and the announcer began describing the usual pre-race details as the post parade for the ten-horse field sauntered by the grandstands.

"It freaked Jarvis out, even though there wasn't a damn thing he could've done to prevent it," Bagwell's voice now intensified above its previous murmur, speaking more comfortably under the camouflage of the announcer's blare. "He blamed himself for the whole damn thing." The writer's tone emulated helpless resignation. "Didn't get back up on a horse for three weeks, and wouldn't go near a race. He knew he was cracking up. He finally went home to his roots. Charles Town, West Virginia. Hoping to work things out."

"It must've helped," Lt. Huber cut in, indicating he knew something of Jarvis's current racing status.

"Jarvis got his start around horses back there when he was just a kid," Bagwell nodded. "Started as a work-out boy at the Shenandoah Downs training track. When he got his jockey's papers and started riding as an apprentice, he just moved up the street to Charles Town Race Track, which, by that time, had year-round racing. Within a couple of years or so, Jarvis became a regular rider on the Maryland circuit — Pimlico and Laurel. Won a bunch of riding titles."

Bagwell paused, looked at the lieutenant and decided it was worth continuing.

"Then, some of the top barns he was riding for moved their summer bases of operation to Mercury Downs when it opened. Jarvis came with them. Been here every summer since. Riding at New Orleans's Fair Grounds during the winter, and coming here every summer. Hell, he's ridden in four Kentucky Derbys."

"Tell you the truth, I didn't know any of that," the lieutenant said with honest gratitude.

"He's always been a natural . . . a great rider," Bagwell acknowledged him, and went on with the details. "And a real cocky S-O-B back in those early years. Give you an example. They call it the Sports of Kings, right? But, that's only for deep-pocketed owners who treat it like a lavish hobby. For the jockeys and the trainers and everybody else connected to the horses, it's their way of putting food on the table, paying the mortgage and sending the kids off to college. It's their livelihood. A business, period."

The announcer's voice was suddenly silent after telling the crowd that there were five minutes left until post time, and urging everyone to make their bets right away so that they didn't get shut out.

"It goes like this. Every time a horse wins a race, its competitive life changes forever," Bagwell's voice suddenly fell back into a softer murmur as both men continued looking out at the infield, only occasionally pausing to look over at each other. "They either move up in class, meaning they have to race against tougher competition next time, or they get more weight put on their backs . . . or both."

"How many people out here today pay attention to things like that?"

"Plus, just the effort it takes to win a race can take one hell of a lot out of a horse," Bagwell accommodated Lt. Huber's question by laying it on even thicker. "Their form can drop off dramatically for a while, until they recover. Some never do. That's the Catch-22 with the past performances you see in Daily Racing Form or anyplace else. That information only tells you what a horse has already done, not what he's going to do next. The Form doesn't come with a crystal ball. They may look big, but Thoroughbreds are fragile animals, not indestructible machines. Hell, they're not all Secretariats or Seabiscuits who can go out there and beat everybody all of the time. And even they didn't always win."

"That much I seem to know," the lieutenant nodded.

"Regardless of what horse it is, it takes a monumental amount of time, effort and money to train it up to the point where it's ready to win a race," Bagwell was now in top form. "That's where handicapping at its highest level comes in. You have to know the tendencies of the trainers. Some trainers will win with a horse as soon as it's ready, regardless of the odds. Others may not push a ready horse until the odds are better so they can collect on a fat bet along with the purse."

Bagwell paused, took a deep breath and looked Lt. Huber in the eye.

"Maybe this'll give you an idea about the kind of guy Jarvis is. When he took a mount on this one horse, the trainer instructed him to get the horse out of the gate in good shape, run him hard for about three furlongs and then ease off. The idea being, if the horse couldn't win with a jockey of Jarvis's caliber on its back, what chance would it seem to have next time when the trainer had planned to put a somewhat lesser jockey up and pull the trigger? This logic should lead to considerably higher odds next time out, and the trainer would have a bundle on it."

Suddenly, the horses for the first race had broken from the starting gate. The blare of the announcer's voice began calling the positions as the horses battled down the backstretch during the opening poles of the seven-furlong sprint.

"Anyway, Jarvis breaks the horse on top, rates him about two lengths in front until they hit the homestretch and then pulls away to win by about six goddamn lengths," Bagwell's description picked up volume again under the umbrella of the announcer's call. "The trainer's having a fit. He didn't have a damn dime on the horse that day. He runs over as Jarvis is bringing the horse back to the winner's circle and yells, 'You'll never ride for me again!' Jarvis just looks down at him, straight in the eyes, and says, 'I'm Cossie Jarvis, sir. I don't ease horses.' Jarvis's attitude has mellowed since then, but his integrity has always been as solid as Fort Knox. He won't take a mount that he doesn't think he can win on, and he still rides like he's hell-bent on winning every race he's in."

The horses for the first half of the daily double had crossed the finish line and the wall of noise from the exuberant crowd that had urged them through the homestretch was subsiding into a kind of beehive's buzz. After the photo-finish sign came down, the results on the tote board confirmed that a 28-to-1 shot had out-dueled the favorite to the wire by a head-bob. As the long shot was being led to the winner's circle for the picture ceremony, the horse was greeted with sparse cheers while the nearby unsaddling of the favorite was being met by hearty rounds of derision.

"Well lieutenant, that pretty much fills you in on Jarvis," Bagwell smiled. "You're probably asking why the hell do you have to know anything about Jarvis. Jace'll tell you what's up."

While the jockey jumped off the winner after the photo snap, Bagwell and Lt. Huber slowly began to pull away from the rail.

"Did you have anything on that race?" the lieutenant asked.

"Are you kidding?" Bagwell chuckled, readjusting his hat. "Daily-double races are a crap shoot, usually. A one-way ticket to going by way of Fat Sam. If you're going to stick around though, check out May's Highland in the seventh. Nice seeing you."

Bagwell was on his way to the paddock area to routinely watch the saddling for the next race without the slightest intent of placing a bet on its outcome. Lt. Huber, meantime, borrowed a nearby spectator's program for a moment, discovered that May's Highland was Number 8 in the seventh race and headed for the betting windows to make an advance wager.

16

HAMMY AND THE CAPTAIN

Carson Bagwell was amicably approachable, but absolutely untouchable, and everybody knew it. Or, they soon learned so. A Mercury resident of fourteen years, each summer he reverently drove twenty-three miles to be trackside by 5:30 every morning. With stopwatch in hand and the strap of his binoculars around his neck, he scrutinized the morning workouts. At daybreak, only a handful of rabid official clockers and a hodgepodge of the horses' connections occupied the otherwise vacant facility.

Pari-mutuel earnings were not his primary source of income, but he stood as ironclad proof that a steady financial profit is indeed feasible from wagering on horse races.

To be sure, Bagwell had a formidable edge. What he did for a living put him at the track every day. Still, most of the steps he routinely climbed during his handicapping analyses were those that, albeit maddeningly dull, were easily available to anyone with the discipline and desire to succeed. Mostly though, the vast majority of horseplayers feverishly stab at every race on the card and then, after they inevitably lose, curse every excuse conceivable except their own shortcomings.

As part of his daily routine at the newspaper, Bagwell published his three preferred choices for every race that day, along with a suggested best bet and top long shot. These selections were always from his analysis of Daily Racing Form past-performance lines in combination with stable tips from various sources, solid rumors

from other sources, and bits and pieces of subtle information gleaned from just hanging around and inter-
preting what he heard and saw. Even so, if he had been
forced to bet every one of his top published picks every
day, even at a minimal $2 per pick, he long ago would
have arrived at poverty row. True, these choices were
his sincerest efforts at how he would bet, if he were
going to bet. But undeniably, nobody can survive by
betting every race, or even every day. Trouble is, most
people's trips to the track are very special occasions,
planned in advance with great anticipation and fanciful
enthusiasm. By the time they arrive, they are frothing
with their craving for pari-mutuel action, not spectator
seating.

An even deeper dichotomy ran between Bagwell's
sense of wagering and his daily job. Trainers, owners
and jockeys eagerly and openly talked with him about
their favorite horses. And, along with interesting histo-
ries and anecdotes about the people and horses at Mercury Downs, he unbiasly filled his columns with the
prideful quotes from this "inside information." On the
other hand, his personal judgment about what to wager
on and when was always a huge step back and discon-
nected from his best effort to carry out the rigors of his
newspaper routine.

Clockers are a sunrise bunch of analytical obses-
sives who, for Daily Racing Form and other published
venues, keep tabs on what the horses in training do
when they break into any semblance of an all-out run
during their morning workouts. Many of these clockers
also are responsible for the detailed accuracy of the
past-performance lines that appear in the racing form.

"Don't take work-out information lightly," Bagwell
had urged his readers in one of his earliest articles after
joining the Mercury Times. "Clockers take their jobs
very seriously, and are fanatics about accuracy. The
information they record appears in Daily Racing Form
and also is easily available from the racing office of the
track where it was recorded. Past performances tell you

what a horse has done in the past — recent workouts can provide a key to what the horse might do next."

"Hi ya, Baggie," Bagwell heard a familiar voice behind him while he watched the horses for the second half of the Daily Double being saddled. "Have a nice little chat with the Gestapo?" Leland Hammerstan queried as Bagwell turned to face him.

"Cut the crap, Hammy," Bagwell snarled. There was only one person who called him Baggie, and he couldn't stand it. "What do you want?"

"Oh, nothing really," Hammy said nonchalantly. "Just thought you guys seemed rather chummy. Thinking of becoming a cop?"

Hammy's sarcasm grated on Bagwell's spine like someone purposely scraping their fingernails over a cheap blackboard.

"Something like that, and I'm going to use you," Bagwell snapped again, cutting immediately to the chase. Hammy had an unnerving habit of irritating him, and Bagwell never wanted to spend more time than he had to around anyone he classified among the mud-dwelling invertebrates.

"Oh yeah?" Hammy snapped back. "What's in it for me?"

"This time, nothing, you slimy, oversized nematode," Bagwell said calmly. "You'll do this one because you love me."

"Sure . . . I love ya, baby," Hammy said with an equally sarcastic smile. "But, you know the drill. For a fee, Baggie, always for a fee."

"Bullshit," Bagwell fired back. "You'll do this one gratis or I'll change my way of giving horses to the security guard. You've made more than enough from me to call in this marker."

"All right, all right . . . don't get personal," Hammy said quietly. "What's it all about."

"Has to do with the Mendoza killing," Bagwell told him, again straightforward.

"Oh shit," Hammy shot back. "That's a bad scene, Baggie. You better watch your ass, man. Word is that it has to do with that big Twin-Tri payoff late last season. I don't know names, but it seems the guys who hit that score are connected. Not top-level cranks. Just sort of middle-management types, if you know what I mean. Word is they're still trying to figure a way to pry that money loose. And, the racing authorities and the feds are just sitting there, waiting for them to try. Anyway you look at it though, those guys think it's their money already, which means it's mob money. And, you do not want to get caught in between!"

The two stared at each other: Hammy with a pleading expression, Bagwell with some apprehension.

"Not only that," Hammy, biting on his cigar, wanted his point taken with no misunderstanding, "Even if they did have Mendoza in the bag, that only knocked out most of the other bettors' chances that day, considering it iced both favorites. They still had to come up with the right combination in both races to get the big money, which means they may have upwards of five figures of their own money tied up. Tell me that alone isn't enough to piss them off? Leave it alone, Baggie!"

"Hell, it wasn't even hit at the track," Bagwell offered. "That ticket was sold at an OTB over by Missouri. Look, all I want you to do is look at the patrol films from a couple of races with me. I want to see if there's any clear-cut evidence that Mendoza was monkeying around. And, if so, how bad."

"Sounds like an easy enough request to square a marker," Hammy nodded with a relieved smile returning. "Can I bring a friend along?"

"Didn't know you had friends," Bagwell tilted his head to the side and forward. "Who?" Anybody Hammy called "friend" was instantly suspect in Bagwell's book.

"The Captain," Hammy answered.

"Who?" Bagwell responded as before, but even more emphatically.

"The Captain," Hammy echoed. "You might not know him by that name maybe, but you've seen him around. Can't miss 'im. He's one of the local railbirds. Here every day. He can see things in a race that I don't pick up on. Always conscious of what lead a horse is supposed to be on . . . whether the jockey's using the whip right . . . what kind of hold he's got on the horse. Things like that. Lemme bring him?"

"OK, but he's your responsibility," Bagwell agreed. "Look, I've got to be somewhere until after the seventh. Let's meet after the eighth at the patrol-film booth. Tell you what, though. If you can track me down just before the seventh, I may have something."

Bagwell knew not to give Hammy anything on May's Highland until very close to post time. Given time, this ever-conniving middleman might use the information to varnish his personal barter network. Half the track would know that May's Highland was solid by race time, and you'd need a microscope to measure the horse's final odds.

The second half of the Daily Double had gone off while Hammy and he were still talking by the paddock. Bagwell spent the next four races in the press box, and then returned to the paddock area to watch the horses being saddled for the seventh. Hammy stalked close by, not wanting to be difficult, but making sure Bagwell remained in his sights and aware of his presence.

As the horses filed toward the track, Bagwell strolled by Hammy and commented that the Number-8 horse looked nice. Hammy bolted for the mutuel windows, while Bagwell continued onto the clubhouse to give Security Agent Ogle a last-minute heads-up on May's Highland.

Hammy's brisk waddle took a circuitous route over to The Captain's usual pre-race perch at the rail near to the mouth of the walking chute that poured the horses from the paddock onto the track.

"Cappy, the 8's a Baggie-lock," Hammy rush-whispered as he passed by and headed for the nearest mutuel windows. Less than two minutes to post, and every window had a sizable waiting line.

"Holy shit, this is all I need," Hammy mumbled to himself as he slid into the back of the shortest line. As a bettor moved away from the window in front of him and another quickly moved into position, the information on the nearby mini-tote board clicked down to the one-minute mark. In rapid succession, two more bettors peeled away from the window. One more now and he would be next. No sweat.

The frailishly thin bettor planted his elbows down on the armrest at the window and, holding his noticeably shaking racing program with both hands, began calling off one-dollar Trifecta combinations. With every call, Hammy's eyes revealed more exasperation and he chewed harder on his cigar. On the tenth ticket the mutuel clerk abruptly stopped the bettor.

"I'm sorry, sir, but the Number-3 horse has been scratched," the women informed him in a friendly manner.

"Oh, my goodness, thank you," the bettor said slowly and graciously, now reviewing his program for some alternative possibilities. "Let's see now."

"Jesus Christ!" Hammy mumbled loud enough for the bettor to hear.

"Oh, I'm so sorry," the startled bettor said timidly to a ferocious looking Hammy, then, turning back toward the clerk, asked, "How much is that?"

"Nine dollars, please," the clerk answered quietly.

With that, the bettor fumbled into his right-hand back pocket for his wallet, nervously brought it up, peered into it and methodically counted out a five and four singles.

"Goddam you, you fuckin' sonofabitch!" a fully enraged Hammy blurted out while the bettor fumbled to get his wallet repositioned in his back pocket and was now backing away, wide-eyed, with the corners of his mouth drawn down and his lower lip protruding to match the sorrowful horror in his eyes. "Where the fuckin' hell do you think you are anyway? In the checkout line at the goddamn supermarket with the rest of the old bags? You walk up to one of these fuckin' windows, you better goddam well know what the fuck you're going to bet and have your goddam money out and ready!"

Red-faced, Hammy quickly turned back to the mutuel clerk with controlled rage and demanded," Five-hundred to win on Number 8!"

The clerk reacted immediately, punching the appropriate buttons . . . but, nothing came out of the machine. As a courtesy, the clerk quickly repeated the process, but she already knew the situation. She had heard the bell; the preoccupied Hammy hadn't.

"I'm very sorry, sir," the clerk said in a charade of sunken sympathy that perfectly masked her hidden satisfaction. "But, the race seems to have gone off. If you could have yelled your bet at me right away, instead of yelling at that poor man, I'm sure I could have gotten it in in time. "

"Holy shit," the visibly shaken Hammy let out a murmur of resigned defeat and, commendably holding back his compulsory "Fuck you" in response to the clerk's unsolicited advice, slowly wandered away. In the midst of raging against the dollar Trifecta bettor he hadn't heard the bell signaling the opening of the starting gate that automatically froze any further betting on the race.

The clerk smirked at Hammy's disappearing back. She had seen similar scenes played out too many times. Plenty of tormented anxiety sputtered in front of her mutuel window every day. With her ticket line now momentarily vacant, she temporarily placed a "Window Closed" sign in front of her machine, stepped back for a mini-break, lit up a cigarette and listened to the announcer's call over the loudspeaker. Silently, and with a tinge of sadism, she rooted for Number 8. At odds of 7-to-1, May's Highland made a strong middle move to get within easy striking distance of the two early leaders and then picked them off in sequence as they faded in the stretch, to win with plenty to spare.

Ω

Hammy and The Captain were waiting when Bagwell arrived at the patrol-film booth. The Captain, who's Christian name was Gustav Olaf Morgenstern, was a fleshy man of a little less than average height. His round, ruddy face showcased a thick red-blond beard and was garnished with thick red-blond eyebrows. This facial bushiness surrounded a pair of steely blue eyes and rubicund nose. The top half of his round body, with protruding belly, was covered by an undersized white, short-sleeved shirt, the buttons straining against the buttonholes. Wrinkled brown slacks and black desert boots encased his bottom half. Black suspenders kept his pants in line. His thick arms and meat-hook hands with stubby fingers also had plenty of red-blond curly hair. He hid his emotions behind a white skipper's hat with a black bill and mirror-coated, prescriptive sunglasses.

Everything was done with his right hand. In his left hand, as if a permanently fused appendage, The Captain always gripped a can or plastic cup of beer that he sipped with quick intervals. He owned two charter sport-fishing boats, the Lively Lady and the Bingo, which he operated out of the Coral Gables area during the height of Florida's tourist season. A master at landing billfish — sailfish and marlin, he had his own way. He never used live or dead natural baits. Relying on an intricately thorough understanding of his quarry's behavior and needs, The Captain prided himself in being able to entice these magnificently prized wall-hangers with handmade artificial lures, much the same as fly-tying trout enthusiasts fantasize. To say that his attention to detail was impeccable was to unfairly understate his acumen.

The Captain made more than enough money during Florida's tourist season to be able to migrate north for the summer and hang over the rail at Mercury Downs every day. He had been trackside since the establishment opened. Nor did he ignore the horse-racing scene during the winter. He was at Gulfstream Park or Calder Race Track whenever gale winds kept his boats at their moorings, and he had openly bewailed the demise of his beloved Hialeah Park. To this day, he still worried over what had ever happened to those infield flamingos.

The Captain had a juvenilish mean streak, which some thought amusing. He enjoyed making fun of people, especially the elderly, preying upon the waning confidence that paralleled their real or imagined failing faculties. Toying with older people's hearing was his favorite. For instance, while obtaining one of his endless beers at one of Mercury Downs's watering holes, he would sidle up near an elderly man and mumble aloud, "Pull your cock today?"

Where upon the startled person would exclaim, "What?!"

The Captain would then answer, "Pretty hot today?"

To which the now self-embarrassed person would quietly answer, "Oh-oh, yes-yes, pretty hot, yes," while The Captain snickered and elbowed the person on his other side.

$$\Omega$$

The patrol-film booth offered horseplayers an opportunity to personally review any race that had occurred so far during Mercury Downs's current racing season. A special brand of horseplayers who fancied themselves as "trip handicappers" were particularly fond of this free service. At their leisure, these self-proclaimed trip-meisters could analyze and dissect any race, forever prepared to pounce on any horse that appeared ready for a winning effort, but had experienced "a bad trip" or had simply used the race as a penultimate sharpener. Next time out, with a better trip and all other things being equal, the horse should surely win, according to these meisters.

Except for the request window, the entire booth was boxed in by specifically numbered TV screens that faced outward. On a piece of paper, any horseplayer could simply submit the date and program number of the race of interest to the booth operator who, in turn, would quickly inform the horseplayer on which screen the race would appear.

At Mercury Downs, each race replay is first shown at regular speed from much the same angle that is usually seen on home TV. The same angle of the entire race is then shown at half-speed, and the finish of the race is shown again in slow motion. Then the entire race is shown from a front view at regular speed. And finally, the start and finish of the race are shown in stopgap sequence. Also, on special occasions, such as when there is a jockey's objection or stewards' inquiry into the running of a race or an accident, the segment of the race where the alleged infraction or mishap took place is shown several times in slow motion. This entire review sequence of a race continues to be repeated until the viewer pushes the stop-button under the TV screen.

Earlier, Bagwell had submitted a special request for the two Twin-Tri races on the day of the big hit last season. This gave the booth operator time to seek out the correct cassette. At the booth operator's instructions, Bagwell, Hammy and The Captain now moved around to Screen Number 7.

"OK. Here we go," Bagwell said as the date and number of the first race in question appeared on the screen. "Now, watch the No. 2 horse particularly closely."

The 2-horse broke from the gate in the middle of the pack. Along the backstretch, the lone front-runner had two lengths on a wall of three horses. Another length back, the 2-horse was stalking behind the wall along the rail. As they came off the far turn and into the homestretch, in unison the three-horse wall pulled even with the front-runner and drove for the finish line. The 2-horse appeared to be blocked when a hole along the rail failed to open and finished evenly in fifth place.

None of the trio of viewers said a word. Hammy and The Captain stepped closer to the TV screen as the various renditions of the race — slow motion, front view, etc. — began to unfold. Bagwell stood behind, watching the two viewers as much as watching the screen.

"I don't know," The Captain turned and said. "Could have just been bad racing luck. I mean, the jockey rode a nice ground-saving trip along the rail into the stretch and then, when he still couldn't find a hole to get through on the inside, just took it easy, not wasting the horse when it seemed hopeless. Either that, or the jockey did an excellent job of masking his full intentions to keep the horse out of contention."

Hammy wasn't buying it.

"Bullshit, sweetheart," he chirped, glaring at The Captain. "That jock went in the tank with that horse right off, and you know it! He never had any intention of doing anything but finishing up the track. He had plenty of horse under him. All he had to do was put him in position."

The Captain drew his head back, furled his left eyebrow, pursed his lips and snorted.

"Up yours, pal-zee," he barked back at Hammy. "Every time you don't cash a ticket, right away the race has gotta be fixed. Oh, be reasonable!"

"Reasonable?!" Hammy screamed back. "If you weren't completely sloshed by the fifth race, you'd know what you were looking at!"

As Bagwell listened to the two banter back and forth, he felt he was overhearing a couple of old married folks carping at each other in a kitchen. Indeed, these two had to be more than just good friends. Then he remembered. Every winter, Hammy would disappear for a couple of weeks or so, and then reappear with a deep bronze tan. Now the pieces of that puzzle made sense.

"OK-OK, let's just say that this one's inconclusive. . . a toss-up," Bagwell urged, stepping in between them after a minute more. He pushed the TV's stop button, signaling the booth operator to insert the other tape.

"This time, watch the Number-6 horse," he instructed.

"Are you fuckin' shittin' me!" The Captain crowed as soon as the horses in the next tape left the gate. "That's jockey stuff for sure."

He looked at Bagwell and Hammy, and they stared back in silence.

"OK, let's watch the slo-mo and the head-on view, and then we'll talk," The Captain asserted impatiently. "Good God!"

In slow motion and from the front, it became obvious that the 6-horse took an immediate left-hand turn out of the gate and had slammed into the 5-horse, and then rode that horse's flank until being shuffled back before the turn.

"Look at that!" The Captain chirped, just a level or so below an all-out shriek. "Look at the way the jockey's holding that left rein down around his leg when they come out. The horse has no option, except what happened. I'll bet you that horse's normal racing style is to go to the front and contend for the lead right out of the gate."

Hammy and Bagwell looked at each other.

"Horses, by their very nature, are herd animals," The Captain said, now calmer. "That's why they can go barreling into a turn all bunched up and nobody gets hurt . . . unless one of them breaks down or a jockey does something really dumb. Each of them is also born with some sort of hierarchy or peck-order complex. Some of them have a rather fragile dominant personality. They've got to have the lead right away and keep it all the way. Once they're headed, they fold up altogether."

Bagwell and Hammy nodded quietly.

"Others with a dominant nature can be rated back off the pace to save their energy until the right time. Once they're turned loose, they're hell-bent on getting to the front and taking over.

"Then there's the real head cases. And there are lots of these. These can run along with anybody, no matter how fast the pace is and no matter how far the race is . . . as long as they don't have to be in front. Good followers or subordinates, so to speak. If and when they are taken to the lead, they get all bent out of shape right away and start looking around for a way out. They'll actually pull themselves up to let another horse take over. That's where the trainer, jockey and precise timing come in. They have to time that very temporary moment when they can get the horse in front so that it occurs right near the finish line. That way, by the time the horse figures that it's time to pull himself up, the race is over."

"That race we just watched," he pointed at the TV screen. "If that 6-Horse was allowed to break the way I suspect it usually does, there's a danger that it might have gotten a long, easy lead. Then, to lose the race, the jockey might have been forced to do something even more obvious than what we just saw. Anyway you look at it, that horse wasn't supposed to win or perhaps even be in the money. Hell, he finished last!"

Bagwell had what he wanted. He signaled to the booth operator that they were done.

"You're absolutely right, Captain," Bagwell said graciously. "Everything in that horse's racing history says that he has early speed from the gate. Nice meeting you."

"Hey, I don't know all the tricks," The Captain smiled. "I don't think anybody does. I sort of take the same position that Supreme Court Justice Potter Stewart did with pornography. I can't exactly define what a stiffed ride is, but I know it when I see it. Hey, neither of those races looked like boat races. Things like that aren't likely to happen at The Merc. No, everybody else seemed to be running their hearts out. Only the two horses you asked us to concentrate on looked questionable. One, way beyond that."

Jesus, the guy's quoting Supreme Court Justices, Bagwell thought to himself with a heightened respect for The Captain.

"Look, if there are any horses on the track that can't be expected to run to any kind of predictable form, it's the nags that the racing secretary sticks in these Twin-Tri races," The Captain started up again. "It's said that there are two kinds of race horses. . . those that are fast and sore, and those that are slow and sound. Well, the rock-bottom nags they put in those Twin-Tri races are slow and sore. Christ, some of them probably can't even see!"

Having heard all that before, Bagwell thanked the two of them as he shook The Captain's hand.

"Heck with that . . . it's the least we could do," The Captain smiled. "Thank you for giving Hammy that horse in the seventh."

"No wonder the odds were only 7-to-1," Bagwell laughed while musing over how many others, besides The Captain, that Hammy actually had gotten to before the gates for May's Highland's race opened.

"Ha, this schmuck got shut out," The Captain jeered, pointing at an instantly flushed Hammy who responded with a sheepish grin and a shrug of helplessness. "I got my bet in with time to spare using one of the automatic betting machines. Bozo here doesn't believe in them. He'd rather stand in line with the rest of the dinosaurs."

"Hammy, you look guiltier now than you ever do after pulling one of your crummy, scummy deals," Bagwell couldn't resist.

"Say, can we buy you a beer or something?" The Captain offered, knowing that Bagwell would consider a crass monetary kickback for one of his tips as a vapid insult.

"Thanks, but I've got to be somewhere," Bagwell answered politely, while glaring sternly over at Hammy like a disapproving parent. "How about a rain check?"

"You're on," The Captain said with sincere pleasure, pointing his right index finger toward Bagwell. "May's Highland got me well for the week, plus some extra. What more could I ask? As Gandhi said, 'The Earth provides enough to satisfy every man's needs, but not enough for every man's greed'."

Jesus, thought Bagwell, *first Supreme Court Justices, now he quotes Gandhi. What's going on with this guy anyway?* Then he looked toward Hammy once more, tilted his head in frowned mock disgust and quietly left the twosome to squabble over the final race on the day's card

No one had said a word about it, but all three knew that they had been looking at Mendoza's handling of his horses — both post-time favorites and both out of the money in those two fateful Twin-Tri races.

17

PSYCH-MAZING

Arriving a little early at Ellen's Runway Lounge, Lt. Huber found the same small, remote table where Maxwell and he had collaborated when the operative had first arrived. Purposely taking the seat that put his back against the wall, the lieutenant was certain that he could, without any obstruction, casually scan the entire marginally lit bar and have an easy view of every booth and other table; an automatic practice with him.

Mercury's detective hadn't completely settled in before Maxwell was quietly taking the seat on the opposite side of the table. The former agent unzipped his light brown leather jacket, but didn't remove his broad-rimmed Stetson.

"Our communication system seems to be cooking," Maxwell said blandly as the waitress hurried toward them. Ordering a couple of Budweiser drafts and some onion rings, they otherwise remained silent until she moved away.

"How's the backstretch treating you?"

"Jess luvlee, bawz"

"I see. Glad I asked."

"I've got a way . . . it's a shot . . . nothing's ever sure . . . but, I can't come up with anything more solid," Maxwell began. "I'm betting this ego maniac we're after can't stand unfinished business or leaving the slightest flaws hanging. Things like that render him obsessively distracted and irritably uncomfortable."

"Sounds like us," the lieutenant said without thinking.

"Yeah. Takes one to know one," Maxwell answered, tilting his head in partial agreement. "He also worries that even small imperfections in his finished jobs will make him look questionable and diminish his value in the eyes of those who pay homage to his sort of services. Hell, he likely ponders what the slightest blemish will do to the underground legend he thinks he's created. Like I said before, this guy's really something."

"I take it back, he's not like us," Lt. Huber narrowed his eyes and shook his head. His frustration was evident. "I'll go along with any damn thing at this point, Jace. We haven't gotten anywhere. Looking pretty hopeless. Compared to the headway we've made, the case is taking up way too much of my department's time. We're letting lots of other things slide."

"That happens when a local crime doesn't have a local cause," Maxwell agreed. "Crimes of passion . . . crimes of abuse . . . situations where the victim and the perp both have local ties. The puzzle parts are all right in front of you, just screaming to be put together."

Lt. Huber nodded his agreement and sat back.

"One thing you've got to deal with, though, If we start with what I'm about to suggest, we'll be trying to bring a God-awful monster back into your jurisdiction," Maxwell, for the moment, became coldly serious. "Whereas, if we'd just leave things alone, likely nothing more would ever happen. We'll be putting some people in harm's way who otherwise would be completely safe here in Mercury. You included. Know who Cosmo 'Cossie' Jarvis is?"

Lt. Huber shrugged his shoulders and nodded quickly.

"Yeah, he was one of the very best jockeys out at Mercury Downs until that Vicone thing happened last year," he answered right away. "Always been right there for the community, too. Fourth of July, Memorial Day, Christmas . . . always in the parades, riding a horse, wearing his jockey's silks, signing autographs. Always helping the police, fire department and civic groups with fundraisers. Visits kids in the hospital, and gets them tickets to ball games and stuff. Even speaks at the schools."

"One of those, huh?"

"Has his own family, too. Couple kids . . . a boy and a girl. Nice wife. Both do a lot on the Q-T. Shy away from any sort of recognition. So much so that you wouldn't know they are doing it unless you happen to be a cop watching over everything that goes on. He doesn't have anything to with this, does he?"

As soon as Lt. Huber put forth his last question with a stern frown, Maxwell began to explain what he had so far. Enrique Mendoza, whose mutilated body had been discovered in the reservoir, had been a top-notch apprentice jockey.

"Back then, his agent had trouble keeping all of his riding commitments prioritized," Maxwell emphasized.

"Look, what I know about this horse-racing stuff you could put in a thimble," Lt. Huber interrupted. "You're going to have to do some extra explaining as we go along."

Maxwell explained that of Mendoza's status as a top jockey tailed off abruptly when he graduated from the apprentice to regular journeyman ranks.

"A loss of ability during that rite of passage isn't uncommon among young jocks."

Then momentarily, for Lt. Huber's sake, Maxwell digressed, telling how, when a jockey first begins riding professionally, his apprentice status allows him to have a weight advantage. For example, the unique conditions of a particular race always designate how much weight each horse must carry. But, a trainer can get his horse into the race with less weight on its back if he uses an apprentice jockey. If a trainer picks an apprentice who has won fewer than five races in his career, that horse gets to carry ten pounds lower than its normal weight assignment. The industry figures that the lack of official racing experience is compensated for by this sort of weight advantage.

Once an apprentice has won five races, his weight break drops to seven pounds, and then after his tenth win drops to five. From then on, the apprentice will keep that five-pound break for one year or, if the jockey hasn't won thirty-five races by then, he or she gets another year's extension. At the end of that time, regardless of how many wins, the jockey automatically graduates to journeyman status and must forever compete with the track-worn men and women riders on equal terms.

Apprentice jockeys are referred to as "bug boys" by racing people because, in the racing programs sold trackside, asterisks will appear next to the weight assigned to any horse they are riding. If the apprentice has a ten-pound weight allowance, three asterisks will appear next to the weight designation. For seven-pounds allowed, two asterisks. And, for five-pounds, one asterisk. These asterisks are referred to as "bugs." Hence, an apprentice with a ten-pound allowance, thereby showing three asterisks in the program, is referred to trackside as a triple-bugboy.

"Every once in a while you get a hot apprentice who can really rack up the wins during that year of grace when he's getting his bug break," Maxwell began getting specific. "From everything I've learned, Mendoza was really good. He was even riding in stakes races and grabbing a good share of the purse money. Everyone thought he was headed for the Southern California or the New York-Florida circuit."

Maxwell suddenly stopped talking. A security breach at one of the passenger check stations had forced the airport to immediately shut down five of its boarding areas and delay all flights at those gates for at least one hour. Out-of-sorts, irritated passengers were moving into the lounge to graze away some time. Within minutes, while Maxwell and Lt. Huber watched, there was standing room only around the bar, and all the tables and booths were taken.

"Then everything went wrong," Maxwell resumed, assured that everyone was too busy with their own problems to pay any attention to what the two men might be talking about. "When he lost his bug, Mendoza seemed to lose whatever magic he had. Like I said, he stopped winning. Trainers who traditionally favored using solid apprentice riders to get the weight break had stopped using him anyway. But, other trainers, those who had used him strictly for his skills — regardless of any weight advantage — soon began looking elsewhere, too."

Lt. Huber signaled that the intruders remained occupied with other things.

"Unfortunately, losing his bug wasn't Mendoza's only downer. His wife left him for an assistant trainer who had taken a top job in Arizona. And, when she went, she took the three kids."

"Real country-western song stuff," Lt. Huber said lightly.

"Mendoza started drinking, something he'd never done before," Maxwell nodded. "People agree that he became pretty depressed. How many times have you heard that one? Last season, he was hanging on by working horses in the mornings and riding in the Daily-Double and Twin-Trifecta races on the cheapest, sorriest nags on the grounds. By then, he didn't even have a regular agent."

"Still, he didn't do what we found to himself," Lt. Huber's impatience was beginning to show.

"Right, here's where we get into it," Maxwell tone was appeasing. "Apparently, on the day the Twin-Tri was hit for megabucks, Mendoza was on the morning-line and post-time favorites in both races. Neither one finished in the top three. Whammo, with the favorites off the board in both races, there was one winning Twin-Tri ticket . . . worth the whole $1.7-million enchilada."

Maxwell suddenly stopped again. This time the waitress was coming toward them. They had been enjoying the lack of attention while she was single-handedly trying to battle the sudden tsunami of disgruntled travelers.

"You boys look like you could use another," she warbled at Jason.

"Yes, bring another round, thank you," Lt. Huber said politely. "No more food though. Getting too close to dinnertime. And, please don't hurry with the beers. We know you got ambushed."

"Thanks, boys," the waitress said sincerely, welcoming their perception with a wide smile.

Maxwell picked up where he had left off, "As usual with these windfall-type hits, the ticket wasn't cashed right away. Usually, they at least want to talk to a good tax lawyer. And, a lot of times the holders will run around trying to get other people involved for relatively small fees in order to bust up the tax bracket created by the lump sum. Who knows? Some want a gaggle of bodyguards to make sure they get home with the money in tow."

"Problems you and I never have," the lieutenant observed.

"But, here's where Cossie Jarvis comes in. He was Mendoza's unofficial mentor during the kid's earlier days. Mendoza always credited Jarvis with talking to him about how to be patient and wait for a hole to open — and then what to do when it does. How to get a horse out of the gate where it was supposed to be, depending on its running style. And, how to use his hands and body to rate a horse — and then to get the most when coming up the homestretch. A zillion other things, I guess. Well, in the jocks' room after the races on the day of that humongous Twin-Tri hit, Mendoza confides to Jarvis that he stiffed both favorites. And, he tells him why."

"That tells me he didn't want to do it in the first place," Lt. Huber nodded.

"Jarvis tells Mendoza that, no matter what trouble he has had before, he's bringing down a whole worse kind with this. Then he advises Mendoza to go to the racing commission immediately. Jarvis sets up a meeting with Commissioner Bill Becker, and late that evening Mendoza and Becker met on the backstretch. Mendoza spills his guts, but he really has no names."

The waitress is back with the two beers.

"I've got this one," Lt. Huber hands her a five-dollar bill with a "Keep the change" appreciation.

"The next morning, all five commissioners get together," Maxwell resumed quietly. "By this time they know that the winning ticket wasn't even sold at the track. The bet was made at an off-track simulcast outlet in southern Illinois, right near the Missouri border.

"The commissioners, along with the State Bureau of Investigations, decide to keep everything hush-hush. They tell Mendoza that he'll have immunity and won't be prosecuted if he'll play along. They just want him to go about things like it's business as usual. Meanwhile, they send out a blanket alert to all mutuel managers in the state, instructing them not to cash that ticket. A hotline is set up to call if there's any attempt. And, they stake out the OTB parlor where the ticket was actually punched. But, nothing. Must have been a leak. The ticket's never been cashed. You know the rest."

Maxwell sat back and took a long sip of beer.

"Yeah, Mendoza ends up dead," Lt. Huber leaned forward. "You got all this just by sitting around on the backstretch, rubbing down horses?"

"Oh, I asked few questions," Maxwell answered with a slight drawl, moving his eyebrows up-and-down twice, and then back up. "Made a few phone calls, too. Did a lot of listening."

"How the hell did you walk in there, out of the blue, and land that job with Harrison's barn?" the lieutenant frowned inquisitively. "He runs one of the best operations out there. You some sort of hypnotist or what?"

"Houdini, I'm not, but I had that rabbit pretty much out of the hat before I even got here," Maxwell answered with a deadpanned expression. "Did my homework. Knew Harrison was topnotch. Also knew about Bright Boy and his leg trouble. All I had to do is wait for them to be close together when I made my push."

"Pretty slick."

"Ye Old Oriental way of doing things. When police surveillance and the threat of grave punishment weren't enough to keep the lawless tendency of mankind in check, ancient rulers sometimes took matters into their own hands. They'd put on disguises and wander out into the market place and see if the system they were trying to implement was really working. They'd go around buying and selling things, ferreting out the cheaters and the thieves and the like."

"Yeah, but you can't bluff that forever," Lt. Huber came back. "What the hell do you really know about race horses?"

"Oh, that," Maxwell was smiling now, eyebrows lifted again. "The house I grew up in was on the outskirts of town. Happened to be right near a Thoroughbred training facility . . . Sagemonte Stables. My brother Arliss and I used to sneak over there, hang over the fences and watch the horses working out around the mile track they had. One day, one of the riders stopped where we were, and, naturally, we started to run. He called us back. Asked if we wanted to work. Hell, I must have been all of ten years old, and Arliss about 13. Even so, they found things for us to do. Around a barn area there's always a broom or a shovel that needs someone on the end of it."

"That's how you learned?"

"Pretty soon though, we started getting closer to the horses. Hot walking them. Feeding and watering them. Helping to give them baths and rubbing them down."

Then Maxwell looked down at the floor to his left, reflecting.

"And there's always some old guy around who, if you're a kid and you show that you're willing to learn, wants to take the time to teach you lots of stuff. Sort of pass things on. Hell, look back over the years. I'll bet you can still name every teacher you had up through high school. Maybe not the college ones that just stood up there and lectured to you. But, certainly the ones who got to you in the classroom and cared about how you did. They couldn't have possibly been in it just for the money. They didn't make any to speak of. They just wanted to influence you, make an impression, leave their mark and make sure you were better for it. Those are the sort of people who, when push comes to shove, realize you can't take it with you anyway. So, it's got to be what you leave behind. What sort of footprint you've left."

"Yeah, you've got a point," Lt. Huber agreed with a far-off look.

"I've always felt that those kinds of relationships are among the strongest unspoken marvels of humanity. And, when you get older, whether you were a teacher or not before, the wanting to leave the best of what you've learned behind becomes very strong, very important. At least, that's the way I see it at this point. God, I don't know what would have happened to me if it wasn't for Mrs. Cranford . . . and my parents were very special people, of course."

"Mrs. Who?" Lt. Huber asked.

"Aa-aa, that's another story," Maxwell replied, gazing off for a second. "In some strange way though, she taught me how to live with those personal conflicts that are never truly going to be resolved."

"Ummm, those. Amen," Lt. Huber nodded in pseudo-jest. "Thank Saint Luke for those haunting regrets that we can't outrun. How else would we avoid sleeping our lives away?" The two men, with eyes downward in concert, became quietly reflective for a long moment, perhaps going over remembrances resurrected by the drifting odors from cigarette smoke and the staleness of dried-up spilt beer.

"All those mistakes and untimely shortcomings . . . all those times when we didn't speak up or step in when we could have helped a situation be different, or stepped back and shut up when we should have . . . always more than enough to occupy us when times get real quiet." Again they were quiet.

"Is that normal?" the lieutenant asked.

"I'd say many, if not most, simply prefer not to deal with thoughts at that level, or, if they do, they really hide it well," Maxwell shrugged. "Most probably lead indefensible lives of avoidance. Just grab what you can while you can, and don't worry too much about how."

"Yeah, so it's up to us, ye ol' social analyzers and moralists, to decide when and how someone ought to be stopped?" the lieutenant shrugged back.

"Get ready," Maxwell quickly urged. "We'll soon be the old ones . . . our time to step up and help the younger ones who care enough to fight off their ghosts and pull through."

"The way I see it, what we're talking about here isn't all peaches and cream," Lt. Huber said with conviction. "This bastard we're after . . . we're banking on his being worried over what sort of image he's leaving behind. We're gambling that somewhere in that sick mind he's inexorably locked onto being the best there ever was at what he does. And, we're guessing that our cooked-up scheme will bring him back here to polish up a residual flaw. In his own sick way, he wants to leave a lasting morbid model of how his sort of things ought to be done. He wants to be the ultimate teacher for those of his own kind. A one-man Hall of Fame."

In unison, the two men snapped back from their reflective meanderings, fending off the beckoning cigarette smoke and stale beer. Yet, that detour had not been a complete dead end. They had reaffirmed that there was more in common between them than just their similar body stature and breadth of shoulders. There, indeed, is a loneliness bottled inside law enforcement people that surfaces only be shared among their own kind.

"Anyway, I learned all about horses' legs," Maxwell broke the silence, returning to the lieutenant's original question. "What they're really made of, how they work and how to rub them and wrap them. When a horse died unexpectedly one day, this old guy — Jeb — chopped one of the front legs off and one of back ones too. Later that day, he took me aside and started to cut one of the legs open and show me all the intricacies of those small, frail bones, and the ligaments and muscles that allow horses to run the way they do. I learned about cannon bones and suspensory ligaments and everything."

"Now it's starting to make more sense," the lieutenant agreed that Maxwell's backstretch abilities were more about substance, less about magic.

"Later, Arliss and I started riding some of Sagemonte's horses and working them out in the mornings. Arliss was better than me, and he stayed smaller. Not small enough to be a serious racetrack jockey, but very good for workouts. That's when I started to gain my deep respect for what jockeys do. I was OK with the galloping. But, when I was supposed to go all-out into a turn, I guess I just didn't have the stomach for it. And, it showed. So, I was used for morning gallops, but, when they really needed to go for time, they'd put someone else up, like Arliss.

"Old Jeb. He must have been 80 years old when he was showing me things. He told me that he avoided death by never paying any attention to it when it came knocking. He'd have none of it. Taking out life insurance . . . Picking out a burial plot or where to put his ashes. . Making out a will . . . Forget any of it. He simply ignored anything that had to do with his dying. Geez, he must be at least 125 by now. I'd like to look him up and see if he still feels the same about everything."

Maxwell deadpanned that last shtick, apologizing with solace that he had more than answered the lieutenant's question about his way with horses. Then, leaning somewhat forward over the table, in a lowered voice he jumped to the reason at hand.

"Cossie Jarvis is psychologically and physically ready to rejoin Mercury Downs's jockey colony," he explained. "But, more than that, Cossie's prepared to help get Mendoza's killer in any way possible."

"What the hell can he do?" the lieutenent asked.

"We've got him under wraps right now," Maxwell explained, using the "we" connotation to include only the two people at the table. "We're going to turn him loose here on the pretense that he hasn't come back just to ride, but also to boldly stand before a Grand Jury and testify about everything that Mendoza told him, including naming names. We're got him housed on the backside, given him a routine to follow while watching him twenty-four hours a day. I'm hoping our monster will take the bait, and that we can orchestrate the time and place to nail him."

"Do you seriously think Jarvis is going to go through with all that?" Lt. Huber said with a wrinkled brow.

"Tell you the truth, Jarvis appears fearlessly committed about this," Maxwell responded. "I'm more concerned that he doesn't go overboard and stick his damn neck out unnecessarily. Either get himself killed or blow the operation, or both. Call it some sort of emotional transference if you want. Sure, he was completely shattered to pieces over that Vicone thing. Now, he's completely pissed off about what happened to Mendoza."

Once again the waitress was upon them.

"You boys want another round?" she sing-songed at them.

"No thanks," Lt. Huber answered, then looking at Maxwell, "Jace, how about coffee or something?"

Maxwell nodded noncommittally. The tide of humanity in the bar had shifted and people were now pouring back toward their respective boarding sites.

"Two coffees, please," Lt. Huber said in a friendly manner, then, again waiting until the waitress was out of earshot, asked, "How the hell do you know a guy like Bagwell?"

"Oh, we have a history, though he didn't know it 'til now," Maxwell smirked. "I was in charge of part of the Secret Service contingent linked with watching over Dukakis's presidential bid in '88. Freedom of the press and all-that aside, we did thorough background checks on any media people who were going to be anywhere near the candidate. Bagwell came up squeaky clean, and then we were able to use him as an undercover mole of sorts. My people spoke to him. He never saw me. Made it clear right off that he wasn't about to rat on his colleagues over every little thing, but agreed to get hold of us if he heard or saw something that appeared to be a real danger."

The waitress returned with the coffees and some on-the-house onion rings.

"That's my side of it. How do you know him in any way other than just a passing nod?" Maxwell asked. "He doesn't seem all that enthralled with what the law-and-order types are doing."

Lt. Huber explained that Bagwell had been instrumental in providing some background information for an animal-abuse investigation that the Mercury police conducted about ten years ago.

"A local know-everybody, know-everything track urchin by the name of Hammerstan put me onto Bagwell, and he really helped break things open," Lt. Huber said. "Some desperate low-life who was living hand-to-mouth on the daily success and failure of his cheap horses became brutally unbalanced when his horses didn't produce enough. A couple of them even died, and they were all marked up in ways that couldn't possibly be accidental. Hell, insurance wasn't even the motive . . . just cruelty. The horses were so cheap, they weren't insured."

"I hate that stuff . . . I know it happens," Maxwell winced.

"Bagwell has a deep love for horses, jockeys and trainers, and even the grooms, stable boys and exercise riders . . . all the hands-on people involved in making racing whatever it is," the lieutenant shrugged. "You don't see a lot of that where gambling's a factor. Usually, it's just predictable mood swings — just gut reactions to the latest winning or losing results."

Maxwell nodded his agreement about Bagwell's overall character.

"Bagwell places a bet now and then," the lieutenant said offhandedly. "Over the years, he's given me ten or so horses, and only two of them lost. And one of those was because the damn horse stumbled coming out of the starting gate, and the jockey fell off. Hell, the horse still finished six-seven lengths in front . . . but, no jockey, no payoff. He gave me one yesterday that won by three lengths, easy."

"Just the short time I've been on the backside, Bagwell's been the most visible media person out there," Maxwell answered. "Everybody likes him and wants to tell him things. I've read some of his columns. They're newsworthy within their sphere, but they also teach you things about Thoroughbred racing. Has he written any books?"

Lt. Huber, picking up the check for the coffees and putting a tip on the table, hinted that it was probably time to break it off, "We better get out of here before we attract too much attention and blow your cover out at the track."

Maxwell smirked and put his right hand up, palm toward Lt. Huber.

"Fat chance," he shrugged relaxedly, while slowly looking around the still lightly-congested room. "Most of these are probably transients who could care less about us. And, even if there are some locals, with the color mix of this whole area, the chance of a cross-culture identification being made is remote. They may I-D you. But then, you're just talking with a black man. At first blush, all black men tend to look alike to white people who live in all-white neighborhoods. They'll ID me by my clothes, not anything to do with my physical features. All I have to do is change into my stable clothes and I'm a totally different person around here."

"That's funny," Lt. Huber broke in with a chuckle. "We had the same idea in reverse when we were kids. We couldn't tell how old black people were, so we figured they couldn't tell how old we were either. We used to go over to the black section of town to buy beer . . . it worked too. We couldn't have been more than 16 at the time. Heck, we had to take the bus — none of us had driver's licenses. They never I-D'ed us."

"Changing the way I talk is getting a little old though." Maxwell shared with a slight smile. "I'll be happy when I can drop the 'Yessuh . . . Ah kin do dat, suh . . . Ah git on it rat away, suh' stuff. Bagwell must get a kick out of it when I talk to him that way. He's got an angle for checking in. Bright Boy's one of the horses I'm taking care of. Apparently a real hotshot prospect before he hurt himself. Bagwell's readers are very interested in when Bright Boy will return to racing. So, he comes by regularly on the pretense of getting almost-daily updates on the horse's improvement."

Lt. Huber had been holding the lounge check while listening to Maxwell's view of cross-culture familiarity. Now he put the check back on the table with renewed comfort.

"You know, this cross-culture thing you mentioned is the reason I can never talk much about my personal conclusion that slavery has been an extremely important and, in the long haul, powerfully beneficial aspect of survival," he said slowly and low.

Maxwell stiffened in his chair, eyebrows up again.

"What the hell? . . . Slavery's a good thing?" he looked at Lt. Huber incredulously. "Jesus, if you want to insult me, why not just try calling me a nigger to my face and be done with it?"

Lt. Huber, chuckling nervously, sat straight up and slightly back, and put a wavy right hand out in front of him. Had he overstepped the bounds of their collective limits of understanding? No, he already knew this man better.

"Whoa!" he blurted out. "That's what I mean! You try to talk about slavery in this country and, right away, it becomes a black-white issue. And, instantly, it slides over into some sort of racial squabble. But, the long history of slavery doesn't have a damn thing to do with race. All you had to do is be on the short end of the stick, and you had a choice — be killed or become a slave to those who, at least temporarily, had the upper hand. Color didn't have a damn thing to do with it."

"It does these days," Maxwell quietly quipped.

"Hell, if prostitution is supposed to be the oldest profession, then people enslaving other people runs a close-up second. I mean, whites enslaving whites, blacks enslaving blacks, and every which way you can think. Hell, back in Greek and Roman times you bartered with your potential worth as a slave. If you needed a loan for something, you could put yourself up as collateral. Strictly financial. Nothing racial about it."

"Hell, I know that," Maxwell nodded. "Anytime you start judging history using modern-day standards you're going to miss a lot of its meaning."

"But, that's not my point about slavery." the lieutenant said, feeling more comfortable about continuing. "When you have a choice of dying instantly or becoming a slave, the prospects of being offered slavery buys you some time. OK, I'll admit it's lousy for the individual . . . unconscionably brutal. Even so, it keeps you in the game, and allows you time to continue passing your lineage onto the next generation. Because that's what it's all about. And slavery, no matter how brutal and controlling, is always a temporary condition."

"I'm sure that's a comfort to them all," now Maxwell was playing.

"Look, when you're used to fighting by using sticks and stones, and you suddenly come up against someone with rifles and cannons, you've got an immediate choice to make . . . if you're lucky enough to be given one."

The waitress is suddenly back again.

"You boys want a refill while you hash whatever it is out?" she says in a friendly manner.

Maxwell, still with some apprehension, nodded to the waitress, and she filled both cups. Although he questioned what Lt. Huber was trying to sell, he was sure he liked this guy. So, he'd listen for the moment. Besides, bigots rarely, if ever, reveal the basic nature of their ignorance in one-on-one situations. They like having the cards stacked heavily in their favor. Even then, they prefer being covered with sheets, he self-quipped. Otherwise, they generally remain hypocritically silent.

"Put it this way, Jace," Lt. Huber resumed as the waitress was leaving. "Say a bunch of space travelers from somewhere actually land here. Now, if they've got the wherewithal to get here, then they sure as hell also can instantly neutralize any resistance we humans could throw at them, including our best nuclear stuff. It would be the old sticks-and-stones versus guns type thing, so to speak. But, if we could show that we were useful to them, even at some very basic level, there's a chance they'll let us hang around."

The lieutenant took a deep breath. Maxwell just listened.

"Now, the one thing that's axiomatic about slavery is that the slaves are always given more and more to do as time goes on, and the enslavers become lazier and lazier. In due time, the slaves figure out how everything works and how to use it, and then they become real threats. Then, either everybody ends up at the negotiating table, working out some sort of equality agreement, or the tables get completely reversed . . . the slaves become the enslavers, and so on."

Maxwell had come off any anxiety he had about the discussion and was calmly waiting his turn. Over the years, he had become certain about one aspect of racism. If it's not talked about openly, it festers in unhealable darkness. He thought about it a lot when trying to decide where to retire. Should he pick a place with an ultra-mixture of people, thus silently demonstrating how tolerant he was of all sorts of racial, religious, political and sexual differences? Or, should he pick a purer atmosphere of singular attitudes and then, whenever they voiced their facade of superiority, needle hell out of them? Which way could he do the most good? *Let's not bring that slant up now*, he decided.

"Yeah, but what about guys who put their foot down, like Patrick Henry with 'Give me liberty, or give me death!' or Martin Luther King Jr. saying 'Life's not worth living until you've found something that you're willing to die for.'?" Maxwell sort of interrupted the lieutenant. "What about that? That doesn't sound like people who are going to stand for having any kind of yoke snapped on them. Instead, they spoke up . . . had their voices heard."

"Yeah, but they were standing on the shoulders of a lot people, plenty of whom died toiling, but who bought time until the situation was right for that give-me-liberty sort of thing to have a chance of meaning something," Lt. Huber came back in cadence, telegraphing that he had thought through all of this way before. "Hell, you walk up to an oppressor who has just taken over and say 'Give me liberty, or give me death,' guess which one you're going to get? No, it was all those nameless people who took it on the chin day-in and day-out, buying the time it took before the Henrys and the Kings were in a position to have what they said stick. Throughout history, how many brave Henrys and Kings were struck down on the spot just because their timing was wrong?"

"There's something to be said for timing," Maxwell agreed.

"No matter where our ancestors came from, everybody got here because things weren't real rosy for them where they came from," Lt. Huber asserted. "They either jumped on a boat or were put on one and came over, or stayed where they were and were worked, starved and taxed to death. Or, imprisoned or ostracized for religious reasons. Hell, the first humans to set foot here came because their food sources were drying up. Out of starvation, they followed the herds across the Bering Strait and into North America."

"A-Ah, maybe we're still slaves," Maxwell said with a smirk, shaking his head slowly sideways as he rose from his chair, signaling that they better go. "What's the difference between that and working stiffs like you and me? Instead of having our food and housing provided, nowadays we get a weekly paycheck to cover those things. We're still slaves. It's just that our standard of living's a little higher."

"Yeah, but with you and me, slavery is self-inflicted," Lt. Huber said, while the two stood next to the table, facing each other. "Still, do you really think that's what it comes down to?"

"No, not really," Maxwell shot back, and continued talking as the two walked slowly toward the cashier's area. "There's a distinct difference that goes along with 'Give me your huddled masses, yearning to breathe free.' Around here, there's relatively few things you're not supposed to do . . . murder, theft, assault, stuff like that. Otherwise, you can do pretty much anything you want to. From what I hear, your whole life is doing police work. Me, too. As long as our essentials are paid for, we'd probably work for nothing. For some goddam reason, we're doing what we want and like to do. That's all that really counts."

Lt. Huber paid the check and, before separating into the parking lot, said, "And, how many people can truly say that? . . . Although they say everyone's got a price that would make them do things they don't want to. What's yours, Jace?"

Maxwell smiled knowingly. Seems everyone in law enforcement has debated this problem with themselves at some time.

"Oh, I used to think maybe a million in small unmarked bills and a one-way ticket to Ecuador," Jace quipped in a low voice, faking a confidential exchange. "From what I hear, there's no extradition from down there. But then, with runaway inflation the way it is, I jacked it up to two million later on."

"Yeah, a million doesn't go as far as it used to," the lieutenant broke in with a huff-laugh.

"Then I started thinking that maybe I wouldn't like the kind of people I'd meet down there," Maxwell continued without missing a beat. "In fact, I've probably had a lot to do with some of them being there. Man, wouldn't they just love to get to their hooks into me under those circumstances? So, what the hell. I figure I better just stay put and do my job . . . working stiff and all that. Good luck."

"Yeah, maybe it all comes down to that," Lt. Huber turned back as the two men had started to depart. "Some people are slaves to their cars, some to their summer homes at the beach and some just to the almighty buck, period. But you and me? We're just slaves to what we choose to do. And that, my friend, is an oxymoron."

It was the last time that the two men would see each other alive.

18

DOUBLE-DATING

As an amicable measure of their growing trust in each other, Bagwell invited Lt. Huber for Saturday evening dinner. Kathi was at the top of her game when "The Hubers" arrived promptly at 5 o'clock. After graduation and an internship, she had moved to Mercury. Bagwell and she had married soon after. With her specialty being large mammals, Kathi too spent much of her time in Mercury Downs's stable area during the racing season.

"Come on in, you two!" Kathi greeted them at the door, with Bagwell off her right shoulder. "So glad you could come, Lieutenant. And, this must be LaVona?"

"Must be," LaVona answered flatly, but not unfriendly.

"The game's still on," Bagwell waved at Lt. Huber, filling him in as the women headed off toward the kitchen. "Sosa's just hit a two-run homer. Cubs are up, 5-4, with the Giants coming to bat in the bottom of the eighth. Bonds is due up first. Wanna bet they walk him? Christ, I saw him intentionally walked with the bases loaded last summer."

The men settled onto the long couch in the living room and began nursing a couple of Southern Comfort Manhattans, while the women basted the finishing touches onto the roast rack of lamb.

"Maybe, if it had happened at some other point in the racing season, I'd have been more alert," Bagwell confided, griping off the cuff about his inability to see through Mendoza's Twin-Tri rides on the day of the big hit. "But, the last few days of any season can get real gummy. You really have to know what you're looking at. Damn getaway money."

"Getaway money?" Lt. Huber, unbuttoning the beige cardigan sweater with the dark brown and white trim that LaVona had bought especially for this occasion, asked. "I've heard of getaway cars. Getaway drivers. Getaway money? What's that? Sounds sort of criminal."

"Uh-uh, track people just call it that . . . tying up their financial loose ends during that final week or so before the place shuts down for the season and everybody's got to move on," Bagwell explained matter-of-factly. "Everybody's going over their books. Summing up their balance sheets. How the season's gone. Lots of people trying to get a little extra to pay last-minute bills and cover moving expenses to their next place. Things get pretty frantic. Lot of weird things happen. Mainly in the cheaper ranks. I've even written about it, trying to wise my readers up."

"Still doesn't sound on the up-and-up," the lieutenant said, telegraphing that Bagwell's brief explanation didn't suffice.

"It is, but you've really got to know what you're looking at . . . a real challenge for a handicapper," Bagwell said as the two also paid cursory attention to the ball game. Bonds had indeed been walked, but the Giants failed to capitalize. With the Cubs already ahead, the promise of any crucial excitement was on hold until Giants came to bat for the last time. "Personally, I tend to lay off betting even more so during getaway days."

"A-ah, even you don't trust it," the lieutenant needled.

"Like I said, watch the claiming ranks. Horses get dropped in way below where they normally run. At a cheaper level, they've got a better chance of winning or at least grabbing a sizable piece of the purse. Also, their current owners aren't excited about taking them to their next place. So, with this drop into cheaper, they're also hoping the horse will get claimed. And if not, they'll try to sell them on the side, real cheap. Then, if still time, the new trainer might drop the horse in even cheaper to win a quick purse."

"Happens everywhere?" the lieutenant cut in.

"Absolutely not," Bagwell answered. "Doesn't in New York or California where, when Belmont and Hollywood close, Aqueduct and Santa Anita open close by. Not many of those stables change locations. Even with the summer breaks at Saratoga and Del Mar, lots of the horses stay and train where they are on Long Island and the Los Angeles area, and just get vanned over when they are going to race. And, the ones that do move, you're not talking Daily Double or Twin-Tri horses. It's mostly stakes stuff. There's little reason for a getaway angle. They're not going anywhere, except next door."

"Mercury Downs is different?"

"Yeah. It's not year-round. There're no other tracks of similar caliber within striking distance. When The Merc's over for the year, everybody ships their stock off to Florida or Louisiana. Mercury Downs shuts down all the way. Hell, you couldn't train a horse here during the off-season even if you wanted to."

"Sounds like a big mess," the lieutenant shrugged.

"Yeah. Getaway time is a real scramble for some," Bagwell agreed, "trying to make ends meet, get rid of excess baggage and get enough together to move on. Sort of problems that aren't top priorities while the season's in full swing. And, everybody's idea of how to get it done is different. As a bettor, probably the best thing to do is watch some of the good old-time trainers. They've been going through that getaway drill long enough to have developed a pattern for relative success. Still, a lot of it depends on how the horses do. It can border on absolute chaos."

"Why the hell don't these trainers just come out with it . . . tell the people what they have in mind those last few days?" Lt. Huber asked with interest. "Seems a fair way to do things."

"No-no. To the horsemen, if and how a person bets is strictly up to the individual," Bagwell took Lt. Huber's question to heart. "They regard the people in the stands as spectators, same as at any football or baseball game. The trainers and jockeys are out there competing against each other for their livelihoods, and they each have game plans for how best to accomplish their aims . . . same as any football or basketball team. Would you consider a football or basketball coach who divulged his team's game plan beforehand as a mark of fair play or careless stupidity?"

"Starting to make sense."

"Imagine a quarterback, after calling the next play in the huddle, turning around and, before going up to the line to take the snap, explaining to the spectators how and why the play is supposed to unfold a certain way?"

"OK, OK."

"Of course the central strategy always stays the same. Get the best out of what you've got. But, the expedience conjured up by the fast-closing end of the season refracts everybody's tactics into a sea of many, many different approaches. What appears to be inexplicable chaos to outsiders is simply a hodgepodge of successful and failed attempts to ease the blow of closure. Most assuredly, this special getaway period is not without its own special risks."

"You're right. It makes sense, when you think about it," Lt. Huber yielded. "Say, these Manhattans are great. What have you got in there?"

"A little different . . . the vermouth's the same, but, instead of the usual rye or bourbon, I use Southern Comfort," Bagwell shared. "Got the idea from a bartender at Penn Station while waiting to catch a train back to Boston.

"I'll keep it in mind," Lt. Huber smiled.

"Another thing," Bagwell frowned, backtracking to their getaway money conversation. "At the end of the season there're always horses that have been brought along on a little slower conditioning schedule. A trainer sometimes wants to get one good race into the horse so it'll be in top form for the next place."

Bagwell, with some impatience, realized that they already had kicked the subject around plenty, but that he needed to get this one final getaway angle in to make the discussion complete.

"If the horse hasn't shown much up until then, it can be a helluva bet. Like I said, the screwy reasons why things happen during those final few getaway days can be incomprehensible to somebody watching from the rail. Nothing crooked about it."

"Just business?"

"Yup, and, for the bettor, it all comes down to knowing what you're looking at. Some of the payoffs are monstrous. A handicapper with some guts and the right kind of perception or imagination can make some real killings, I guess. My advice, though, is always to be ultraconservative, and especially so during getaway time. Always protect your money. There's always another race."

As usual, Lt. Huber was more content to listen than to speak, but Bagwell's last comment called for a response.

"Well, you can't get any more conservative than I am at the track," he laughed lightly, intending to agree with Bagwell's ultraconservative philosophy. "What I know about Thoroughbred horse racing, or any other kind of racing, is that I know I know nothing. Hell, the only time I ever put my money on a horse is when you tell me to."

"Whoa, I'd never tell you anything like that!" Bagwell couldn't help but laugh back. "Christ, you make it sound like I take the money out of your pocket and push it through the window for you. The only thing I want to get across whenever I tell you something is that I have stronger than usual feelings that the situation might be right for taking a reasonable chance."

"Jesus, ever think about going into politics?" Lt. Huber humorously baited.

"Horse racing's far simpler," Bagwell smirked. "The outcome's usually a lot more clear-cut . . . and gratifying. Lately though, I've been working the political scene a little with my editorials, trying to needle the state into lowering their take-out from the betting pools. It would certainly benefit the entire industry. But, with the Republicans in there now, it's tougher. Had a better chance with Clinton and the Democrats. Hell, Clinton's mommy, Virginia Kelley, was a devoted horseplayer. A fixture at Arkansas' Oaklawn Park every spring."

"Yeah, but it strikes me that Clinton didn't always have his mind on business," Lt. Huber quipped.

"What the hell," Bagwell shrugged. "I never got upset over how he took his breaks. He cared about balancing the books and what was important over the long haul. Greenspan, supposedly a bedrock Republican, liked him a lot. As for his indiscretions with the chippies, the only thing that showed me was we have very different tastes. Ever get a good look at that Paula Jones? Ouch!"

Lt. Huber laughed out loud. "No accounting, huh?" Then, coming down, he spoke more seriously, "I don't know, though, perhaps if Clinton had picked another vice president, besides Gore, the Democrats might still be in there. I mean, everybody squawks about the election ending up in Florida's hands. But, Jesus, Gore couldn't even swing his own state! I have yet to fathom the collective mind of the Tennessee voters. They liked Gore representing them in the Senate, but preferred some out-of-stater in the White House? A Texan, no less. Doesn't make any sense. Hell, the last time Tennesseans tried to do Texas a favor, they got all shot up and bayoneted by Santa Anna's soldiers at the Alamo."

It was Bagwell's turn to return the laugh, "I have no clue whether that final Florida count was on the level or not. I hope it was. But, as a handicapper, if the final count comes down to one of the candidate's brothers presiding over the counting, which way would you bet?"

"Supposedly, the brother stayed out of it," Lt. Huber winked back, "and let the chads fall where they may."

"Yeah, and there's a bridge in Brooklyn that's for sale anytime you're interested," Bagwell couldn't resist before returning to his racing-needing-help-from-politics theme. "Bush apparently used to own a piece of the Texas Rangers ball club. How the hell that would improve horse racing's fate I don't know. But, at least he seems sports-minded."

"Lots of luck."

"Seriously though, who's in the White House doesn't mean squat as far as what a track's take-out is. It's up to the individual states how they want to regulate that. But, the guy in the White House sets the national mood. And, right now, I don't think that's helping my cause."

"You know, pari-mutuel betting strikes me as a lot like blackjack, which I fancy myself understanding and being pretty good at." Lt. Huber said soberly. "We both get instant gratification from our judgments, and we like to think that our judgment sharpens with concrete information. Maybe the most important thing that we both realize is that, no matter how good we are at what we do, it's not a life-changing avocation . . . unlike a goddam lottery hit might. No, we're grinders . . . plodders. Except for hitting a blackjack, when I win, the payoff just matches my bet. Nothing more. You do better with those pari-mutuel odds. But then, I only have to beat the dealer. You're trying to beat however many other horses there are in the same race with your bet. You've got more work to do each time to find the edge you need."

"You've got me there," Bagwell yielded. "I wouldn't walk into a casino with your money. Even into a sports book to bet a horse."

"Well, I've read about and listen to everything I can on blackjack," Lt Huber answered, sticking to his guns. "But, what I really get a kick out of are these guys from the casinos who get on TV and try to teach people how to play the game. Isn't that sort of like teaching you how the electric chair works by having you sit in it while they pull the switch?"

"If played right, pari-mutuel betting, and perhaps blackjack, unlike other gambling hooks, are beatable games," Bagwell offered.

"I know blackjack is, because the casinos reserve the right to pry anybody away from a table without having to back it up with any reason," the lieutenant asserted. "Usually though, the reason is card-counting, which is a skill, not an illegal scam. Card counters can smell when the remaining part of the deck has drifted into being significantly rich in high cards. Trouble is, they usually give themselves away by changing the size of their bet, really sending it in when the deck is ripe."

"Then the bouncers move in," Bagwell surmised correctly.

"Lately, there's been more hubbub than usual over teams of counters who swarm onto the tables like voracious locusts after months of being masterminded and trained at MIT. But hell, that team concept's not new. I read about it back in the mid-80s. Instead of one guy sitting at a table and attracting a lot of attention by changing his bet with the drift of the deck, these teams station a sentinel of sorts at each table. This only works in casinos that have lots of tables, like Vegas, Atlantic City or maybe Monte Carlo."

"Got to have plenty of action?"

"Wouldn't fly very well in Deadwood or Cripple Creek. The way it works, the sentinels stationed at the tables just keep betting the minimum and watching the drift of the deck. When they see it going their way, they send up some sort of signal to cue their high-rolling whale. He's the roaming teammate with fistfuls of chips or cash who swoops down and plays only at the opportune moments. When things are really cooking, these teams can put a helluva dent in a casino's blackjack balance sheet in a hurry."

"That's gotta attract attention."

"The team operating back in the 80s was finally caught by a security officer named Nunez. He did it by simultaneously watching all of the TV screens connected to the surveillance cameras above the blackjack tables.

"The omnipotent eye-in-the-sky."

"Correct-a-mundo. He picked up on the team's signal system. Sternly presented with the facts, the whole bunch apparently was happy to 'Get out of Dodge' unscathed.

"Now, there's an independent troubleshooting outfit — the Griffins — employed by the casinos to roam around and ferret them out. It's gotten to be a real cat-and-mouse circus. Once the real faces of these team members are in the troubleshooter's book, they try to keep going by using disguises. Beyond wigs and beards, some of these guys even dress up as women."

Then, suddenly jumping scenarios, Lt. Huber continued.

"Christ, I hope our team isn't flawed. Jace seems to know what he's doing, but I don't know about the rest of us. We haven't much experience with this sort of thing . . . maybe our professionalism will pull us through."

"Yeah, if you can call what Hammy does a profession," Bagwell interjected with serious concern.

"Oh, he's the best I've seen . . . at whatever it is that he does," Lt. Huber said, unable to conceal some reservation. "He takes care of certain needs and doesn't flaunt it. That's all I ask. Most of all, he controls what goes on around here and keeps it clean. If there's any trouble, he makes sure it's taken care of before my office ever gets wind of it. There's none of this stuff about addicts robbing and burglarizing to feed a habit, or street-hustlers hanging out on every corner. In fact, a couple of times, there were instances that could have turned in that direction, but Hammy tipped us off so we could put the clamps on it. Things could be a lot worse without Hammy around. He's like you in at least one respect. If I need him, I always know where to find him."

In the kitchen, meanwhile, the women were on less familiar terms. Kathi whipped the potatoes while LaVona checked the crown roast.

"They're both spending a hell of a lot of time on this Mendoza thing," Kathi broke the ice.

"Yeah, so what if they have different reasons," LaVona didn't hedge her response or disguise her irritation. "Carson because it happens to involve a jockey, and The Lieutenant just because it happened in his beloved jurisdiction. But God, I'll be glad when they get this thing the hell out of the way, one way or another."

"I don't like it at all," Kathi agreed. "Carson's been having trouble sleeping, and nothing ever fazes him. I don't think you and I are in real danger, though. It's not like we have a serial murderer or rapist prowling around. From what Carson tells me, this is a whole different cup of tea."

"Yeah. The Lieutenant never brings his work home, but this one has him twenty-four/seven," LaVona shared anxiously, unmasking her inner frustration. "He's really taken it as a slap in the face that Mendoza was dumped in his reservoir. He's turned it into some goddam personal vendetta. We may be in less trouble, but our men are in deep shit. Political correctness aside, that FBI guy keeps telling him this bastard that tore up Mendoza is a whole different sort of motherfucker."

"I know," Kathi, unfazed by LaVona's colorful language, said sharply. "Carson's tried to assure me that he'll stay strictly background. Regardless of what happens, he says he won't be in the line of fire. I mean, Jesus Christ, he's never had damn thing to do with law enforcement, one way or the other."

"Apparently this sonovabitch has a track record of killing jockeys who get involved with the wrong people," LaVona snarled. "He does what happened to Mendoza for a goddam living. You know, we're never going to talk either of our men out of what they're doing . . . Hey, this rack is ready."

"That's what we're waiting for," Kathi smiled with a flick of her eyebrows. "You get the men to the table . . . I'll bring in the stuff."

During the opening minutes of the feast, the two dying conversations had trouble leaving any offspring. But, loosened by the cold Bordeaux that Lt. Huber had picked up on the way over, an astute observation was made.

"I notice an overall neatness around here, and lack of toys . . . no kids, huh?" Lt. Huber said with a half-jest. "Or are they all grown up and gone, like mine?"

Bagwell just nodded in the negative. Kathi jumped in.

"Oh, Carson and I continue to give it very serious thought," she offered politely, "but, we're not sure, time-wise and financially, if we could give kids the attention they would deserve."

"Christ, you sound like you're buying a car," Lt. Huber said in a tone that signaled that he was now completely comfortable with his hosts. "Hell, if you wait until you think you can afford 'em, you'll never have 'em. What I don't like are these people who think all there is to having kids is a good screw. Who cares if it's followed by a couple of decades of abusive neglect or outright abuse."

The Lieutenant was in high gear. He had seen too much not to, aided by a little fine wine, speak out whenever he had the chance.

"There they are . . . as far as the rest of the world is concerned, a happy couple with a couple of cute brats. The ideal American family. And then we end up with them at the police station with their fully hyper teenagers . . . hell, even earlier nowadays. First time, what the kid's done usually isn't too bad. So, we call the parents in, trying to work with them before things really get out of hand. But, you know what? As often as not, when we start to explain our intentions, all of a sudden the crap that's coming out of the parents' mouths is the same as what the kid was pulling. All we can think is, 'Oh Christ, no wonder the kid's the way he is.'."

Kathi nodded empathetically and waved her right hand, finger-spread palm out.

"I know exactly what you mean," she said in an agreeing tone. "Some of the wives of the trainers whom I treat horses for are middle-school or high-school teachers. They take jobs at the track during the summer to supplement their incomes. It fits in great with their schedule. Sometimes, when we're having lunch, they'll moan about the same thing happening at parent-teacher conferences. They'll lay out the kid's poor work and lousy grades, and then try to get into how the parents and the teachers could work together to help the kid improve. Right away, with the same attitude and tone that the kid was using in class, the parents attack the teacher, blame her for the kid's sorry performance and even threaten to go to the principal about it. Christ, by the time they leave, they're yelling about suing the school for slander. Talk about a no-win situation!"

Lt. Huber poured himself some more wine. After everyone else waved across the tops of their glasses, he leaned back.

"Down at the station, when we get a situation like that, we joke about starting a pool on how soon we'll have the kid back in there again. Like you say, it's not funny. But, how in hell do you break that cycle before it's too late. I mean, it seems to start out subtly enough. Like the guy we're after in this Mendoza thing. He couldn't have always been the way he is now. There had to be some subtle cues before that behavior full-blooms and becomes so entrenched that the personality develops into a lifetime way of doing things. It's not one day he's a well-integrated, nice guy and then the next he's a full-blown sadistic monster."

The others were listening with interest.

"Oh, I know that fellow Whitman, the one who got up in that tower on the University of Texas campus some years ago and started shooting, was that way. He was a nice guy, supposedly. All of a sudden he kills his wife and mother, and pulls a trunkful of guns and ammo up into that tower and starts shooting. No one in particular. Just anyone in range. When they autopsied him, they found lesions on his brain. He even left a note pleading that they autopsy him. Hell, he knew something had gone wrong . . . Hey, did you happen to notice if the Cubs held on?"

"Actually, no," Bagwell shrugged. "We were talking along there, and when I looked over, apparently the game was over. Six o'clock news was in full-swing."

"What!" LaVona blurted out. "What the hell were you two hens cackling about that made you pass up a crucial sports moment. Is Neanderthal masculinity dying as we speak?"

Bagwell and the lieutenant stared at her, sad-eyed, as if discovered with their hands in the cookie jar.

"This guy we're after, I bet we don't write this one off as a reaction to brain lesions," Lt. Huber, without a direct rebuff to LaVona's judgment, resumed his previous line. "This isn't some guy who suddenly has a psychotic break and decides to even the score by going into a restaurant or the place where he worked and blasting away. He's not a mass murderer. . . and not a serial killer, either. No, it's way deeper than that. . . real deep. And, there's no real pattern to his methods. That's because he doesn't decide what he's going to do. Lets the job tell him. Then he just comes up with a how, to fit the who, when and where. The real why doesn't matter. Strictly business."

"Sounds hopeless," Bagwell almost whined. Kathi and LaVona looked on silently.

"This guy's used society as his campus and carefully — I mean carefully — learned his trade. He's the valedictorian. Even so, there's got to be early signals, if anybody's paying attention and knows what they're looking for. Hell, he probably learned a lot about how to get things across just by sitting in a regular classroom."

The lieutenant paused for a deep breath, then looked directly at Kathi.

"Your teacher buddies there have got an impossible job," he pointed to her. "A teacher will say something to twenty-thirty kids sitting out there in their seats, and she'll have very specific and special intentions about what she's trying to get across with her words. Regardless of how dryly they are defined by Webster's, her words will hit those thirty kids in thirty different ways. Pictures are conjured up in each kid's head strictly on how their individual experiences relate to those words. Sure, the whole classroom is using a common language. But still, there will be thirty different interpretations going on out there. And, who the hell can guarantee that they'll always be good ones?"

"So, the cops and teachers are at the core of it!" Kathi baited, with no takers.

19

WHY DO YOU?

"What is the matter with you? Don't you care about us?" LaVona unleashed anxiously, then paused with an intensive stare. She barely had waited until they were pulling away from the curb, still waving and smiling their happy good-byes while the Bagwells stood at their doorstep.

"Why in God's name are you doing this?" she exclaimed. "What possible good can there be? You're not fooling around with some half-assed local break-in or domestic squabble. This goes way beyond any usual danger. And, you're trying to bring it here. Courting it, for Christ sake! Bringing it down on yourself and everybody else around you."

At the end of each of her sentences, each of which was accompanied by a discernible gap of silence, Lt. Huber side-glanced toward her for an instant, while continuing to focus straight ahead as he drove west along Ellsworth Avenue, keeping within the 30-mph speed limit. The darkness ahead was still and crisp, sharpened by the near-full moon's illumination from directly above.

As usual for this time of the evening, rain or shine, Mercury's small-townishness was accentuated by the absence of traffic. After dark, "Mercury rolls up the streets and puts 'em away 'til morning" was the common mantra about the town. A few residences had vehicles parked in front as he cruised steadily along the two-lane, one-way thoroughfare, placing his faith in the stop signs that governed the north-south traffic as he passed by each intersection. When he was certain that an actual lull had arrived in the stop-and-go of LaVona's fervent pleading, he took in a long breath and let it out even more slowly.

"It's not that late — let's go for a beer," he said, without asking. He knew that the issue at hand couldn't be discussed fairly at either of their living quarters. This called for neutral territory and even-handed treatment, unencumbered by any mixed-in deference to cordial-host and gracious-guest facades, real or imagined.

As he spoke, he turned his Ford's steering wheel to the left at the next intersection. Three blocks later, he turned left again and began driving east along Belgrade Avenue.

The Dew Drop Inn had remained his in-town refuge among the public for several years now. Everyone who frequented the tavern was familiar with his off-duty demeanor and relaxed tolerance toward the constantly boisterous kibitzing that ranged a decibel or two below irascible rowdiness.

The couple hadn't shared a single word since his suggestion. Quietly, they settled into a booth near the bar. Beneath the constant chatter at the pool table, dartboard and shuffleboard, the twang of country-western music in the background and the murmur of an unwatched television program, they knew that they could converse comfortably in this atmosphere of open privacy.

The lieutenant held up two fingers and Saul the bartender knew instantly to bring two jumbo-size Budweiser drafts.

"It's what I do," Lt. Huber shrugged, "and you already know that. I don't pick and choose which situations I want to become involved with and which ones to avoid. If I ever start feeling like that, I hope I'll know enough to step aside so someone else can do the job the way it's supposed to be done."

"Wait a minute, Bob," LaVona was ready. "You're not just investigating or getting involved. We're way beyond that. Christ, you're trying to create a situation that wouldn't even happen otherwise. That's got to be wrong!"

"Wrong?" Lt. Huber said in slightly louder voice. Then, quickly catching himself, he leaned forward in a quieter tone. "How in hell can you say that? We're not talking about right and wrong here, or good and bad, or any of that stuff. Someone else'll figure all that out later."

He took a long sip of beer, sat back and spoke again, "Look, all I know is that we have a real chance to get this menace off the street before someone else gets killed. That's it. That's what it's all about. It's a little late in the game for me to be asking questions about things I gave answers to a long time ago."

"The world doesn't need you, but the people of Mercury do," she offered instantly over top of his pause. "You've got yourself mixed up with federal agents and racing commissions and who knows what sorts of organized crime. And you're right there in the thick of it, way beyond just being cooperative so the others can do their jobs. Look, that's not what's going on here. You're pissed off. Making this personal. Dammit, Bob, you know better!"

"Look, how the hell can I avoid this?" he answered evenly. "That dead jockey was dumped in my jurisdiction. And, very likely, he was mutilated and tortured somewhere else here, too. If I don't do everything I can, I don't belong here. It's the reason I was brought here in the first place."

Another sip of beer, then he used LaVona's silence.

"The people of Mercury are my people. They see me everywhere — here at this bar, at restaurants, on the street, talking to their kids . . . everywhere, dammit. And that, by itself, makes them feel safer. If I don't do something now . . . just let it fester . . . they'll soon look at me very differently. They'll start thinking, 'As long as this bum's in office, we're not safe.' And, they'd be right, too."

"Yeah-yeah," she wasn't buying it. "How the hell safe are they going to feel if you're not around? Period? Not around because you put your ass in a sling when you shouldn't have."

Her face was reddening, the area around her squinting eyes becoming puffy.

"Hell, that even holds when selling houses. I'm always concerned . . . I always care about the people. Even so, I never get involved personally. When they tell me things about their situation, it helps me to find the kind of home I think they'll fit best in and be happiest with. But, when they just go on griping about their lot in life, trying to get me to listen because no one else will, that's when I cut it short. It's as simple as that."

"Hey, Officer Bob," Ronnie Kart, a crack dart player, approached the couple's table, also acknowledging La-Vona.

"Hi, Ronnie," the lieutenant smiled. "What's up?"

"Me and Jim are working those two over there," Ronnie confided in a low, hushed tone. "But, we haven't got them quite where we want 'em yet. Too early to — you know — lower the boom."

The lieutenant nodded knowingly, "You mean to say you found two pigeons in this place who know about you and Jim and are still stupid enough to challenge you?"

Ronnie chuckled quietly, "No-no. These two clowns are just passing through. Came in here, right away started throwing the darts and bragging how great they are. Me and Jim started by taking up their invitation of friendly 6-11-Bull for who buys the next round. Since then it's escalated to small side-bets, plus the beers. That's gone far enough." Ronnie, looking at LaVona, pulled his right palm down over his face, exchanging a grin for a stone face in the process. "We're just about to — you know — stick the harpoon in."

"Luckily, we've got a front-row seat," LaVona whispered, half-kiddingly.

"Officer Bob, I could use some advice on another matter," Ronnie said, disregarding LaVona's attempt at wit. "I've got dog trouble with one of my neighbors. Maybe it doesn't sound like a big deal, but it's got me riled. This neighbor's got one of those yappy little things about the size and shape of a Scotty dog, but it's got long brown hair all over. Looks like a damn mop running along. Anyway, the neighbor's constantly losing control of the damn thing. She won't put it on a damn leash. Anyway, I've got two huge locust trees in my backyard and, in between them, a whole garden full of all sorts of beautiful irises that I've swapped bulbs to get over the years. Man, the color contrasts are out of this world when they're in bloom."

"I've seen them, Ronnie," LaVona smiled. "They're worth looking forward to every year."

"Gives you an idea how I feel about them," he nodded briskly to her. "Anyway, that little yappy dog spotted a squirrel or two in those trees once. Now, every chance it gets, it comes yapping over to those trees, charging back-and-forth between them whether the damn squirrels are there are not, and tearing hell out of my irises . . . "

"Hey, Ronnie, you going to play or not?" His partner, Jim, yelled from the dart line. "These guys think you're having second thoughts . . . chickenin' out!"

"I'll be there in a damn minute, dammit!" Ronnie yelled back. "Does it look like I'm going somewhere? I'll be right there."

Then, turning back to the lieutenant, "Sorry about the interruption. My iris bed is completely destroyed for this year."

Everyone at the table was silent for a mini-moment, trying to determine whose turn it was to speak.

"Some of my other neighbors and friends remark how I put an awful lot of work into my flowers, lawn and shrubs," Ronnie readily sliced the silence. "Hell, I tell them it ain't work at all when you finally see the results. But man, it sure all of a sudden feels like nothing but work when you get everything set and then someone else — or their damn dog — comes along and wrecks everything before you even have a chance to enjoy your handiwork."

For a milli-moment, while the erstwhile dart shark was explaining his gardening plight, the lieutenant's attention drifted into wondering what havoc Marcus might be creating for his neighborhood whenever he disappears through the back door. Over the years he had fielded more than a few citizens' complaints about various cats that were indiscriminately defecating in other people's petunia patches or their children's sand boxes. Simply because he was a police officer, were his neighbors perhaps too kind, too respectful or too apprehensive to complain openly about Marcus?

"Dammit, Officer Bob, I spoke to this neighbor about her friggin' dog lots of times, and even explained about my irises and everything," Ronnie continued to describe his woeful dilemma, and the lieutenant immediately refocused. "All she does is look at me sad-eyed and say she's sorry. Hell, I've fantasized a number of times about having my 12-gauge close by when that little bastard comes running over. Only fantasized, mind you. I'd never so much as make a move in that direction."

"I know. You're to be commended for your self-restraint, Ronnie," the lieutenant took the opportunity to interject his true concern.

"What am I supposed to do now?" Ronnie pleaded, looking at the lieutenant, then over to the dart board as if he were suddenly in a hurry, then back to the lieutenant.

"Let me make the next move, Ronnie," the lieutenant said softly, but directly. "Which house is it?"

"The one next to mine on the north side," Ronnie said, all ready on the move toward where the other three throwers waited. "Thanks, Officer Bob."

"Dogs in flowers?" LaVona chided. "Do you do kitties stuck in trees, too?"

"All right, all right," the lieutenant shrugged and smirked. "Very funny. But, that's what I'm driving at.

These are my people. They believe I can take care of things. They feel safe with me around. Christ, that kind of stuff doesn't just come with the job. Got to be earned."

As he finished his remark, the lieutenant picked up his beer glass and clicked it against LaVona's. Then abruptly, "Geez, sorry I didn't introduce you. I just assumed you knew Ronnie."

"Heck, anybody who's got a car knows Ronnie," LaVona answered, with assuring disinterest. "He fixed my starter about a month ago. Remember?"

After a brief span of silent reflection, the couple turned in unison toward the dart area, which suddenly had become conspicuously quiet. The transients seemed to have traded in their jovial braggadocio for troubled consternation. What was funny earlier was now unfunny. And, vice-versa. Ronnie and Jim were now at the top of their game. And, Ronnie had an extra reason to smile. His iris dilemma was being attended to.

"So much for showing the local hicks how it's done," Lt. Huber winked at LaVona.

"I've got to admit, I'm a little confused," he shifted to a more serious tone. "When we went around the block on something like this before, you took the completely opposite position."

Oh really," LaVona shot back. "When was that?"

"When we talked about women who've been raped," he answered

"Oh? What the hell's that got to do with this?"

"Well, if I recall — without putting words into your mouth — you advocated action at almost any and all cost," the lieutenant began choosing his words very carefully. "We agreed that many, if not most, raped women are extremely hesitant to take any formal action, legal or otherwise, because of the hellish frustration and embarrassment involved."

"Right, but women have to get past that," she began before he had finished. "You can't allow those goddam freaks to get off Scott-free. They've got to be stopped.

They've got to pay. What's a little embarrassment along the way?"

"First of all, the perpetrator generally leaves her with some sort of threat about being killed if she says anything to anybody," the lieutenant calmly answered. His lifelong training gave him a home-court advantage in discussions of this sort. "Then, the cops will grill hell of her, trying to determine whether it was just a lovers' spat gone wrong or some other provocation. On top of that, she knows that, if it goes to court, the defense lawyer is going to paint a graphically horrendous picture of sluttishness. Not to mention the long-range, perhaps permanent, way she's going to be viewed differently by family and friends. Add up all that crap, how can you blame anybody for wanting to cover things up?"

"For crying out loud, welcome to the twenty-first century," LaVona grimaced, unable to contain her dismay. "There are concerned councilors, law-enforcement rape specialists and a whole bunch of other support mechanisms these days."

Pausing, she then calmly asserted, "Those freaks are banking on what you just pointed out. The tables have to be turned."

"Do you hear what you're saying, for Christ sake," he countered with exhilaration. "All I have to do now is shut up and rest my case. You demand that these women not only have reasons to take action, they've got obligations. Given all this, how in God's name can you question my present position? Does my commitment to law enforcement stop short of some invisible barrier?"

Straight-faced, head tilted to the right, the lieutenant sat back in his chair. Then he slowly shrugged once, both palms up on the table.

"Pretty convincing, Officer Bob," LaVona answered with sincere acquiescence. "I believe you've got me by the short hair here. Except for one thing, my position on rape is a generality. It's for the general good of all, not personal. I don't know what the hell my reaction would be if I were the one raped. One thing for certain, I sure as hell wouldn't set up a situation where I could be raped again."

"We've got the setup . . . we've got control," he said easily. "No surprises this time."

"Besides, it's one thing to provide local background support so the feds can move in and get the job done," LaVona remained unconvinced. "Like Bagwell's doing. Wanting to help, but staying the hell out of the line of fire. Not you, Officer Bob. You're out there leading the friggin' charge, for Christ sake. Keeping the peace in Mercury is a far cry from baiting . . . luring . . . inviting, for the love of God, some marauding psycho killer! Control, my eye! Let the feds handle it, for crying out loud. That's what they're good at."

Meanwhile, across the room, Ronnie was counting out Jim's share of the take, while the two transients were slurping down the last of their beers in preparation for a hasty exit. Nodding to Jim with the last of the split, Ronnie quickly looked over to the couple at the table, craned his neck forward, stuck his tongue out of the right side of his mouth and gave a long wink. Inwardly though, Ronnie was a little sorry that Jim and he had stuck the harpoon in so deeply, so quickly. With more surgically refined patience, more wool very likely would have been shorn from these two willing lambs before the slaughter was completed.

"Jesus, talk about your win-ugly," LaVona commented about Ronnie's victory gesture.

"At the risk of sounding facetious, I've got to say something," the lieutenant said with easily detectable apprehension. "Back when we were in Reno that time and you were describing your attempt at marriage, I thought — but dared not say at the time, of course — 'she liked the idea and the image of marriage, but not the commitment'."

"Funny, I didn't think you were listening that closely," LaVona said, surprising him with her quiet, even-keeled manner. "But, this isn't about me."

He took in the last of his beer, and then, carefully returning the oversized glass to its coaster, said, "You so sure about that?"

20

TRUE SPORT

"The Hubers," as Kathi insisted they were, though they had never hinted to anyone the slightest inclination toward tying the knot, had cheerfully departed shortly after 9 o'clock. While Kathi filled the dishwasher, Carson, invigorated by the evening's conversations, headed off to his den with hopes of producing some inspired prose.

"That was enjoyable, dear," Kathi broke the human silence ten minutes later, leaning against the door-jam of his den with the whirring cycles of the dishwasher in the background. "We should have people over more often."

"Yes, it was nice," Carson agreed without turning from his PC. "Offhand though, I can't think of anyone else besides Bob and LaVona who would fit in so nicely." Then turning toward her, he mumble-chuckled with a touch of fiendish delight, "Ought to bring Hammy and The Captain over. That'd cure any heavenly hostess delusions in a flash."

As part of the Bagwell household's regular after-dinner routine, Kathi usually cleared the dining table so she could spread out the medical records of the horses she was currently attending. Meanwhile, Carson predictably moved down the hall. Crammed into his niche was a small desk supporting his personal computer and printer. The cabinet above the desk contained his disks, style manuals, reference books, a rarely used thesaurus and two dictionaries, although one of the dictionaries was usually somewhere else in the house, wherever he happened to have last depended on it. He was obsessed with the necessity for a clear interpretation of the English language and the precise meaning of words.

A small, floor-to-ceiling maple bookshelf rose across from his desk. This eight-level fixture held books that Carson regularly used and those that he had recently read for the first time. The space between the desk and the bookshelf barely gave him room to sit down and then pull his chair comfortably back in front of his PC. His chair was a small, hand-stained walnut piece with a completely movable, thin beige cushion.

Carson wrote all of his columns, editorials and feature stories at home. He steadfastly argued that if he ever tried to write such pieces at his desk at the Times, frustrating interruptions by visitors and phone calls would likely drive him to hurting someone psychologically or physically long before he accomplished the task at hand. Indeed, having a personal temple in which to cultivate his thoughts, devoid of interruption, was one of the prized parts of Carson's life. Kathi mostly respected this.

"Why in Heaven's name are you involving yourself in this?" Kathi, knowing that her question was hopelessly rhetorical, stared at him with deadpan seriousness. Prior to this evening, he had given her only sketchy explanations about his collaborations with Lt. Huber and Agent Maxwell. He also knew that she hadn't come down the hall just to revel over the evening's enjoyment with The Hubers.

Familiarity had bred a cache of instinctively stock answers for these moments, beginning when they had originally dissected and mulled over his move from the New York metro area to Chelsea. They had rehashed the same script a couple of years later when he decided to jump from Chelsea to Mercury. Unlike the vast majority of his journalistic ilk, Carson seldom kicked an idea around openly until he had decided upon a firm approach. Before reaching that point, he broodingly churned each issue in silence. Consequently, by the time he opened up, his position was usually close to immutable. Kathi knew this from their private arguments; and she knew it from the articles that he published.

As part of her monogamy with Carson, Kathi had unyieldingly withstood the waves of disappointment expressed by her family, especially the long-range volleys about her living arrangements with him after she arrived in Mercury. She knew that, as personalized as their criticisms appeared, their motives were without real concern for her, but only how her openly unconventional behavior might reflect upon the family's good name.

Whenever Carson gazed into those lavender eyes, they reminded him of the improbability of Kathi and his togetherness in Mercury. So much precious time apart had to pass. Too many chance interactions of companionable convenience had to be hurdled. Once, when he tried to stammer his fathomless amazement into words, she had quietly interrupted, "Anything worth having is worth waiting for."

For sure, while completing her educational commitments without him, a conveyor belt of suitors presented themselves to her in endlessly imaginable postures, only to be icily parried in the germinal stages each time. Some didn't take this affront to their naked egos in stride. They lashed out, such as spreading gossip that they had mistakenly asked a lesbian for a date. This only added to their troubles. Kathi had made friends right away among her fellow interns at the NY-RA, both men and women, and they, along with auxiliary staffers, closed ranks. Soon, those brave enough to chance an offer of dinner and a movie knew very well to lick their rejection wounds in silence.

When she and Carson had finally decided to go through the pretense of a marriage ceremony, only her brother, Harold, had flown into Mercury to attend. Carson had made him his Best Man, in deference to his own brother, Richard, whom he put in charge of escorting Momma Bagwell. Dr. Bagwell stayed away. The rest of Kathi's clan anonymously receded into silent closure.

During his second year at the Mercury Times, his father had died while Bagwell was in the midst of his first meaty story, a designer-drug scandal at the race-track.

As a matter of policy at Mercury Downs, after each race, the winning horse and one randomly chosen other entrant were taken immediately to the test barn for urine and blood analyses. Trouble was, the racing commission's lab only tested for substances on a pre-published list. If a trainer could get hold of a painkiller or performance enhancer that wasn't on the list, chances were good that the horse could get by the test barn without being detected. This time though, the cer-tified testers had received a tip on a specific new stimu-lant that horses were being "juiced" with about eight hours before they were scheduled to race. Immediately, the track's lab began testing for the drug without any prior warning. During the first week, two leading train-ers had purses withheld, and both were suspended in-definitely until either formal hearings could be held or appeals granted.

Right away, lawyers on both sides began having a field day. Sabotage, entrapment, retroactive incrimina-tion, libel, slander, character assassination, misuse of the public's trust . . . day-by-day the air thickened with new claims. Carson alone was on top of the daily sal-vos, as well as the opinions of astute bystanders, when news of his father's death reached him. He knew that if he left, even for a few days, someone else would have to take over the story as it unraveled by the hour. He would have to turn over all of his notes and any prelim-inary drafts. When Kathi asked him with bemused con-cern why he had not attended his father's funeral, he flatly replied, "We haven't given a damn about each other for years. No reason to start up now."

A month later, brother Richard visited Carson again, this time for two days. He solemnly detailed how their father's estate had been divided three ways, will-ing half of everything to their mother and one quarter to Richard. The other quarter, presumed to have been originally earmarked for Carson, was instead bequeathed to the local hospital where Dr. Bagwell had served as chief-of-staff for several years.

"Well, perhaps some good will come of it," Carson said blankly to Richard. "Tell Mom I'll try to get back there for a visit when the racing season's over here."

Before he had his chance, his mother suffered a stroke and died within a matter of hours without ever regaining consciousness. After the funeral, with Richard as executor, her estate was divided equally between the two brothers.

"Richie, I can't remember when was the last time I wept for anyone or anything," Carson confided to Richard before stepping onto the plane back to Mercury. "Maybe it was when one of our dogs died."

"Well, you won't have any trouble about that now," Richard consoled him with a departing hug.

As she sagged against the entrance to his den, Kathi knew he was beyond becoming involved in the "Mendoza thing". She also was comforted by knowing that, when making any taciturn decisions along the way, he would take her feelings into account.

"You know how I feel about jockeys, Kath," Carson quietly replied, sincerely trying, as always, to win her understanding. The couple had celebrated their tenth anniversary three weeks earlier, and his passion for her burned brighter with time.

"I know you love them . . . even have great respect for what they do," she answered awkwardly. People openly gossiped about the "Mendoza thing" while she made her daily rounds of the barn area. Although the information never completely added up, she had developed grave misgivings about the entire incident. "But, so what? This Mendoza thing is so horrible!"

"Oh, hell, Kath, we both came from extremely protective backgrounds," he cut right in as she left off. "We could have hidden behind wealth and privilege forever. Anytime things got a little rough, we could have just receded behind our families' money if we had wanted to play our cards that way. All we would have had to do is be nice, behave ourselves and do what we were told."

"Carson, we've gone over this a hundred times," she interrupted with growing impatience. "So we're the rebellious brats of the bunch. Big deal. Doesn't mean we have to go around tempting fate at every turn."

"Rebel, hell, we didn't run away from anything," he asserted with mild irritation. "We ran toward what we wanted. You love your animals. And, I've got jockeys, trainers and horses to write about. Besides, if I, along with Lt. Bob, Agent Jace and the rest of them, don't do something about what happened to Mendoza, who the hell will?"

"Mendoza was a grown man . . . knew what he was getting into was wrong," she yelled back at him. "Now, from the damn grave, he's pulling all of you in with him."

"Mendoza was down on his luck," he copied her escalated intensity. "Some slime balls saw that he was vulnerable. Took advantage of what they thought was easy pickings. Got mad when things didn't go their way. Had him killed. And not just killed!"

"Being a turf writer, even a good one, is a long way from that," she said in a lowered unsympathetic voice.

"Don't worry . . . Ah, nobody understands my feelings about jockeys when I try to explain it in jockey terms." he shrugged. "Baseball seems to be the great American Rosetta Stone for explaining all other things to an erstwhile neophyte, sweetheart."

"Don't try sweethearting me now," she said sharply. "Baseball analogy . . . Rosetta Stone . . . Heaven help me!"

"He might not, but I'll try," Carson laughed. "Back before college baseball was a strong enough game to serve as anything close to a minor league system for the pros, much the way college football and basketball always had, high-school kids who showed any promise at all with a bat and a glove were immediately signed up by the major-league teams and shoved into their farm systems. Very few were fortunate enough to climb up through the minor-league ranks and make it into the big time. The rest — the overwhelming numbers who didn't, either because they simply didn't develop and mature as expected, or sustained a career-ending injury — were cut loose . . . unskilled, uneducated and lacking the training to do anything else. Baseball's come a long way since. The caliber of college-ball competition has blossomed to the point where kids are jumping from college right into the majors."

"You're telling me what everybody in America knows, even without a Rosetta Stone," she said, growing noticeable edgy with the conversation. "Everyone knows how much Barry Bonds, A-Rod and Roger Clemens make per minute."

"Jesus, that's not my point, dammit," he grumped, showing she was making him edgy. "Nowadays, if they happen to fall by the wayside, college baseball players have an education to fall back on. Even if they do make it, that college degree is always there after they're through playing."

"The money they make these days . . . they can ride the gravy train for the rest of their lives," she said with open disapproval.

"Yeah, well not so with jockeys," he kept on, ignoring her tone, as well as her logic. "If they're small enough and, from looking at their parents, don't seem that they will go through any massive growth spurt, they're grabbed up early and put to work with the horses, usually as exercise boys to start with. To get their jockey's apprentice license, they have to be at least sixteen years old and show proof that they worked as a stable rider for at least a year."

"That's no excuse for not pursuing a formal education," Kathi argued. "Lots of people do things and still find the time to educate themselves."

"With the nomadic nature of the racing industry, these young kids really don't have much chance for a solid education, even if they do make a special effort to stay in school," he shook his head. "They do so much jumping around, school to school, as the seasons change that there's never really the kind of continuity and stability that it takes to become focused on a useful education."

"Don't the people around them care anything about them?" Kathi shook her head, finding his explanation unsatisfactory. "Or, is it just another sad case of 'What can you do for me right now?'"

His silence gave her question creditability.

"Look, Kath, I promise I'll stay out of harm's way," Carson, after a long moment, assured, dearly wanting her to realize his awareness of her concern. "I can't just stand by. Oh, I'll admit that I usually don't put myself in this sort of position, in the midst of murder and crooked gambling and all that."

"Harm's way? How're you going to know where to draw the line?" her tone pleaded. "Why not stay out of it altogether?"

"Even with my writing, whenever I've felt that I had no recourse but to take a shot, I took it," he reminded her. "Regardless of whom I might make mad — or how it might hurt my career, as they say. I've always had to do what I felt was my job, or get the hell out."

"But, we're not talking life-and-death?" she chided.

"One I'll never forget happened a quarter-century ago," he persisted, ignoring her jab. "I got really upset over the outcome of the Preakness. A huge-hearted filly named Genuine Risk won the Derby two weeks earlier. Then, around the far turn at Pimlico, she was moving up to the lead. As they came off the far turn, Codex, a big strong colt with Hall-of-Fame jockey Angel Cordero aboard, went very wide, taking Genuine Risk outside of him. She lost her momentum and Codex finished first. The stewards' 'INQUIRY' flashed in the infield right away."

He took a deep breath, adjusting himself in his chair,

"Hell, I'd seen Cordero pull stuff like that a hundred times. Rough-and-tumble Latin-American riders like him take pride in those sorts of tactics. Race-riding they call it. All part of the game, they say. If you can't take it, get out of the way, and that sort of stuff. Well, after an unusually long review, the 'INQUIRY' sign came down and the race was declared official, with Codex's number staying up there as the winner. I had a fit."

"I can just imagine," Kathi smirked knowingly.

"Don't get me wrong, I didn't have a penny on the race," he assured her, but she already knew that wasn't his point. "I wrote a seething editorial, calling for the firing of Pimlico's stewards on the spot. And I strongly suggested that the Maryland racing commission go after the people responsible for hiring such incompetence and fired them too!"

"Think I remember you mentioning this incident a time or two before," Kathi said, not trying to cut him short. "But, not in this way."

"People started avoiding me like the plague," he smiled. "I'm talking about the run-of-the-mill writers who hang onto their jobs by schmoozing and looking for the next patronizing puff piece to scribble about. Actually, the good ones rallied around me. Some even admitted that, while they might not have the guts, they were glad I did. It had to be said, they confided. Times like that, you find out who's who."

"Stand up and be counted!" she cheered with urgency.

"Heck, none of the jockeys or trainers ever held it against me," he said quickly, parrying his satirical cheerleader. "Oh, Codex's trainer, D. Wayne Lukas, was a little sensitive about it right off, but he never treated me badly. Same with Cordero. Those two guys are as professional a pair as I've ever run into."

"There're lots of people who look upon jockeys as slimy little opportunistic scumbags who would sell their souls or their grandmothers for a nickel," Kathi countered. "You know the sorts of abuses, verbal and worse, they take in the saddling areas. And the trainers always seem to be bawling them out."

"Yeah, but trainers take their share of abuse, too," Bagwell chuckled. "Anytime people put their money on the line and it doesn't pan out the way they think it's supposed to, there's hell to pay."

Trainers have a lot in common with baseball players, too, he asserted.

"Ah, the ever-reliable Rosetta Stone," Kathi quipped.

"Yeah, it takes all kinds to make up a baseball team," he proposed, while begging her forgiveness for again falling back one of his favorite crutches. "Just look around a diamond . . . all the different sizes and shapes out there. Different talents. Different skills. Nobody who can do it all. Outfielders don't make very good second basemen. Catchers don't make good pitchers . . . Same with horse trainers. Some are good with certain leg ailments. Some are better at the way they use blinkers. Some specialize in developing turf horses, while many others do better on dirt in America."

Diplomatically waiting for a genuine lull, Kathi gleefully lunged at this obvious moment to talk about something that had always irked her.

"When I first started working with the horses in The Downs's barn area, I'm sure some people felt they could take advantage of my newness," she said, standing up straight, away from the door jam, waving her right hand in front of her, palm up, with the index finger extended. "On more than one occasion, someone whom I didn't recognize would walk up out of the blue and, in an ultra-friendly tone, ask me about some horse I happened to be attending. Luckily, one of the first principles they taught us in New York was to treat every horse with doctor-horse privilege, exactly the same way any doctor should respect their human patient's privacy. It took a little while, but word got around and I wasn't bothered anymore."

Bagwell nodded his agreement that human nature will always look for an angle, try anything to gain an advantage.

"It's especially noticeable in the claiming ranks," he slowed his speech, lending to an air of mystery. "Trainers watch everything about other people's horses. They watch, not as drooling admirers, but with the eager pursuit of a willing suitor seeking fulfillment."

"Good lord!" Kathi grinned at his non-baseball analogy.

"They watch for subtleties and tendencies in individual behaviors," he described, unperturbed. "In the saddling paddock, as the horses march toward the track and during the post-parade procession, how they warm up during the fading moments before a race and, of course, every aspect from the time the gate opens until they have passed beyond the finish wire. All of it. They also watch them gallop out afterwards and how they return to the unsaddling area near the finish line."

"So they watch," Kathi wasn't impressed.

"Occasionally, a deft trainer will see something — a quirk or something — some aberration that he is skilled at correcting and capitalizing on. Things that are imperceptible to most others, including the horse's current connections."

By now, Bagwell knew that he wouldn't be writing anymore tonight. Turning again toward the screen, he copied what he had produced onto his file and began shutting his machine down while continuing to speak. In the habit of treating almost every outside demand while he was in his niche as an indefensible intrusion, that code turned upside-down whenever Kathi appeared. She knew this, and tried hard not to use the advantage frivolously.

"Some great stories have come out of horses simply changing hands," he smiled. "I guess Seabiscuit's everyone's favorite. Hell, Sunny Jim Fitzsimmons was one of the greatest American trainers ever, but he never came close to figuring Seabiscuit out. Maybe it had to do with being so darn successful by doing things a certain way. Or maybe it would have taken too much time, and Sunny Jim was just too damn busy. But, old 'Silent Tom' Smith looked into Seabiscuit's eyes and saw what others had missed, and he knew what to do about it."

"I liked the movie a lot, if you'll recall," she chortled. "Except when they Hollywooded-up the details in the last part. The real way it happened would have been quite enough."

"Sounds simple, doesn't it?" Carson managed to stay with the issue, ignoring her cinematic critique. "If so, in lesser terms, there's a lot of race horses out there just waiting for the right trainer to come along and turn them into future Seabicuits. Geez, want a more recent case? Look at the job McAnally did with John Henry after that one had been through the mill."

"Too bad he was gelded," she interjected quickly.

"Like Kelso. Seems being gelded was the only way to make him into a racehorse," he jumped in just as quickly, then returned to making his point. "Sometimes, too, a horse suddenly takes a quantum leap forward in its ability without changing hands. Just takes an insightful adjustment. That's what happened when Shug McGaughey moved Lure from the dirt onto the turf. Hell, the horse won back-to-back Breeders' Cup Mile races. Billy Mott did the opposite with Cigar — turf-to-dirt — and all hell broke loose. Cigar turned into an all-time tiger! Twice Horse of the Year while matching Citation's record of sixteen straight stakes wins!"

Kathi stuck closer to what she had been implying.

"It's one thing to know what your job is," she said, "and it's another thing to have the intestinal fortitude to do it."

Bagwell knew exactly to what situation she was referring.

"Another hot potato popped up in '88," again he tried ignoring her reference. "Ironically, it involved the Preakness again . . . and another Lukas-trained horse. That big Derby-winning roan filly of his, Winning Colors."

He recounted for her how, back then, Lukas was still regarded by hardboot Kentucky traditionalists as a snotty upstart from the quarter-horse ranks. Winning a Preakness or even a Belmont was one thing, but not their beloved Kentucky Derby! Apparently, the two weeks between the two races brought the anxiety over Lukas's Derby success to a super-boil. When the gates for the '88 Preakness opened, Forty Niner, ridden and trained by Hall-of-Famers Pat Day and Woody Stephens, respectively, surged forward along the inside of Winning Colors, keeping her in midtrack all the way down Pimlico's front stretch. She never got near to the rail the way she had done right away during the Derby. Then, as they were supposed to head into the clubhouse turn, Forty Niner kept going straight, taking Winning Colors extremely wide.

"Because of that recklessly purposeful maneuver, Winning Colors lost all chance of winning," Bagwell asserted with respect, "To her credit, she was game enough to finish third behind Risen Star. Forty Niner, who had finished a hard-charging second in the Derby, crawled home way up the track — last, if I recall — completely spent by that early foolhardiness. Classic cut off your nose to spite your face stuff. Before the race, there were many who believed that, with a little better timing, Forty Niner might have reversed the outcome of the Derby. Instead, the horse's chances were sacrificed to make some stupid point."

"And, when 'The Carson' doesn't like something, he does something about it!" Kathi pitched in, using her kindliest tone of mockery.

"Yeah, you got it . . . Again, I went ballistic," Carson responded, taking a sip of cooling coffee while remaining quietly serious. "Horseracing, to me, has always been 'The Sport of Kings'. That day it became 'The Sport of Shame'. In those moments along the front stretch at Pimlico, horseracing fell from the sporting heavens of 'My horse can beat your horse!' into an abysmally spiteful hell of 'I don't care what happens to my horse, as long as I make damn sure yours doesn't win!'."

"Zoom! Captain Do-Good races home to his mighty typewriter!" Kathi's tone changed very little.

"That day, the late Frank DeFrancis, Pimlico's owner and president at the time, had given me seats that I couldn't have picked any better if I'd owned the place," he reflected, unmoved by Kathi's pleasant attempt at ridicule. "One of only two times I ever watched a Preakness from any place other than the press box. A great day. Even so, as I was walking over to do interviews after that Forty Niner incident, I felt racing had momentarily sunk to one of its lowest levels."

"The way you love the sport, how could you have felt any differently?" she could no longer mask her adoring familiarity with loose lightheartedness.

"I wrote three or four articles and editorials about it, all with the mission of helping to make sure nothing like that ever happened again. Word was that the orders for that travesty had come down from Forty Niner's owners, located in the heartbeat of Kentucky's bluegrass country."

"I gather they are not listed among your friends these days?" she stated what she thought was obvious.

"Goes with the territory . . . If you do the job right, you don't have many true friends," he answered matter-of-factly, "I never asked either one of them directly, but through the grapevine I heard first that Day and Stephens said that they were both just following the owner's instructions, same as they always did for any client. Later though, I guess after a lot of lingering remorse, they agreed that, if they had to do it all over again, they would never have gone through with that sordid plan."

Kathi always enjoyed his slant on the racing community's more provocative history. Through the everyday backstretch gossip, she was familiar with Genuine Risk's and Winning Colors' Preakness stories. Even so, she marveled in his personal interpretations. Kathi loved his need to tell a story as precisely and truthfully as he perceived it, without any sugarcoating or out of deference to people of presumed importance. She knew his approach had cost him several opportunities and created some enemies. She also knew that those so-called opportunities would never have made him happy or involved people that he would otherwise call friends. She loved this about him.

Most evenings about nine o'clock, the couple would reconvene on the couch for a nightcap tea in front of the TV and an episode of "Law and Order" or "CSI". She never failed to arouse him from the half-trance of doing battle with his latest plague of thoughts. Within minutes he would be sprawled on the living-room couch, forcing Kathi to hop to the nearby reading chair if she wanted to concentrate on the TV episode. With her light lemon-yellow bathrobe accentuating those lavender eyes and strawberry blonde hair flowing over her shoulders, Carson remained eternally convinced that there was no place on Earth he would rather be.

Under a delightful excuse, the distracted couple had allowed this evening to sneak into its later regions. Entertaining the Hubers had pushed their practiced ritual aside. By the time they gathered for the late news, the broadcast was half over, and the promo for the next slot on the channel promised a rerun of a Law and Order episode from previous seasons.

"Oh my God! It's one of their earliest," Carson moaned. "We've seen this one at least a couple times."

Kathi nodded in agreement, "Yes, no one did it. Turns out to be death by misadventure."

Carson, still stretched on the couch, rested his head in his right hand above his crooked elbow and smiled over at her.

"Hemingway insisted that there are only three true sports — bullfighting, mountain climbing and auto racing," he shrugged while the day's sports scores were scrolling across the screen.

In response, Kathi quietly clicked the off-button.

"Only those three, he said, force the participants to truly put their lives on the line as a regular part of attempting to compete and excel. To Poppa, all other so-called sports were merely forms of recreation . . . even football, our national pastime of vicarious violence. Sure, there are plenty of broken bones, torn ligaments, damaged muscles and concussions. He's right though. With the equipment and rules that control football's violence, the reaper's hand isn't in on every snap of the ball."

"Hey, Mr. Hemingway made his judgments from the comfort of a spectator's seat," she chimed in. "I don't see him in the thick of it at Indy."

"Be that as it may, I've always felt that he missed a bet by excluding what jockeys have to endure," he said, while nodding in agreement to Kathi's indictment. "Just getting into one of those heavy-duty-steel starting stalls atop more than a thousand pounds of keyed-up horse-flesh would melt most men into babies."

"Me, too!" she chirped, pointing to the middle of her chest.

"Then, charging from the starting gate at breakneck speed over four spindly legs that could snap at any moment," he continued to build his case while recognizing her feelings. "Want more-than-thousand pounds to come crashing down on you or roll over on you or toss you under the steely hooves of the other horses? Hell, jockeys are as rawly courageous as any mountain climber, bullfighter, or race-car driver."

"I think they have to be nuts — all of 'em," she nodded with conviction, while stifling a yawn.

"Christ, in what other sport does an ambulance chase close behind the entire event as it unfolds?" he said with more seriousness. "To me, jockeys are the biggest people in the world. And they do it with their musical, magical hands. It's how man and beast communicate while cruising along at about 40 miles per hour. Shoemaker was all about his hands. The reason women jockeys like Julie Krone, Patty Cooksey, Donna Barton and the rest of them are successful is their hands. With a gentle firmness, they gain their horse's confidence and make them to want to perform at their best. Hell, brute force and abuse can get any dumb animal to go through the motions. But, you'll never bring out a Thoroughbred's innermost competitive will with a threat or a beating. They store that magnificence in their hearts, only to be openly celebrated during a two-way communication of a very different level."

"Trading control for two-way respect?" she asked in summary.

"And jockeys do it with their legs, too, in stirrups tightly dangling from the sorriest little strip of synthetic leather ever called a saddle," he gritted his teeth, letting out a harsh breathe. "Hell, the evil bastard that mutilated Mendoza knew all this. He used it as the method for his message. The hands being cut off didn't have a damn thing to do with avoiding fingerprinting. Along with the cut-off legs and sewn-shut mouth, that whole ungodly ritual was a special warning. A warning to all jockeys. How horribly sacrilegious what Mendoza was put through! If I can help get the guy who did it, I'll certainly do my damnedest."

Kathi stared at him, trying inadequately to hide her concern with a slight smile. There was a long silence then. Both looked downward, lost in separate thoughts of a common plight, at an unseen spot between them.

"So, Mrs. Bagwell, that's the long and the short of why I care so very deeply about every jockey . . . because of what they must do," he broke their silence.

"Well, I'm going to bed," Kathi abruptly announced as she rose from her chair, then leaning forward, put her head next to his and squeezed, quickly adding a kiss to forehead. "Coming along?"

"Sounds like a plan," Carson quipped quickly. "I'll be up in a minute."

21

CHARLEEN'S STORY

The early-to-mid-afternoon racing cards at Mercury Downs dovetailed nicely with the daily downtime for the local ladies of the evening. Accustomed to sleeping late, many of them gravitated toward the clubhouse to enjoy being with friends and perhaps arrange an amorous hookup for later. They all knew Hammy, and he knew them all.

Wherever there is a racetrack, loose money waits to be counted.

Same as how he conducted his other business, Hammy's liaison with the ladies was as their quintessential go-between. And, it worked. Differing from their metropolitan compatriots, the ladies of the Mercury scene were rigidly independent. When not making direct contacts, they relied on the judgments of the motel clerks and taxi drivers. And Hammy was connected in every way. If a motel clerk got a request for a special kind of service, he didn't have to worry about which ladies did what, with whom and how well. Just call Hammy. As soon as he knew what was up, he knew whom to get. And his litany of resources wasn't limited to trafficking with only the ladies. If a thoroughly checked-out request involved genuine adult sex of any nature, Hammy always guaranteed a satisfying connection.

Charleen MacDonell, formerly Helen Kuralski, left an abusive home life at age twelve, and moved in with her grandmother. From the time when she was first aware, Charleen, while still Helen, had been told that her daddy was dead. She also was informed that bachelorette Aunt Martha had moved in to share in the financial burden and chores, and to broaden the perspectives of an erstwhile single-parent environment. The trouble was, no bright, inquisitive preteen remains quietly convinced of anything when glaring contradictions continually abound. Finally, with Helen approaching her high-school years, her mother was situationally forced to confess that the father probably was not died, but had disappeared without further contact, abandoning the family only weeks before Helen was born. Furthermore, "Aunt Martha" was not an aunt in the true sense. She turned out to be Mom's live-in lover.

As disquieting as these confirming revelations were to digest, the explanations at least made more sense to Helen.

Matters worsened as Helen grew. "Aunt" Martha's doting fondness toward her was becoming more than affectionate . . . and frighteningly obvious to Mom. To fend off the brewing disintegration of her reconstituted household, Mom quietly convinced Helen to move in with Gramma Kuralski and share her nearby apartment suite.

Battling self-imposed guilt brought on by an abandoning father and a secondary position on Mom's love list, the transplanted preteen found a nurturing haven at Gramma's.

"Why in God's bane should we accept that we're only born to serve men?" hedonistic Gramma was quick to ask rhetorically. "Oh, men are OK. They do indeed serve a purpose. But, that doesn't mean by any stretch that you have to get married to any of them."

As a sought-after commercial artist by trade, and also a published poet, Gramma had never married. Instead, she constantly trifled with a global stream of naive suitors.

"Oh hell, they may not have invented them," Gramma claimed with a trained look of wisdom on her brow. "Still, the Jews and the Christians insist on keeping those absurd chauvinistic traditions alive and well.

Hell, they never invented anything. Just stole earlier ideas and changed the names. It's all a crock."

Instinctively avoiding the damning mediocrity of peer-pressure popularity, Helen sailed through her high-school years as her class's valedictorian and student council president. With near-perfect SAT and ACT scores as a springboard, she earned a bachelor's degree in Chemical Engineering at Florida Polytech while on full academic merit scholarship. The following fall, after turning down offers from several corporations, she enrolled in the department's graduate program.

To supplement her scholarship money, Helen turned tricks on the weekends and during the summers, using the "stage name" of Charleen, and remaining meticulously adept at juggling these two aspects of her college years. The protective shadow of Gramma's wing had included a tutelage on how to skillfully survive in an easier dollar bracket while enduring the poverty-stricken pursuit of a college degree. Sure, later she would make millions, but for now . . .

Midway through her second year, in the midst of putting the finishing polish on her Master's thesis, Helen, along with five of her closest campus activists, concocted, over coffee in the student cafeteria, a plot to heist enough computer equipment to comfortably cover all their expenses for the rest of their grad-school careers. All they had to do was pry the equipment loose. Tommy, the instigator of the plan, cheerfully assured the others that he had a surefire connection poised to instantly move the booty for a considerable lump sum.

Financially, Helen's scholarships and Charleen's personal income more than adequately satisfied everything she needed. Still, Tommy's clandestine frolic awakened a murkier side of the camaraderie between the campus's grassroots pseudo-intellectuals.

Realistically, no one in the group would have carried through on his or her own power. But, they had transgressed. The collective snowball of suggestions, which grew with each passing minute during the group's original blueprint meeting of their coffee conspiracy, gripped and propelled everyone beyond the bluff zone of no-return: Either in all the way, or be forever ostracized as just another vacuous impostor.

"See, it's a piece of cake," Tommy, like some transparent cheerleader, urged everyone. "I'm so sick of worrying about where my next cup of coffee's coming from. An hour's work and that's all taken care of. Besides, the place is probably insured. So, nobody gets hurt."

Helen still could have pulled out. She didn't need others nearly as much as they courted her. It was the call of adventure and the promise of a momentary break from the humdrum of everyday campus routine that became too absorbing to be ignored. Three days later, the group met briefly to confirm that all were still in. The next day, after another intricate verbal rehearsal, their final plans took on the aura of a ceremonial blood brotherhood.

"As soon as we load the stuff, we take it right over to the fence and get our money," Tommy whispered with satisfying assurance. "He'll be waiting. No questions. No names."

Tommy and one other hid inside when the store closed for the day. The six's combined surveillance homework had documented when the local police cars routinely passed by on normal patrol, and when, where and for how long the patrolmen took their nightly coffee breaks. The Stone Age burglar alarm system could be easily neutralized by anyone inside the store, and there was no evidence of guard dogs.

Dressed in all-black, in an exhilarating near-farcical masquerade as seasoned cat burglars, the two insiders were abruptly cornered when stumbled upon by the armed night watchman. Everybody had failed to account for him. Meanwhile, the outside four in the adjacent alley, including Helen, waited with nervous anticipation for the side door to open so that they could begin hand-conveying the boxes of merchandise toward the dark green pickup's bed. Instead, a police car, with lights flashing and siren silent, coasted onto the street shoulder at the end of the alley, blocking the still empty pickup's lone exit from the cul-de-sac. Abruptly, upon hearing the watchman's excited commands through the building's wall, the quartet scattered, leaving the two hapless insiders to their wits.

Predictably, led by Tommy, the two insiders quickly implicated the others, naming names under promises of leniency. Soon, all six were standing with a pro-bono attorney at an arraignment, begging for leniency in front of Judge Raymond Blake's stony stare. Pled down from attempted burglary to breaking-and-entering, the six, all first-time offenders, squirmed away without jail time. The two canaries were given probation periods exactly half as long as the others. The sentences also demanded considerable community service of the outside four.

Most unfortunately, Florida Poly's Dean of Students immediately was made aware of the convictions. All six were summarily expelled, with notations made on their transcripts in case they should ever apply elsewhere.

The blow was particularly severe for Helen, the only dedicated student among the group. Sadly too, the caper itself had held little interest for her beyond testing its practical soundness against the hypothetical. When push came to shove, her overblown sense of comradeship and inability to say "no" had, in an instant, shattered the pathway to her dearly envisioned future. Embroiled in bitterness, Charleen left Helen behind forever.

Tall, just under six feet, strawberry blonde, which she tinted more toward the red end, and athletically built, she fell back on the skill that had provided steady support during her school years. Routinely photosynthesizing beyond her vitamin D threshold on Broward County's beaches during late mornings, she began spending her afternoons with the social crowd who congregated at Gulfstream Park.

Green was Charleen's color. Covering her thin, curvaceous figure, a mid-thigh skirt gave way to sleekly tanned legs sculpted by the flex from four-inch stiletto heels. Topped with a frilled, short-sleeved white blouse and black leather vest, men's minds wandered as she passed by, regardless of whom they happened to be with at the time. She deplored the use of foul language by men or women. Her soft, deep, comely green eyes changed in an instant to steely emeralds to telegraph her disapproval of any nearby obscenities. Of course, when in a client's best interest, she could talk dirty with the best.

During the second year following her expulsion, with the blunt pain from that ordeal having waned somewhat, Charleen began enjoying late-morning brunches with Howard Mitchell, a top Thoroughbred trainer who overwintered his stable at Gulfstream Park and shipped a portion of his stock to Mercury Downs during the summer. Her skirts began taking on a more mid-calf discreteness

The cream of Mitchell's stable, usually owned by racing's blue-blooded traditionalists, was sent to the New York circuit for the big-pot, historically prestigious races at Belmont Park and Saratoga. While there, these horses were always overseen by Mitchell's two hand-picked assistants, Walter Keyes and Carlos Ceranti. Meanwhile, Mitchell, known throughout the industry as "Mitch," traveled with the horses that eventually were stalled at Mercury Downs. Mostly, these were his more unsettled horses, requiring his additional observation and analysis of minute details before making further decisions about their daily training.

Charleen and Mitch were married two days before Gulfstream Park's season ended.

"She must be some woman to have put the bit in your mouth," Tad Cooper, Mitch's best man, chided just before the small, quickly arranged ceremony began. Mitch silently answered with an agreeing nod and smile.

As the meet's second-leading trainer, he had been on a high edge the entire time. Best of all, Mitch was saddling the most talented three-year-old colt that he had ever trained. With seemingly effortless command, Shining Image had won the Hutchinson Stakes early in the meeting, then been caught at the wire in the longer Fountain of Youth Stakes.

Following that surprising loss, Mitch firmed up the colt's endurance base with brisk longer gallops. Then, nearing the Florida Derby, he had the colt's regular jockey put Shining Image through two sharp four-furlong workouts. With his colt as the co-favorite to win, Mitch and Charleen were married the night before Gulfstream Park's showcase prep race for determining Triple Crown worthiness.

The next afternoon, Shining Image grabbed an un-contested two-length lead midway around the club-house turn and began to rate kindly, setting reasonable mid-race fractions over the notoriously slow Gulfstream surface. Halfway through the far turn, as Mitchell watched through his binoculars, the jockey brought out the whip. Coming off the far turn, five stalking contend-ers fanned out behind Shining Image and, in concert, swallowed up the early leader's advantage. Midway through the homestretch, the jockey stopped urging Shining Image as he faded farther and farther to the rear, eventually hand-ridden past the wire next to last.

Mitch slumped, devastated.

In the unsaddling area, the jockey described how Shining Image had begun, for no apparent reason, struggling and shortening his stride approaching the seven-furlong mark. Under all-out urging, the colt had kept his momentum for another half-furlong, but surely was unfit for the classic distances demanded by the Triple Crown series.

Mitch canceled his personal plans for New York. In-stead, he would follow his usual routine, heading for Mercury Downs and again turning the New York por-tion of his stable over to his two able assistants.

"Mercury! Where is that?" Charleen exclaimed upon having the bright lights of New York suddenly jarred from her immediate expectations.

"Ah, you'll love it there," Mitch assured her. "Those people are real. No phoney-baloney pretense. I'm se-riously thinking of moving there when I retire."

"What about us?" she reacted automatically. "Don't I count?"

"Ah-h, trust me, you'll love it!"

Ω

Shining Image was one of the horses Charleen and he took with them. Mitch still hoped to develop what he felt was the colt's yet-untapped potential and do well in a handful of softer midwestern derbies, thereby enhancing the animal's resume for the breeding shed.

Without any previous hint, soon after Mitch and Charleen arrived at Mercury Downs, Shining Image's owner sold the colt. The new connections abruptly shipped the colt to their preferred trainer stabled at Chicago's Arlington Park.

"Image's been sold," Mitch moaned to Charleen about his former owner's decision, as if a ton of bricks had been dropped on him. "I was never even consulted."

"Is that the way it's usually done?" she asked with sympathetic concern.

"Probably more often than I'd like to admit . . . this can be a cruel, unforgiving business at times," his sad tone carried an uncharacteristically philosophical tinge of accepted defeat. "Among the other trainers, I'm seen as a big deal. But, with owners, I'm just one of the hired help."

The uprooting of Shining Image signaled the beginning of the worst summer by far that Mitch ever encountered during one of his annual northward treks.

After suffering through a twenty-seven-race slump, Mitch finally made it the winner's circle with one of his cheaper claimers. Enticed by recently published morning workouts that sharpened the mare into winning form, three trainers had dropped their names into the claim box before the race. Alas, Mitchell's first success of the meet was haltered away as soon as the winner's circle photo was snapped, before he had an opportunity to capitalize on the extent of the horse's sharpened form.

€

Sitting at the small auxiliary bar in the clubhouse shortly after arriving at Mercury, Charleen spotted a classmate from her college days, one who had supported herself in a similar fashion. Charleen didn't know the woman's name; she hadn't been part of Charleen's intellectual in-group. Still, the sight recognition between the two was instantly there.

Obvious, too, was the woman's daily routine. She was a local courtesan. However, to an unknowing eye, the only constant in the woman's trackside routine was when, once or twice a week, she could be seen talking earnestly and at length to a slovenly dressed, mustached man with refractively prescriptive black-rimmed glasses and a cheap cigar smell.

Ω

As his disastrous Mercury Downs season was mercifully ending, Mitch shipped most of his remaining stock back to Florida. A few, before completing the trek to Florida, he and Charleen took to Louisiana Downs, near Shreveport, which raced Thoroughbreds through the end of October.

Charleen was finding married life with Mitch to be alarmingly different than the late-morning brunches that had sparked their union.

"Is this what it's like for everybody?" she caught herself asking in silence several times a day, and more often as time oozed by. "How does anybody stand it?"

Her waning interest in the intricacies of any aspect of horse racing, which had never been very high, and the long hours that her brand-new husband's chosen profession demanded day-in and day-out, were shredding any passion that she might have felt for him.

On top of it all, Mitch's fortunes as a trainer continued to crumble during the next Gulfstream meet. Disenchanted owners began stabling their stock with trainers who were exhibiting more success. The usual string of promising young colts and fillies that had previously breathed hope into his stable for the coming season now went to other handlers. And, Mitch began coming home even later, mostly more than a little tipsy and flushed from trying unsuccessfully to schmooze superficial clients toward his barn.

As his Gulfstream disaster spiraled downward, the trainer's out-of-control drinking was forcing former connections to nervously avoid him. By the time the meet was over, Mitch's two assistants, Keyes and Ceranti, had formed their own stable and were heading to New York completely independent of him. With the few unaccomplished horses that remained, his usual summer sojourn to Mercury Downs didn't make sense, financially or otherwise. Instead, he decided to remain in Florida for the summer and race the horses he had left over at nearby Calder Race Track.

Charleen had always found excessive drinking to be as offensive as obscene language. Accordingly, they had spoken very little during the Gulfstream meet. As Mitch's behavior became more distraught, she had taken on more of their burden. She took charge of keeping the financial records of his business. Daily, she cornered him — either late at night or before he left in the morning — to collect receipts, pay bills and account for all of his income. His business may be in shambles, she thought, but his records are indisputable.

She also had been supporting herself financially and paying the rent on their flat since early in Gulfstream's meet. Another's dilemma had become a window of opportunity for her and she had jumped at it.

The Chamber of Commerce for the nearby newly incorporated town of Obelia Cove had been set adrift when its original director embezzled the organization's entire working capital. The money was gone, even though the Chamber's books still indicated that a mid-six-figure balance was available. Lamenting over the Chamber's lot to Charleen while trackside two days after the travesty was discovered, Councilwoman Lottie Hargen, overcome with exasperation, confided, "I don't know what we're going to do!"

Nowadays, Charleen was rarely at the track. Her avoidance was part of a growing disgust with her life conditions, in general. She was at the track today only because Mitch had a horse entered in the next race. Last night, the horse's owner had given her a roll of money to bet. Most of it was for himself, but also included was enough to cover sizable Win bets for the trainer and jockey. Some owners did this out of superstition, others felt that it fanned encouragement.

"Where's that person now? In custody?" Charleen asked with a growing measure of interest. She and Lottie had moved over to one of the vacant benches. "Where's the money?"

"Gone. All gone," the councilwoman answered with a resigned whimper. "She's gotten away, I guess. Police are baffled. Vanished completely. The entire account's cleaned out."

At first, Charleen halfheartedly had played the part of a sympathetic ear, hoping the subject would change shortly. Something about her seemed to attract these sorts of soul-baring confessionals. This time though, as the councilwoman continued to elaborate upon the details of the town's misery, Charleen began imagining herself in the position of troubleshooter. Moments passed. She gazed toward the floor in front her. Lottie fidgeted.

"I've been handling Mitch's books for a while now," Charleen offered quietly. "Lottie, I've got time on my hands. Appoint me as your interim director or something. I'll go over things and see what we can do. One thing, though, once a week I want to convene with you and any other council member you bring along."

"I can get all of them," Councilwomen Hargen chirped with renewed vigor.

"No-no. Too many cooks . . . we'll never get anything done," Charleen advised. "You, Lottie, and one other one would be best — even better if the other member is different each time."

"That's the way you want it, Charleen, that's the way we'll do it," Lottie said, looking toward the ceiling, her anxiety visibly defused with relief. "Oh, thank you, Jesus!"

"I'll bet anything that's where the hitch was," Charleen said sternly. "You — not you, personally, but your council — hired someone whom you didn't check up on at all, or had some half-baked recommendations. Then you turned that person loose in the office without any system of checks-and-balances or any accountability whatsoever."

"Sounds as if you've been around more than we have," Lottie remarked helplessly.

"You've got to know one thing going in," Charleen said, all but ignoring Lottie's comment. "Some people are terrific . . . except when they get around money. I don't know what it is. Maybe they think they're just borrowing. Maybe they're angry about what they're being paid and feel that they deserve more. A self-imposed raise so to speak. Apparently it's like drugs. They just won't stop, or can't, unless you simply keep them away from the till. I mean totally. They're excellent workers otherwise. Just can't be around other people's money. I'm sure a psychologist could put it in better terms."

$$\Omega$$

During the next two months, Charleen convinced a solid majority of Obelia Cove's Chamber-member businesses to donate another half of what they had originally paid in annual dues to get the organization back on its feet. A picnic-in-the-park fundraiser, showcasing several local rock bands, added another nice piece of change to the Chamber's coffers, all of which was earmarked toward economic development and growth for the new town.

"The same thing is true here as in the horse business," Charleen told Lottie when they were alone after one of their meetings. "Our hiring practices might be OK. It's our firing practices that always seem to need work."

"We simply didn't take control over things the way we should have," Lottie nodded, agreeing that Charleen was clarifying the obvious. "Too trusting."

"A person might otherwise be acceptable . . . you know, well-behaved, respectful and with a good appearance . . . but still, at some point, jobwise, if they aren't cutting it, you've got to stop making excuses and cut 'em loose."

Ω

Just before leaving for the track on the Monday daybreak of Gulfstream's closing week, Mitch announced his decision to stay in Florida for the summer and run the remains of his stable at Calder.

"A trip to Mercury just doesn't add up this time. It'll be the first time in eight years."

His decision finally gave the situationally estranged couple a key to moving beyond their sickening silence. She was still awake when he came in late that night. For weeks now, she had been sleeping on the couch

"Mitch, we've been through for months," Charleen said quietly, sitting on the edge of the pullout couch. "I'm not sure we ever really got started. What sounded like a wonderful idea, at least to me, never really happened. We haven't been to bed together for weeks, and, even before that, we'd been ignoring each other."

"I know, Babes," Mitch said with an agreeing monotone. "I thought I'd be a better husband to you. Better than this, anyway."

"Oh, Mitch, we're both at fault," Charleen said with impatient resignation. "I'm to the point now where I just feel stupid hanging around here. When you make your move over to Calder, it's probably a good time for us to split up, too."

Mitchell, not once attempting to interrupt, stared at her with a tired, boozy look of defeat.

"What will you do, Babes?" he murmured offhandedly, seemingly beyond being affected by whatever her answer might be.

"You can probably keep this place," she answered. "The move between Gulfstream and Calder is of no consequence, distancewise. Everything's paid for. The rent's right. With your daily rates and your percentage from purses, you'll be in OK shape. Not rich, but making a living. Mitch, please make time to go over the books . . . every night, if possible."

"What will you do, Babes?" he murmured again, continuing to stand next to the nearby chair.

"Well, I'm not staying around here. I'm so sick of Miami and Florida, and everything about it," she said plainly. "Funny maybe, but I'm thinking about going back up to Mercury. I liked it there. Made some friends. And, I'm thinking about going back to school."

"You should," he said with a more emphatic tone. "You've got a lot on the ball."

"So do you, Mitch. Be yourself, for God's sake. Lay off the booze. That's not you."

The cat caught his tongue. She waited in vain, then answered more of his question.

"I'll let you know where I am as soon as I get settled. That way, we can take our time working out any legal details. I don't want anything but my freedom and to get on with it. We're in a self-made limbo here. If we don't do something soon, we'll wake up late-middle-aged, asking ourselves what the hell happened. By then, it'll be too late to matter."

Charleen winced at having resorted to using the word, hell.

"What kind of horseplayer am I?" Mitchell answered. "If I knew anything at all, I'd have seen this coming. All along, I just wouldn't give it the attention it deserved."

"I know . . . I know," Charleen answered, sadly sympathetic. "I'll have my stuff out of here by the time you get home tomorrow."

Then the deadening silence. As he moved toward the bedroom, she sank back into the couch.

When she arose in the morning, Mitchell had beaten the dawn as usual and already departed for the track. He left no note.

"You can tell by the number of payments you still have the community's confidence and respect at this point," Charleen said assuringly to Councilwoman Hargen over lunch at the local Arby's on her way out of town. She hadn't taken long to load the smallest trailer that U-Haul offers. Mostly clothes and toiletries, along

with a small redwood table-chair set and the wildly colorful lamp from "Aunt Martha". Her books and book-
shelves had been loaded first.

"Through it all you've been able to hang onto a
hundred-percent participation in this new round of
membership dues from the local merchants. But mark
my words, Lottie. If something like that ever happens
again, your Chamber of Commerce would be dead as a
doornail."

Lottie shook her head with an expression of quiet
thankfulness as Charleen handed her the bankbooks
accounting for the merchants' latest payments to the
Chamber.

"I'll make sure we form a review committee of three
council members to watch over the Chamber Director's
business . . . every step, just like you said," the councilwoman assured with stern determination. "Charleen,
I can't tell how much we all appreciate what you have
done for us. We were just too trusting before. I think
now, because of you, we've learned our lesson." Then,
after an uncomfortable gap of silence, "I'm so sorry
things didn't work out between you and Mitch."

"Seems we both fell into something that just wasn't
there," Charleen said awkwardly, revealing her disappointment. "Some sort of time trap, I suppose. I don't
know. Society seems to dictate when and how we're
supposed to do certain things to carry on a so-called
normal life. Whatever that is. A time to be born, to be in
school, to leave home, get married, have kids, so-on
and so-on. Sort of a predetermined destiny with built-in
pressures. For my purposes, I had left home earlier
than usually expected. Maybe I was just too desperate
to get back on track, get back in step with what people
expect you to be doing at a certain stage of life. Who
knows? If Mitch and I hadn't ever married, we might
still be enjoying some sort of happy relationship."

Starting up Interstate-95 after lunch, Charleen felt
that her time in south Florida hadn't been a total bust.
A failed marriage had been balanced by helping an entire community of well-meaning citizens regain their

self-respect and restore their fundamental vision of their future.

Ω

Driving under clear, crisp mid-Spring weather conditions all the way, and particularly mindful of hauling a trailer for the first time, Charleen reached the lights of Mercury on the evening of the third day. While passing by Valdosta, Georgia, early the first evening, after having swung over to Interstate-75 through Orlando, her usually trusty Plymouth began bottoming out when she pressed down on the accelerator. Then a terrible knocking sound.

A helpful gas station attendant correctly diagnosed the problem as a bad fuel pump, also recommending that she get a new passenger-side front tire. Unable to obtain a rebuilt pump until the next morning, Charleen overnighted at the nearby Comfort Inn. By noon, she was back on the road, fully confident that she was ready for anything that life's imps might throw in her path.

Though Mercury Downs's live-racing season wouldn't open for two weeks, Charleen found a clerk's position at the track's gift shop very convenient to her needs. The manager remembered her from her connection with Mitch and was happy to have someone he could trust. While the "real horses" weren't running yet, the track still catered to a year-round simulcast clientele, and enough souvenir business was routinely transacted to justify keeping the gift shop open.

Predictably, after the opening weekend's flush of frenzied enthusiasm, The Downs's trackside attendance never hit full stride until the Mercury Derby, which, along with California's Santa Anita Derby, was contested a week before the traditional Super Saturday series of prep races in Kentucky, Arkansas and New York. The Mercury Derby provided a final prep for trainers who wanted an extra week of rest before reaching for the Holy Grail of Thoroughbred racing.

When The Downs's racing season started, the gift shop added its other clerk, May Belle Atchafalava from

Louisiana's bayou area, who spent her winters as a mutuel clerk at New Orleans's Fair Grounds. She had been coming north and working in the Downs's gift shop ever since the track's first season.

May Belle was a degenerate horseplayer from top to bottom. Betting the ponies consumed her life, but not without some saving limitations. She always paid her bills and covered her living expenses first. Only then did she dump every remaining penny through the mutuel windows. Mercifully, she never borrowed.

May Belle knew all of the buzz words connected with insider trackside know-how. Unfortunately, she never bothered to learn the origins of the jargon or how it was supposed to be applied at any particular moment. Nor did she seem to care about the source of the information. As long as the "right words" were connected with a tip, that was enough to impress May Belle and have some of her money flow in that direction. When The Downs closed after the long Labor Day weekend, May Belle faithfully traveled back to Louisiana and stayed with her widowed sister in Hammond, across the river from New Orleans, until the Fair Grounds opened during the Thanksgiving Holiday weekend.

Ω

On Sunday during the Memorial Day weekend, Charleen spotted the same classmate whose name had escaped her the previous summer. She was talking to that same cigar-smoking track urchin whom Charleen had seen her with earlier.

"Hey, I know you!" the woman chirped as Charleen walked toward her after she had broken away from the cigar smoker. "We went to school together."

Some say there is honor among thieves. Well, the same can be said for the instant comradeship among ladies of the evening. If they aren't immediately into exchanging embellished descriptions of some of the quirkier Johns they've entertained, they are swapping stories about some aspect of how they got into the business. Charleen learned that the woman's name had been Carla O'Malley during her Florida Poly years. Now she was Bobbette Garvey.

"Call me Bobbie," the woman cheerfully insisted.

During a couple of her mid-afternoon breaks from the gift shop, over coffee, Charleen became cued in on the local scene. Bobbie said that mostly she worked through Hammy, but never for him. He served as her "information man" and her go-between, but all "Mercury gals" of any repute worked independently. Hammy wanted no part of being a master pimp over a stable of hopelessly dependent women. Nevertheless, all the ladies knew that the safest way to comfortably operate smoothly within The Downs's subculture was to maintain a constant line of communication with Hammy.

"I'll let him know you're interested," Bobbie said as the two pulled away from the table. "He'll never even give you a look if you come at him straight on." Then she giggled, "You've got to be properly recommended."

The following Thursday, while Charleen was checking her cash-drawer count, a muffled voice murmured to her.

"I'd like one of those red-and-white sweaters with the Mercury Downs logo," Hammy said, putting out his cigar in the upright cylindrical ashtray. "I'm not sure what size."

"Right this way, sir," Charleen answered, calmly leading the way to the folded sweaters along the back wall of the shop, and out of May Belle's earshot.

"Bobbie tells me you're a standup gal," Hammy said quietly, quickly looking her up and down. He knew how to look past an outer cover. "Christ, you could get a grand or more if you're any good at all. Bobbie said she filled you in a little. It's really that simple. You're on your own at 70-30. Fifteen percent allows me to eat and the other fifteen takes care of everything else. You know . . . protection, look-the-other-way stuff . . . Hell, you know what I'm talking about . . . You know the drill."

The entire time the two conversed, Charleen slowly kept busy, taking several sweaters down from the shelves and holding them up to Hammy's shoulders for sizing and approval. While talking astutely about the qualities of each sweater she suggested, her silent expressions assured Hammy of her familiar acceptance with what he was spelling out.

"Let's get one thing straight," Hammy kept his low tone while maintaining his usual slouch. "You're managing yourself. You're independent. I'm just one of your expenses. I'm just the information guy. All I need to know is what you're willing to do and where you draw the line. That way I can prioritize. When I get something, I just call and tell you where and when. All you have to be is confident that I won't put you into something you don't want. After that, how you handle business is up to you."

Throughout this elaboration of details, Charleen kept nodding with an expression of patient recognition. Hammy paused at momentary intervals while chomping down on a newly uncellophaned, unlit cigar, thereby feigning disapproval of each sweater she sized against his shoulders.

"I want my thirty percent as soon as it's convenient," he said in a whisper. "You won't work too often, but you'll make good money when you do. All tips are yours. I just want what's coming. Period. You go to the client's place, and, if there is ever any funny stuff, get out as soon as you can. But, for the record, I've never had any trouble with anyone. Things are cross-checked too much before you ever show."

With that, Hammy said he'd be back later for a sweater and departed. Charleen rejoined May Belle near the front of the shop.

"There's a queer duck," May Belle surmised.

"Yes. After all that, couldn't make up his mind," Charleen answered with practiced offhandedness. "Said it was for a friend."

Throughout her first summer at the gift shop, Charleen fastidiously maintained her plain, bordering on stodgy, image. Her carefully tinted long strawberry blonde-red hair was dutifully wound into a bun on the back of her crown. She usually wore soft-colored pantsuits and white frilly blouses, with a neutral broach on the lapel or a gold chain necklace with a small gold cross high on the chest. Her gaudiest item was her winged eyeglasses. In this fashion, she sculpted the cookie-cutter pretense of somebody's no-nonsense, frumpy secretary.

When she got a call from Hammy, down came the hair, in went the tinted contact lenses, up went the skirt to mid-thigh, and on went the pushup bra and the stiletto heels. By night's end, everybody was happy.

Charleen's upscale apartment was part of Bramblewood Estates, located off the far turn of the racetrack and considered to be a suburb of Goldspar. Every day, Bramblewood's elementary and secondary kids were bussed to their parents' choice from among several of Goldspar's private schools. To a person, Bramblewooders did their weekly shopping in Goldspar.

On a nice day, Charleen was within walking distance of her gift-shop job. She preferred renting to buying her own house or condo, grounded by the visceral grit that all of life's conditions are temporary. And, if so, why seek a pretense of permanency?

Her daily schedule made time for enrolling in early morning and evening classes at Mercury Community College. She was completing some basic pre-law degree credits. Beyond that, to obtain the pre-law degree that she wanted, she knew she would have to attend a four-year college or university. The closest available curriculum was one-hundred-fifty miles away, in another state, and would most certainly require that she leave her very satisfying gift-shop routine. So, she quietly, but fervidly, hoped nothing bad ever happened to Hammy.

For now though, Charleen had settled in as an integral part of the trackside community. In particular, her supervisor always voiced his thankfulness that she was one of his clerks.

"Your cash drawer always comes out to the penny, every day," he said one late August afternoon. "Truly commendable. May Belle's never comes out right. Doesn't seem to have her mind on what she's doing all the time. If it's any consolation though, she's over half the time, and under the other half. Guess it sort of cancels itself out over the long run."

"I don't know about all that," Charleen interjected directly. "But, I do know I like being around her as a fellow employee. She always treats people right."

The supervisor acquiesced immediately, putting his palms out in front with a nod to signal apologetically that he was sorry for having brought up the issue.

After the racing season ended and May Belle had headed for Louisiana, Charleen fell into a rigid schedule of schoolwork in the mornings, Monday through Friday, and opening the gift shop at noon, Wednesday through Sunday. Even her arrangement with Hammy had slowed to once every ten days or so, tailing off completely while Hammy went on his annual sojourn to Florida.

For Charleen, this otherwise insignificant span of banality became uniquely stamped when Mitch's and her divorce was finalized. Uncontested down to the bare bones by both sides, the agreement was simply a matter of exchanging signed documents through the registered mail ways. They had spoken very little over the phone during the entire process. When they did, each had been sincerely concerned about how the other was getting along. Then on Sunday evening, two weeks before the opening of The Downs's next live-racing season, she received an unexpected call from Mitch.

"Hi, Babes. How ya doing?"

"OK," Charleen answered with a tinge of apprehensive inquisitiveness. "How'd the Gulfstream season treat you?"

"Great . . . heckova lot better than last year," he said, pouncing on the opportunity to report his recent upturn. "A lot of my old owners have come back. Guess the grass wasn't any greener where they went last year. Picked up plenty of new business, too. Got one helluva three-year-old I'm going to ship up to New York for the Wood Memorial as his final prep. Had to scratch him out of the Florida Derby . . . a little heat in one of his joints. Didn't miss hardly any training, but didn't want to risk running him hard right then. All cleared up now. He's training terrific."

As much as she remained uninterested in all aspects of horseracing, Charleen found that she was truly happy to hear Mitch bragging about his return to success.

"I'm probably going to ship some horses to Mercury for the summer, too. That's how good things have been. I'm going to send this new assistant I've got with them. I'm going to New York. Ever been there?"

"No-o-o-o," Charleen answered, skeptically waiting for an involving punch line of some sort.

"Well, it's a great place," he said without changing stride. "Like the song says, 'If you can make it there, you can make it anywhere.' But, that's not the reason I called, Babes. . ."

Charleen responded with silent anticipation.

"There's some real bad crap going around down here . . . about you," Mitch said in an unwilling tone. "You know that Obelia Cove Chamber bunch that you were hooked up with? Well, apparently they're missing a lot more money."

There was an uneasy pause. This time Charleen broke in.

"Dammit! I told Lottie Hargen to be sure about the character of the next director they hired," she hissed into the phone. "That council was supposed to set up a watchdog committee to prevent that sort of nonsense."

"No-no," Mitchell cut in. "From what I hear, that's not it at all. It was when it came time for them to start collecting the next round of annual membership dues from their local businesses. They did an audit beforehand, and found no money in the Chamber's account. Nothing."

"Look, Mitch, there was more than two-hundred-thousand in that account when I left," she asserted. "I gave Lottie Hargen the bankbooks the morning I left. What you're talking about is just a bunch of idle gossip cooked up between you and the rest of your boozing buddies."

"No, no, no, Babes," he retorted. "Haven't had a drink in months. Learned my lesson about that. Never liked the stuff anyway. Just thought hobnobbing around the bars was a big way to drum up business. The more it slipped, the more desperately I drank. That's just so much history now."

"I'm glad to hear it, Mitch," her tone was fueled with encouragement. Shouldering the phone to her right ear, she hurriedly buttoned her white frilly blouse. Very soon, she was expected at the gift shop. Her supervisor could, of course, easily take care of any early customers. Regardless, she hated being late for anything.

"Christ, I didn't call you to blab on about that stuff," he said apologetically. "Look, when they did that audit, they found that all that money had been missing since the day you left."

"Oh, my God!" Charleen blurted, suddenly frozen with her left arm through the jacket of the light turquoise pantsuit she had chosen.

"They've got some half-assed statewide warrant out on you," Mitch said, ignoring her excitement. "Knowing you the way I do, I know the whole thing's bullshit. Apparently, after the first time money was missing, no formal complaint was ever filed against that director. And the cops never really made any effort to find her. Never even issued a warrant."

"Mitch, this really stinks," Charleen shot back. "This isn't a case of corrupt hired directors with their hands in the till. This is an inside job! And that Lottie's in the thick of it. Damn, she's some actress. The cops, too, for a chunk of the action!"

"One thing, Babes," Mitch pitched in. "Nobody down here seems to know where that first director went. Not a trace."

"Probably dead . . . shark or gator bait," Charleen said matter-of-factly. "Geez, I had car trouble just after I got into Georgia and had to stay overnight. They may have been laying for me farther up the line, maybe back over on I-95, thinking I wouldn't be turning west until

Savannah. When I didn't show as expected, they must have figured I'd already gone by or took another route."

The line was silent for a long moment.

"Looks like that whole town was created to line the pockets of the racketeers running the show, including cops," she said.

"If you haven't been bothered by now, they're probably willing to live and let live as long as you stay away and shut up about everything," Mitch said, attempting to smooth the situation.

"Is that what you would do, Mitch?" she answered impatiently.

"Hell, don't know what I'd do," he answered frankly. "I'm the kind of guy who wouldn't put myself in a position like that in the first place, for crying out loud. That's the trouble with you, dammit. You're always willing to be so damn helpful, without really looking before you leap. Caring about people who don't deserve a ounce of your attention . . ."

"Oh, cut it out," she snapped back.

"Christ, the only reason I'm back on my feet is because of the way you managed the details of my business and kept my books in order," he had plenty more to say. "When I began pulling myself together, everything was right there in black and white. All I had to do was start being a trainer again, the way I used to be . . . What are you going to do, Babes?"

"I don't know," Charleen responded with complete honestly. "A network like that . . . cops and everything. I'm going to sit tight, for now. What about your assistant? The one that's coming up here? He's bound to spot me. I'm working at the track."

"Armond? Don't worry about him. He knows the score. He's on our side all the way," Mitchell assured. "Some of the information he picked up was very helpful in putting the pieces of that Obelia Cove nonsense together. If you need to get a hold of me while I'm in New York, he's your man to see. That's about it, Babes. If anything more comes up, I'll be in touch right away."

"I'm happy for you, Mitch," she said with sincerity. "You're a great trainer. One of the best."

"Oh, yeah. I'm real great with horses," he agreed sourly. "If I only could've handled us as well while I had the chance."

Again the line was silent for a long moment.

"I know, Mitch, me too," she finally answered softly. But, by then the party at the other end had hung up and a new dial tone was blaring back into her ear.

22

SQUEAK!

"Ah gots tah tawk to 'em in persun," Maxwell drawled quietly, scuffing a dusty path as he approached Bagwell. Stopping by the Harrison barn area with the pretense of checking on Bright Boy's improving condition had become a semi-regular part of the writer's after-the-races beat. He normally had about four hours in between the last race and the deadline for next day's column. The final race on Sunday's card had gone off only minutes before and, since the track was dark on Mondays except for holidays, most of the backstretch help already had vanished, getting a jump on a day off. In the midst of the mass evacuation, the late afternoon shadows were stretching to absorb every open space.

Maxwell needed to talk to Hammerstan in person, and seemed troubled over how best to set up the meeting. He couldn't risk one of those across-the-table-type chats that he used with Lt. Huber. Hammy's street reputation lugged too much baggage.

"Try this on," Bagwell proposed after Maxwell mentioned his dilemma. "Spread the word that Bright Boy is being readied for sale by the current owners. I'll bring Hammy around as a prospective buyer. If we're careful, no one should suspect. Under normal circumstances, Hammy personally wouldn't be caught dead talking to the likes of you. I can guarantee this though, he doesn't like what happened to Mendoza anymore than I do."

Maxwell frowned at what Bagwell's "the likes of you" might be suggesting, then brushed all inferences aside.

"That's not far off the mark," he winked at Bagwell quietly, slipping out his barn-area dialect. "What the owners seem to have in mind is bringing this colt back fit enough to win first time out. They do want to get rid of him, and they're hoping a good performance will inflate his value. We don't have anything running Wednesday. Should be pretty dead around here all afternoon. Bring Hammerstan over anytime after the first post. I'll be here with Bright Boy."

The following Wednesday, Bagwell pried Hammy away from The Captain shortly after the horses came onto the track for the third race, but not without some balking.

"Are you fuckin' kidding me!" Hammy said in a harsh whisper. "You want me to talk to some goddamn cop I don't even know?"

Bagwell quickly got his way by stroking Hammy with the facade that he would be playing the part of a prosperous horse buyer.

"Ya know, I've thought a lot about owning one of these nags," Hammy said, sort of gazing upward. "I mean, standing in the winner's circle, getting my picture took and all that. Hell, let's do it. I'm depending on you, Baggie, that this one's on the up-and-up. No bullshit, right?"

Bagwell automatically knew that the best time to get other things done unnoticed was from the time the horses first appeared on the track until just after the race had been run. Everyone's focus narrowed to a frantic fever caught between watching the horses and navigating a path to the betting lines early enough to avoid being shut out.

Bagwell assured the elderly gate guard at the barn area entrance that Hammy was there strictly on business and would be with him at all times. The guard hesitated, then acquiesced with lingering reluctance.

The grayish overcast and light drizzle gave the afternoon a quieter, earthier backdrop, and heightened the smell of straw and horses. The air was absolutely still as the two approached the exhibiting shed where

Maxwell and Bright Boy waited. Bright Boy, covered in a red-and-white Harrison Stable blanket, nibbled at the grassy area inside the walking ring, seemingly unconcerned with human activity.

After acting out a ritual of introductions, Maxwell motioned for them to follow. He tied Bright Boy with a long lead to one of the braces under the outdoor shed roof of the showing stall, and then the trio of men walked back along the chain-link fence into the slight drizzle.

"There. Now we can talk," Maxwell murmured with a smile. "Nobody can get close enough to hear without us seeing them first."

"Aren't you a little concerned about letting that horse just be there on his own?" Hammy asked Maxwell directly.

"Oh, he's a damn ham," Maxwell answered, pointing over to the rigidly haughty Bright Boy who now appeared to be strutting, but in reality was standing perfectly still. "Conformationwise, he's an extremely attractive animal, and he knows it. As long as he thinks we're watching him, he'll stand there quietly and keep posing. Like the owner told me, 'Just bring him out when prospective buyers are around. He'll sell himself.' Personally, I like showing him off."

Hammy looked at Maxwell for a long moment, then at Bright Boy, and then back at Maxwell. "Talking to a cop is like going to the dentist, knowing you've got cavities," he winced at Maxwell.

"Carson said you wouldn't get a kick out of this," Maxwell smiled out of one side of his mouth.

"I don't know what Baggie told you to expect from me, but I can't be of any help," Hammy said. "Believe me, if I could finger anyone for you, I'd do it. What was done to Mendoza is the pits. Look, all I heard is that some connected jerks thought they could get their hands on some easy money with Mendoza's cooperation. The commission got wind of it almost as soon as it happened, and told the track to hold the payoff. Apparently there was a leak . . . and I'm telling it to you the

262.........Getaway Money/Joule

same way it was coming down to me from various sources . . . no names, no nothing. Anyway, the play-boys got wind that the payoff had been frozen and that the Illinois simulcast outlet where the ticket was sold was being staked out. Probably other places, too."

Maxwell interrupted. "How the hell did the info about it being an Illinois spot get out?"

"Are you kidding?" Hammy said. "The amount of attention that Twin-Tri pot was getting during the days it kept swelling up became a nationwide promo for the track. They were loving every minute. Nothing that big had ever happened here before. Hell, as soon as the payoffs were officially announced after the second half of that Twin-Tri, the track's PA announcer told every-body there was only one winning ticket and that it had been sold at that Illinois outlet. Computers know that stuff automatically. Welcome to the world of hi-tech."

"I know, I know," Maxwell backed off willingly, sorry that he had asked. "It's the same way we were able to find which window the bet was made and which mutuel clerk sold it. She said, yeah, she remembered selling it, but her description of the guy kept changing a little each time she told it. We ended up with white male . . . average height and weight . . . maybe dark-brown hair, forget eye color . . ."

"Hmm, immediately narrows it down to under fifty-million guys . . . Makes your work infinitely easier . . . We should expect an arrest any moment now?" Bagwell nodded to Maxwell, taking the opportunity to get his two-cents in.

"Yeah, but they never announced that the payoff was frozen," Hammy picked up again, having heard enough of Bagwell's sarcasm to know when to ignore it. "That leaked somehow. I'd say you've got internal prob-lems. Hell, if I ran my business that way, I'd be out of business. And probably dead."

Pausing momentarily, Hammy realized he felt com-fortable with Maxwell. Without urging, after neither of the other two chose to speak, he went on.

"Right away, the playboys hunkered down and started stewing over ways to pry the payoff loose. As time went by, that just got them madder and madder. Seeing it's kinda hopeless, in a fit of frustration, they decide to send a message. What happened to Mendoza wasn't a simple rubout. It was a fucking ritual. Christ, talk about throwing good money after bad. It must have cost them a shitload to hire the sadistic mechanic who did that one. These guys aren't worried about the payoff anymore. They're into the principle of the thing."

"Few things worse than that," Maxwell rolled his eyes.

"Look, whether they ever cash that ticket or not, those guys think that money's theirs. Period," Hammy was deadly earnest. "Start fucking around about that, and start praying."

"Ah, bully tactics won't work here," Maxwell scoffed. "More likely to get them caught."

"A couple of things I've put together from what I've heard, but I don't see how they can help," Hammy tried another approach. "Number one, the bet was made at that Illinois outlet, so I think the guys who master-minded this thing with Mendoza — if you can call it that — are out of Chicago. Also, once the cat was out the bag, I think these guys went up a notch or two and pled their situation. This Mendoza thing was ordered and financed from above, maybe not right at the top, mind you. No matter, you guys keep monkeying around with this, it's gonna get real messy."

"It isn't already?" Bagwell interceded.

"Already is one thing, Baggie," Hammy shot back. "What could happen is something else. God, you do not want to fuck around with these people. You've got to know where to draw the friggin' line, Baggie! They don't."

Maxwell intervened suddenly, "Sh-sh, someone's coming closer."

Two men unfamiliar to Maxwell hurriedly walked past the trio and took up positions along the fence at the end of the stall's walk area. They began looking toward Bright Boy straight-on, pointing and chatting vigorously.

"Look, Mister," Bagwell said in regular tone, directing his facade toward Maxwell. "You say this horse is a good horse. You'll have to do better than that. What the hell does good mean?"

"Wall-l-l-l, ya know, suh," Maxwell drawled, reverting to his backstretch dialect. "Gudt means gudt. Reel fine racehaws. He kin go like hell."

"Yessiree, that tells me everything . . . thank you," Hammy said with mocking sarcasm. "They're going to be asking the upper part of six figures. maybe even seven for this horse. If I'm going to shell out that kind of cash, I want a little more assurance than he's a nice horse."

"Actually he said he was a good and fine horse," Bagwell grinned back, trying to help fill the air with meaningless conversation. "Nice might not have anything to do with it. You're switching one word for another altogether. But, I'm more concerned about the differences in meaning for the same word. What means good to this fellow might not mean the same thing to you."

Hammy and Maxwell both stared at him inquisitively with slight smiles.

"Look, take the word 'gay' . . . There's a great example of how a word has rapidly evolved into a totally different usage in our culture," Bagwell pressed on, watching Hammy begin to nervously shift his feet back and forth, while Maxwell smirked and picked up a nearby rake. "Somebody walks by and says in passing 'How you doing?' If you answer 'I feel gay,' that's probably going to give the other person reason to pause."

"So, what's the point?" Maxwell played along.

"Half a century ago, no one would have batted an eye," Bagwell portrayed equal seriousness. "All the word meant was that you were happy . . . exhilarated. Can't be used that way at all anymore. No siree. Gay is strictly part of the homosexual vernacular these days."

As the level of conversation among the trio rose, the two men at the end of the fence began looking over.

"Well hell, I've seen enough," Hammy said with harsh irritation. "I'm going back over to the grandstands where I can smoke. I'm still going to wait and see how this sonafabitch runs in a race before deciding anything."

As Hammy began walking on the path toward the barn area gate, the two men at the end of the fence moved in the other direction, down the row of fences and away from Maxwell and Bagwell. Maxwell folded his hands over the top of the rake handle, leaned down on it and rested his chin on his hands.

"Yep, words are powerful if you know how and when to use them, or not use them," he smiled. "That O.J. trial showed that. When that showboat lawyer — F. Lee Bailey — asked that investigating officer — Detective Mark Furman — if he ever used the word nigger . . . and Furman got all flustered and said no, he never had. Geez, how the hell can you be a law-enforcement officer in a large metropolitan place like Los Angeles and say that you never used the N-word?"

"Seemed strange, didn't it?" Bagwell smiled.

"Strange? You realize how many bar fights there are every Saturday night in a city like that?" Maxwell answered. "Hell, Furman didn't have to be using that word in anyway derogatorily . . . just descriptive in his reports. Hell, you get a bunch of more-than-half-drunk hotheads together, and pretty soon a couple of them are going to be squaring off. Somebody's gonna call somebody else a nigger and then the fun begins."

"Yeah, all Furman had to say was that he never used it a way that was meant to demean anyone," Bagwell nodded, "and then explain how he had to use it professionally. The way he came off by saying that he never used that word, the reaction from anyone with any sense was 'Bullshit, I'll bet he uses it all the time!' Forget whether the bloody glove was planted. The way he answered that part was enough to discredit him."

Although the drizzle had let up just before Hammy departed, the afternoon remained blandly gray and still, and now the two men from before returned to their spot at the end of the fence and were eyeing Bright Boy again.

"You know, that N-word isn't going to go away, no matter how much the politically correctors scream," Bagwell said in a regular tone. "It might be losing some of its fightin'-mad steam, but it's going to stay out there. Not as much as fuck, of course. That has to be the king of futile expression. Geez, as a noun, verb or adjective . . . sometimes all in the same frigging sentence."

"What would we do without it?" Maxwell smiled.

"Nowadays though, on prime-time TV sitcoms, with the right timing in the right situation, with the right tone and inflection, the N-word gets a cascade of laughs."

"I know . . . I've seen and heard it," Maxwell responded plainly. "Even so, there are plenty who still think it's never a good idea. Also, whenever you see that sitcom stuff, it's always one black calling another that. Anytime you see a white calling a black that, it's either right before or in the midst of violence."

They both paused for a moment, looking over at the two men at the end of the fence who were just standing quietly.

"I feel the same way about the N-word as what we were talking about with 'gay' before," Bagwell took up again, consciously lowering his voice while making sure it could still be heard from a distance. "It, hopefully, will evolve into a very different usage, too. To me, the word is colorless."

"You're losing me," Maxwell tilted his head.

"In one of the places I lived before coming to Mercury. . . and I won't say where because it doesn't matter. . . on our block there were these two families side-by-side. One black, the other white. The black family kept their place immaculate. Always cut the lawn, had cheerfully beautiful flowers all over the place and nice hedge, and a big Irish setter that the kids took turns walking. Right next to them was this white family's place that was a real eyesore from a long way off. Three or four vicious dogs chained at various places along the sides of the house. No shelter. Poor things barked incessantly, rain or shine, day or night. Couple of cars jacked up on the front lawn. Lawn, hell! Dirt and weeds . . . fine crop of dandelions. The house needed a paint job and a lot of stuff fixed. Get the picture?"

"Seen it plenty of places."

"To me, the white family was a bunch of niggers and the black family fine upstanding citizens who made a positive contribution to the neighborhood and were an asset to the entire community just by being there."

"Shakes out that way, doesn't it?"

"And, that's what I think a nigger's going to turn out to be in the long run. Anybody who can't take care of what he's already got and is responsible for, and yet keeps right on grabbing for more without any regard for anyone else. Nothing color about it."

"You've got a heavy chore on your hands."

"Hell, those guys from Enron, Tyco, WorldCom and the rest of them who were indicted for grabbing millions and millions of dollars, and ripping people off? They're all white guys in white collars, as far as I know . . . and they're all niggers, too."

The two men at the end of the fence apparently had seen what they came for. They pulled away from the fence and began walking toward the entrance to the inside.

"Sounds like a tall order to me, sport," Maxwell nodded amusedly to the side. "Trying to turn white folks into niggers. But, who can say?"

As the two others entered to inside of the barn, a tall man in an ordinary beige raincoat and felt hat stepped out from the shade and approached them.

"What are those three fellows out there talking about?" the man asked them directly.

"You wouldn't believe it," the one in the red and black flannel shirt answered. "Some stuff about homosexuals being gay, and something about white people being niggers. Funny thing though. That stable boy's accent seemed to change when the subject did. We really weren't paying much attention. We heard that nice looking bay colt out there is for sale. You the owner?"

The tall man glared back as he pulled a cigarette from a half-empty packet of Winstons and lit it with a cylindrical blue Bic lighter.

"No," he said sharply, and walked back into the darkness of the shed area. In the midst of the grandstand crowd on this dank afternoon, his raincoat would dissolve him into a sea of anonymity, especially if he removed his hat.

The two men frowned at each other, shrugged and walked toward the gate.

"This Hammy fellow seems like the type to keep his mouth shut when he wants to," Maxwell said quietly. "Fill him in as much as you need to, and get him to spread our story about Jarvis and the Grand Jury. If he's all that you say he is, that might stir up the monkeys."

Bagwell stayed with Maxwell for a few more minutes, then headed back over to the grandstand side. Hammy was waiting.

"What the hell kind of crap was that!" he shrilled. "He already knew everything I could tell him. That's all I need . . . being seen standing around shooting the shit with some goddam cop."

"Christ, Hammy, keep it down," Bagwell murmured as they walked over to the trackside rail and leaned against it, looking toward the infield tote board. "You're the only one who knows he's a cop. I'm the one who told him you could be trusted. Besides, you're right. He won't bother you again. If you get something, tell me . . . and, if need be, I'll relay the message. But, keep shooting your damn mouth off and you're right. You'll attract attention. Now, here's the real reason I took you over to see the cop, as you put it."

Thoroughly, Bagwell explained the details of the Jarvis ruse and what he wanted from Hammy.

"Just put it out in the form of a rumor . . . that should be enough," Bagwell suggested. "Jarvis'll be around the barn area for people to see, which should help confirm your rumor."

Hammy gazed at Bagwell through his thickly pre-scriptioned bifocals and gave a deep sigh. "Well, OK," he nodded, then chuckled. "I'll bet you don't even have a horse for me in the next race?"

"No," Bagwell said flatly.

"Great . . . so answer me this, Mr. Wordsmith?" Hammy said, turning around and looking up into the stands as he leaned against the railing with his elbows propped on top. "Can't a gay guy also be happy? Are being happy and gay mutually exclusive? Must the word mean one thing, but not the other? Can't there be a gay, gay guy?"

Bagwell smiled and headed for the paddock.

23

COURAGEOUS OR BRAVE?

The twelve-horse field for the third race had finally been safely led into Mercury Downs's starting gate. As a maiden-special-weights race for two-year-old fillies, literally two-thirds of the field were first-time starters. And this new, impossible-to-rehearse experience had been overwhelming. Frantic apprehension had boiled behind the gate. Ten minutes had ticked past the designated post time, but now all twelve fillies were jitterly in line.

Patiently working through the erratic hesitations, balkings and rearings, and a vet inspection of one of the fillies after she had blasted through the shut front door of her starting stall, the assistant starters and gate crew had performed with their usual yeoman-like persistence and genuine horsemen's savvy.

Now the head starter, with his finger on the electric start-button, watched from his infield-apron platform, waiting for all the lower legs below and heads above the separate starting doors to become still. At the same time, he listened for the barking shouts from his gate assistants to say all was ready from their side.

Suddenly, the Number-10 filly reared straight up. The thrown jockey grabbed for one of the stanchions on the left side, missed and fell into the stall, underneath the upright horse. With the full weight of her upright body, the frantic filly's left hind hoof drove into the jockey's upper right leg, snapping and shattering the femur as he lay on his back.

Using his left leg and elbows, the jockey wriggled desperately for safety, dragging his other now-useless leg. Before he could squirm free, the same hoof pile-drove downward again, this time into the middle of the lower part of the already ruined right leg, smashing the tibia and fibula and tearing the calf muscle away.

The panicked filly then reared over completely, coming down squarely on her back inside the stall. In the instant before the horse's body came crashing down, the jockey had semiconsciously elbowed his way from under the stall and now lay motionless in the dust in front of the starting gate, unaware of those silent, gut-wrenching seconds of eternity before the emergency crew arrived. In the background, others of the gate crew rushed to attend to the shrill cries of the inverted, terror-stricken filly as she kicked and arched her neck in a claustrophobic frenzy of thrashing helplessness.

"Oh God, no!" the assistant starter, at Sammy's side within seconds, blurted while turning away in stupefying anguish. Imprints from a smashing, grinding horseshoe were welling up with blood in the upper and lower parts of the jockey's pant leg. Both areas of impact appeared flattened into the dirt. "Hurry . . . please . . . hurry!" the assistant pleaded as the first-responding paramedic raced toward the jockey from the standby surveillance ambulance.

Ω

At 2:12 p.m. on Wednesday, August 9, 1995, Sammy Perez's potentially Hall-of-Fame racing career was smashed into the puffing dirt in the time it takes for a can of Pepsi to roll into a vending machine outlet after the select-button has been pushed.

Sammy Perez began riding at El Comandante racetrack in San Juan, Puerto Rico, on weekends when he was fourteen. Reaching a pact with his apprehensive parents, they begrudgingly agreed that he could ride only if he promised to stay in school. He was an excellent student and an even better jockey. And, despite his young age, Sammy had realized the value of being good at both.

At sixteen, Perez rode Gato Negro to win the Caribbean Triple Crown. Three years later, on Mercury Downs's ribbon-cutting day, he rode two horses for trainer Will Harrison and was immediately put under contract by Harrison's Conquering Karma Stable. Allowed to freelance whenever Conquering Karma did not have a horse entered, Perez became Mercury Downs's winningest jockey during the track's second season. His remarkable ability to find the winner's circle remained above the rarefied twenty-percent level. He won the second-annual Mercury Handicap aboard Harrison's versatile mare Bappy Booker; and soon he was shipping with Mercury Downs-based horses to tracks on the East and West Coasts to ride in big-purse races.

During the mornings before his accident, Perez had been personally working all three of Harrison's topnotch two-year-old colts, hoping that at least one would develop enough promise to be his first Kentucky Derby mount the following year. As he lay in the emergency room, passing in and out of consciousness, Perez pleaded with the doctors not to amputate his horribly mashed leg.

Along side two crescent-shaped titanium rods — one fastened by screws just above the ankle and below the knee, the other just above the knee and a several centimeters below the hip joint — doctors hoped enough adjacent bone mass was still viable to eventually knit and fuse for support. During the ensuing eighteen months of excruciating therapy, devotedly urged on by his wife Sondra, Sammy began to take steps without assistance. The nerve damage to the injured leg curtailed some of the potential pain; and, with a movable brace at the knee, he could manage on his own. Having retained free movement at the knee and hip joints, and by re-strengthening his lower-body muscles under the uncompromising guidance of Reggie, a militant physical therapist, Perez developed a unique gait for getting around with remarkable agility and swiftness. With his damaged leg permanently bowed inward, he wobbled to the left when swinging his right leg out and forward. Once firmly planted, he would straighten up and send his undamaged left leg directly forward.

Certain that Sammy was the best jockey that he had ever given a leg-up onto a saddle, Harrison, with his financial assistance and moral support, had helped the broken rider through his entire rehabilitation. Quietly accepting the truth that Sammy would never ride in a race again, Harrison patiently sat with the jockey through his predictable psychological journey of realization, despair, seclusion, self-pity, hatred, suicide contemplation and, ultimately, acceptance and determination.

"You're darn lucky to be here, son," Harrison confided to Sammy when he felt the time was right. "That filly's razor-sharp hoof missed severing your femoral artery by millimeters. Hell, you could have bled out right there on the track."

When Harrison, with agreement from the doctors, felt the time was right, he assigned Sammy to some general duties around Conquering Karma's barn area. Sammy responded by becoming a bubbling magma of red-hot energy. First mucking out stalls, doing some hot-walking and keeping the tack in immaculate condition, Harrison soon put him in charge of the physical operations for the entire stable.

Rather than heading over to the grandstand side when the afternoon's racing started, Sammy quietly wandered through the barn area, visiting with workers from other stables, sharing racing stories and giving hints on how they might make their places look a little better. The entire backside became his personal territory.

Sammy was like a kid during those December days approaching Christmas — a self-appointed scout and surveyor of all things under the tree. At every split moment, a kid always knows exactly how many presents are there and whom they are for. And, he knows within microseconds when a new one has been added, even if he wasn't nearby when the actual placing happened.

Mercury Downs's stable area became the gift pile beneath Sammy's Christmas tree every day of the racing season. He knew right away when someone had been hired, fired, promoted or changed jobs. He knew the names of all the horses, along with their exercise riders, trainers, owners, race-day jockeys, vets and grooms. He knew all the track officials and racing commission people. He knew when the delivery trucks were supposed to arrive, and when the garbage and stable muckings were supposed to be trucked away. He knew what cars, pickups, campers, vans, trailers and RVs belonged to whom and where they were supposed to be parked.

In the horseman's cafeteria, Sammy knew what everyone usually had for breakfast, and whether they drank coffee, tea, soda, milk or beer. He never gossiped. Everyone felt safe talking around him. Even more so, they came to feel safer by knowing that he was around.

During every racing season since his life-changing accident nine years ago, Sammy lived on the backside, while Sondra continued to maintain the family household in town. He also got into the habit of strolling the barn area at night as a sort of self-appointed extra security guard. He could move as well as anyone on the backside, swinging that right leg outward to the side and then forward in that wobbly gait which he now accomplished quickly and without pain. And, he added a smile and a nod whenever he passed by someone.

Ω

Bagwell's and Sammy's days together began when he was Mercury Downs's leading jockey. Bagwell had written several exclusive stories about the rider's meteoric rise through the jockey ranks, highlighting what the various horses he had ridden were like and what his favorite race had been so far.

Sammy had confided that he hoped his all-time favorite race was still somewhere in his future; but, if he had to pick one at the moment, it was certainly winning the Mercury Breeders' Cup Handicap aboard Rasp. Though he had gone on to win that same race twice since, it was his ride aboard Rasp, a big gray long-striding five-year-old gelding, that resided in his heart. That eleven-horse field had had a solid mix of front-runners, stalkers and closers for the nine-furlong race, with a guaranteed purse of $200,000.

True to form, Rasp and Sammy had fallen back into last by the time the horses headed into the clubhouse turn. Midway down the backstretch they were still there, as Rasp continued to obey Sammy's cues to stay relaxed. Suddenly, with only mild urging, Sammy said he could feel his height from the ground "drop down a level or two" as Rasp instantly lengthen his stride and began grabbing at the track. Hugging the rail, Rasp rapidly cut down seven opponents by midway through the far turn and was taking dead-aim on the leaders who were three-abreast across the track. Approaching the wall of horses as they came off the final turn, Sammy had urged Rasp to stay in along the rail, expecting racing room to open up inside as the horses fanned out off the far turn for the charge to the wire. Instead, Rasp defiantly bolted to the outside as the trio in front jammed in on the rail. As Rasp roared to the front, Sammy looked to his left and saw that the hoped-for opening along the inside had never materialized.

"I've never been on a horse before or since that was so intensely competitive and knew exactly what he had to do to win," Sammy told Bagwell in clear, distinct English with only the slightest trace of a Caribbean accent. "No matter how great of a jockey you think you are, if you don't have a great horse under you, it ain't gonna happen, baby. Bad jockeys can make good horses look bad, but it takes a good horse to make a good jockey look good. That day, Rasp made me look as good as I've ever looked."

With the hope of landing a Kentucky Derby mount ever on his mind, Sammy also told Bagwell that two of the greatest rides he had ever witnessed were Shoemaker's masterful surge between horses at the top of the Churchill Downs stretch and then through another momentary inside hole in mid-stretch to win the 1986

Derby with Ferdinand, and Bailey's flawless threading of Grindstone through traffic from fourteenth to first in the 1996 Derby, nipping Cavonnier at the wire by a gnat's eyelash.

"One error in judgment or effort, no matter how small, would have spelled defeat in either case," Sammy reflected with a longing sparkle in his eyes.

In a more recent interview, when Bagwell was doing a feature piece on the rough-and-tumble harshness of being a jockey, Sammy had reflected on his career-ending catastrophe.

"Eddie Arcaro once told me that the greatest fear for a jockey wasn't being killed out there," Sammy shared with a pause. "It was being so severely injured that you became a paraplegic and had to spend your remaining days in a wheelchair. Eddie said no, if something like that was going to happen, he'd rather go all the way. Becoming a paraplegic was a more horrible thought for someone with a jockey's super-aggressive, competitive nature. And Eddie must have been sincere about those feelings. Later, I saw him saying the same thing on national TV.

"But, you know, that day . . . and I still don't remember everything that happened . . . when I saw that horse coming down on me, I never wanted to live so much in my whole life."

24

EVERYTHING COUNTS

As soon as Cossie Jarvis agreed to act as a decoy for Jason's plan, Bagwell told Sammy to be doubly on the alert for anyone who didn't fit the daily backside routine.

"My good friend, are you implying what I usually do isn't good enough?" Sammy needled.

"I don't care how trivial or stupid it might seem or sound, old friend," Bagwell insisted, not in the mood to quibble with Sammy, "get ahold of me right away — anytime, day or night. Please don't worry about intruding on my privacy or any of that damn nonsense. Get ahold of me, please!"

Bagwell also had successfully cajoled and coerced Hammy into clandestinely spreading among his various no-goodnik colleagues the cooked-up reason for Jarvis's return, hoping the misinformation would flow to the planned target.

Exactly ten days after Bagwell had urged, something out-of-the-ordinary caught Sammy's attention during his evening meanderings. He came upon a rather small, plain-looking fellow in the vicinity of the Harrison stable. Sammy kept his distance at first, stepping into a darker place. The man quietly kept rechecking his watch. Suddenly, from the opposite entrance a familiar face appeared. Jarvis was casually making his nightly 10 o'clock visit to Bright Boy.

"Howdy," Jarvis nodded in passing. The man nodded a silent response. As Jarvis turned with complete affection to the colt, the man silently slipped into the shadows on the left side of the walkway and continued checking his watch.

Now Sammy made himself known.

"May I help you, sir?" he asked dutifully.

"Uh, . . . I hope so," The Churchmouse answered, startled for a millisecond, then stepping forward in a friendly manner. "Actually, I seem a bit lost. I'm just trying to find my way back out to the parking lot . . . without much luck."

"No problem, sir," Sammy answered dryly, masking his complete distrust of the man's stated intentions. "Just follow that path over there. You'll come to the security gate. The parking lot starts just beyond."

"Thank you very much," The Churchmouse smiled thinly as he began to hurry toward the path.

Sammy approached Jarvis who was still leaning at the side to the door of Bright Boy's stall, stroking the colt gently along the lower right jowl and talking softly.

"You know that guy?" Sammy asked.

"Never saw him before," Jarvis shook his head, continuing to stroke Bright Boy. "Maybe he's a buyer. Didn't say a thing to me though. Why? What's up?"

"Ah, probably nothing," Sammy said. "But, watch yourself. You never know."

"Yeah," Cossie answered, returning his attention to the colt. "Ya never do."

Sammy called Bagwell right away.

"Let's not screw around," Bagwell leapt into extreme urgency. "Grab the tape. Meet me at the paper. Bring Cossie with you."

Ω

Surveillance tapes became a security measure for many barns along the backstretch after Dancer's Image was disqualified from winning the 1968 Kentucky Derby. Following a lengthy succession of court battles, Calumet Farm's Forward Pass, the runner-up, had been declared the winner and awarded the Derby's first-place purse money. Dancer's Image was summarily disqualified because his post-race test showed a positive pres-

ence for the then-illegal pain-killing medication Butazo-
lidin, commonly referred to as "Bute."

Considered to be an aspirin for horses, Bute is regularly given to relieve soreness in leg joints. Back then,
horses could legally train while medicated with Bute,
but they couldn't compete in any official races in Kentucky with the substance in their system. Rule of
thumb was that Bute shouldn't be given within forty-
eight hours of a race in order to allow its residual af-
fects to wash out and not be at a detectable level during
post-race blood and urine testing.

The final outcome of the 1968 Derby had irritated
many bettors and elated many others. Because the results of the Kentucky Racing Commission's reversal
were not announced until the Monday after the race,
the results as "officially" declared on race day remained
the "official" payoffs. With a sting of irony, anyone who
had held onto their Dancer's Image win-tickets after
Monday's ruling could still cash them, even though the
horse had been disqualified. Likewise, tickets on new-
winner Forward Pass remained losers.

The yearlong series of appeals that ensued over the
commission's disqualification also showcased other
measures of unhappiness. Aside from accusations that
the commission had frivolously bent in favor of Calumet
Farm because of that stable's pervasive reputation in
American racing lore, at least two reasons worth considering were proposed for Bute having shown up in
Dancer's Image's test. No one seriously believed that
trainer Louis Cavalaris had purposely applied the drug
just before race time with the cavalier hope of getting by
the detention barn's analysis. Some felt that perhaps
Cavalaris had played the "Bute game" too close to the
forty-eight-hour threshold or that the horse was meta-
bolically slow in washing the residue out within the
usually assumed grace period. The other hypothesis
was sabotage. Had someone gotten to the horse with a
syringe while no one was looking?

Whatever the real reason, surveillance equipment of
all sorts was stepped up in barn areas everywhere

throughout America's racing circuit. Some of the stuff approached a sophistication worthy of national defense. Indeed, a strategically placed videotape camera or two might have helped Cavalaris's cause.

As a preteen, Bagwell had sat by the TV with his mother, watching Stage Door Johnny run away from Forward Pass in the homestretch of the 1968 Belmont, thereby denying the Calumet colt an immortalizing Triple Crown pedestal. To his credit, Forward Pass had won the middle jewel, the Preakness, while Dancer's Image had been disqualified from part of the purse again, this time for impeding other horses in the homestretch. His mother cheered the outcome of that Belmont, insisting that politics had influenced the "official" finish of that year's Derby more than who crossed the finish line first. Those Kentucky hardboots, Momma said, couldn't stand having an outsider like owner Peter Fuller from Boston win their beloved Derby.

Turned out Momma may have been more right than she knew, Bagwell had mused. Seems that the chemist in charge of those post-race Derby tests gave conflicting testimony during the yearlong investigation that followed.

Ω

By the time Sammy and Jarvis arrived at the newspaper office with the tape, Bagwell, Lt. Huber, Hammy and Charleen were already there. The early quartet could hear them coming up the stairs, Sammy cursing Jarvis when he tried to lend assistance.

"I never go any place where I can't make it on my own, dammit," Sammy scowled. "That way, I always know I can get the hell out of there on my own if need be!"

"OK-OK, suit yourself," Cossie shrugged. "Don't blame me if you fall down and break your damn neck."

"What the hell is he doing here?" Sammy barked as soon as the two reached to the top, glaring at Hammy and instantly mollified over being in the same room.

"Relax, he's on our side for now," Bagwell said sternly. "He hates what happened to Mendoza as much as the rest of us."

"You trust this creep?" Sammy said, not being put off in the least by Bagwell's show of confidence. "Guys like this are what give the track scene a bad name. I can't stand any of them. Christ, if you ever have to shake hands with one of these bastards, get your hands wet and then rub them in the sand before taking hold or else the bastard'll just slip right out like some slimy damn eel."

Hammy, having been called much worse, unflappably stepped in.

"Hey, Sammy, be nice" he said, calmly trying an appeasement approach. "Let's just call a truce for now. We can get back to who's more slimy than who later. OK? At least I don't go around sticking my snoot into everywhere it doesn't belong."

Bagwell, after waiting a long second to see if the duo had anymore to go over, turned the format over to Sammy.

"The Harrison stable area has one surveillance camera that scans the fronts of all its stalls and the entire walkway every twenty-four seconds at normal speed," Sammy explained. "The recorder has a capacity for two six-hour tapes. When the first one is full, the second one kicks in automatically. So, we change the tapes about every twelve hours as part of our normal workday. This routine continues during The Downs's entire racing season. We keep these tapes for at least a year before beginning to tape over them during the next season.

"Now, the one I phoned Carson about earlier tonight has all the earmarks of what he said I should be looking out for. Something about this guy bothered me a lot. Here's what I'm talking about."

The segment that Sammy was alluding to showed Cossie walking toward Bright Boy's stall with the horse's head and neck already protruding through the opened top half of the Dutch door, apparently in expectation of the jockey's nightly visit. None of the other horses along Harrison's row were in evidence. In the shadows across the walkway to the left, a shorter-than-average man stood. Then, from the right, Cossie spoke to Bright Boy and they nudged each other affectionately. Stroking the colt gently on his jowl, Cossie began talking quietly.

"We'll both show 'em, right out of the gate, won't we, boy?" he said in a low, confident tone while producing a peppermint from his pocket for Bright Boy.

Then, from farther to the left, there was Sammy slowly making his way toward Cossie. Suddenly, the man in the shadows and Sammy saw each other. The man in the shadows stepped forward. Sammy stopped the tape right there.

"He came toward me and said he was lost," Sammy described. "Said he was trying to find the security gate to get out. I think he was staking Jarvis or Bright Boy out, or both. Bothered hell out of me, especially with you telling me to be on my toes for anything strange. Then I remembered . . . after calling you, Carson . . . I think I've seen this guy before. I think he said he was lost back then, too!"

"Could it have been around the time when Mendoza got killed?" Lt. Huber broke in.

"Could've," Sammy answered hesitantly, trying to be carefully accurate, rather than overly accommodating. "Can't say for sure. But, it probably wouldn't be on the Harrison tapes anyway. Mendoza was staying in the general quarters with the backstretch help."

"Hold on a minute, you guys. I know this guy," Charleen, having remained silent and farthest away from the TV screen, suddenly spoke up.

"I thought you might," Hammy flicked his eyebrows and nodded. "That's why I practically insisted you come along."

"Yes. Well, he's not much," Charleen kept on. "I mean, he just lays there on the bed and plays with my undergarments and himself while I walk around the room naked. Didn't want me to go anywhere near him.

Big tipper though. Said he wished I had been around last time he was in town. Trouble is, I can't tell you where he might be staying. One of those rare times when I made the arrangements for the room and he showed up. You remember, Hammy?"

"Yeah, I remember," he growled. "Just the other day. But, I never saw him in person. Shaky picked up the request, checked him out and got hold of me. Shaky's out of town somewhere now. Won't be back for about a week or so. Damn, he probably knows where this guy's holed up."

"Before I started with this creep, we chatted a little," Charleen broke in. "A lot of them think they have to break the ice that way. Geez, you'd think they were getting ready to ask me to the prom."

She paused briefly, recalling details, then. "Said he was in town on business, but then wouldn't say anymore about it . . . even though, as always, I pushed it a little. Usually, they want to brag a bit. Play the big shot. Part of getting in the mood. But, this guy clammed right up."

"But, Jesus, as out of place as this guy might have seemed, he sure doesn't look like he could harm anybody," Sammy said, noticeably puzzled.

"Bingo, you just won the kewpie doll," Lt. Huber blurted out before he could catch himself. "Sorry for the outburst, folks, but that's precisely what makes guys like this so successful . . . and hard to catch. Few people ever notice them. Even if they do, they're always grossly underestimated. Appearing absolutely harmless is their biggest advantage. Don't look like they could harm a fly."

"He probably can't," Hammy agreed, taking on an urgent aura of wisdom as he pointed to the screen. "This guy's a go-between . . . a scout, an advance info man. Doesn't want any part of being around for the ruff-stuff."

"Yeah, you know all about that, don't you," Sammy glared, as Hammy reached for a cigar.

"OK, knock it off," Bagwell interceded. "And, there's no smoking in the building, Hammy. Especially those cheap ropes."

"What do you think, Baggie," Hammy said kiddingly, apparently unoffended by Sammy's or Bagwell's comments. "Does this Bright Boy get your vote for Horse of the Year? I keep reading in your columns about he's the right stuff and he's ready."

"I don't vote for Horse of the Year anymore," Bagwell reacted with bland seriousness. "Haven't since 1990, when Calumet's Criminal Type got the vote over Unbridled."

"What the hell's that got to do with anything?" Hammy frowned.

"Any horse who wins the Kentucky Derby and Breeders' Cup Classic in the same year has got to be Horse of the Year in my book," Bagwell was in full form now. Hammy had hit upon an open sore. "Oh, I know, Criminal Type won five stakes in the middle of the year, including back-to-back million-dollar purses. But, conveniently perhaps, just when the other serious contenders were gearing up for those big fall races, Criminal Type came up with a career-ending injury. He wasn't around for a lot of the head-to-head combat with the big boys. Oh hell, I'm not saying Criminal Type wasn't a nice racehorse . . . and Lukas did a helluva fine job training him. But, he didn't even carry top weight in his races, let along start dragging around a whole bunch of pounds like the real top ones end up doing. I just think politics did Unbridled in. The Calumet factor again. Anyway, in my best childish fashion, I got peeved and told the Eclipse outfit where to put their Horse-of-the-Year ballots in the future."

"That fixed 'em, didn't it?" Hammy chided.

"Ironically, even with yet another Horse of the Year in tow, Calumet, because of absurd mismanagement through marriage, soon collapsed into an irrevocable bankruptcy," Bagwell wasn't about to let his mental archives on the subject remain unfinished. "Their golden-goose stallion — ultra-insured Alydar — was mysteriously found with what turned out to be a life-ending injury. And, that was just the tip of the iceberg. The whole crumbling mess was a drama of Gothic-horror proportions to anyone with a sincere appreciation and love for the underpinnings of American horse-racing lore."

Bagwell paused, stared at the floor and shook his head sadly, "Calumet."

He had been speaking mostly for Lt. Huber's and Charleen's benefit. The others already knew a lot about Calumet's crash-and-burn.

"How the hell did this guy know enough to be there right when Cossie was making his nightly visit to Bright Boy?" Sammy asked, urging everyone back on task.

"Simple. Did his homework," Hammy assured him. "These guys are wizards at walking into a local bar or one of the watering holes at the track, ordering one beer, and coming out of there with enough info to fill a bible."

"Must be more than pretty good at cutting the bull-shit from the fact, too," Lt. Huber noted with a confident tone of experience.

"With this Bright Boy-Jarvis thing, hell, all he'd need to do is go to our public library and dig up Bag-well's columns from the local newspaper," Hammy said, looking directly at the lieutenant. "In nothing flat, he'd be a damn expert on the subject."

"Yup, you never know in what way your words are going to reach people," Bagwell said as an expression of approval for Hammy's line.

"He was probably just shoring up a few details when you caught up to him in the stable area," Hammy said, nodding toward Sammy. "Don't ever think these guys are stupid or inept. They only look harmless."

"Sammy, start the tape from where you left off," Bagwell requested with some irritation.

The continuing tape showed The Churchmouse walk away to the left, and Sammy go over and briefly visit with Cossie and Bright Boy. After Sammy left, Cossie stayed with Bright Boy a few moments more, patted him gently along his neck and then said good night.

"Wait a second," Bagwell said to Sammy hurriedly, tapping him on the upper arm. "Run that back! Go back to just after you walk away."

Everyone, their attentions having begun to wane, now moved in closer to the screen with renewed interest. No one said a word.

Sammy rewound the tape to where Bagwell asked. Again, Sammy walked away and Jarvis bid Bright Boy good night.

"Same as before," Hammy sniped. "So what?"

"There!" Bagwell suddenly pointed. "What's that? Run that part back again."

During the next sweep of the camera, after Jarvis had walked away, there was no mistaking. Ten feet farther to the left, and deeper into the darkness than The Churchmouse's initial position, suddenly the burst of flame from a lighter and then the red-glow tip of a tall-from-the-ground cigarette ember. Then, when the camera swept by again anxious seconds later, nothing but a hefty puff of smoke drifting into the lighted walk area.

"Run it back again," Bagwell ordered. "This time, stop it and zoom in."

This time, when the lighter flicked on, the faint midsection of a dark shirt and an equally indistinguishable striped tie were seen against the glow. Worse, when the lighter was raised to the cigarette tip, no hint of facial features could be developed.

"What the hell is that all about?" Hammy broke the silence while several more rewinds and enlargements were failing to add any clarity.

"It seems to go like this," Lt. Huber offered plainly. "Jarvis was watching the horse, Mr. Lost there in the shadows was watching Jarvis, Sammy ended up watching Mr. Lost . . . so then, what the hell was Mr. Cigarette watching? I'll bet you anything, Mr. Lost didn't know Mr. Cigarette was there, and doesn't know who it is."

"So then, where does this Mr. Cigarette fit into all this?" Sammy asked with worried impatience. "I never even knew he was there! I don't like that."

"I've never seen that Mr. Lost before in my life," Hammy said, telegraphing that he had seen enough and wanted to go anywhere where he could smoke a cigar in peace. "Maybe Mr. Cigarette's just a straggler who didn't feel like being seen. Who can say? If there's nothing else, gentlemen, I'd like to scram. I've got people to see."

"Me, too, gents," Jarvis said. "Coming, Sammy?"

"Think I'll stick a while," Sammy answered. "Thanks for the lift out here, though."

Jarvis followed Hammy and Charleen down the stairs. Charleen, at Hammy's urging, had agreed to be part of the gathering only after reaching the understanding that Bagwell would approach Lt. Huber later about her Florida situation. She wanted the lieutenant's advice and, if possible, his help. Bagwell had promised to do his best.

"I'm sorry, Mr. Bagwell," Sammy said after the three departers were out of earshot. "I hope I didn't disrupt things too much. But, that Hammy's such a sleezeball of the first order. I swear to God, he's so crooked that when he dies they're going to have to screw him into the ground to bury him."

"Sammy, I don't agree with Hammy's chosen life-style," Bagwell answered. "In all fairness though, he didn't like being here, either. So happens he's as pissed off as the rest of us about what happened to Mendoza. Wants to help in any way he can to nail the sons-of-bitches. If it gets out, Hammy could very well be looked upon as a rat by a lot of the people he does business with on a daily basis. Man, that wouldn't be pretty."

Silently Bagwell wondered what the odds were that the six people who had convened here tonight would ever come this close together again. These people weren't just ambivalent toward one another. Hell no. They actively avoided each other.

"Mr. Lost there," Lt. Huber motioned to Bagwell, then pointed at the now-blank TV screen. "I've seen him a couple of times recently at Charlie's Wagon Wheel, during the dinner hour. I tend to believe Hammy's right. This guy's the setup man on some sort of relay mission. Very likely he's done his job and is getting ready to fly the coop, if he hasn't already. We're going to have to move fast . . . tonight. Get me the best shot of Mr. Lost's face you've got and make some prints. If he's eating at the Wagon Wheel, chances are he's also been staying in one of the joints nearby, along motel alley . . . I don't know what the hell to make of that Mr. Cigarette. Looks like somebody's watching all the watchers."

25

FRAILTY OF FORTUNES

"Look, I know it's late as hell." Lt. Huber roused his on-duty staff with the gruffness of a locker-room inspirationalist as soon as he arrived at the station. "We've got to do this tonight. Hope to hell we're not too late already."

He gave copies of The Churchmouse's close-up portrait and full-length photo to the two regular-shift patrolmen while explaining how the three of them would split up and begin canvassing the motels in the Wagon Wheel restaurant's neighborhood. While he briefed the dispatcher with some procedural details, she in-turn assured him that two part-time patrolmen were on their way in, ready to cover for the two regulars now heading out on special detail.

"This guy doesn't look like he could blow over a feather, lieutenant," the patrolman closest to Lt. Huber shared quietly.

"Oh Christ, you, too?" Lt. Huber barked back. "Look, you clowns, for your own safety and survival, the last thing you want to do is underestimate the guy in this picture. Stay on your toes, dammit!"

The room fell silent. Satisfied that he had made his point, he began reiterating the obvious.

"You're probably going to have to wake the desk clerk up at each place. They gonna be a bit squirmy. Don't let them put you off. You know these guys — and gals — operate in some sort of don't-ask, don't-tell zone. Make sure they take a good long look at these pictures. If you have any doubts whatsoever about how they

react, stay on them and keep at them until you're satisfied. If you catch a break, notify me immediately. And
then keep the damn clerk in sight until I get there. I
don't want them volunteering any help to their patrons.

"One other thing. Before you do anything at each
place, cruise the parking lot. Check for airport rentals
and which doors they're parked in front of."

The two patrolmen were the youngest, most inexpe-
rienced on the current Mercury police force. Accordingly, they regularly pulled the weekday night shift. For
tonight's purposes, however, their youthfulness didn't
bother the lieutenant. Both had come to the force with
glowing credentials from the state police academy. They
had been out on patrol when radioed to return to the
station ASAP. An hour after midnight the trio began
contacting their first motel clerks. All three, now
dressed in plain clothes, drove unmarked vehicles.

Right off, Lt. Huber came up dry. The clerk, still in
his chair behind the desk, instantly assured the detective that no one fitting Mr. Lost's description was staying at Restful Nook. In keeping with the clerk's assurance, the desk log indicated that everyone staying there
was a first-nighter. Convinced that the clerk's explanation was on the level, Lt. Huber still wondered whether
Mr. Late might be changing motels every night or so to
cleverly diminish his chances of being traced or becoming well-recognized simply through familiarity.

With the neon-red vacancy sign still lit out front,
the front desk was dark at Lt. Huber's second stop, the
E-Z Inn. He pushed the night-bell button hard. Getting
no response, he rang harder. Soon, a short, swarthy
fellow with ruffled, thinning black hair and black-
rimmed round glasses approached the front door while
still fighting to put on his pale blue terry-cloth bathrobe.

"Veddy gute, sir," the man smiled sleepishly, opening the door. "I hab a cuppel of dubbels left."

"No-no, Najindra " Lt. Huber said cordially, feeling
just a twinge badly that he had aroused the drowsy little man. "I just need your help with something special."

Over the years, Lt. Huber had, during routine rounds, become familiar with most of the local motel clerks. Najindra Rao and his wife and four daughters were the sole operators of the E-Z Inn, on call at all hours every day. Each year, shortly after The Downs's season was over, the Rao family shut down their motel for a month and traveled to the old Bombay vicinity to visit close relatives.

Lt. Huber showed the man Mr. Lost's pictures and produced his detective's shield at the same time simply as a matter of protocol. Instantly, the man's eyes widened. He was fully awake now.

"Have you seen this man around?" Lt. Huber asked quietly.

"Hee's a baad mahn?" the clerk's accent quickened.

"No-no, we'd just like to know if he's here," Lt. Huber asserted calmly.

"I beliebe dat is Meester Barner in Room 144, down arun dee back," the man pointed in a wide sweeping arc for emphasis.

"Make sure, OK," Lt. Huber urged, holding back a sudden rush of hope. "How long's he been staying here?"

The clerk held up his right hand with the index finger pointing upward and, with a nod, walked over to the guest log.

"Hee's bin heer since las Turzdee, sir," the clerk said after several moments. "I beliebe hee's in hees room right now."

With all due respect to Najindra's accent, Lt. Huber mused, the guest log indicated that Mr. Lost actually had signed in using the name Thomas Varner. Makes sense that Mr. Late would do most of his scouting on the weekend when track attendance reaches its peak congestion. Blending in almost anywhere he wanted to go would be easier.

"Najindra, I'm depending on you not to contact this Mr. Varner for any reason," he requested strongly, yet congenially, to the little manager. "We might be around here for a few hours. Please don't become alarmed, Najindra. This has nothing whatsoever to do with you. I just need your cooperation."

"Veddy gut, Officer Huber," the clerk smiled nervously. "You hab my vard. My lips are see-elled"

Within minutes the other two officers met Lt. Huber at the entrance to the E-Z Inn's parking lot, parked their vehicles and climbed into his back seat.

"The clerk said that Mr. Lost probably is alone in Room 144," the lieutenant explained as he pulled into a parking spot between a pickup and a compact, directly across the lot from Room 144. From there, they had an unobstructed view of the door.

"We'll watch from here for a while," Lt. Huber instructed with a relaxed murmur. "I'll bet that compact in front of his door is his cheap rental. Budget conscious little bastard."

"Who isn't?" Lt. Huber wasn't sure which one muttered it.

"I'm hoping that a bigger fish will show up," he explained quickly. "If all we end up with is Mr. Lost, we're going to up a friggin' creek without a friggin' paddle. Have your pieces ready."

The two patrolmen traded glances.

"Neither of us have ever fired our pieces at anyone, lieutenant," Patrolman Don Keifer chirped from directly behind. "I've never even pointed it at anybody."

"Neither have I!" Billy Powell agreed, looking over worriedly from the back passenger's side.

"Look, just be ready," the lieutenant said calmly. "I'm not expecting Gunfight at OK Corral. Just remember the things you learned at the academy . . . and don't shoot me. "

For long minutes, the lieutenant cultivated the silent contemplation that consumed the vehicle, then he spoke again.

"He's all paid up at the motel, so he's probably planning to head out early. If he starts to move, I'll dump you two where your cars are parked. We'll use a tail relay on him."

The three leaned back in their seats, quietly watching the door. A half-hour passed, during which several cars pulled into parking spots and patrons went into their rooms.

"The bars must be closing," Officer Keifer flatly broke the silence, then abruptly changed the subject. "Do you think bastards like what did Mendoza in go to church?"

"It's a non-issue . . . forget it," Lt. Huber said matter-of-factly. Still, Keifer's question was one more indication how much the Mendoza killing had scarred local feelings. The lieutenant hadn't so much as hinted to either of these junior patrolmen that tonight's activities had anything to do with that particular case.

"Why, lieutenant?" Keifer seemed sad.

"You start worrying about everybody's private lives, you'll go nuts. You'll get enough of that without going looking for it. Let it go."

"No. Evil people can't possibly hope there's a hereafter with any sort of accountability? Can they, lieutenant?"

"I suspect you've had a debate of this nature with your college buddies . . . more than once I'd say. Didn't get much solved, did you?"

Officer Powell hadn't said a word, and didn't intend to. He hated any discussion that tampered with his beliefs. He silently begged for an end to it.

"We never changed each other's minds, if that's what you mean?" Keifer shrugged. "We always figured there were other people who knew more about those things."

"Yeah, right," the lieutenant scoffed. "Look, we have our hands full getting bad people off the streets and making good people feel safe. Are they breaking the law or not? That's plenty. You start monkeying around with what else everybody's doing . . . well, I don't know what to tell you. Where do you go with that?"

Ten minutes of an eerie silence passed before the lieutenant spoke again.

"Tell you what, boys. Let's take a hypothetical. Suspects like the one we're tracking tonight aren't common thugs. They're more crafty and clever than you can imagine. They never come straight at you. In some ways, I'd think they'd be probably more likely to go to church than most."

Lt. Huber gave the appearance of being completely relaxed. The other two shifted positions frequently with frayed uneasiness.

"Sons-of-bitches like that work hard at appearing to be well-respected members of the communities where they live. Makes sense that going to church would be part of it all. And, they'd make sure it was the right church, too.

"Right church?" Powell, now sitting in the front passenger's seat, asked. "What in the world's that mean?"

"Something mainstream for the place and time," the lieutenant responded coolly. "You know, like Catholic, Baptist or Methodist. Nothing that's going to raise people's eyebrows. Creeps like this, they're geniuses at blending in. Making everybody feel comfortable."

"Sounds like friggin' politics to me," Keifer spoke up, looking straight ahead and shifting in his seat.

"Everything's politics, for Christ sake," the lieutenant growled.

"Yeah, Plato says Man is a political animal," Keifer leaned forward from his back seat.

"Ha, so some of that book-learning did sink in," the lieutenant jostled calmly. "Lot of difference between them describing how it's going to be and when you're really in it. Am I right, boys?"

"Maybe so, but how could anybody like that really believe in a hereafter?" Powell inquired thoughtfully, slowly tapping the fingers of his right hand on the dashboard. "They can't possibly justify what they do with an outlook on a glorious afterlife. They spend a lot of time trying to escape judgment."

"How does that make them different than a lot of the rest of us?" Lt. Huber asked abruptly. "Look, all this hereafter stuff and other supernatural hocus-pocus aside, it's not good to judge people by the way they go through the motions — attending church or anything. Some, if not many, probably go because they like to be with other people and sing the hymns. Otherwise, they really don't give it much thought."

"But faith is belief, not thought," Keifer asserted, leaning back against his backseat.

"Beliefs . . . thoughts . . . who knows?" Lt. Huber said evenly. "All that stuff aside, right-minded members of the clergy can be pretty solid pillars of any thriving community. Hell, I've worked with most of them in Mercury at one time or other. They're great with kids and domestic quarrels, especially kids who have developed some sort of mistrust about parents and cops. But . . . that doesn't mean that there's an afterlife or that holy spirits are fluttering close by or any of that."

"You don't believe in God?" Keifer inquired anxiously.

"Who the hell knows what to believe?" Lt. Huber snapped back. "That's the nice thing about it. You can believe whatever you like. But, I've found, if you want anything done, you better do it yourself. Sitting around praying doesn't get it."

"You don't ever pray, even when things are tough?" Powell said with a look of worry. "No such thing as the power of prayer?"

"I've been around long enough to remember when the horror of polio was scaring the pants off everyone," the lieutenant answered reflectively, still not changing his tone noticeably. "The ones it didn't kill, it mangled horribly. There was a hell of a lot of praying going on. But, it took Jonas Salk and his vaccine to put a stop to all that fear. Damn . . . never have figured out why he didn't get a Nobel Prize. Didn't have to be the prize for medicine either. Could have gotten the Peace Prize. It was immeasurable, what he did for Mankind."

The inside of the car was silent again, as quiet as the rest of the parking lot. After a long moment, Lt. Huber took up again what had suddenly become a one-way conversation.

"Look, even if there is a God, I don't think he's terribly interested in what I'm doing right now or at any other particular moment," he said evenly. "Hell, I don't remember having too many problems before I was born. I don't think I'll have many after I'm dead. Just a case of how fast the worms can get into the coffin."

"Geez, how can you live like that?" Keifer said, now increasingly disturbed. "Don't you have any faith that there's something better out there?"

"Better? Out there?" Lt. Huber answered with a slight shrug, struggling hard not to be facetious. "Joe E. Lewis, an old-time Vegas standup comic, once said, 'We pass this way but once, but, if you do it right, once is enough.' Actually, he was answering someone's question about his views on reincarnation. But, it fits any of this hereafter stuff."

"Standup comic, huh?" Keifer objected with distain.

"Why put off doing things you would like to do, or should do, simply because you think you're going to have another shot at it in some other lifetime? Sure there's questions that haven't been answered to my satisfaction. When did time start? Where does space end? How did the first something get made out of nothing? Stuff like that. Until some of that's answered, I'm not coming to any final conclusions about God or any of the rest of it."

"Gosh, that's pretty heady stuff, lieutenant," Powell broke in, while a silent Keifer remained mildly frenetical.

"Look, one common thread runs through all religions. The endless battle between good and evil," Lt. Huber acquiesced. "God versus Satan, or the Zoroastrians' Ormazd versus Ahriman. All the same. And, it's the reason we're sitting out here on this damn dreary, drizzly night while most guys with any sense are home in a warm bed with their wives. Tell you what, boys. If you don't have those kinds of convictions about why you're a policeman, maybe you ought to be finding another line of work."

"We're both in this for the same reasons, lieutenant," Powell stopped tapping, speaking for Keifer as well. "You just say it a little differently."

"Don't be fooled, just because we seem to be in the backwaters of high crime here in Mercury," Lt. Huber was now convinced his conversation was working. "At any time, you might be called on to kill somebody in a split second, either to save someone else's life or your own."

"We're told all that at the academy," Keifer blurted out with assurance. "I hope it never happens."

"Hey, I don't know what the hell they're teaching at the academy these days, but, they used to teach you that, if you draw your gun, you better be ready to use it. Hell, the day you graduated and strapped that thing on your hip you better had already decided that you're ready to kill someone without any reservations. You wait until you draw that gun to decide, there's a good chance you're the one that's going to end up dead."

The inside of the car became contemplatively quiet. The daylong gloomy overcast had turned into a drizzle shortly after midnight and had since become a steady, windless downpour, turning the otherwise eerily quiet outside into a bothersome tap-tap-tap cadence.

"You know, everybody thinks the scum we're after are easy-to-spot ugly looking creatures with red eyes and green teeth who lay coiled in wait for night to fall so they can put on their black capes and scurry out onto the moor, under the sardonic grin of moonlight, to perform unspeakably horrible deeds," the lieutenant enjoyed painting this picture, using a purposely creepy voice that bordered on overt comedy. Then the voice turned extremely serious.

"Unspeakable horror . . . right. The rest of it's pure bullshit. Couldn't be farther from reality. Take the guy we've got staked out here. He wouldn't draw your attention one way or another if he was standing right next to you. Strictly part of the passing scenery."

"Yeah, but we picked up on him," Keifer chided, not liking being treated like a complete neophyte.

"It's all internal with these guys," Lt. Huber stayed the course. "Whole different ballgame. Remorseless. Completely impersonal. No emotional axe to grind. Nothing like your garden-variety textbook serial murderer or mass murderer. Usual profile stuff? No, with guys like Mr. Lost here — and whomever he's hooked up with — their only motive is their current assignment. That's it. Just a job to do. It's always business as usual. They don't bother anybody until they're asked to. Then, watch out!"

"Sounds like you're trying to scare us, lieutenant," Powell said quietly.

"Yeah!" Keifer chimed in with a more disturbed tone.

"Oh, you can scream or plead all you want, or just keep quiet . . . Makes no damn difference," the lieutenant kept on as if uninterrupted. "They're not listening anyway. Once they've got you in their sights, they just keep methodically going about their business. Like a lioness after she's picked out the antelope she wants. The antelope can do anything it wants. The lioness is interested only in completing the mission at hand. Once she locks on, pretty soon the party's over. Simple as that. All very modern."

"You talk to us like we don't know anything," Powell said flatly.

"Yeah," Keifer echoed, sounding a bit deflated.

"I'm sure you do," Lt. Huber responded earnestly. "There can come a point though, out here, when knowing's not enough. Doing's what rules. Can save lives, including your own."

"You seem to have come through all right," Powell observed in a tone with a questionable hint of subtle humor. Keifer remained quiet.

"Guys like this, they make sure they have things all their own way," the lieutenant brushed aside any insinuations. "They put a helluva lot of energy into making sure of that. Different breed. Probably couldn't survive the way they do without today's transportation and communication."

"So . . . we're on top of that stuff," Powell began tapping again.

Keifer was silent, except Lt. Huber thought he heard a yawn.

"This guy here in Room 144? Consensus is that he's an advance man." Lt. Huber, unimpressed, had more to say. "Here just to scout things out and set things up for an accomplice. This guy might not even like the sight of blood. That's for someone else. A real assembly line division of labor. Yes siree, a modern-day monument to the teamwork concept."

The lieutenant paused, bringing the momentary silence to bear with his special brand of sarcasm. The two officers respected the pause, quietly exhibiting their intentions to keep listening.

"These guys never carry weapons that you could put your finger on without an argument," Lt. Huber took more silence as a hint to move his tuition-less lecture forward. "Never guns. Maybe a knife, but it'll be something arguable. Not a big-ass Bowie or the like. Mostly, they plant what they're going to need ahead of time at the site where they are going to do the job. The advance man might even take care of that. Sort of like a wife sending a husband along with a shopping list." Again the lieutenant announced another quick pause. Still no response from the two urgently intent officers.

"Good thing is, once you corner them, it's over," Lt. Huber was becoming aware of talking too long without conversation. "They become like an owl that has hunted too long and suddenly is caught out with the sun up. Blindly out of their element, they just fold their wings and take roost without the benefit of proper cover. Man, you want to hear a real racket? Come across a too-long-out owl that has been discovered by a flock of crows or blackbirds. Jesus, soon every damn bird within earshot is on the alert. Without things his own way, the owl just sits and takes it, including the dive-bombing assaults. Same with the birds we're after. Catch 'em out. Then, just walk up and arrest 'em. The battle's over at that point . . . none of that hoodlum shoot-out stuff. Hard part is catching up with the smart sons-of-bitches, not apprehending 'em."

Ω

As dawn arrived and the rain had broken off, Lt. Huber's gaze remained fixed on the door of Room 144. He let the other two sleep. Daybreak announced a cloudless cover. Soon the sun would begin baking away the remains from the overnight dampness. Not an hour later, The Churchmouse dutifully appeared, carrying a suitcase and overnight valise.

"Reveille time, boys! Here we go," Lt. Huber's barked in a low voice, his nudging observation instantly rousing Keifer and Powell into action. "As soon as he's on the move, I'll drop you two by your cars and keep after him. Get on your radios. Use our special frequency. I'll want to switch off with one of you as soon as I can."

The Churchmouse's rental Neon moved around to the front of the building, then through the front entrance and turned right.

After hurriedly dropping the patrolmen off, Lt. Huber filed into the light early morning eastbound traffic. On weekdays, most early traffic became westbound as Mercury's out-of-town workforce funneled in for the day. Soon, Powell's and Keifer's cars were in his rearview mirror.

"Move up, Officer Powell," he said, as he faded back into the traffic. "Let him go a little farther. As soon as we're sure that he's heading for the airport, we'll nail him. Let's make sure he's not going somewhere else to meet someone."

"Hey, Lieutenant, if he's going to the airport, maybe we should we let him go all the way?" Keifer came back. "Maybe he'll be meeting somebody inside?"

Lt. Huber smiled to himself. This was the sort of professional candor that he worked particularly hard to develop in the people whom he supervised. Within his comfortable sense of propriety, opposing suggestions were always welcomed. Never taken as a threat to his ultimate authority.

"Not likely he's meeting somebody there," Lt. Huber's voice calmly moved into a pedagogical tone. "I played it down before, more likely is he's got a gun with him. We don't want him waving that around in the middle of the terminal, maybe even escalating into some sort of half-assed hostage situation. Nah, all things considered, our best bet is to take him out here in the open . . . if only in the interest of public safety."

"I read you, Lieutenant," Keifer answered firmly.

A few minutes later, Lt. Huber gave his next orders.

"Officer Powell, pass him and stay ahead," he commanded. "Officering" them with their surnames was his way of emphasizing the professional immediacy of the moment. "Officer Keifer, move into where Officer Powell was."

Mr. Late was boxed in now — Powell in front and Keifer behind, with Lt. Huber trailing Keifer, ready to pounce into the outside lane. Five miles later, with the airport's central tower in sight, Lt. Huber made his move.

"OK, Officer Keifer, drop back, and then pull in behind me when I stop him," he ordered. "Officer Powell, after we get him stopped, grab the first U-turn and come on back. Keep watch from the outer westbound shoulder."

Satisfied with the fired-up "yes-sir, Lieutenant" answers that came back, Lt. Huber drove out along the driver's side of The Churchmouse's Neon, flashed his badge and pointed for him to pull over. Without the slightest resistance, The Churchmouse obeyed instantly.

"Sir, I'm Lt. Huber of the Mercury Police Department," the detective spoke directly and calmly, keeping his badge in plain sight. The Churchmouse rigidly agreed that he was Thomas Varner. "We'd like you to come to the station with us and answer some questions."

"Surely we can handle this right here, officer?" The Churchmouse said calmly. "I can't imagine I've done anything wrong. I have a plane to catch very soon."

"What time's your flight, sir?" Lt. Huber asked, knowing it didn't matter. "Where're you headed?"

"It's shortly before noon to Chicago, and it's on time . . . I checked a little while ago," The Churchmouse explained, nervously beginning to sense that his answers were not helping.

"Well now, it looks like you're going to have to miss your flight, sir," the detective said, almost before The Churchmouse had finished. "Nice thing is, if you call right away when we get to the station, you'll have time to reschedule for a later flight today without any penalty. I'm sure there's a couple more flights to Chicago today. Probably even a red-eye. Weekdays in that direction, seats should still be open."

"Am I under arrest?" The Churchmouse blurted out, his face now fully flushed.

"Not now . . . do you want to be?" the detective suggested smoothly.

Deflated, The Churchmouse slouched and allowed himself to be guided into the back seat of Lt. Huber's vehicle.

"Keifer? Follow me back to the station with Mr. Lost's car," Lt. Huber ordered, his speech becoming more relaxed and made more obvious by his having dropped the "Officer" bit from his instructions. Then, hurrying across the two eastbound lanes as soon as the light traffic allowed, and over the grassy median to where Powell was parked. "Powell, stay put while I send someone to drive Keifer's car back. Nice going, both of you."

"Is he the right one, Lieutenant?" Powell asked with pride.

"He's the one we wanted," said the detective with a faint smile.

26

SQUEAL!

Lt. Huber U-turned. Keifer followed, and the two-car caravan headed back toward Mercury.

On the way to the station, Lt. Huber watched The Churchmouse nervously twitch and shift his eyes from side to side.

"You seem a little worried, my friend?" His needling was met with a revealing silence and sad gaze toward the side window.

Entering the station, Lt. Huber and The Churchmouse were joined by Patrolman Keifer in the conference room farthest down the hall to the right. Chief Millington watched through the observational mirror.

"Do I need a lawyer?" The Churchmouse stammered.

"It's not my call," the detective answered rhetorically. "Do you want one?"

"I want to go to the airport."

"Answering a few questions should help that."

"Answer questions? I don't know what you're talking about. What do I know that could possibly be of interest to anyone here?"

The Churchmouse seemed to be gaining a bit of footing.

"Try this. What were you doing on the backstretch at the race track at 10 o'clock last night?"

Any temporary footing The Churchmouse had gained now gave way in an instant.

"I . . . I was looking to buy a horse."

"The one the guy was talking to and petting?"

"Yes . . . yes"

"So, you wanted to get a jump on everyone? Rumors that the horse might be up for grabs had just surfaced?"

"That's it, precisely."

"Why didn't you talk to the guy with the horse, instead of hanging in the shadows."

"He looked pretty small. Like he was a jockey, not an owner."

"You're pretty small. Are you a jockey?"

"No."

"Look, we can keep this up as long as you like. A lot of planes will come and go in the meantime."

The Churchmouse's willfull energy was completely drained. He had no script for this. He never ad-libbed. He always knew his mission and had complete control. Those around him where supposed to be completely in the dark. He stared at the table top between them in silence.

"Look, my friend, we really don't give a damn about you," the detective said, continuing to convincingly push his thinly-laid foundation. He was now into his fortieth hour without sleep. "We're really interested in who you're working for. Simple as that. Tell us what we want to know and there's a good chance you'll be on a plane for home later today. How about some coffee?"

"I don't feel good. I'm going to be sick."

"Keifer, take Mr. Lost to the restroom. I'll bring him some coffee or a soda, if he wants"

The Churchmouse followed Keifer out, completely oblivious of the "Mr. Lost" connotation.

Moments later, Lt. Huber left the room, too.

"Bob, you don't have a damn thing but a lot of half-baked circumstantial crapola on this guy," the chief whispered, catching up with Lt. Huber on the way to the coffee pot. "That doesn't go around here, and you know it, dammit.

"Right now, I'll admit, it's a bit of stretch," the detective whispered in agreement. "He doesn't know that. He's scared shitless. He's about ready to crack, and he hasn't really asked for a lawyer."

"You know I can't let this go on forever," the chief advised in his unmistakable tone of agitation. "If you don't start getting somewhere fast, I'm going to have to order you to cut him loose."

Lt. Huber brought two coffees and a Pepsi back to the conference room. The Churchmouse and Keifer were waiting. He knew from their years together that the chief had said what he said for the record. The detective also knew that the chief respected his instincts and had his back. How and for how long he should continue applying pressure on The Churchmouse was summarily under his control.

"Why are you picking on me?" The Churchmouse blurted. "I've done nothing wrong."

"Oh, let's see," the detective said with his practiced subtle tone, accompanied by unblinking assertiveness. "You rented the motel room under the name of Varner, but you rented the car under another name. Stanton, wasn't it? And purchased your airline ticket under yet another . . . Greenstreet. Doesn't that seem a little odd? Or, do you have some sort of illness we ought to know about? If so, I sure hope it isn't catching."

The Churchmouse quivered. Frantically, he did not want to be in the area when The Talon arrived. How much do these people really know?

"Promise you'll let me go?" he pleaded, completely broken now. The detective marveled over how little pressure it had taken. Time to play the helping hand with personal sincerity.

"I'll do what I can. Depends. Tell us about Cossie Jarvis."

"Look, I was just doing the make-up on the guy . . . that's all . . . just sort of a profile work-up and mapping out his routine," The Churchmouse stammered. He was gripping his coffee cup on the table with both hands, giving no sign that he wanted to drink from it. "I'm not responsible for anything that happens later. I'm never even there, I swear. I don't even want to know."

"Yeah-yeah, I know," Lt. Huber said with mock sympathy. "Funny how the prosecution starts tossing around accusations like accessory, premeditation, even co-conspirator in cases like this."

"Cases?" The Churchmouse squealed. After a few moments of silence, he began a detailed description of relevance.

As he recorded the voluntary monologue, Lt. Huber sat back in his chair in silent awe at The Churchmouse's attention to detail and elaboration. The little man quietly began by telling how he and The Talon met, how long they had been together, then about some of their capers. The detective wondered when he'd had an easier time getting so much voluntary information from a suspect.

"What about things having to do with jockeys?" Lt. Huber asked, attempting to move the conversation.

"Yes." The Churchmouse answered alertly. He corroborated his involvement in the jockey deaths in Maryland and California. He was so thorough that Lt. Huber seldom interrupted with a question or a request for clarification.

Strangely though, The Churchmouse was unwavering in his insistence that he didn't know anything about a jockey's alleged overdose in New Orleans. Nothing in the South. That had to be someone else's work. And then he described his thoroughness in tracking Mendoza on Mercury Downs's backside the previous summer.

"And you're sure he's on his way here right now?" Lt. Huber re-established about The Talon's pattern.

"He always comes in very soon after I leave so that the information I give him is at its freshest," The Churchmouse nodded slightly, signaling that he was completely spent and, for reasons of his own, serenely relaxed.

Calling the airport from the station, The Churchmouse was assured that he had a seat on the 4:45 flight to Chicago, with the same stopover in Cincinnati.

"Keifer, follow Mr. Lost, or whatever, to the airport and make sure he gets on his plane safely," Lt. Huber directed, while The Churchmouse nodded incongruously, again not understanding the "Mr. Lost" reference in the slightest.

"And, you," the detective pointed his finger at The Churchmouse. "No phone calls to anyone. Understand?"

"I wouldn't know where to call now, anyway," The Churchmouse answered, exuding a wellspring of relief. "Once these things are in motion, there's never any talking. No way to stop it from my end."

"We'll see about that," Lt. Huber gritted. "Let me tell you how this is going to work. Drive your rental back. Just like business as usual. You're being escorted from nearby to the airport by my men. No funny stuff, you hear?"

The Churchmouse nodded without the slightest objection. The lieutenant had his undivided attention.

"You'll be watched on the plane . . . Stay in your seat while you're on the ground in Cincinnati. When you land in Chicago, you'll be met by a couple of our men and detained until I give them the high sign. Any suspicious behavior on your part and we'll put the clamps on you so fast . . . Another thing. Take a good long piss or whatever you've got to do before you get on that plane. There'll be no using the in-flight restrooms. As they say, have a nice trip."

27

THE ONCE-OVER

He was an uncontested master at keeping up appearances. Between the time he had launched The Churchmouse into his latest scouting mission — the broken protocol of a uncharacteristic return trip to Mercury — and had received the details about how best to encounter Cossie Jarvis, The Talon also had, with a routine air, accepted another unrelated assignment. Although comparatively uncomplicated, this newest agreement was one that he had no intention of honoring.

Unbeknownst to everyone, The Talon already had singularly and privately decided that his personal Mercury mop-up of the Jarvis situation would be his swan song. From there, according to plan, he would directly and immediately fade into the quiet cotton-candy limbo of untraceable anonymity.

Going back into Mercury ran diametrically counter-current to his self-imposed absolute of never returning to the location of a previous atrocity. In most other respects, too, this was not one of his regular assignments. No patron had called. This one was strictly on him; on his own time and at his own expense. To minimize any questions about his business-as-usual operandi, he had already forwarded The Churchmouse's fee to the regularly designated location.

This would be neither an act of vengeance or a vendetta. None of that useless emotional frailty. This personal project at Mercury Downs would be the final statement of his impeccably enduring craftsmanship as The Talon.

"Indeed, wherever I go in the future, it will not be a happy time if I do not take care of this one last little chore," he counseled himself accurately.

"Hey, Talon, dis is Skinny Marvin," the voice at the other end had urgently spoken into the voice-mail recorder. Sitting by, The Talon had let the phone call run through all six regular rings, then relay to his answering machine. He seldom took calls directly, choosing instead to determine who was calling and what, if anything, they had to say. This call from Skinny Marvin was no exception.

The uninterrupted message did not require a return call. Within the cognitive realm of The Talon, Skinny Marvin was not a person. He was a thing, a throwaway tool.

"Ya know dat jockey ting up at Mercury dat ended up in da commissinah's office? Whal, frum da wurd on da street, it seems he also had a sordda Dutch uncle — ya know, another older jockey — who he tode everyting ta. Now, it seems dat dis older jock — name of Jarvis, Cossie Jarvis — is pissed off ta beat all hell about how Mendoza ended up. He's back in Mercury ta squeel ta da Gran Jury. Names an-all. Look, I had nuttin ta do wid any a dis. But, I know how ya like ta heer about dis stuff A-S-A-P. And, I still appreciate what ya dun fer me dat time. See ya around. Oh, I got dis info from a guy who goddit straight from a guy name Hammy up dere in Mercury. Dis Hammy guy has put me onta stuff before. Never a bad turn. No bullshit."

Most of the calls, of course, concerned his real estate holdings and motel business, all of which he managed from his office-in-the-home. The Talon stored these message tapes in a perfect chronology, in case any IRS problems arose. However, tapes that also contained messages of the type he had just received from Skinny Marvin were destroyed without delay after he quickly memorized all of the information. Physical records of such calls simply were not allowed to exist.

Taken to the backyard cookout pit, and helped by a couple of briquettes and some squirts of lighter fluid, this sort of potentially incriminating evidence was melted into an amorphous oblivion. Early on, he had debated erasing these messages and just recording over them. But perhaps there was, or soon would be, a technology that could conjure up the ghosts of record-ed-over evidence. Better to be terminally safe.

Skinny Marvin's information had always proven to be rock-solid, The Talon mulled. *What of it? What could this Jarvis pygmy possibly hurt? I'm certain the guys who approached Mendoza had enough smoke in their identities that the poor bastard had no idea who the hell he was really talking to. They let their upfront hook mon-ey do all the identifying needed. What if this little Jarvis runt sings his head off in front of some goddam Grand Jury? What of it? No problem. Besides, I'll be long gone.*

Regardless, The Talon knew that the searing de-mons who had molded him would never let go this way. It wasn't because his mother hadn't doted on him, or because his father was never there. Completely over-looked in the early nurturing, his inner life had begun as an unresponsive vacuum. From birth, a seemingly rehearsed facade reflected itself in his infectious smile, masking any evidence of the usual sociological at-risk red flags. In time, he willfully became the architectural-ly perfect engine of crafted evil. Soon after he took his first breath, any vestiges of social emotion had been eternally sentenced to an unlockable steel cage in the backwaters of his psyche.

An excellent student, he explored and discovered meaningful applications from every subject he was ex-posed to. He viewed all things, living and nonliving, as equally stony pieces awaiting manipulation. He moved among them, through them and around them only to suit his uncompromising inward satisfaction and basely gratified ego. Protected by layers of self-schooled socia-lization, his toyingly depraved core surfaced only when called upon professionally. Then it was time to go to work. And, a pockmark of the likes of this "Jarvis thing" had to be attended to in some orderly fashion. Above all, absolute subjugation, under an uncontestedly cruel supremacy, must always be maintained.

"Who does this little bastard Jarvis think he's fooling with?" The Talon broodingly self-counseled with a clenched jaw. *"Christ, I worked that little spic-jock over the way I did to teach the rest of those little fuckers to keep their goddam mouths shut and do what they're told. Well, they will now, when this is over. Hah, this Jarvis crap is a textbook opportunity to create permanent dread for what happens to anyone who takes it upon themselves to cross the wrong people."*

The stimulation of how to liquidate his motel holdings with as much profit as possible was working in other ways, too.

"Besides, how could I do otherwise and still think of myself in the same league with those who gave me so much of what I know?" The Talon snorted to himself. *"One-Shot Lenny, Primrose Ernie, Westside Lloyd, The Catskill Panther . . . all the rest. They damn well didn't show me everything so I'd back away from unfinished business!"*

That this foray would be a non-contractual freebie made it even sweeter. Every step would be his own call. No outside instructions about what to do or how far to go. Carte blanche in every way. Expenses? No matter. He already had more than enough resources salted away to last two luxurious lifetimes.

Ω

Immediately after The Churchmouse contacted him, detailing Jarvis's whereabouts and movements, along with suggestions for closure, The Talon decided to carry through with a decoying charade. He would personally launch his advance man into a new assignment — the one he had absolutely no intention of carrying out himself. In the end, The Churchmouse would be holding the bag on that one. Small price to pay for the sake of appearances. Anyone who knew of the working alliance between the two would keep assuming business as usual while The Churchmouse went about his routine advance work. Instead, it would serve The Talon's convenience of even more time to severe himself from the tiniest roots of any former reality.

The Churchmouse had mentioned the flight he would be departing GIA on, a regular precaution between the two, specifically to prevent an awkward chance of both being spotted in the same place at the same time. This time though, The Talon wanted to catch up with The Churchmouse. If his connections weren't seriously delayed anywhere along the way, The Talon was certain he could intercept The Churchmouse at GIA in plenty of time to divert him from his flight to Chicago via Cincinnati, instead sending him through to St. Louis.

Beginning his circuitous route to GIA with a hop from Pensacola to Houston, he had waited two days at that Texas stopover for The Churchmouse's detailed targeting of Jarvis in Mercury. He then had grabbed a red-eye onto GIA, arriving hours before The Churchmouse's scheduled departure. Plenty of time for bogus planning.

Ω

While waiting for his after-midnight flight to begin boarding at Houston's George Bush International Airport, The Talon's silent revelry drifted to the previous Wednesday when he was approaching the fourth tee at Richwater's Beau Rivage Country Club. The players making up the day's foursome were all skillful regulars who were on the tee most Wednesdays — Father Franklin Reeves of Richwater's First Presbyterian Church, local orthodontist Dr. Joshua Yonnadi and Rod Altentrop, top investment strategist with the People's Bank of Richwater.

"You're up, Richard . . . made the rest of us look pretty sick on that last hole," Father Reeves jovially informed Pierce, completely unaware, of course, that he was addressing The Talon during a morning of carefully scheduled relaxation. "That continues to be the stiffest par-five I've ever played on. You made it look easy . . . darn near birdied it!"

"It's the second shot with that three-wood," Pierce confided in a friendly manner, with Altentrop closest by. "A pro at a course I used to play early on handed me that club one day and sternly urged me, 'Learn this club.' I went through Hades."

"Three-wood, huh," Altentrop said attentively. "Got one in my bag. Never use it."

"Kept reverting back to my old three-iron after a few fairway fits . . . then I'd try the wood again," Pierce nodded with serious recall. "Must have bounced back and forth between those two clubs a dozen times. Finally, I started stepping back a little, letting the club do the work. The pro had told me that right off. Just took a while to sink in. Nowadays, depending on the course I'm playing, my game's four, maybe five, shots better than it was before."

"Wow. Next time I'm at the range I'll try it," Dr. Yonnadi said with newfound enthusiasm.

"Staying out of the bunkers would help you two fellas, too," Pierce needled Altentrop and Father Frank. "The good doctor seems to be the only one who knows how to hit a ball straight."

In a tight second-shot group, after teeing off, the four began walking down the fairway of the dogleg-left par four. They wouldn't have to fan out for at least one-hundred-fifty yards. As homage to a healthy lifestyle, the foursome divulged their aversion to carts one early morning in the clubhouse. As they were preparing to head out, the assistant pro voiced a hearty concern that they didn't use carts.

"Look, sonny, we'll pay the rental fee for the damn carts, if that's what's bothering you, sonny," Altentrop had snapped back in obvious disgust. "Then, please let us alone so we can walk the damn course." After that, nobody mentioned anything about carts to these four.

"Anything new and exciting on the real estate horizon, Richard?" Dr. Yonnadi had asked while they strolled leisurely, perhaps inflated by Pierce's compliment of his accuracy in the fairways.

"You know, now that you mention it, there is one thing," instinctively, Pierce pounced on an opening when he heard one. "Sort of by coincidence, if you believe such things exist, several well-established motels have come to my attention all at once. I'm putting them together as a package — merging them into a regional chain, so to speak, as a ready-made cash cow. Actually, two of them are mine. The Emerald Oasis and Picturesque Palms."

"I know them both," Altentrop said with pleasure. "When I have people in from out-of-town, I usually put them up at one of those."

"Only happy to hear that," Pierce quipped in good jest. The conversation couldn't be going better, he thought. "I've done the math. The management at each location is steady and solid. With regular upkeep and maintenance, the package should pay for itself in four years. . . tops. After that, there'll be many ways to go. Sit back and enjoy a hefty profit as far into the future as I can see. Or, sell the package at a windfall. The public's clamor for nice, reasonably priced staying space along Florida's coast won't be going away. Only going to get better and better. You can bust up the package. Sell some. Keep some. Why, you guys interested?"

By now, the foursome had paused into a tightened cluster of captivated interest in the middle of the fairway. By rights, the foursome behind them could have started yelling. But, they were businessmen, too. After all, it was Wednesday.

"I don't know, Richard, I'm a little long in the tooth to be investing long-range," Father Frank spoke first. Normally, being part of the community clergy is not a ready-made ticket to affluence. However, Father Frank came from money and had been inheriting chunks from it during the past ten years.

"Geez, Father, you'd think you had one foot in the grave," Pierce exclaimed. "You're just entering middle-age, for crying out loud. I'm only talking a few years."

Father Frank gave no sign.

"How about you, Doc?" Pierce turned, looking over at Dr. Yonnadi. "There are poor teachers and poor lawyers, but no such thing as a poor dentist, right?"

"I'm not saying yes, not saying no, for now," Dr. Yonnadi answered quietly. "Doesn't sound bad, except I haven't heard anything about, you know, money. Feel like taking a look at it, Rod?"

"It's what I do, Josh," Altentrop answered calmly. "Sounds like Richard might have something. Turning a conglomeration of differently owned motels into a mini-chain might be the way to go here. If so, maybe between us, we can come up with something. We'll probably want to include Kevin Wentworth and Jason Horn, too. I'd like to look into it. What do you say?"

Father Frank and the good doctor bobbed their heads in unified approval.

"You're farthest away, Father," Pierce observed. "You go first." Abruptly, the call to board the red-eye beckoned The Talon back to the present.

Arriving at GIA with time to spare, The Talon claimed his small suitcase in his usual unassuming manner and, after heading back up the escalator, took a seat that provided an easy visual of the security lines leading to the concourse where The Churchmouse's flight would board. Today's edition of Mercury Times, featuring a Front Page story about the county's first National Guard troops leaving for Iraq, fortified his intentions to keep his head down, thus minimizing chances for an offhand familiarization.

Ω

Not consciously aware that nostalgia was clawing at his decision to back away from the life that had honed him into the lone member on the A-list of his kind, he reflected about how he had earned his bones, as they say. When had he become The Talon?

Shortly after One-Shot Lenny was assassinated, Big Mike agreed that the Arachnids were through. The two survivors shook hands in farewell and promised to stay out of each other's way. Never much for casino games, Pierce always enjoyed the shows and food that Las Vegas offered plenty of. With absolutely no prospects on the horizon, he took up residence at the Flamingo Hotel. Perhaps Bugsy Siegel's "vision in the desert" would provide some osmotic inspiration.

On the third evening, while queuing into the Flamingo's reliably eclectic buffet, he spotted Ned "Sharpie" Sharpstein, a more-than-an-acquaintance friend from the old Chicago neighborhood. Those days he was still called Frankie X., before he became the prosperous Richard Pierce of Richwater. In the old neighborhood, Sharpie was known as Jew-Boy, a derogatory practice that Pierce never subscribed to.

Since losing contact with Pierce several years back, Sharpstein had made his way to Sin City as a freelance journalist. He, however, thrived within his standard of living by being an intermediate cocaine mule, transporting bricks of the nose candy by car from the mosaic of makeshift dark-of-night airdrops stretching west into the San Bernadino Mountains. Taking these bricks from on-foot receiving teams, Sharpie then smoothly met the distributors at various predesignated exchange points just beyond the neon reach of the Vegas octopus. Everything was in two coded messages: Where and when to pick up, where and when to drop off. The slightest hitch and everyone simply receded back into the velvet darkness, holding onto what they had, awaiting newer instructions.

Without acknowledging each other in the slightest as they waited in front of the iced mountains of succulent snow crab and boiled shrimp, Sharpie relayed his phone number. Supping at the same place the next evening, the duo loosely hung in line together without a word, then had a hostess seat them at the same table.

After Sharpie laid down a handful of yellow overnight sheets from the Stardust Race & Sports Book between them, the two began a charade of analyzing the next day's races. In fact, they spoke of old times in the neighborhood and compared notes on what they had been doing since.

"Anything in the mix out this way, Sharpie?" Pierce interjected out of the blue. "I'm not broke. Just suddenly find myself unemployed. I'm also Richard Pierce now."

Sharpie, while running his right index finger slowly down the information on one of the Stardust's sheets and intermittently tapping his finger as if to emphasize a point, described in detail a current dilemma that had some of the old boys very upset.

"This three-man pod that seems thinly connected to the Russian mob is muscling their way into the local prostitution action," Sharpie murmured, leaning forward and not about to mince words now. "They're trying to get control of the illegal traffic on The Strip and The Gulch first. Christ, Frankie, they're bold as hell. Plugged two street pimps right in front of their girls."

"Real wild-west stuff, huh?" Pierce smirked. "Sounds very messy. Crude."

"That's part of the problem," Sharpie pointed to Pierce. "They're so obvious. So open. They act like they have some backing from higher up. A pretty thorough check has turned up nothing though. Nobody's willing to take credit. Personally, I think they're on their own . . . especially how they go about doing things. Christ, Frankie, these cowboys openly brag about taking over every legal bordello outside the city limits. Big plans, these guys."

"What kind of connections have you got out here, Sharpie?" Pierce asked slowly. "This is exactly what I'm looking for. Can you get me a green light? Just me?"

"Lemme see what's up," Sharpie nodded with a slight smile, still keeping his hand on the overnight sheet. "From the looks of you, I get the feeling you know what you're getting into. Meet at the same time tomorrow night over at the Rio's buffet. If you haven't tried that one yet, I think you'll like it."

Pierce gave his OK with a slight nod.

Ω

"Try some of each over at the exotic sections, just for the hell of it," Sharpie cheerfully instructed as they began by filing into the Rio's salad line the following night. "Just take it and try it. Don't worry what it is."

Sharpie was bubbling over as they sat down to start on plates piled with the salad course.

"I put the word out to my best places before going to bed last night," he whispered clearly. "By noon today, your green light was lit solid. You've got a bit of a rep. It's good. I'd even heard about some of your stuff out here. Christ, you've never even been questioned?"

Pierce shrugged slightly with a hard smile as Sharpie spoke.

"These three Ruskie clowns aren't into gambling. They're rather go clubbing with their favorite chippies. They seem real fond of that new one, Panthers & Pussycats, in between the Morocco and the Riviera."

"Yeah, I've passed by it when I jog up to the Sahara and back in the morning, early," Pierce spoke, while pointing down to information on a sports-book sheet he had brought with him. "Hard to get a feel for the joint at that hour. Pretty quiet."

"Well, it's noisier that hell at night," Sharpie emphasized. "That joggin' doin' you any good?"

Pierce sat up straight. "What do you think?"

"Looks like it, I guess."

"Yeah, and it wouldn't hurt you to lift a few weights once in a while, too."

Sharpie decided that was enough of that.

"There's not a lot of front to it, but it stretches back off the strip for almost a damn block and a half. Two bands going all the time, near to either end so they don't drown each other out. One's rock, the other's country."

"Whole damn town was built on noise." Pierce preferred progressive jazz.

"Yeah, OK. These bands hang about eight-nine feet above the floor on thick Plexiglas, perforated platforms so they don't take up any dance room. You can move back and forth between the two-step and the twist. Lots of slow stuff at both ends as the night goes on. When you hear a number you like, just dance your dolly right under the band. Really pick up the vibes. The platforms have a million one-inch holes to let the sound drift down. The place is always packed."

Sharpie had given him enough to start. For the next four nights, Pierce quietly bumped and shoved his way around the Panthers & Pussycats, hidden behind three changes of disguise. By the end of the fourth night, with the help Sharpie had given him, he had the three no-goodniks pegged.

"Jesus, they're boisterous and crude, without even bothering to be flamboyant," Pierce silently self-counseled while pretending to listen to the rock band from the edge of the dance floor, nursing a half-filled glass of beer in his left hand. *"Trouble is, they think they're too tough. They're to the point where they think they're so smart they don't have to prove it. Friggin' lazy! They even lose touch with each other. Don't know what smart is. Nothing like Lenny and Big Mike taught."*

Nearing midnight of his fifth visit to the Panthers & Pussycats' musical chaos — a sweltering summertime Wednesday that guaranteed the place would be packed, but the entranceway waiting line wouldn't be prohibitively long — Pierce moved from the centrally located men's room to the rock-end dance floor and then to a floor-side booth. Silently and swiftly, he'd covered the route in less than four minutes. In the dimly lit, sardine-packed ambiance, he nimbly opened the carotid and jugular on one side of each Ruskie's neck with a downward slice that also left the trachea gaping and gurgling.

Having approached from behind, he paused after surreptitiously opening the pompously unsecure racketeer wannabe seated in the booth. As he pushed the gushing Russian's head over to the shoulder of the woman sitting with him, she wide-eyedly gawked with a massive inhalation, her mouth agape in a silent scream, momentarily pseudo-atrophied with terror. He put his right index finger to his pursed lips and glared.

"Just look straight forward, Hon, for a couple of minutes without a sound or I'll cut you too," he demanded gently with an icy glare. "After that, scream your head off, if you think it's worth it."

As throbbing tremors of consuming horror began pulsating from the base of her spine, she obeyed in cold perspiring silence. Her unblinking gaze seemed blurrily directed onto the dance floor. In a disbelieving stupor, she stayed numbly fearful of what might be unfolding behind her.

He reflected with amusement how easy the first of the three had been — trapping the Russian in that men's room stall and leaving without a drop of blood splattered on himself. The difficulty had been getting to the second target before discovery of the first took hold. Swimming through the endless sea of gyrating sardines as the seconds ticked away, the next Russian had fallen to the floor with his left hand covering the sliced right side of his neck. Under the raised glass floor of the rock band, the self-involved sardines closest to the prostrate, quivering Russian had continued to writhe uninterrupted as the blood pool grew. Surrounded by this panorama of undulating narcissism, Pierce had anonymously, and with hawkish focus, been able to swiftly circle behind to his final quarry at that floor-side booth.

As the mass of sardines behind him began slowly simmering with a collective realization of his work, The Talon nonchalantly smiled and nodded as he passed by the bouncer at the south door and began blending into the strolling bromide of humanity along The Strip's east sidewalk. Slowly and systematically, he removed the bushy black mustache and sideburns, reversed his blue jacket into white, while donning a pair of tortoise-shell glasses and running his hand through his sprayed hair to fluff it. Behind him in the growing distance, a nauseating chain of panic was spreading through the club.

28

AMBITION MEETS ABILITY

He had driven southeasterly through the night in the Nissan Sentra provided by Sharpstein, delaying twice at rest stops in Arizona, at Kingman and then Flagstaff, for brief breathers before reaching the outskirts of Albuquerque early the following afternoon. After quietly enjoying the earthy New Mexican tribal flavor of Old Albuquerque and very reachable Santa Fe for a week, he cautiously phoned Sharpie for a make on the fallout from the Panthers & Pussycats bloodletting.

"Where in the hell are you?" Sharpie exclaimed. "Christ, they're looking high and low for you!"

"Yeah, I'll bet they are, and I'm damn well making sure they don't find," Pierce reacted evenly. "I'm just checking, Sharp. I'll be the hell out of here before they ever chase this call down."

"No-no, wait!" Sharpie shouted, hoping he wouldn't hear the receiver click in his ear. "It's not what you seem to think, Richie. Nobody gives a damn what happened to those Ruskies. The people who count are damn happy. Everybody knows they were mobbed up."

"Made a damn mess, didn't I?" Pierce, feeling better about things, started fishing.

"Cops don't lose sleep over mob hits," Sharpstein began spelling out the obvious. "Christ, you know that! Oh sure, they didn't particularly like having it happen in one of the clubs, especially on The Strip. They get over that stuff quick. Part of Vegas's charm — attracts even bigger crowds. What I'm talking about are the guys who gave you the green light in the first place. They want to know where to send your money."

"God help you if you're putting me on, Sharp?" a still apprehensive Pierce spoke back flatly.

"Look, they just need to know where you can be reached," Sharpstein took on an even more friendly calm. "So help me God. They've got a runner ready to deliver your payoff, plus a bonus, within ten hours. When he asks 'Once in a blue moon?', you just answer 'The second full moon of the month.' That's all there is to it."

"I'll call you back in a few minutes, Sharp," Pierce abruptly hung up. At the front desk, he found that the room to the right of his was vacant. He rented it under the pretense that he expected a couple of business associates later in the day. Then he called Sharpie to give him the number of the ghost room.

"Hey, Richie, you can keep the Nissan, too," Sharpie said, before hanging up. "It's legit. Not hot. Just use the title in the glove box. You're on your own for the insurance."

"When I get mine, you'll get yours," Pierce assured Sharpstein. "You already know that."

"Yeah, well, should be a pretty tidy sum," Sharpstein said, referring to the size of the package Pierce could expect. "A bunch of grateful others were happy to sweeten the pot. A load off a lot of people."

"How the hell do you know all that?"

"It's what I do, Richie."

"Watch you don't stick your beak in where it shouldn't be. I like having you around, Sharp."

"Appreciate your concern, Mother."

"OK, but don't blame me if you end up with an ice pick in your eye," and with that, as Pierce hung up, he heard, "You take care, Richie."

That was the last time he had seen or heard from Sharpie. Not that anything disastrous had happened in the meantime. There simply hadn't been any reason for their paths to cross.

After getting a nearby take-out pizza, Pierce settled into the room that he had originally taken and waited. Toward sundown he heard a stern knock at the other room's door, and, after a brief lull, another, more intense knock.

Opening his door, Pierce saw a boy in his late teens, perhaps early twenties, standing squarely in front of the other door. He had a cube-type package under his left arm.

"Can I help you?" Pierce asked directly.

"I don't think so, sir," the apprehensive youth answered.

"The second moon of the month?" Pierce smiled.

Stunned, the youth mechanically responded, "Once in a blue moon."

Pierce nodded and took the package. The youth, confusedly concerned over the reversal of the arranged code, silently scurried away.

Right away, he sent Sharpstein ten percent of the package. Early on, Pierce had learned the wisdom of squaring an account as quickly and conveniently as possible. Sharpie hadn't asked for anything. All the same, Pierce knew the score.

"Never leave something hanging so it becomes a favor owed," One-Shot Lenny had told him right off. "Let them owe you. Never the other way around."

"Makes sense, I guess," Pierce had answered without attention.

"Look, let somethin' ya shoulda took care of right off grow into a hangin' favor, and ya don't know what the hell ya might be called upon to do down the line ta square things," Lenny explained impatiently. "It might be somethin' ya'd easily want to say no to if ya didn't owe a favor. Got it?"

Within a month after getting the package from the runner, Pierce had settled into the newly incorporated Florida town of Richwater, which would rapidly grow into an attractive Gulf-side tourist stopover and begin providing a solid workforce as a suburb of the Tampa Bay area to the north. By year's end, he had acquired his first two motels, and had begun renovating their ramshackle neglect and upgrading their appearance. Then he called Big Mike.

"Mike, I need you to put me in touch with someone who's involved with calling the big shots."

"Nice work you did out in Vegas, buddy" Big Mike broke in. "Things went back to normal real quick. Looks like there wasn't really much backing by the Ruskie higher-ups, so to speak. Just three yo-yos trying to branch out on their own."

"Guess I helped change the old saying 'Nobody ever gets killed in Vegas' to 'Nobody ever gets killed in Vegas that doesn't need killing'," Pierce answered, approaching as close to humor as he ever did.

"Look, Richard, you know I'll do whatever I can," Big Mike said with a hint of a laugh to acknowledge the gist of Pierce's comment. "Your stock is way up with the boys after Vegas. That was really something. Christ, I couldn't have done it."

"I did put my mind to it," Pierce said in a deadpan tone. "Look, Mike, I know you'll do your best. You can always reach me at this number."

Three days later, while cooking breakfast for himself in the manager's home-office of his recently acquired motel, the phone rang.

"Pierce?" the voice had a rough directness.

"Speaking," he answered.

"This is The Pink Candle," the voice said, sounding like a bastard file gouging out a good-sized groove in a block of wood. "What's on your mind?"

It was the call he had hoped for.

"Special jobs that you need the best for, and can't afford to have messed up," Pierce said, trying to mask his exuberance. "Get my drift? Otherwise, I'm just your average Florida motel entrepreneur."

"You'll probably hear from someone, sometime," the abrasive monotone droned. "From now on, you're The Talon."

Seventeen years had passed since that phone call, filled with millions of dollars of immaculately successful "jobs." All local attention had been successfully diverted by his creation of a synthetic chain of apparently lucrative motels to explain his perceived wealth.

Ω

Instantly, he snapped back to the present as The Churchmouse's departure time grew nearer. Inwardly, The Talon was becoming agitated. Several times he had checked the "Departures" schedule on the TV screens in the middle of the huge walkway leading to the security line. "On Time" continued to be the message next to The Churchmouse's flight number.

Departure time came and went, but no Churchmouse. And, the TV screen had insisted "On Time" all along. The Talon quickly made an inquiry at the Information Desk as to the status of Flight 439 to Chicago via Cincinnati. The attendant confirmed that the flight had left on time.

Donning his best puzzled look, The Talon went to the baggage check-in and staging counter. "I have a couple of salesmen in town, one of whom was going to leave today on Flight 439, while the other stayed behind," The Talon calmly said, bluffing a smile to the attendant behind the counter.

"What are their names, sir?" she smiled back.

"Garth?"

"No-o-o-o . . . I'm sorry, sir, there's no Garth listed here," the attendant answered after quickly scrolling through the names of Flight 439 passengers on her screen.

"Then it must have been Greenstreet?" The Talon said quickly, knowing that The Churchmouse always departed under one of those names.

"Ah yes! S.G. Greenstreet," the attendant suddenly responded with the delight of a treasure-hunt discovery. "Mr. Greenstreet called more than an hour before departure to reschedule. He will now be leaving on Flight 471 for Cincinnati at 4:45, and then on to Chicago. And, so far, Flight 471 is on time, sir, coming in from the West Coast."

"Something's up . . . this sort of change never happens," The Talon grimaced inwardly while smiling calmly at the attendant to acknowledge her courtesy.

Moving more quickly than usual now, he headed back down the escalator and past the baggage claim area to the row of car rental booths. Scanning each booth, he knew that The Churchmouse always chose compact economy cars from the company with the cheapest rate. Some of these companies offered low up-front rates, then gouged a client with mandatory "this-and-that charges." The Talon knew all about those, and he knew The Churchmouse did. Valu-Rate Wheels seemed right up The Churchmouse's alley.

"I've been waiting for a Mr. Stanton," he told the young woman behind the counter, aware of The Churchmouse's chain of name changes, having been the one who taught him that fail-safe routine. "I know he's rented a car here in the past few days. Has he returned it yet?"

"I can check that for you, sir," she said accommodatingly, and then "No, sir, Mr. Stanton hasn't," shaking her head with tight lips and slight shoulder shrug. "He has the rest of today before he's overdue. Is there anything else I can do for you?"

"*Something's fucked up here*," The Talon thought without changing his expression. "*This never happens.*"

"Yes, I'd like to rent a car?" he asked plainly. "Also, could you tell me the make, color and license plate of the car that you rented to Mr. Stanton? There's a couple of places he might be, and knowing that information would help me locate him. It's rather important."

Several minutes later, after signing the appropriate agreements and finding the Valu-Rate Wheels' nearby parking lot, The Talon was driving out of Goldspar International Airport, toward the city of Mercury. Instinctively, his infallible gut stirred with a decisive hunch. Oh, The Churchmouse might have had an accident or illness, but that would be only the second worst reason for deviating from their years of ironclad planning. He could always check into that later.

The Talon thrived by making the right move at the right time. Relentless as a stalking jungle cat focused on the scent, his body and mind were hard-wired for reading and adjusting immediately to every nuance. He knew when to sit tight in ambush and when to prowl and pounce. Twenty-five minutes later, he was driving down Mercury's main north-south thoroughfare looking for the police station.

"There it is!" The Talon whispered to himself as he spotted The Churchmouse's rental Neon. *"The cops have him. That little sonovabitch! What the fuck is he doing at the cop station? How the hell did he let himself get tangled up with a Mickey Mouse outfit like the Mercury police?"*

He drove around the block and then parked across the street from the station so that he could observe the front door head-on.

"He's been nailed . . . he'll start singing like a frightened little canary," The Talon was sure. "But, he doesn't know when I'm supposed to arrive, or when I'm going to hit that little runt jockey. Only that I'm going to."

A half-hour later, The Churchmouse came out of the front door of the station and put his left hand on the railing that ran down the middle of the five concrete stairs, splitting the two lanes of foot traffic that led to and from the sidewalk. Right behind him was the much larger Lt. Huber. Then, seemingly in response, The Churchmouse stopped midway down the stairs, turned to face the detective and leaned against the railing as the two commenced talking. From afar, The Talon's advance man did not appear to be particularly upset. He spoke with the law officer for a moment, then nodded, turned and walked toward his car.

"Last minute instructions, huh . . . that little fucking sellout!" The Talon silently cursed to himself, putting his Neon in gear.

"Hell with this," he mumbled loud. "Forget this Jarvis. Get the next plane. I'm gone, and they'll still be waiting around for me to show up. They may even start thinking The Mouse is a nut. Just wasted their time. That in itself ought to be worth the price of admission. Watch the little bastard squirm."

Turning left at the light, The Talon drove around the block once more, turned onto Belgrade Avenue and headed back out to the airport. He knew he could not leave. *"My God, Mousey, how in the hell did you ever let this bunch of goddam yokels get wind that you were even here? Even existed?"* The Talon mulled hatefully as he drove on. *"You sloppy little son of a bitch."*

Pulling into Valu-Rate Wheels' up-close parking lot, The Talon parked his Neon in a slot that had four other open slots nearby and waited. The Churchmouse had a 4:45 flight to catch.

As The Churchmouse drove into the special parking area for rental-car drop-offs, Officer Keifer, who had been trailing him at an inconspicuous distance, peeled off and headed up the ramp to the right, toward the passenger drop-off area. Flashing his badge, he quickly abandoned his parked vehicle and hurried inside to the customer service booth where The Churchmouse would check in his luggage and have his rescheduled plane ticket validated. The Churchmouse would only be out of sight for a harmless moment or two, Officer Keifer surmised.

The Talon calmly emerged from his car and moved toward The Churchmouse's Neon as it turned into the parking spot three slots away. As The Churchmouse reached for the glove compartment to get his rental information, The Talon tore open the passenger's door and slid in. The Churchmouse's eyes bulged and his mouth gaped as he lurched away with his back against the driver's side door.

"What kind of greeting is that?" The Talon growled venomously. "I thought this would be a happy surprise for you. You sold me out, didn't you, you little bastard."

The Churchmouse just stared back, taking three short, choppy breaths before exhaling. "No," he whimpered. "Please."

In an instant, The Talon's push-blade knife sliced through the right side of The Churchmouse's neck. As he ripped the razor-sharp blade forward, the opened neck painlessly exposed the gaping esophagus and trachea, as well as the sliced carotid and jugular. Moving away, he reached over with his left hand and grasped The Churchmouse by his hair, twisting his head forward. The blood gushed onto the steering wheel and the dashboard. Very shortly, the gurgling and trembling stopped. The Talon shoved the limp head to the side with disdain and slid out through the passenger's door. He had things to do . . . quickly.

29

PIECE OF CHEESE

The nape of the lieutenant's neck tightened and became clammy as he listened to Officer Keifer's call.

"Mr. Lost is dead . . . his throat was slashed while still in his rented Valu-Rate Wheels car."

An old feeling, unfelt since coming to Mercury, visited the lieutenant. With siren blaring and lights flashing, he sped toward GIA. Why the hell did Officer Keifer let Mr. Lost out of his sight, even for a second? He'd attend to that later. Right now though, unable to reach Maxwell, he called Bagwell.

"Carson, the guy we're after name is Pierce, Richard Pierce . . . goes by the mob moniker of The Talon," Lt. Huber explained in a noticeably hurried pitch. "He's here, dammit. The guy who spilled the beans on him . . . you know, the one we caught on tape . . . you know, Mr. Lost ? He's dead. Found murdered at the airport a short time ago while he was dropping off his rental car. The way it was done, it's gotta be our boy."

"Hammy's dead, too," Bagwell blurted back. "Found in a stall in the men's room under the grandstand. Throat slashed, too. A short-bladed pushbutton knife was just laying there. They can't find his buddy, The Captain, anywhere."

"Yeah, we found that kind of knife at the airport scene, too," Lt. Huber said, the back of his neck growing tighter and clammier. "I can't raise Jace."

"I'm at the track. I'll go see him. Fill him in."

"With those bodies laying around, you know this guy's gotta move fast," Lt. Huber shouted "He's gonna go right after Jarvis, if we're right, and disappear. We'll never get him." After pause, he lamented, "Oh Christ . . . Hammy?"

"Yeah, I know," Bagwell echoed, matching the detective's tone. "Somewhere along the line . . . clever as he always was . . . he talked to the wrong person once too often. I think he knew it, too. He stuck his neck way out a long way for us. He must have gambled that we'd close this thing out before . . . What are you going to do?"

"I've got an idea," Lt. Huber replied, then demanded, "Just make sure Jarvis stays safe."

"Oh, man, watch yourself," Bagwell urged forlornly.

"You just take care of your side of the street, let me take care of mine," the lieutenant's voice dropped, abruptly restored to its routine level of professional directness.

If the profile that Maxwell and he had created was psychologically accurate, and now in motion, then The Talon was on an inexorable collision with Jarvis when the rider made his routine nightly visit to Bright Boy, the lieutenant calculated. All he had to do now was play into the script, and be in place when those two creatures of habit converged. But, that wouldn't be until well into the evening.

Ω

Bagwell found Maxwell at his regular afternoon post near the Harrison stalls. The trainer was talking at length with the principal owner of Bright Boy and two other people whom he didn't recognize. Maxwell was intermittently posing and parading the flashy colt back-and-forth in front of trio.

Harrison, now moving off to the right, seemed visibly deflated. Apparently Bright Boy was being sold. The argument had boiled down to whether the current owners would keep the colt until Saturday and run him in an allowance race as scheduled, or turn Bright Boy over right away. If sold today, Bright Boy would be sent directly to the breeding shed without ever again seeing the inside of a starting gate.

"What if he reinjures himself, or worse, dammit?" the older of the two interested parties asserted boisterously, obviously trying to impress the two women who seemed only casually interested from a distance.

"It's this way," Bright Boy's owner answered. "If he hurts himself, you have the option of not buying him. Simple as that. But, if he wins, you're going to pay half again as much."

"Oh, come off it! If he wins, you get the purse, I get the horse for what we've agreed to," the man chirped back, trying to be witty, but pitching more like an auctioneer without the power of a gavel.

"Hell, the winner's end of that purse ain't near what I'm talking about," the owner barked back. "You want the horse? Then go along with what I've laid out."

Maxwell and Harrison had taken up positions near each other along the fence and were exchanging microglances and frowns while the two squabbling parties fired their bullying salvos. The horse would be sold. Who was the better horse trader was at stake.

"Besides, if he wins Saturday, the boss won't need these clowns," Harrison quietly stepped closer and whispered to Maxwell. "Plenty of others'll come running."

"God," Bagwell thought, *"If it weren't for the jockeys, trainers and stable people . . . and, of course, the horses. . . there are some parts of this horsy set that are hard to swallow."* He also knew why Maxwell hadn't answered Lt. Huber's calls. He wouldn't chance having his cell phone ring in the midst of something like this. Stable boys with untimely cell-phone calls could draw unnecessary attention. Even if not answered.

When Maxwell gazed nonchalantly in his direction, Bagwell flicked the index finger of his right hand, signaling that he wanted to talk as soon as the coast was clear. Maxwell acknowledged with a slight nod.

The two flesh peddlers continued to rattle their sabers for another half-hour. Time and again, one side threw versions of buying a lame horse into the mix, only to be countered with the breeding lines alone being worth much more than the asking price . . . and, if Bright Boy proved that he could run on Saturday, that should double his value. The two women had long since cashed in any interest, giggling among themselves with small talk.

Finally, a truce decided that Bright Boy would run for the current owners Saturday, after which the principals would resume their negotiations.

"Christ," Bagwell thought, *"After all that; nothing!"*

"Put Bright Boy to bed, George," Harrison said in a tiring tone. "I'll see you in the morning."

"Yessuh, Missuh Bill," Maxwell dutifully replied.

Bagwell's approach toward Maxwell, as the others receded into their separate ways, didn't draw any special attention. He had been checking on Bright Boy's progress quite regularly. If anything, he showed worthy respect by staying well in the background while the entrepreneurial wannabes had been in full bloom.

"Hey, don't be too hard on Mr. Owner there," Maxwell advised quietly, pointing to the horseman's back as he disappeared into the barn. He had read Bagwell's silent disapproval from afar. "It's his hobby alright, but he treats it somewhere between that and a business. Has to. If you don't, something like this can put you in the Poor House in a hurry."

"Sounded like all business to me, with plenty of ego mixed in," Bagwell shrugged. "Not much thought about the horse or people's feelings.

"That's where you're wrong," Maxwell explained while they led Bright Boy back to his stall. "Look, that buyer made him an offer he shouldn't refuse. He stalled on accepting it anyway. For only one reason. He's well aware of how much attention and care Harrison has put into this guy." Maxwell stopped and patted Bright Boy on the nose. The colt playfully tossed his head.

"Looks like Harrison's not the only one who'll be sorry to see him go," Bagwell smiled with a new understanding.

"Harrison's just glad he'll get to run him once more before he leaves . . . he's not a greedy man," Maxwell asserted. "Jarvis is happy, too. This Bright Boy thing has made him a new person. Whole again. Back to being himself."

Bagwell filled Maxwell in on the recent events, relaying Lt. Huber's opinion that Pierce would finish with Jarvis at the earliest opportunity.

"Hard to believe he's here already," Maxwell said. "Not his style. Either Bob's wrong, or something very strange is in the wind. Either way, I'll get Jarvis the hell out of here and baby-sit him. Where the heck is he right now?"

"Safe for the moment," Bagwell assured. "Over at the jocks' room behind the paddock. Plenty of people around. I'll get him to come over."

"Too bad about Hammy," Maxwell called out. Bagwell, who had begun walking away, turned and took a step toward the agent.

"I'm going to have to live with that one," the writer lamented sincerely. "Hammy stepped over the line doing me a favor. If I'd have let him alone, he'd be alive. You can't live like he did, then expect to get away with what he did for us. He knew it, too. I should never have let it happen."

Some coaxing was necessary for Bagwell to pry Jarvis away from the eternal poker game in the jocks' room. Soon though, while escorting the rider over to Harrison's barn area, the writer was outlining what Maxwell had in mind.

"I'm not buying it, for crying out loud!" Jarvis screamed when the three came together at Bright Boy's stall. While Maxwell stood silently by, Bagwell had detailed to Jarvis what had happened to Hammy and The Churchmouse.

"Dammit, I didn't come all the way back here only to slink off and hide somewhere when the chips are down and we can nail this sucker," Jarvis grimaced

"Look, you don't get this bastard by being a hero or just plain stupid," Maxwell interceded sternly. "He's always got the jump on us to begin with. One step ahead. We're following his lead, waiting for him to make a mistake. If Huber's right, he's made one by being here right now. We've got him cranked up the way we planned. I don't want to miss. It's already cost two lives that we know of. They just got in his way while he's going after what he really wants."

Jarvis tilted his head inquisitively.

"You!" Maxwell asserted, pointing his right index finger into Jarvis's breastbone. "Why make it easy for him?"

"OK, but let's not lose him!"

"Look, he's way off his usual script right now. I'm betting he's never allowed himself to get into a situation like this before. What started out as a simple case of pride in his work has turned into an ugly massacre. No way he wanted this to happen. The one we're calling Mr. Lost? He probably triggered it. Now this S-O-B will keep coming. The more we make you unavailable, the more frustrated he'll become and more likely he'll be provoked into a making a fatal error. Look, if you're so insistent about getting in the way, at least pick your spots. Stay the hell out of the way, except when I can cover your ass."

On edge since the news about Hammy, Bagwell had had enough, thoroughly convinced at this point that he had done his part.

"Need somebody to get out of the way, huh?" he hurriedly told Maxwell. "I'm your boy. Sounds like you two want to make things a little hot around here. And, I'm sure you don't need my help."

As Bagwell strode briskly toward the security gate, heading over to the comfort of grandstands, Maxwell and Jarvis disappeared into the shadows of the shed area.

"He's not a hero or stupid, but he's got courage," Maxwell lectured to Jarvis, while halfheartedly pointing back toward Bagwell.

"Yeah, so did Hammy," Jarvis answered with biting sarcasm.

30

NIGHTLIGHTS AND NIGHTHAWKS

Lt. Huber could only assume that the meeting at Bright Boy's barn area took place. Bagwell had assured the lieutenant that he would call back if he couldn't locate Maxwell. No such call had been received. What he did know was that The Churchmouse had staked out Jarvis's routine and had spoken to The Talon about the jockey's nightly check of Bright Boy, suggesting it would provide the optimal moment.

The detective also knew that the only open path into the barn area was through the security guard's gate. Otherwise, the entire area was encased in a seven-foot chain-link fence, topped off with eighteen inches of inward angled, three-stranded barbwire.

Shortly before nine o'clock, he pulled into a parking place near the security gate, with cars on both sides and plenty of open spots close by. From there, he had an easy view of any activity that might take place at the gate.

The entire cloudless, moonless sky teamed with a stellar spillage of infinitely varying intensities. Above, slightly to the west, the Big Dipper poured forth, and five widths from its pointer stars rested the North Star, marking the tip of the Little Dipper's handle. Sister planet Venus smiled conspicuously from halfway up in the west, but Jupiter, in the southeast, was even brighter.

The lighting along the parking lot perimeter was directed downward by overhead reflecting hoods on tall metal poles. Time-controlled to a daily schedule, these lights had been on for a while and were now hosting their nightly visits from moths and a countless roster of other nocturnal insects. Three nighthawks rose and dove in relays in the warm stillness, feasting on the salad of flying morsels under the lights. Originally designed to provide blanket security over the entire lot, the lighting system appeared to have been the victim of severe cost-effective cuts. Just below each pole, the lighting was most effective, but the intervals on both sides of each pole quickly became engulfed in darkness. A person could do things within these obscuring patches without being noticed.

"How will he try to get back there?" Lt. Huber asked himself. *"Is he going to park and walk through, or drive up with some sort of half-assed I.D. pass?"* Twenty minutes later, his question was perhaps about to be answered.

A dark green rented Neon compact pulled into the parking place located two cars to the right of Lt. Huber's on the same side. The lone occupant, a slightly bigger-than-average male, got out and stepped toward the location of the security gate. Then he paused, pulled a cigar from the left breast pocket of his dark jacket and began lighting it.

"That's him all right," Lt. Huber murmured. "Just like Mr. Lost described." Certain of his quarry, he jumped quickly from his car seat and walked briskly toward the man, drawing his pistol.

"Sir, Mercury police," Lt. Huber barked with authority, holding his badge up with his left hand. "Please keep your hands where I can see them."

"What's this all about?" the man asked with remarkably quiet inquisitiveness. Outwardly, he appeared startled, dropping his cigar and putting his hands up shoulder high, palms out. It was an act. He instinctively understood the rarified symbiosis that had brought the two of them together at this crossroads. He welcomed this.

Meanwhile, the detective remained dutifully unaware.

"I don't see where I've done anything wrong. I assume this is a public parking area."

This guy's a carbon copy of Mr. Lost, the lieutenant observed. Once you expose them, they fold up like busted kites and crash in a helpless heap. I'll bet this one starts singing, too, as soon as I get him to the station.

"Sir, I'm putting you under arrest for suspicion of murder," Lt. Huber asserted while returning his badge to his left shirt pocket and producing a pair of handcuffs. "Exigent circumstances. If, as you say, you are innocent, you have nothing to worry about. Please put your hands behind you, sir."

The Talon calmly slid his left hand down and behind him. Otherwise, he remained perfectly still.

"Murder? Preposterous! There's some mistake, officer," the man said, maintaining his level and now friendly tone. "I'm only here to look at a horse. I have permission."

"You have the right to remain silent," Lt. Huber began as he moved around the man to left. "Anything you say can be held against you in a court of law . . . "

"What is this? Am I going to need a lawyer?" the man asked, his question overlapping Lt. Huber's reading of the first of his rights. The Talon smirked at his self-irony in forecasting the next Miranda warning.

"You have the right to an attorney," with methodical disregard for The Talon's commentary, Lt. Huber continued to speak while reaching down to attach the handcuffs. "If you do not have . . . "

As the lieutenant reached down, The Talon whirled one-hundred-eighty degrees to his left and the razor-sharp, push-blade knife from his right-hand sleeve slashed deep into the policeman's throat. Realizing what had happened before feeling it, the lieutenant grabbed for his neck with both hands and caught the blood flow as it gushed at an angle. His handcuffs clattered to the ground. The Talon kicked him squarely in the solar plexus.

Lt. Huber's retching, gasping body slammed against the driver's-side door of the nearest parked car and slid slowly to the ground.

"You poor bastard," The Talon, grinning, spoke quietly above the gurgling sound. "You're lucky you ever even got in the same place with me. How does it feel to feel your life spilling out in front of you? Relax, dammit. Won't be long now. Hell, every drop of blood travels around the whole body in less than a minute . . . Or in your case, spills out."

Lt. Huber grew limp and quiet. The Talon reached down and grabbed him by the upper part of the back of his shirt and then his belt at the base of his back. Using both hands, he dragged the leaking dead weight toward the unmarked police car.

"Actually, you were very good at what you did," The Talon chuckled to the unresponsive body in the past tense as he opened the driver's side door. "Just not nearly good enough," heaving the body across the front seat "Too bad." as he wiped his prints from the door handle with his tie.

The Talon was certain that he would be well away before anyone discovered his deed in the morning. Meticulously, he assured himself that he still had no visible blood on his clothes, Brandishing a new cigar, he resumed his leisurely stroll toward the security gate.

He paused again. Why had he done that? He never acknowledged his quarry on equal terms. They were opaque objects, not organisms. If perceived at all, any feelings by his quarry were completely inconsequential to the coolly determined end at hand. Discourse added a familiarity that simply didn't matter.

Perhaps the gut-level disappointment from The Churchmouse's cowardly betrayal had triggered this unplanned outburst of dialogue. Preoccupation with verbal consternation had carried through while having to unexpectedly dispatch the lieutenant. That was new, also. Never before had he seriously considered killing an officer of the law.

He had even muttered surly epithets to Hammerstan while slashing him. *"Don't let this be a sign of some sort of inefficiency,"* The Talon now self-counseled.

Ω

Put into Bagwell's terms, The Talon was in the midst of a "Getaway Week," which, for his particular purposes, would be compacted into several volatile hours of a single day. With brutal satisfaction, his getaway currency would be coined during the horrid finality of his special, unspoken self-terms. In the backwaters of his relentless scorn for unattained human kindness stirred the ingredients of those macabre rules, and only he knew what those rules were. Did he hold to them?

"Good evening, sir," The Talon smiled and waved cordially to the elderly guard, unassumingly approaching the security gate entrance to the barn area. "I have permission to look at a horse. The owner knows I'll be leaving very early tomorrow and said it would be OK to look at the animal tonight. He told me where the horse is stabled. I'm sure I'll find it."

"Well, sir, I'll still have to see some written permission and your identification," the rosy-nosed retiree was drowsily pleasant, yet unwaveringly direct about doing his job by the numbers. Unfortunately, the guard also fancied himself as one the track's prominent good-will ambassadors. Instead of routinely raising the front window of the booth, he opened the door and stepped into the archway with a greeter's smile.

"Of course . . . how thoughtless . . . I have a note from the trainer right here," The Talon calmly assured, then reached into his shirt pocket and handed the guard a note identifying Harrison as the author.

"Strange," said the guard. "Mr. Harrison usually puts out his written communications on special paper with the Karma Stable letterhead."

"Yes, well, maybe he didn't have any with him," The Talon remained calm, but direct. "We were at a restaurant having dinner earlier today, and he asked the manager for the notepaper that's on." He pointed to the note.

"Oh no, sir, you must be mistaken," the guard shook his head in amused disbelief. "Mr. Harrison has two horses running in stakes races up in Chicago today and tomorrow. I know for a fact he left here yesterday."

"Look, can you help me out, pal?" The Talon turned to a sad-eyed plea. "I'm on a tight schedule here."

"Let me call the horse's owner, Mr. Ratliff," the guard reached for his personnel directory. "Let me see some identification."

"I have it right here," The Talon said quietly, reaching into the inside pocket of his jacket.

He drove his knife into the lower midsection of the guard's chest and ripped upward. He then immediately pushed the guard against the back of the booth. Holding the gasping body upright with his left hand over the man's mouth, The Talon amusedly watched the startled guard's bulging eyes glaze into relaxed unawareness.

As he slid the limp body onto the floor of the booth, out of range of the upper-half observation panes on all four sides, The Talon turned off the inside light.

Slowing only to check his watch and light a fresh cigar, he knew that he still had ample time to become part of Jarvis's predictable nightly pattern with Bright Boy. Even in the pervading darkness, The Churchmouse's verbal details of the focal area were pictorially precise and instructively complete enough to move The Talon along with confident familiarity.

Barn D was within easy walking distance of the security gate, closest to the clubhouse turn of the main track. A special make-shift opening along the outside railing midway into the turn allowed horses from Barn D convenient on-and-off passage during early morning workouts. As one of The Merc's leading trainers and key spokesman for backside issues during the past several years, Harrison had earned the honor of stabling his horses in Barn D. In traditional fashion, Barn D was a wide-mouthed, high-ceilinged artificial tunnel open at both ends, with rows of stalls running along both sides. Approaching from the security gate direction, Bright Boy was housed in the third stall on the right side. Amid the purposely quiet atmosphere, garnished with softly calming night lights, the crisply painted yellow-and-white decor of Harrison's stable area reflected the essence of spotless care.

"Mousey said that some little cripple might also be sniffing around, too, sticking his nose into things," he reviewed in silence as he approached the Harrison shed-row. *"Can't be much to take care of, if need be."*

Ω

Jarvis checked his watch again. The time was nearing for his usual late-evening visit with Bright Boy. Where the hell was George?

"This is his idea of safekeeping?" Jarvis muttered, impatiently scanning the bleak provisions of the under-cover agent's special stable-boy compartment adjacent to the backstretch's general quarters. *"Safe from what? I wouldn't be caught dead in a place like this! A real rat's nest, for Christ sake. George knows I want to see Bright Boy, especially now that we're sure to lose him after Saturday's race. Hell with this. My horse needs me."*

Ω

The Talon stepped into the shadows of an empty equipment cove diagonally across the central walkway from and to the left of Bright Boy's stall, quickly survey-ing his surroundings.

"Mousey's the best," he marveled over the precise-ness of the phoned description from his murdered ad-vanceman as though he were still alive. *"Any one of these empty stalls behind me will do just fine."*

The Churchmouse also had suggested a similar set-ting for the "Mendoza job," but back then The Talon had required something very different, more remote for his purposes. Now though, any one of these empty stalls would do. He'd simply need to get Jarvis quietly inside and shut the door. The rest would be easy and relatively quick. The Talon had a commuters' plane to catch before sunrise.

Almost to the expected minute, the jockey appeared. Sounding like a free-floating cuckoo, Jarvis walked slowly toward Bright Boy's stall with high-then-low chirpish whistles.

Bright Boy instantly appeared through the front of his Dutch-door stall and extended his head forward, inviting Jarvis's hand by nuzzling the air with his outstretched upper lip in a sort of joyful grin. The Talon let the mutual display of affection settle into a soft horse-human consummation of gentle nuzzling, stroking and patting.

"Hey, fella," The Talon momentarily approached from the darkness with a relaxed greeting.

"Me?" Startled, Jarvis pulled away from Bright Boy and stiffened, his back to the stall.

"Is this horse the one they call Bright Boy?"

Without answering, Jarvis began creeping backwards along the stall doors.

"What's the matter with you, boy?" The Talon gnashed at the jockey while sidestepping quickly to his right, cutting off the frightened jockey's intended retreat.

"Yes-yes . . . this is Bright Boy," wide-eyed and drained, Jarvis saw no exit.

Time to quit the facade and get on with it, The Talon mused.

"You poor little runt. I hope to God that you've already squealed to that Grand Jury. It'll make this that much sweeter. Make a move and I'll slice you into pieces right where you stand. Let's go."

Closing in on Jarvis, The Talon nodded toward his left shoulder while pulling a small rope from his back pocket.

"All right, that's enough of that," a voice from inside Bright Boy's stall calmly demanded. "Stop right where you are or, so help me God, I'll drop you right where you stand."

The Talon, unsure of where the voice had origi-
nated, stopped where he was. His widened eyes darted
left, then right. Jarvis bolted, sprinting into the darkness in the direction from where he had entered. Maxwell tilted his broad-brimmed Stetson back and patted
Bright Boy on the neck while he rose at the front, inside
the horse's stall, his pistol pointed squarely at The Talon's upper torso.

"We'll just stay right this way until the others arrive," Maxwell said, preparing to quick-dial the Mercury
Police station. "You're through, pal. I was betting that
you wouldn't be able to leave matters alone . . . a loose
end, even the illusion of one, was going to grate on you
until it drove you nuts. I know, you think you're hot
stuff. But really, you're pretty much just a type."

Enraged, The Talon dropped the small rope. With
one of his ready-to-arm knives now concealed in the
palm of his left hand, he came toward Maxwell with a
friendly smile.

Coolly, without uttering another word, Maxwell
fired at his approacher's right leg.

"Can't say I didn't warn you."

Blood poured from a hole just above the knee. The
Talon lurched to the right and grabbed his leg with both
hands, letting out a long grunting gasp. With a dull
thud, his knife fell to the dirt floor beside him.

Alarmed, Bright Boy threw his head up with a loud
defensive snort at the ringing report from Maxwell's 40-
caliber pistol. Then, with his head lowered and craned
outward, and back legs spread, as Maxwell watched,
the colt swaggered nervously backward into the perceived safety of the darker end of his stall. A loud
thump as his rump collided with the back wall, then
silence.

"I'm not going to kill you, old chum . . . though you
might like me to . . . now," the operative said with complete command, quickly returning his attention to The
Talon, who remained bent over, clutching the wounded
area of his disabled leg and quietly wincing. "No, we've
got to go over things. We'll want to know all about you."

"God damn you," The Talon growled, his hands scarlet with blood. "You black bastard!"

"How nice of you to be so politically correct in your hour of need," Maxwell hesitated in making his call, relishing the moment. "Except, my parents were happily married. Did you even know yours?"

The Talon had the bleeding under control and had steadied himself. He knew all about pressure points.

"I warn you, pal," Maxwell said with authority, a reminder of who was in control. "I'm not going to fuck around with you. You're type has to be stopped, one way or another."

"You'd have never gotten close to me if I hadn't come back here, dammit," The Talon grunted above his pain.

"Yeah, but you did . . . I had you the day you were born, pal," Maxwell said subtly as he unhitched the lower front of the stall, stepped out and then leaned against the reclosed door. "It was never a case of if; the only question was when. Man, you were the monkey to my grinder."

In the shadows to left, on the opposite side of the walkway, the sudden yellow flash-spike of a cigarette lighter shot upward and, after a second, instantly disappeared, leaving the glow of a tiny red-orange ember in its wake.

"Come out of there!" Maxwell shouted, swinging his pistol around to the direction of the surprise as a rolling puff of smoke reached out from the shadows. "Show yourself!"

The Talon, wincing with short, harsh breaths while maintaining his center of balance, immediately sensed that Maxwell's attention was distracted. Stealthily picking up his knife, he surged forward.

With calm reflex, Maxwell fired at his attacker's left leg, again inches above the kneecap. The Talon gave a high-pitch groan of excruciating pain and collapsed into the dirt in a sobbing quiver, now clutching his left leg with his bloody hands. Bright Boy, from the darker reaches of his stall, snorted in response at the second gunshot, and otherwise remained eerily still.

Maxwell heard, in the shadows to the left, the fading footsteps of an unhurried exit. A door opened with a creaking whine, then slammed shut. Moments later, a car started and slowly rolled away in the gravel.

With his pistol trained on The Talon, the retired operative quick-called the Mercury Police Station and ordered the desk officer to dispatch backup officers and an ambulance.

"I can't get Lt. Huber to answer his phone," Maxwell said, as he moved toward The Talon, kicked the knife away and stooped to examine at the leg wounds. Both femurs had been shattered where the bullets struck, but the nearby major arteries were intact. The Talon lay on his left side, staring straight ahead in a quiet glassy gaze, his folded hands loosely pressed against his right knee in sort of a sideways fetal position.

"We can't either, sir!" the desk dispatcher exclaimed worriedly. "He won't even answer his car phone!"

EPILOGUE

Seated at Lt. Huber's vacated desk, Agent Maxwell used the better part of a work-week to complete his Mercury reports. His Washington bureau was anxious.

Murmured conflicts of lingering shock and sorrow constantly swirled around him. Transcendental loyalties found action in combative whispers. Why had this sudden intruder chosen to work from The Lieutenant's space? A measurable group looked upon this perceived trespass with seething indignation. To them, the well-worn mahogany desk was sacrosanct — a shrine to be solemnly genuflected toward while given a wide berth. Not a pen nor paperclip should be moved from the exact positions where Lt. Huber had last placed them. The leaves of his daily desk calendar should have remained frozen on the date of his demise.

Others felt there was no better way to reach closure for the unseemly death of their beloved comrade than by using his workplace to recognize its finality. To them, the desk had always been a hallowed site for pursuing justice.

Either way, glazed eyes and stiff jaws amid eerily noticeable gaps of silence were the unmentioned order of the day throughout the building.

Clara Brown, appointed chief dispatcher by Lt. Huber upon his arrival in Mercury, broke into an uncontrollable sob and had to be helped to the ladies' powder room. Mostly though, amid their grief, everyone remained accommodatingly blue and solemnly carried on with their tasks. That's the way The Lieutenant would want it, they knew.

Constantly the focus of this silently adamant barrage of opposing perceptions, Maxwell remained friendly and unapologetic all week. Chief Millington told everyone on his staff to take as much time off as they needed. He took two days himself, in no mood to begin deciding how to fill his department's cataclysmic vacuum.

By week's end, Maxwell was no closer to identifying the apparition with the cigarette who quietly and confidently had dematerialized into the night while Pierce was being taken down. Beyond a doubt, this was the same faceless, soundless puff of smoke — less than fondly referred to as Mr. Cigarette — whom Bagwell had caught an amorphous glimpse of while viewing the Harrison stable surveillance tape at the newspaper office.

Using the meager information that Pierce had on his person and in his rental car, along with Lt. Huber's information from The Churchmouse, Maxwell methodically retraced the nomadic assassin's web of diversion back to his Richwater residence. With warrants in hand, bureau agents from the Florida office were systematically combing through Pierce's home, interviewing neighbors and other members of the community, and delving into his obscure real estate and motel holdings. So far as they could figure, there was plenty of money squirreled away under mysterious codes, likely disguised in far-off deposits.

At 6 o'clock on any summer morning, the operative knew where to find Bagwell. The trackside benches nearest to the finish line were unoccupied except for a single cleanly dressed, Trilby-topped chap with a stop-watch.

The early sun's face had just become a bold tangerine glare above the eastern horizon. Bagwell, using a small hand gesture, signaled the approaching FBI operative, who, in-turn, shading his eyes under his right-hand palm, followed the writer's gaze into the glare at the far turn of the backstretch.

A silhouetted horse and rider suddenly surged from a breezy gallop into an all-out drive. On cue, Bagwell clicked his watch as the duo streaked past the half-mile pole. He stalled his digital watch momentarily at the quarter pole and checked. 23.32! Still under a comfortable drive, the brisk workout continued through the homestretch, passing by the finish line in 47.76.

That solid time for a handy four furlongs would be the one reported publicly by the official clockers watching from the skyline press box. Bagwell knew better. What Harrison really wanted was an extra-quick burst over those first two furlongs. And, he got it. With that tightner, Bright Boy was sure to break on top during his return to racing this coming Sunday. As long as the colt was ready to break from the gate cleanly, his stamina and heart would take care of the rest.

A muddy track had forced Harrison to scratch Bright Boy from his originally planned return the previous Saturday. A fortunate stroke, Bagwell felt. The extra time likely helped the colt get over any lingering anxieties from Maxwell's gunplay.

"You ought to stick around, Jace," Bagwell nodded. "This one can't miss."

"Sorry, pal, I risk enough on the job," Jace huffed, all but ignoring Bagwell's invitation, while showing a small photo of Arliss's family as a ruse. "When I get time off, I find a nice warm beach and a nice cool drink with one of those little tiny umbrellas sticking out the top." Then he pointed toward the top of the clubhouse turn where Bright Boy was snorting and blowing into an easy gait. "Listen, chum, while you were home sleeping with your wife, I was bedding down with that one."

Bagwell shook his head, improvising that, while the people in the photo were nice, he didn't recognize any of them.

"They're still waiting for somebody to try to claim that Twin-Tri money," Maxwell said. "But, they don't seriously think anybody's going to be that stupid."

Bagwell tilted his head apprehensively.

"Don't let them relax completely," he said in earnest. "That much money's probably oiling the wheels of stupidity somewhere as we speak. Else how did this whole rotten mess ever get started in the first place? One thing though. The time limit should be coming up pretty soon?"

Maxwell agreed.

"A year from the date any ticket is sold, any unclaimed money automatically goes into the track's coffers," he recited for Bagwell, knowing the scribe was thoroughly aware of the policy. "But, the track won't be keeping it all this time. Most of what actually went on here hasn't made its way into the newspapers . . . yet. And, it promises to stay that way."

Oh, really!" Bagwell retorted with mock facetiousness. "How the hell is that supposed to happen?

"If Mendoza's family gets a third and the Don Mac-Beth Memorial Jockey Fund for helping injured jockeys gets a third," Maxwell nodded and winked. "The track's been very cooperative so far. They don't like any talk about, shall we say, race tampering getting into the papers."

"Why are you telling me this?" Bagwell whined with mock disgust.

"Because newspapers just love to play that sort of stuff up for all it's worth," Maxwell stayed the course. "Remember that Miami paper that stirred up that Kentucky Derby buzzer story a few of years ago without a shred of reasonable evidence?"

While Bagwell silently nodded his awareness of the incident, Maxwell changed direction. "I'm heading back to Washington with my report."

"Just keep me out of it, will you?" Bagwell urged emphatically, looking back out at the track to reconnect with the action. "I don't need the hassle."

"I'll do my best to be minimal," Jace promised, then chuckled. "As long as you don't try to out-scoop me. Besides, I'll always know where to find you."

"I'll go along," Bagwell said in a tone that telegraphed his gratefulness for what Maxwell had done.

"Look, if things get even a little funny, do not hesitate to call me directly," Maxwell said with stern eye contact. "I mean, the slightest thing. Mr. Cigarette's still out there."

"Hey, wait a minute, I was never out front in any of this," Bagwell registered concern. "I was the creep-around messenger boy. Certainly didn't attract any attention, did I?"

"Oh, so in your clairvoyant omnipotence you know precisely where this Mr. Cigarette did and didn't do his watching," Maxwell growled impatiently. "For God's sake, how many times did you come see me at Harrison's barn?"

"If he's such a big deal in all this, why didn't he take you down while you had The Talon in your sights?" Bagwell asked, turning to be squarely in front of Maxwell, while delighting in using The Talon's underworld moniker, instead of Pierce. "I mean, what the hell was he doing with all this watching anyway, if he wasn't going to put it to good use sometime? Seems he had the perfect opportunity."

"Hey, I'm still learning what makes these guys tick." Maxwell answered quietly. "I'll admit, it gets to me sometimes. When it does, I take a breather. I'm always drawn back in. I do know that these guys like to work on the sub rosa. Cockroaches in an unlit kitchen. That gangland Roaring 20s stuff, with guns blazing up and down Main Street? A bunch of crap, these days. The Talon and perhaps Mr. Cigarette are Baby Boomer gangsters. My guess is that Mr. Cigarette was here to just watch and report back. Pierce probably didn't even know he was here. Even if he was given an OK, he probably figured stepping in would only make a bigger mess than it already was."

"Whud did ole Missuh Harrison say about yore suddin depawchoor, bawz?" Bagwell chided, using his best attempt to mimic Maxwell's backstretch facade.

"You kidding?" Maxwell chuckled with amusement. "I couldn't have gotten to first base without him. He was in with us from the start. Mendoza won some big races for him. The way that boy was killed broke Harrison's heart."

"So he and Jarvis and you were our backstretch team from the get-go," Bagwell said as a statement, not a question.

"Jarvis? No way. He's too damn obstinate to reason with. Fortunately, he's also a creature of habit. I could at least keep track of him, which turned out to be just as good. Jockeys are funny that way. They don't understand danger the same way the rest of us do. Maybe if they did, they'd never get into a starting gate."

Maxwell handed Bagwell a card with his private number, and began walking toward the parking lot.

"Hey, he won't ever get out, will he?" Bagwell called to Jace, referring to The Talon.

Agent Maxwell stopped, paused, then turned and came back.

"He's worse than most . . . still a basic type though," Maxwell chose his words carefully in a low monotone. "Always quiet and very independent as long as they have things their own way. When they lose that, they become unglued. Their egos turn in on them. Some just clam up . . . sort of code of silence. Others start singing like canaries. That's when the shrinks and that sort get real interested. Got its own problems, too. Separating the truth from the bullshit."

"That's all very nice," Bagwell said with mild urgency. "As long as it all happens in some deep hole somewhere far off."

"Guys like that very seldom converse straight across with anyone," Maxwell all but ignored Bagwell's plight. "They see things one of two ways. They're either in complete control or they aren't. Somehow, they grew up that way. When you look at the big picture, all we did here was treat a symptom. A little revenge, perhaps. A little justice, maybe. The disease is still out there. Next week, there'll be another Pierce on the loose."

"Comforting thought," Bagwell exhaled.

"Hell, Pierce is a product of modern-day transportation and communication, but the root cause goes back to the cave days when the first group of sadistic malcontents banded together to take advantage of the pleasant side of human nature."

"That's crap," Bagwell barged in. "There's nothing political about this. Strictly money."

"Money and power . . . control," Maxwell corrected. "I'll bet the money that Pierce made from his first trip to Mercury wasn't for just killing Mendoza. There's plenty of goons to do that real cheap. Nah, Pierce was paid for what he did to Mendoza, then leaving the body where he did without a trace. It was meant to scare hell out of every jockey on the continent and beyond. I guess those killings that first caught my eye — Delaware, California and Louisiana — weren't done horribly enough to get the point across. I'd venture to say that Pierce might have been paid upwards of half the amount of that big Twin-Tri payoff or more to do what he did to Mendoza."

"I guess it takes a lot more to scare some other people," Bagwell said with a rhetorical tone. "Even so, money didn't get him back here."

"Ah, anyway you look at it, Pierce was just a tool," Maxwell lingered, realizing this opportunity was rare. "Those behind the whole thing are in business for the long haul, and the amount they paid Pierce, no matter what it was, was a pittance compared to what they expected to bring in, in the future, with every jockey quaking under their ruthless thumbs."

"I know jockeys who wouldn't stand for it, no matter how much pressure you put on them," Bagwell chirped.

"Hell, everybody's got a breaking point," Maxwell reflected. "Just because Mr. Cigarette backed away doesn't mean that it's over. They might try to get at Pierce, afraid of how much he knows, and not trusting what he might do or say. That's why we've got him in the deep-deep freeze right now, at least until the shrinks have a chance to squeeze him."

"You think Mr. Cigarette will take over where Pierce left off?"

Maxwell shook off the question, and pointed his right index at Bagwell's face. He still had a point to make.

"Then, if things go according to Hoyle, they'll continue bickering over whether Pierce is genetically predisposed toward his life's work or he has some sort of a behavioral glitch. You know, some traumatic early aberrant exposure. Some sort of scarring abuse. Then they go about fighting over whether he was really responsible for his actions. Was he simply a victim of his horrible past? Was just acting out accordingly? I'm way out of the loop on that stuff."

"Hell, we fight about that stuff down at the newspaper," Bagwell agreed. "Everybody does that. Nobody really does anything bad. They're all just misunderstood. Are we crazy!"

"Meantime, I've got to go figure myself out," Maxwell's voice quieted to an almost imperceptible murmur. "How the fuck can I get down on the same level of inhumanity as a remorseless, guiltless, sadistically clever piece of scum like Pierce and, win or lose, still feel that I'm an OK guy when I come out the other end?"

For an instant, the two men explored each other's eyes in earnest partnership, neither able to reach the next words. The retired operative slowly and resolutely blinked with a slight grimace, turned and walked away.

"You're a good person, Jace," Bagwell called after him. "We seem to run into each other about every 20 years. Next time ought to be a real kick."

Maxwell hesitated, looked at the ground in front of him, smiled silently, then continued walking.

Ω

"What did he want?" Zimmerhoff whined, waggling up behind Bagwell just as the writer was returning his attention to the horses on the track.

"You're up early," Bagwell snapped.

"Never mind that," Zimmerhoff chirped with impatient worry. "He's been putting pressure around here."

"Oh, he showed me a picture of some people," Bagwell spelled out slowly, in vaguely truthful terms. "I'd never seen any of them before. Then he gave me his number in case I remember something. Said he's leaving town. That's all."

"Sooner the better. Do us all a favor, will ya, and don't ever call that number under any circumstances," Zimmerhoff chittered and scampered away.

"Hey, if you haven't done anything wrong, what have you got to hide?" Bagwell called after the scurrying Zimmerhoff, smirked and turned toward his horse world.

Ω

Agent Maxwell had one more appointment and plenty of time to keep it. His flight to Washington wouldn't board until mid-afternoon.

"I don't know what to say, except something that doesn't come close, like I'm terribly sorry," he quietly commented to LaVona while they sat across a table at the far end of the Ellen's Runway Lounge, away from the cluster of other customers. "I know how much you loved him, and how much he loved you. It's why I couldn't leave without seeing you. You learn that you can't just shrug something like this off and go about your business as if it didn't happen or matter. Things have to be said. You have to touch bases, see people, try to talk about things."

"You're not that cold calculating bastard-robot after all?" LaVona interjected, trying to lighten the situation. Neither was buying it.

"I do know that he was doing what he had to," Jace didn't miss a beat. "It doesn't make sense, does it? A fine person gets killed, and I do my damnedest to keep one of the most cravenly despicable forms of humanity alive. God, I'm going to have to answer one hell of a lot more questions about why I shot that SOB in both legs than I ever would have if I'd just put one between his eyes. In some weird way, right there in front of me, Pierce decided the party was over. I know he was trying to get me to kill him with that second shot . . . maybe even with the first."

"I truly believe Bob would have preferred dying on the job to anything else . . . but not now," LaVona shared in a melancholy tone. "We had plans."

"We know nothing about what really happened here, or why. When greed and fear nourish the level of evil that . . ." Jace winced without finishing. "Can we ever, with any degree of certainty, detect this absurd disregard for humanity before it gets to this? That's why, with everyone screaming for quick and final justice, we have to take a long look at the likes of a Pierce whenever we can. There's a trigger there, just waiting to be pulled. If we can spot that before a finger ever gets put on it . . . well, there are experts in other fields who should be talking about this. Not a front-liner like myself."

"Maybe that's just what's needed," LaVona suggested. "Someone looking down the throat of pandemonium. I'm no expert either. How can you afford to mess around when there's a chance something like that might get loose again?"

"I have no feelings for either side of the old punish-ment versus rehabilitation argument," Maxwell shrugged. "For me, by then it's too damn late anyway. By then, somebody's been raped, severely beaten or killed, or they've been abused in some horribly tortur-ous way for a long time."

"Rehabilitation!" LaVona stopped him. "You honest-ly think you can fix something like a Pierce? Even if you think you could, could you trust it?"

"No, you're right," he agreed without hesitation. "If we want to get anywhere, we have to begin stopping things before they get started. Think my home office will buy that's why it was two slugs in the legs instead of one between the eyes?"

"Depends how far away from the trees they are, I suppose."

After finding out from the top agent at Florida's of-fice that Pierce had been cooking a real estate facade to garner his good standing in the Richwater community, Jace had called upon LaVona for general background information about the profession. When he finally un-derstood enough of the details, the setup was really ra-ther simple. Pierce had been juggling ten motels along Florida's Gulf Coast, two of which he maintained in his own name at any particular time and eight more under other phony corporative titles.

Through accelerated depreciation and bogus guest lists, he was able to show solid annual profits, testifying to his financial position. Even had a profit-sharing scheme, with half the net annual proceeds being di-vided among employees who demonstrated a certain level of loyalty. With time-lapse regularity, every three years or so he would, on paper, sell his two currently owned motels to one of his ghost corporations, and, in turn, purchase two others from his bogus corporative glob to put under his personal name.

He kept impeccable, albeit crooked, books and al-ways paid his state and Federal taxes on time and to the penny. Even so, his real worth was safely salted away offshore — somewhere such as the Cayman Islands, Jace surmised, and perhaps Swiss accounts.

"He was in the midst of unloading everything . . . all his motels . . . his house, too," Jace confided with La-Vona. "There was even a woman and two adopted children. My guess is that he was going to leave them high-and-dry. Jarvis was some sort of unscheduled last loose irritant. He already was making his final getaway when his twisted recipe of professionalism and narcissism got in his way. What made him so good at what he did, finally did him in."

"Yeah, and it was predictable enough so that Bob and you could built a rather elaborate trap around it."

"Bagwell explained it to me in track-talk terms one afternoon. During 'Getaway Week,' things that don't normally make sense the rest of the time start coming to the surface with predictable regularity . . . or something like that anyway. If Pierce had just let our cooked-up Jarvis scheme alone, or had succeeded before we nailed him, I don't think we'd have ever caught him. He'd have disappeared forever, delighted and proud of all that blood on his hands."

"You couldn't just let it go, could you? Not only Bob and you. It took all of you . . . Cossie, Hammy, Bagwell and the rest . . . Anyone of you hadn't agreed and it might not have been a go . . . Bob would still be here."

"Would you have loved him the same? What was bothering hell out of The Lieutenant was the complete lack of evidence at the Mendoza discovery scene," Maxwell's voice became extra-low again.

"Don't I know," LaVona nodded quietly. "It kept driving him nuts right up to the end."

"It had me, too . . . until I discovered that some of the summer cottages on the far side of the reservoir had a few rowboats for rent," Maxwell spoke with sincere respect. "One of the fellows I showed Pierce's picture to said 'maybe', but he couldn't be sure. Pierce probably used a bit of a disguise, and, of course, he wouldn't have used his real name to sign for a boat. There was one rented from the Winchell residence by a Raymond

Pearl at about six o'clock the evening before Mendoza's body was found."

"Wasn't lugging that body around a little obvious?" LaVona seemed bewildered.

"With the hands and lower legs gone, the jockey's body couldn't have weighed more than eighty pounds or so. Easy enough for someone of Pierce's physique to move around without catching any attention. As long as it was covered properly."

"Maybe so."

"Also, he was an absolute genius at controlling blood trace. You know, the night he was taken down he didn't have drop of blood on him, except his own and the gatekeeper's. By the time he got to the gate, he was no longer worried about being sneaky, We know he wore the same clothes all day, and was involved in at least four up-close knife murders."

"You're nothing, Jace, if you're not one heck of stickler for detail," LaVona's compliment had an artificial tone.

"Anyway, the boat wasn't returned until after 9 o'clock that night," Jace's description now had an air of forgiveness. "Plenty of time under the cloak of darkness for Pierce to pick an ideal spot to ease the body in from the waterside of the boat. That part of the reservoir is pitch black after dark, anyway. I got the number of the boat. A team from the regional office is going over it. My bet is, we won't find anything conclusive."

"It really had Bob," she re-emphasized. "Leaving that body in his jurisdiction had him steamed. He hated what he thought it implied. It was very unlike him . . . a big case of revenge stewing."

"Yes. Got him too far out on a limb . . . nobody there to watch his back," Maxwell said, surprising himself with how sincerely straightforward, rather than cryptically consoling, he was becoming here. LaVona's confrontational directness was comfortingly contagious. He never spoke openly about cases. God forbid, one still open! He knew why. It was time to stop skirting the real reason why he had come.

"Long ago, I lost someone who meant everything," he just poured forward bluntly.

LaVona studied him, then asked, "What did you do? How were you able to put it behind you?"

"I never have," he said with stern blandness. "I let it almost destroy me. In the end, I'm not even sure it changed me. I think it made me more resolute about what I was supposed to do. To be. All I know is, you don't leave something like that behind. You bring it along with you the rest of the way. It's part of who you are . . . what I am."

"Who watches your back, Jace?" she came back to him.

He usually answered "Smith & Weston" or "Mr. Colt" to this line of inquiry. Now, he just shrugged in deference.

"Where to next, Jace?" she asked with warm interest.

"I've got a flight back to Washington in a few hours," the agent answered, agreeably receptive to her concern while sitting straighter. "They're dying to talk to me. I wanted to have a pretty good handle on my reports before I got there. My room's right here at the airport. The government gets a special rate. As a habit, they always liked me close by in case they wanted me to catch the next available flight to somewhere. Not much chance, now that I'm retired."

"It's nice to be depended on by someone, or something," she reflected.

"After Washington, I plan to spend a few days or so in Pierce's Florida neighborhood, just kinda snooping around. Try to answer some loose ends. If all that motel stuff is really true, maybe I can figure a way to funnel some of the proceeds from any sales to that woman and her two kids . . . if I'm satisfied they were nothing more than innocent props for his local facade."

"Yes indeed, appearances count for a lot," she let him know she was listening.

"Then I want to slip over to the other coast . . . a place called Obelia Cove," unsure he should be elaborating. "Through that fellow Hammy, using Bagwell as a go-between, Charleen made Bob promise to look into some alleged funny stuff going on there. The only way she'd agree to be part of that get-together at the newspaper when that videotape fingered the late Mr. Lost."

"The more we talk, the more the bodies pile up." LaVona winced.

"It's possible some federal improprieties are linked to this Obelia Cove thing," he had a point to make. "If I can help clear that stuff up, it might be safer for people like Charleen to move around more. She's deathly afraid to leave Mercury, let alone go near Florida."

"I know Charleen," LaVona nodded. "She's a stand-up gal . . . with her own ideas about how life should be lived. If she says there's something there, there probably is. I like her. Trust her horse sense."

They explored into each other's eyes softly in silent agreement.

"Is it always like this for you?" she asked. "Do you ever rest? Take a break? Is there someone waiting for you?"

"Yes. Yes. Yes . . . and no." Jace responded flatly to her rapid-fire quartet of inquiries, again acknowledging his appreciation for her concern. Handing her a small white card, "This is my very private number. Call me anytime, for any reason. I mean it. Don't hesitate for a moment. This Pierce thing might still have some real legs to it. If you don't reach me right away, just say your first name after the beep. I'll get back to you as soon as I hear. Come on, I'll walk you to your car."

Jace stood up and pushed his chair against the table.

"Thank you, Jace, but no. I want to sit here alone for a while," LaVona pleaded with a grimacing smile, her glazed eyes looking up. "I need to be away from everything for a few moments. Here's as good a place as any."

"From the looks of it, I may have to be back through Mercury sometime soon," Maxwell said quietly. "Would you mind terribly if I called on you?"

"I'd like that very much, Jace," she answered softly, with welcoming eyes.

Maxwell nodded with a slight smile. As he disappeared into the noise of the main concourse, LaVona put her face in her hands and slumped over the table to muffle the sniffling chokes and to catch the tears.